# JANE AUSTEN'S S

Jane Austen is renowned for the economy of her art: for the close focus of her romantic plots and the precision of her writing style. Exploring that economy stylistically and structurally, this book traces Austen's keen interest in narrative form. Anne Toner pinpoints techniques that are fundamental to the distinctiveness of Austen's fiction, many of which have been little explored to date. Toner argues that Austen's conciseness in terms of plotting, narrative description and the depiction of dialogue also contributed to her innovations in representing thought, expanding the novel's capacity to depict consciousness. Narrative and rhetorical features are presented clearly and accessibly and will open up some new ways of thinking about prose style with implications for the study of fiction beyond Austen's own.

ANNE TONER is a fellow in English at Trinity College, Cambridge. She is the author of *Ellipsis in English Literature: Signs of Omission* (Cambridge University Press, 2015).

# JANE AUSTEN'S STYLE

*Narrative Economy and the Novel's Growth*

ANNE TONER

*University of Cambridge*

CAMBRIDGE
UNIVERSITY PRESS

**CAMBRIDGE**
**UNIVERSITY PRESS**

University Printing House, Cambridge CB2 8BS, United Kingdom

One Liberty Plaza, 20th Floor, New York, NY 10006, USA

477 Williamstown Road, Port Melbourne, VIC 3207, Australia

314–321, 3rd Floor, Plot 3, Splendor Forum, Jasola District Centre, New Delhi – 110025, India

79 Anson Road, #06-04/06, Singapore 079906

Cambridge University Press is part of the University of Cambridge.

It furthers the University's mission by disseminating knowledge in the pursuit of education, learning and research at the highest international levels of excellence.

www.cambridge.org
Information on this title: www.cambridge.org/9781108424158
DOI: 10.1017/9781108539838



First published 2020

Printed in the United Kingdom by TJ International Ltd, Padstow Cornwall

*A catalogue record for this publication is available from the British Library.*

*Library of Congress Cataloging-in-Publication Data*

Names: Toner, Anne, 1971- author.
Title: Jane Austen's style : narrative economy and the novel's gowth / Anne Toner, University of Cambridge.
Description: Cambridge ; New York, NY : Cambridge University Press, 2020. | Includes bibliographical references and index.
Identifiers: LCCN 2019026050 | ISBN 9781108424158 (hardback) | ISBN 9781108424158 (ebook)
Subjects: LCSH: Austen, Jane, 1775-1817--Literary style. | English language--19th century--Style.
Classification: LCC PR4038.S8 T66 2020 | DDC 823/.7--dc23
LC record available at https://lccn.loc.gov/2019026050

ISBN 978-1-108-42415-8 Hardback
ISBN 978-1-108-43940-4 Paperback

# *Contents*

# *Illustrations*

# *Acknowledgements*

My first debt of gratitude in writing this book is to Trinity College, Cambridge. Trinity was generous in aiding my attendance at conferences, for which, and at which, much of the material for this book was developed. Trinity was also generous in giving me leave from teaching, following a period of maternity leave, facilitating a period of research at a crucial time in my professional life. I am grateful to my colleagues – Joe Moshenska, Adrian Poole, Anne Stillman, Ross Wilson, Susan Daruvala and Sachiko Kusukawa – for supporting this period of leave.

Linda Bree has been an extraordinary source of encouragement for this project. Her enthusiasm for this book, as well as her expertise as an Austen scholar, were crucial to its development. I am grateful to many others at Cambridge University Press, especially Bethany Thomas, who took on the editorship of the book, Natasha Burton, Carrie Parkinson and at the production stage, to Sarah Lambert. I also owe a great deal to the expert guidance and detailed advice of the Press's readers, to Leslie Connor for such careful reading of my text and to Priyaa Menon for much practical help. My ideas have taken shape through the support and input of other scholars working on Austen; in particular, I am indebted to Susan Allen Ford, Serena Baiesi, Joe Bray, Emma Clery, Carlotta Farese, Katie Halsey, Peter Sabor, Francesca Saggini and Bharat Tandon. I have found Chawton House Library a hospitable and inspiring place to visit and discuss ongoing work and I would like to acknowledge the efforts of Gillian Dow in particular. The Cambridge and South-West branches of the Jane Austen Society kindly invited me to present my work-in-progress. Jan Melissa-Schramm and Emma Widdis have continued to be unfailing sources of guidance and good sense. I am also grateful to the many students with whom I have spent time talking about Jane Austen.

I have published several essays on material that has been reworked for this book. These are 'A "Said He" or a "Said She": Speech Attribution in Austen's Fiction', *Persuasions*, 34 (2012), 140–9; 'Landscape as

Literary Criticism: Jane Austen, Anna Barbauld and the Narratological Application of the Picturesque', *Critical Survey*, 26, 1 (2014), 3–19; 'Apophatic Austen: Speaking about Silence', *RSEAA XVII–XVIII* (2017) 179–97; 'Free Speech: Jane Austen, Robert Bage, and the Subversive Shapes of Dialogue', in *Textus. English Studies in Italy*, 30, 3 (2017), 167–87; and 'Jane Austen Jotting: the Manuscript of *Sanditon* and the Question of Style', in *Persuasions On-Line*, 28, 2 (2018). I owe thanks to the editors of these journals for permission to republish this work in revised form here. I am also grateful to the staff at the Bodleian Library; the British Library; the Hampshire County Archives; and especially, Cambridge University Library. James Clements and Patricia McGuire, Librarian and Archivist respectively, at King's College Cambridge have always gone out of their way to help.

Jane Austen's juvenilia reveal the delight she took in writing dedications. This book is dedicated, with love and gratitude, to my family: to Arthur and Florence, and to Jerry whose support and generosity seem without bounds. It was he who suggested that I write down the ideas that I had about Austen and then helped me find the time to do so.

# *Abbreviations and Conventions*

All quotations from Jane Austen's fictional works are from the Cambridge edition of the *Works of Jane Austen*, eds. Janet Todd et al. (Cambridge University Press), unless otherwise noted. Full details of these volumes are listed in the bibliography.

## Abbreviations

| | |
|---|---|
| *E* | *Emma* |
| *J* | *Juvenilia* |
| *L* | *Jane Austen's Letters*, collected and ed. by Deirdre Le Faye, 4th ed. (Oxford and New York: Oxford University Press, 2011) |
| *LM* | *Later Manuscripts* |
| *MP* | *Mansfield Park* |
| *NA* | *Northanger Abbey* |
| *P* | *Persuasion* |
| *P&P* | *Pride and Prejudice* |
| *S* | The manuscript of *Sanditon*, in *Jane Austen's Fiction Manuscripts: a Digital Edition*, ed. Kathryn Sutherland (2010). Available at https://janeausten.ac.uk/index.html. ISBN: 978-0-9565793-1-7 |
| *S&S* | *Sense and Sensibility* |
| *W* | The manuscript of *The Watsons*, in *Jane Austen's Fiction Manuscripts: a Digital Edition*, ed. Kathryn Sutherland (2010). Available at https://janeausten.ac.uk/index.html. ISBN: 978-0-9565793-1-7 |

## Conventions

References to the works listed above will appear parenthetically within the text. *Jane Austen's Fiction Manuscripts: a Digital Edition*, ed. Kathryn Sutherland (2010), is cited whenever the quotation of manuscript works involves reference to revision or specific orthographic practice. Pagination follows that provided by Sutherland's digital edition of the fiction manuscripts. Jane Austen's spelling and punctuation are followed as closely as possible, when quoting from her manuscripts.

The occasional distinction I make between double and single inverted commas is between verbatim quotation of source material and quotation with slight grammatical alteration for the purpose of quotation. All emphasis within the text marked by bold type is my own, unless otherwise noted.

# *Introduction*
## *Austen and the Economy of Art*

Jane Austen has always been known for her economy of art. The author who described herself as composing on "the little bit (two Inches wide) of Ivory [...] with so fine a Brush" (*L*, p. 337) has been praised, as well as criticized, for the circumscribed focus of her plots, the precision of her writing style, for her miniaturism. Nineteenth-century readers compared her fiction with Flemish painting and with instruments of reduction, the microscope that examines tiny details, and the sieve, filtering away all extraneous matter.[1] Austen's fiction yielded "no redundancy or waste".[2] By contrast, critical writing today emphasizes the expansiveness of Austen's view. Austen's scene no longer solely consists of the marriages of the English gentry; rather it reverberates with national and global politics: with banking, wars, scandal, slavery. Nevertheless, Austen's skill remains in the minimalism of her approach, her intimations and taxing hints. Her art is one fundamentally characterized by exactitude and compression.

This book does not study Austen's economy thematically. Rather it takes as its subject a series of technical principles that shaped her fiction and its content, and that galvanized the representational powers of fiction. From the beginning of Austen's writing life, in the stories that she wrote as a teenager, matters relating to the size and scale of fiction preoccupied her and these matters constitute in no small part the brilliance of her early writing. The radical contractions of Austen's early fiction provide clues to her technical accomplishments later on. There are many surprising formal continuities between the drive to brevity of the juvenile writing and

[1] On the last of these, see R. H. Hutton, unsigned review, 'The Charm of Miss Austen', *Spectator* (1890), in B. C. Southam (ed.), *Jane Austen: the Critical Heritage 1870–1940*, vol. 2 (London and New York: Routledge & Kegan Paul, 1987), p. 196.

[2] Unsigned articles, 'Miss Austen', *Englishwoman's Domestic Magazine* (July, August, 1866), in B. C. Southam (ed.), *Jane Austen: the Critical Heritage* (London: Routledge & Kegan Paul, 1968), vol. 1, p. 206. Further references to *Jane Austen: the Critical Heritage* are by volume number.

Austen's lengthened-out published fiction. Austen made concision a rationale for her novels and both Austen's private and public writing provide a strong body of evidence to support this.

There are very few extant comments made by Austen about her own novels. There are, however, two series of letters which are especially revealing as to Austen's own technical practices. The first series comprises parts of two letters that Austen wrote to her sister, Cassandra, on the publication of *Pride and Prejudice* in 1813.[3] These two letters give unique access to Austen's thoughts about one of her completed novels on first seeing it in print and offer a raw account of the formal and stylistic decisions that she had made. These letters to Cassandra are celebrated for Austen's palpable excitement and pride on the arrival of this "my own darling Child", a novel that she playfully claims to be "too light & bright & sparkling". Yet Austen also comments on much more practical matters: the exclusion of a narrative superstructure when writing dialogue, the value or otherwise of matter extraneous to the story, the novel's length (how it is shorter than *Sense and Sensibility*) and the respective length of individual volumes following the process of 'lopping and cropping' that she had undertaken in preparation for publication. Cassandra Austen, after her sister's death, noted that *Pride and Prejudice* was published "with alterations & contractions".[4] How striking it is that on reading through *Pride and Prejudice*, Austen turns over different aspects of the novel's formal "contractions" and even betrays anxieties about her choices. At the same time, she delights in what she characterizes as the "Epigrammatism of the general stile".

The second series of letters to reveal Austen's compositional practices are the five letters written by Austen to her niece Anna Austen over the summer and autumn of 1814 concerning the novel that Anna was writing, 'Which is the Heroine?'. Austen wrote to Anna with her and Cassandra's opinions of the novel-in-progress, along with her own views regarding principles of success in fiction. At this point, Austen was an established author of three published novels, with the composition of *Emma* under way.

[3] Friday 29 January and Thursday 4 February 1813; (*L*, pp. 210–12).

[4] Cassandra's memorandum is held in the Pierpont Morgan Library, New York. It is transcribed in Kathryn Sutherland, 'Chronology of Composition and Publication', in *Jane Austen in Context*, ed. Janet Todd (Cambridge: Cambridge University Press, 2005), pp. 12–22, p. 16. Sutherland comments on the memorandum being possibly drawn up soon after Austen's death, perhaps towards the end of 1817, to help Henry Austen prepare his 'Biographical Notice' of Jane Austen accompanying the posthumous publication of *Northanger Abbey* and *Persuasion*; in James Edward Austen-Leigh, *A Memoir of Jane Austen and Other Family Recollections*, ed. with an introduction and notes by Kathryn Sutherland (Oxford: Oxford University Press, 2002), p. 219, note 44.

These letters have been called Austen's "art of fiction"[5] and this is an art that is alert to the superfluous, in terms of inconsequential circumstances and "wandering" plot, but also at the level of the sentence. Austen repeatedly criticizes overly descriptive or detailed writing. Prosiness and minuteness are singled out as errors. Instead, Austen firmly recommends revising and paring back. "[H]ere & there," writes Austen carefully to Anna, "we have thought the sense might be expressed in fewer words" (*L*, p. 280; 10–18 August 1814). Reading a later instalment, she recommends that Anna look back over her writing so as to "curtail" and 'scratch out' that which is "prosy & nothing to the purpose" (*L*, p. 288; 9–18 September 1814). In the same letter, Austen writes: "You describe a sweet place, but your descriptions are often more minute than will be liked. You give too many particulars of right hand & left.—" (*L*, p. 287).

Austen knew from her own experience the importance of identifying and reducing passages that "are more minute than will be liked". This is an overt if overlooked topic in a number of her extant letters, where she reflects on the problem of detail: how much to include and how much is sufficient to interest. The paradox of a formal economy in any kind of writing is the abundance that can accompany restriction of scene and subject, as the details that constitute that scene come more vividly into view. Austen was attracted to the minute and enjoyed in her correspondence the protracted details of the everyday, but she was alert to the dangers of excess. This book will argue that her fiction explored and navigated this dynamic in many different ways. More particularly, Austen had overt stylistic strategies – the subjects of each of the chapters that follow – that prioritized concision and exclusion, and by their means she found a new denotative capacity for detail, which had a profound impact upon the English novel.

## The Economy of Art: Austen's Reception

A number of early critics of Austen's work identified a principle of exclusion governing her fiction and recognized a consequent dilatory effect. What was new about Austen's work was the absence of excitable incident and plot, but this was an omission that was filled by a new emphasis on character.[6] The writer of the first article of a series on 'Female Novelists' in

[5] Kathryn Sutherland, *Jane Austen's Textual Lives: from Aeschylus to Bollywood* (Oxford: Oxford University Press, 2005), p. 248.

[6] In 1862, Julia Kavanagh surmised that "Miss Austen knew that she excelled in character, and probably guessed that she might not excel in adventure". Julia Kavanagh, 'Miss Austen's Six Novels', in *English Women of Letters* (1862), in *Jane Austen: the Critical Heritage*, vol. 1, p. 183.

the *New Monthly Magazine* of 1852 conveyed the relation between reduction and growth within their own style, dismissing in one short, simple sentence Austen's minimizing of plot, to build instead in an amplifying manner towards Austen's attention to "processes", "evolution" and the "gradually wrought" within her new form of fiction:

> Plot she has little or none. If you only enjoy a labyrinthine *nexus* of events, an imbroglio of accidents, an atmosphere of mystery, you will probably toss aside her volumes as 'desperately slow'. Yet, in the careful, artist-like management of her story, in the skillful evolution of its processes, in the tactics of a gradually-wrought *dénoument*, in the truthful and natural adaptation of means to ends, she is almost, if not quite, unrivalled. Nothing can be more judicious than her use of suggestions and intimations of what is to follow.[7]

The microscope was the best analogy for Austen's capacity both to limit her field and enlarge the characters within it: "The field of view may be in some sense a small one; but like that of a good microscope in able hands, there is abundance of light, and the minutest markings of character are beautifully shown in it".[8] According to R. H. Hutton in 1869, Austen's is a dizzying play of scale, a "minifying instead of a magnifying medium" that reduces the scale of life, "while really multiplying its humours".[9]

But for others, Austen was too minute and, in consequence, overwhelmingly diffuse. Richard Whately, in one of the earliest appreciations of Austen's fiction, describes how her "minuteness of detail has [...] been found fault with".[10] William Charles Macready in 1836 complained that *Mansfield Park*

> has the prevailing fault of the pleasant authoress's books; it deals too much in descriptions of the various states of mind, into which her characters are thrown, and amplifies into a page a search for motives which a stroke of the pen might give with greater power and interest.[11]

[7] Unsigned article, the first in a series on the 'Female Novelists', *New Monthly Magazine* (May 1852), in *Jane Austen: the Critical Heritage*, vol. 1, pp. 137–8.

[8] W. F. Pollock, from 'British Novelists – Richardson, Miss Austen, Scott', *Fraser's Magazine* (January 1860), in *Jane Austen: the Critical Heritage*, vol. 1, p. 168.

[9] Hutton, 'The Charm of Miss Austen', in *Jane Austen: the Critical Heritage*, vol. 2, pp. 195, 196. See the description of Austen's "microscopic observation of foibles", from an unsigned review of Harriet Martineau's *Deerbrook*, *Edinburgh Review* (July 1839), in *Jane Austen: the Critical Heritage*, vol. 1, p. 121. George Saintsbury suggested that "for all the 'miniature'" in Austen's delineation of the pettiness and selfishness of men, "there is something gigantic"; from 'Preface' to *Pride and Prejudice*, illustrated by Hugh Thompson and published by George Allen (1894), in *Jane Austen: the Critical Heritage*, vol. 2, p. 217.

[10] Richard Whately, unsigned review of *Northanger Abbey* and *Persuasion*, *Quarterly Review* (January 1821), in *Jane Austen: the Critical Heritage*, vol. 1, p. 98.

[11] William Charles Macready, diary entry, 9 July 1836, in *Jane Austen: the Critical Heritage*, vol. 1, p. 118.

It is perhaps unsurprising that an actor and actor-manager such as Macready would have been displeased with Austen's elaboration of states of mind instead of character in action or in speech. But unusually, at this early stage of Austen criticism, Macready pinpoints Austen's amplifications as not depicting character broadly, but excavating characters' interiority and the workings of the mind. Henry Wadsworth Longfellow called Austen's fiction "a kind of Bowditch's Laplace in the romantic astronomy", referring to Pierre Laplace's five-volume edition of *Mécanique Céleste* (1799–1805) with its extensive notes and commentaries.[12] Far from being "a small, thin classic" as Mary Augusta Ward would have it,[13] Austen's work swells for Longfellow into encyclopedic tomes, incapable of leaving anything to the imagination. Like Longfellow, Virginia Woolf described Austen as refusing to leave gaps: she "stuffs up every chink and cranny of the fabric until each novel is a little living world".[14]

It was George Henry Lewes who coined the phrase "economy of art" for Jane Austen's fiction, in 1859 in *Blackwood's Edinburgh Magazine*, and in doing so he established the developing orthodoxy that Austen's brilliance lay in her artistic concentration. Lewes's essay sought to extend Austen's reputation beyond a coterie readership and he promoted Austen as an unequalled practitioner of minimalism in fiction:

> no novelist has approached her in what we may style the 'economy of art,' by which is meant the easy adaptation of means to ends, with no aid from extraneous or superfluous elements.[15]

Having endorsed in previous publications Macaulay's view of Austen as comparable with Shakespeare, in 1859 Lewes claimed that Austen was unsurpassed even by Shakespeare in dramatic presentation. That is, Austen rejects the easy option of description and instead leaves her characters to present themselves through speech. Criticism of Austen often pointed to omission. Lewes's is an example: he lists the "absence of breadth, picturesqueness, and passion"[16] in her fiction and dwells on what she fails to describe,

[12] Henry Wadsworth Longfellow, from his journal entry, 23 May 1839, in *Jane Austen: the Critical Heritage*, vol. 1, p. 117.

[13] Mary Augusta Ward, 'Style and Miss Austen', *Macmillan's Magazine*, 51 (December 1884), 84–91, p. 91.

[14] Virginia Woolf, unsigned review of W. and R. A. Austen-Leigh, *Jane Austen: Her Life and Letters*, and Sybil G. Brinton, *Old Friends and New Faces*, *Times Literary Supplement* (8 May 1913), in *Jane Austen: the Critical Heritage*, vol. 2, p. 244.

[15] George Henry Lewes, unsigned article, 'The Novels of Jane Austen', *Blackwood's Edinburgh Magazine* (July 1859), in *Jane Austen: the Critical Heritage*, vol. 1, p. 152.

[16] Ibid., p. 160.

whether it be the physical appearance of her characters or details of scenery. But this results in the unrivalled economy of her writing, "the truest representation, effected by the *least expenditure* of means". The following year, Lewes returned to Austen in *Blackwood's Edinburgh Magazine*, once again to praise her "principles of Economy and Selection", "nothing is dragged in, nothing is superfluous".[17]

Lewes began admiring Jane Austen in print from the early 1850s and over the next decade his appreciation of Austen's formal restraint developed into a thesis of economy to be applied more broadly to literature. In 1859, he asserted how "almost all defects in works of art arise from neglect of this economy" and how "[i]n novel-writing, as in mechanics, every obstruction is a loss of power; every superfluous page diminishes the artistic pleasure of the whole".[18] The sharpening of the economic metaphor in Lewes's literary criticism was indebted to Herbert Spencer's 1852 essay 'The Philosophy of Style' and would result in Lewes's own 1865 *Principles of Success in Literature*, first published as a series of essays in the *Fortnightly Review*. Using the analogy of the "mechanical apparatus", Herbert Spencer argued that stylistic accomplishment made the least claims on the resources of the reader.[19] Writing should aim in its syntax and figurative language at efficiency, brevity and ease of comprehension, and minimize "friction" and "inertia".[20] Spencer was mainly attempting to rectify obscurity of meaning due to poor expression, but he nonetheless advocated more generally ease of interpretation as a merit of reading. That Austen claimed with respect to *Pride and Prejudice*, "I do not write for such dull Elves" / "As have not a great deal of Ingenuity themselves" (*L*, p. 210), is one counter to Spencer's desire for saving a reader's effort, as Austen clearly demanded, indeed by means of economy and omission, an intellectual endeavour from her audience. In *The Principles of Success in Literature*, Lewes modulated Spencer's philosophy by querying any rigid sustainability of literary economy, even as he established it as the first of his fives laws on which such success depends.

In describing the 'Law of Economy', Lewes employs Spencer's mechanistic notion of the undesirability of any "friction" in the process of reading, so as to exclude the retarding effect of the "superfluous". Lewes does

[17] George Henry Lewes, unsigned article, 'A Word about *Tom Jones*', *Blackwood's Edinburgh Magazine* (March 1860), in *Jane Austen: the Critical Heritage*, vol. 1, p. 175.

[18] Lewes, 'The Novels of Jane Austen', *Jane Austen: the Critical Heritage*, vol. 1, pp. 153, 162.

[19] Herbert Spencer, 'The Philosophy of Style', in *Essays: Scientific, Political, & Speculative* (London: Routledge/Thoemmes Press, 1996; first published in the *Westminster Review*, October 1852), vol. 2, pp. 333–69, p. 335.

[20] Ibid., p. 336.

not refer to Austen by name in *The Principles of Success in Literature*, however, his repeated emphasis on Austen's eschewal of the "superfluous" in previous writing fed into his theory. But Lewes here registers the difficulty of an absolute exclusion of "superfluity": "[e]conomy is rejection of whatever is superfluous; it is not Miserliness" and in a paradoxical turn "redundancy" can be salvaged in the name of clarity:

> Perhaps the very redundancy which he [the author] lops away might have aided the reader to see the thought more clearly, because it would have kept the thought a little longer before his mind, and thus prevented him from hurrying on to the next while this one was still imperfectly conceived.[21]

In fact, the "best economy" allowed in places for "liberal expenditure" when "dictated by a generous impulse, not by a prodigal carelessness or ostentatious vanity". The economical writer judiciously permits expansion, even something like repetition, so as to aid a reader towards a vividly delineated apprehension and by consequence to allow variation in pace and cognitive progress.

In many places, Austen's private writing about fiction seems strikingly close to Lewes's theories of economy in *The Principles of Success in Literature*. Her comments cohere with Lewes's focus on the importance of revision,[22] 'striking out' and 'lopping' (Lewes) or 'scratching out', 'lopping and cropping' (Austen) anything which "will not carry away any of the constituent elements of the thought" (Lewes) or is "nothing to the purpose" (Austen). Austen's literary criticism also seems to correlate with Lewes's fundamental dislike of redundancy, as redundancy diverts attention towards "collateral detail". Under the 'Law of Simplicity', Lewes recommends that for a successful narrative structure "parts of novels should have organic relations". He continues:

> Push the licence to excess, and stitch together a volume of unrelated chapters, – a patchwork of descriptions, dialogues, and incidents, – no one will call that a novel; and the less the work has of this unorganised character the greater will be its value, not only in the eyes of critics, but in its effect on the emotions of the reader.[23]

Austen rejected precisely such "unrelated chapters" when she joked with Cassandra that *Pride and Prejudice* "wants to be stretched out here &

[21] George Henry Lewes, *The Principles of Success in Literature*, with an introduction by Geoffrey Tillotson (Farnborough, Hants: Gregg International Publishers, 1969; first published in the *Fortnightly Review*, May–November 1865), p. 70.

[22] Ibid.

[23] Ibid., p. 74.

there with a long Chapter [...] about something unconnected with the story" (*L*, p. 212). Yet we can see Austen in her letters, especially her early letters, also drawing attention to the dilemma of what in fact constitutes the extraneous and reflecting upon the management of what deserves elaboration or otherwise.

## Jane Austen's Letters: "That Choosing Instinct"

In 1885, Mary Augusta Ward published a hostile review of Lord Brabourne's edition of his great-aunt Jane Austen's letters. The review, 'Style and Miss Austen', is, following Lewes, the next major assessment by a well-known literary figure of Austen's economical style. Ward contrasted Brabourne's edition unfavourably with Austen's "determining quality" of "self-restraint".[24] The very act of publishing two volumes of personal letters containing the common events of day-to-day life was contrary to the "virtue of literary reticence".[25] Regarding the editorial matter, Ward claimed that Jane Austen herself would have been bored by the inappropriate lists of family pedigrees.[26] Ward also noted the lightness of tone characterizing Austen's letters as muted by the effect of the introductory chapters with their long lists of names and "wandering" criticism.[27]

In 'Style and Miss Austen', Ward, as much as Lewes, saw economy as a universal standard by which to judge the worth of a literary work and whether it is a "classic".[28] The terms of praise employed by Ward are "concentration" and "condensation", and she viewed Austen's genius as a confirmation of a historical process of ongoing literary refinement and distillation:

> The progress of literary expression during the last two hundred years has on the whole [...] been a progress towards concentration. Literature tends more and more to become a kind of shorthand. The great writers of this generation take more for granted than the great writers of the last, and the struggle to avoid commonplace and repetition becomes more and more diffused. The mind of the modern writer is on the whole most anxiously concerned with this perpetual necessity for omission, for compression. It will never describe if it can suggest, or argue if it can imply. [...]

[24] Ward, 'Style and Miss Austen', p. 91.
[25] Ibid, p. 84.
[26] Ibid.
[27] Ibid, p. 85.
[28] Ward writes of Susan Ferrier: "Miss Ferrier is scarcely read now [...] and will gradually drop more and more out of reading. And it is very easy to understand why, if one does but approach her books with these qualities of expansion and contraction which go to make up a classic in one's mind. She has little or no faculty of choice, nothing is refused that presents itself"; ibid., p. 90.

> It was her possession of the qualities of condensation that made Jane Austen what she was. Condensation in literary matters means an exquisite power of choice and discrimination – a capacity for isolating from the vast mass of detail which goes to make up human life just those details and no others which will produce a desired effect and blend into one clear and harmonious whole.[29]

There is a great deal of truth in this for Austen's fiction, including Austen's place in a broad formal trajectory towards compression. Novel writers of Austen's generation were rethinking the heritage of Samuel Richardson whose profuseness played a central part in his innovative transformation of English fiction, as he sought to capture human life through such a "vast mass of detail" or in his own words, the "minute". Jane Austen's brother Henry noted her admiration for Richardson, but her dissension from his prolixity.[30]

George Henry Lewes accounted for Austen's economy largely in terms of what she chose not to describe. Mary Augusta Ward dwelt upon Austen's concentration in matters of language. Austen's style indicates "the perpetual effort to be content with one word rather than two, the perpetual impulse to clip and prune rather than expand and lengthen".[31] A process of revision is acknowledged here ("clip and prune"), but Ward repeatedly envisages Austen's powers of condensation as a "gift" or an "instinct", the insights of which are spontaneous: Austen "seizes at once upon the most effective image or detail and realises at a glance how it will strike a reader".[32] Ward writes in the tradition established by Henry Austen, that his sister's compositions arrived fully formed. For Ward, the best of Austen's letters show "the perfect spontaneity of the writer".[33]

Ward felt that the most revealing letters in Brabourne's edition were the girlish ones that record flirting with Tom Lefroy and others. These come closest to the vitality of *Northanger Abbey* and remind us of the spirit of Catherine Morland, giving "glimpses, as it were, into the workshop which produced the novels".[34] But there are other letters, many of which were included in Brabourne's edition, that not only give glimpses of the workshop (which Ward conceives of as the subjects and tones of the later fiction), but

[29] Ibid., p. 89.
[30] Henry Austen, 'Biographical Notice of the Author' (1818), in Austen-Leigh, *A Memoir of Jane Austen and Other Family Recollections*, p. 141.
[31] Ward, 'Style and Miss Austen', p. 90.
[32] Ibid., pp. 90, 91.
[33] Ibid., p. 85.
[34] Ibid., p. 86.

that reflect on the abilities and tasks of the worker. Austen thinks through the matter of selection, tempering Ward's view that condensation was a spontaneous and innate talent. Austen herself did not always feel that she had the gift of a "choosing instinct".[35] But she was mindful of its importance.

What often comes to the surface of Austen's letters are reflections regarding the distribution and delivery of the writer's material: that is, the dynamics between the letter's content, the quantity or extent of that content and the stylistic means of conveying it. She muses on her desire for detail and she jokes about being boring. The much reprinted letter-writing manual *The Complete Letter-Writer* advises tradesmen to be concise in letters of business, while the writer of familiar letters is instructed to range widely through a variety of subjects. There is no guidance, however, about managing the line between enjoyable detail and prolixity.[36] Austen, by contrast, frequently comments on it. Writing a good letter to a known correspondent is inevitably different from writing a good novel, yet the processes of embracing or fending off material, engaging or boring a reader are germane to both.

The letter that Ward uses as an immediate example of the workshop of Austen's fiction, written in 1796 when Austen was twenty, is certainly familiar to a reader of the novels in its subjects of flirting, marriage and gossip, but also in its satirical register and knowing self-contradictions. But that very letter opens with the revealing address to Cassandra:

> My dear Cassandra,
>
> I shall be extremely anxious to hear the Event of your Ball, & shall hope to receive so long & minute an account of every particular that I shall be tired of reading it. (*L*, pp. 7–8; 5 September 1796)[37]

This comment, however playful, reveals a consciousness about the proportion of detail to interest and the reader's remuneration or reward for the time spent reading. What readers might think they desire through curiosity might soon be satiated. This is a subject that recurs in Austen's letters and indeed her fiction. In fact, the opening of this letter is strikingly close to the debate between Catharine and Camilla Stanley in Austen's unfinished manuscript 'Catharine, or the Bower', composed a few years

[35] Ibid., p. 91.

[36] *The Complete Letter-Writer; or, Polite English Secretary.* [...] *The Twelfth Edition, Improved* (London: for Stanley Crowder; and Benjamin Collins, in Salisbury, 1768), pp. 35, 32.

[37] This letter is included in *Letters of Jane Austen*, ed. with an introduction and critical remarks by Edward, Lord Brabourne (London: Richard Bentley & Son, 1884), vol. 1, p. 138. Further references to this edition are listed as 'Brabourne'.

earlier in 1792. There the two young women discuss Charlotte Smith's novel *Ethelinde*, with Camilla objecting to its length:

> "Besides, Ethelinde is so long—" "That is a very common Objection I beleive, said Kitty, but for my own part, if a book is well written, I always find it too short."
>
> "So do I, only I get tired of it before it is finished." (*J*, p. 249)

In this passage, the sentiments of which Austen liked enough that she reworked them for *Northanger Abbey* and *Pride and Prejudice*, Austen registers, again in a comic mode, the same interplay between detail and interest, description (for which Smith is celebrated) and length as she does in her letters. Camilla is the butt of this comic dialogue for being a superficial reader, but Austen could recognize and identify with the sentiment of becoming "tired" with a style of writing that is both desired and enjoyed.

In another letter to Cassandra about a ball (also included in Brabourne's edition), Austen reflects upon how minuteness may be a matter of time-limited enthusiasm for events, which are quickly excised by the memory:

> Your desiring to hear from me on Sunday will perhaps bring on you a more particular account of the Ball than you may care for, because one is prone to think much more of such things the morning after they happen, than when time has entirely driven them out of one's recollection. (*L*, p. 63; 20–21 November 1800)[38]

Much later, when recording for Cassandra the *exact* page number reached in each proof volume of *Emma*, it is uncertain whether she is stating straightforwardly Cassandra's sisterly interest in the last detail of her proof-reading or whether she is apologizing for straying too far into minutiae that can interest no one but the writer: "A Sheet come in this moment. 1$^{st}$ and 3$^{d}$ vol. are now at 144.—2$^{d}$ at 48.— I am sure you will like Particulars" (*L*, p. 312; 24 November 1815).

The magnifying element of Austen's fiction, her predilection for observing the minute that her nineteenth-century critics pointed to so often, has a corollary in this repeated enjoyment of "particulars" in letters. She repeats in her correspondence her pleasure in detail: "You know I enjoy particulars, & I was particularly amused with your picture of Grafton House" (*L*, p. 300; possibly late December 1814).[39] "[L]ittle events" form the substance

[38] Ibid., vol. 1, p. 241.

[39] This scrap from a letter was probably written to Anna Lefroy (*L*, p. 445–6). Austen's niece, Anna Austen, married Benjamin Lefroy on 8 November 1814.

of a good letter (here an admirably "long" one from Cassandra).[40] They may also give a writer a structure:

> I shall now try to say only what is necessary, I am weary of meandering—so expect a vast deal of small matter concisely told, in the next two pages.[41] (*L*, p. 179; 30 January 1809)

Austen not only tells Cassandra that she is going to get to the point, but seems to think out on paper, however casually, the nature of the content ("small matter"), its quantity ("vast deal"), and the compensatory time of telling ("concisely told"). That Austen is alert to the opposing spatial relations she invokes – between "vast deal" and "small matter", "little matter" and the "long" – is most obviously demonstrated when she acknowledges that to write "at large", to write more fully, is also to write "at small", with more precise detail:

> I can now answer your question to my Mother more at large, & likewise more at small—with equal perspicuity & minuteness, for the very day of our leaving Southampton is fixed—[42] (*L*, p. 170; 10–11 January 1809)

Austen adopts a verbal play that acknowledges one spatial extreme to be inevitably productive of another.

While Austen relished minuteness, she also acknowledged in her letters that it can be tedious (as any reader of Richardson would know), as well as "foolish". Miss Milles, whose conversation Austen recorded when staying at Godmersham, has been identified as a possible prototype of the garrulous Miss Bates in *Emma*. Austen states:

> She undertook in three words to give us the history of M[rs] Scudamore's reconciliation, & then talked on about it for half an hour, using such odd expressions & **so foolishly minute** that I could hardly keep my countenance.[43] (*L*, p. 255; 26 October 1813)

But a couple of weeks later, when still at Godmersham, Austen uses the same expression, consciously or unconsciously, mirroring her vision of Miss Milles in her own potential to give excessive detail:

40 "You are very amiable & very clever to write such long Letters; every page of yours has more lines than this, & every line more words than the average of mine. I am quite ashamed—but you have certainly more little events than we have. M[r] Lyford supplies you with a great deal of interesting Matter (Matter intellectual, not physical)— but I have nothing to say of M[r] Scudamore" (*L*, p. 136; 20–22 June 1808). This letter is included in Brabourne, vol. 1, p. 356.

41 To Cassandra Austen. Included in Brabourne, vol. 2, p. 73.

42 To Cassandra Austen. In Brabourne, vol. 2, pp. 54–5, noted as 10 January.

43 To Cassandra Austen. Included in Brabourne, vol. 2, p. 196.

> My dearest Cassandra,
>
> Having half an hour before breakfast—(very snug, in my own room, lovely morn^g, excellent fire, fancy me) I will give you some account of the last two days. And yet, what is there to be told?—I shall get **foolishly minute** unless I cut the matter short.—We met only the Brittons at Chilham Castle, besides a M^r & M^rs Osborne & a Miss Lee staying in the House, & were only 14 altogether. My B^r & Fanny thought it the pleasantest party they had ever known there & I was very well entertained by bits & scraps. —I had long wanted to see D^r Britton, & his wife amuses me very much with her affected refinement & elegance. —Miss Lee I found very conversible; she admires Crabbe as she ought. (*L*, p. 261; 6–7 November 1813)

Conscious of the dangers of the minute as Austen is, the letter exemplifies small matter "concisely told". Austen narrates her visit to Chilham Castle by moving in brisk sentences between the individuals that she met there. However, she finds herself straying into the very minuteness that she finds displeasing: while Lady B[rook] is described as getting away from a visit to a concert with admirable promptness, it is Austen who finds herself 'dawdling' in writing about her:

> Lady B. was much what I expected, I could not determine whether she was rather handsome or very plain.—I liked her, for being in a hurry to have the Concert over & get away, & for getting away at last with a great deal of decision and promtness [*sic*], not waiting to compliment & dawdle & fuss about seeing <u>dear Fanny</u>, who was half the even^g in another part of the room with her friends the Plumptres. **I am growing too minute, so I will go to Breakfast.**[44] (*L*, p. 262; 6–7 November 1813)

The subject of this letter may be the trivial everyday matter that Mary Augusta Ward identified as uninteresting; that is, the "ordinary chit-chat of the ordinary gentlewoman". But surely Austen's self-consciousness about what she thought to be the requisite amount of detail to interest does have relevance for understanding her fictional economy? In December 1808, Austen approved of Mr Deedes's epistolary style in a letter to Cassandra:

> He has certainly great merit as a Writer, he does ample justice to his subject, & without being diffuse, is clear & correct; —& tho' I do not mean to compare his Epistolary powers with yours, or to give him the same portion of my Gratitude, he certainly has a very pleasing way of winding up a whole, & speeding Truth into the World.[45] (*L*, p. 162; 9 December 1808)

Austen repeatedly measures success in writing by some rule of concision and this enjoyment of a letter "speeding Truth into the world" proves

[44] Included in Brabourne, vol. 2, pp. 209–11.
[45] In Brabourne, vol. 2, p. 39.

consistent with many of her novelistic choices. Whether Austen had an unfailing "instinct" for the concise is moot, but she did admire it in different forms, and in the earliest fiction that she wrote, as a teenager, she seems to have been strongly motivated by it.

## Jane Austen's Juvenilia: the Contractive Imagination

By and large, Austen's teenage writings retain their reputation as being distinct from her mature fiction.[46] This is because of their often outrageous narrative events, including murder, bigamy and drunkenness, and their highly burlesque tone that is only occasionally evident in the satirical portraits of the mature work. The style of the juvenilia is most commonly thought to re-emerge in the caricatures of Austen's last work *Sanditon*, especially in its improbable hypochondriacs.[47] But Austen's critique of contemporary fiction in the juvenilia undoubtedly shaped her mature art. Through her parodic dissent from aspects of sentimental fiction of the day, she created the terms of her own style. Not only that: the teenage writings prove to be, formally, a foundation for all that she writes later. It is in Austen's early writings that we see most clearly her radically contractive thinking and her formative interest in narrative acts of concision, diminution and acceleration.

As a teenage writer, Austen was motivated by the possibilities of contraction. Her interest in reducing famously enormous works speaks volumes. Any reasonable expectation of length one might have for a history of England, based on the historical exemplars of the day, whether David Hume's six-volume or Oliver Goldsmith's four-volume histories, or even their popular three-hundred-page abridgements, is overturned by her own 'The History of England', written in a mere thirty-three, illustrated and capaciously spaced manuscript pages. The most entangled narratives of succession are summarized with blasé compression, as with the Wars of the Roses: "for Henry Tudor E. of Richmond as great a Villain as ever lived, made a great fuss about getting the Crown" (*J*, p. 179). Aiding her young niece Anna, Austen depleted the seven volumes of *Sir Charles Grandison* to five small dramatic acts and a mere fifty-two manuscript pages.[48] In the juvenilia as a whole, the notoriously lengthy genre of the

46 Peter Sabor closes his 'Introduction' to the Cambridge edition of Austen's *Juvenilia* with a description of the style of these early writings as "quite unlike the work of any of her contemporaries, and equally unlike her own mature novels" (p. lxvii). Conjectural dates for the composition of individual pieces within the juvenilia are taken from *Juvenilia*, xxviii–ix.

47 Sabor, *Juvenilia*, p. xxiv.

48 The short play is in Jane Austen's handwriting and it is likely that Austen transcribed her niece's composition (*LM*, p. cxvi). For the history of the attribution of the play *Sir Charles Grandison*,

novel was repeatedly reduced, most ruthlessly in *Volume the First*. There, one complete novel reaches fifty-four manuscript pages ('Jack & Alice'), but, excluding the 'Detached peices', the prose fiction in this volume averages at fifteen pages apiece. Austen's completed work, 'The beautifull Cassandra' (also in *Volume the First*) displays most ostentatiously the project of reduction, consisting of twelve chapters, with no chapter running to more than four sentences or six manuscript lines. The novel takes up four manuscript pages, excluding the dedication (see Illustration I.1).[49]

In her teenage fiction, Austen channels the same questions that she would raise in her letters, regarding the distribution of words to event, towards a bravura comedy of narration. She achieves this through a deliberate disequilibrium between details and their significance. The comedy of the early writing often consists in compressing narrative that anyone would expect to be protracted by means of absurd flights through time. In 'Frederic & Elfrida', Charlotte receives and accepts two proposals of marriage in the space of three tiny paragraphs (*J*, p. 9), while in 'Amelia Webster', three courtships are conducted in seven miniscule letters to close with a triple wedding. Austen also ridicules fictions that make absurd claims for plenitude. Inset tales, where characters tell of their previous lives and adventures, were common into the nineteenth century and frequently satirized by Austen who reduces these often lengthy, contextual episodes into a formulaic hyperbole that delivers nothing:

> At the request of your Mother I related to them every other misfortune which had befallen me since we parted. (*J*, pp. 134–5)
>
> As soon as she had complyed with my wishes in this particular and had given me an accurate detail of every thing that had befallen her since our separation (the particulars of which if you are not already acquainted with, your Mother will give you) I applied to Augusta for the same information respecting herself, Sir Edward and Lady Dorothea. (*J*, p. 135)
>
> I informed them [Philander and Gustavus] of every thing which had befallen me during the course of my Life, and at my request they related to me every incident of theirs. (*J*, p. 137)

see *LM*, pp. cxi–cxviii. Brian Southam gives the alternative view that Austen was the author of the play: *Jane Austen's 'Sir Charles Grandison'*, transcribed and ed. by Brian Southam; foreword by Lord David Cecil (Oxford: Clarendon Press, 1980). As elsewhere, page counts of Austen's manuscript texts exclude title or other prefatory pages.

49 Jane Austen, 'The beautifull Cassandra', in *Volume the First*, pp. 115–19 in *Jane Austen's Fiction Manuscripts: A Digital Edition*, ed. Kathryn Sutherland (2010). Available at www.janeausten.ac.uk. ISBN: 978-0-9565793-1-7. In their edition of Austen's *Teenage Writings*, Kathryn Sutherland and Freya Johnston describe the first notebook as suggesting a writer "testing how sparely and cryptically a piece of fiction might be assembled and retain the elements necessary for comprehension", in Jane Austen, *Teenage Writings*, ed. with an introduction and notes by Kathryn Sutherland and Freya Johnston (Oxford: Oxford University Press, 2017), p. xvi.

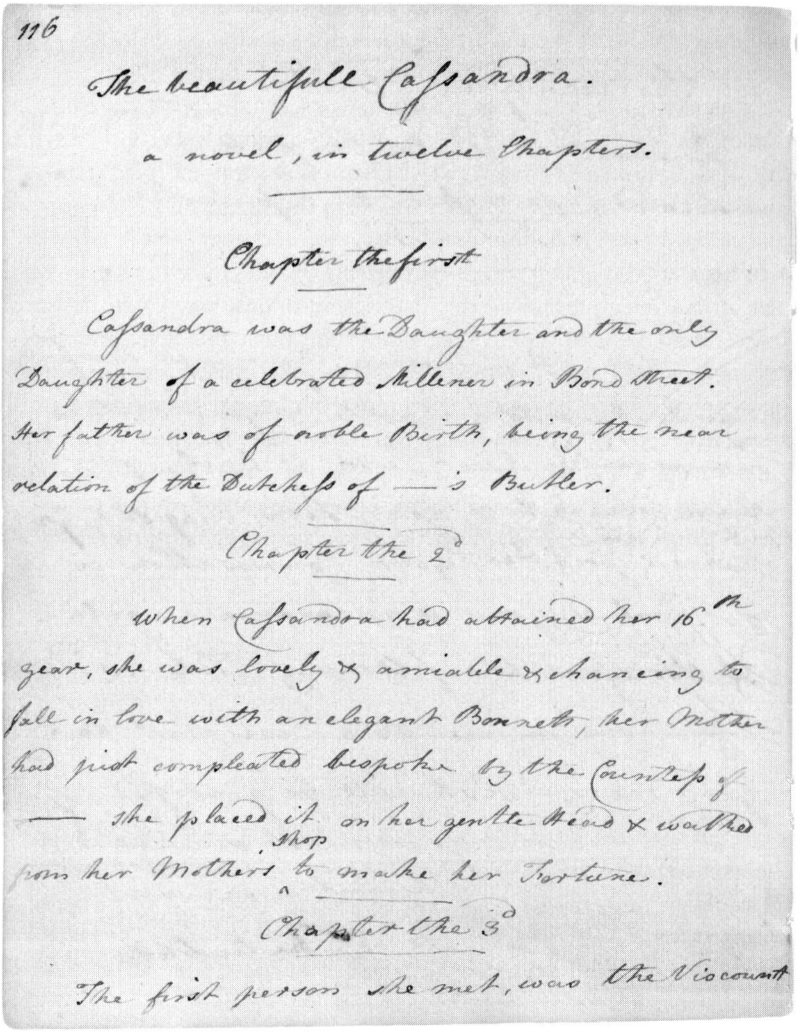

116

The beautifull Cassandra.

a novel, in twelve Chapters.

Chapter the first

Cassandra was the Daughter and the only Daughter of a celebrated Millener in Bond Street. Her father was of noble Birth, being the near relation of the Dutchess of ——'s Butler.

Chapter the 2d

When Cassandra had attained her 16th year, she was lovely & amiable & chancing to fall in love with an elegant Bonnet, her Mother had just compleated bespoke by the Countess of —— she placed it on her gentle Head & walked from her Mother's shop to make her Fortune.

Chapter the 3d

The first person she met, was the Viscount

Illustration I.1 Jane Austen, 'The beautifull Cassandra', in *Volume the First*, p. 116. By permission of the Bodleian Libraries, The University of Oxford. MS.Don.e.7

Inset histories, while promoting inclusiveness, can make a novel distractingly heterogeneous. Austen reduces *ad absurdum* such narrations that must inevitably be briefer than promised.

Alongside such contractions of the extensive are ostentatious irrelevancies. Both strategies serve as commentary on the novelist's need for selection. Importantly, Austen's satirical irrelevancies are never quite permitted to become fatiguing in themselves, as they are contained by the briefest of narratives. In 'The adventures of Mr Harley', the minute narrative which amounts to a total of sixteen lines, space is given to the fellow travellers of Mr Harley in a stage-coach – "A man without a Hat, Another with two" – along with the woman he remembers to be his wife (*J*, p. 46). It is impossible to say in cases like this whether there is any biographical relevance to such strange details, but to read these manuscript narratives as existing for eyes beyond a family coterie – and Austen was imagining them in part as published works – details like these remain tantalizingly obvious non-starters. The travellers and their hats, about whom we learn nothing else, are miniature emblems of those circumstances in fiction "of apparent consequence, which will lead to nothing" about which she would much later write to Anna (*L*, p. 281; 10–18 August 1814).

Elsewhere in the juvenilia, Austen creates narrators who more ostentatiously are unable to select and sieve, most egregiously in the 'Memoirs of Mr Clifford: an unfinished tale—' which begins, conventionally enough, with a journey to London:

> Mr Clifford lived at Bath; and having never seen London, set off one Monday morning determined to feast his eyes with a sight of that great Metropolis. He travelled in his Coach and Four, for he was a very rich young Man and kept a great many Carriages of which I do not recollect half. I can only remember that he had a Coach, a Chariot, a Chaise, a Landeau, a Landeaulet, a Phaeton, a Gig, a Whisky, an italian Chair, a Buggy, a Curricle and a wheelbarrow. He had likewise an amazing fine stud of Horses. To my knowledge he had six Greys, 4 Bays, eight Blacks and a poney. (*J*, p. 51)

The narrator skips over the dangerous fever that incapacitates the hero for five months, to describe Mr Clifford resuming his journey with another routine inventory of its ensuing stages. In 'Edgar & Emma', Austen fuses narrative listing with irrelevant protagonists to present intertwined stylistic and structural infelicities. It is difficult for the reader even to find the hero Edgar Willmot from a catalogue of family simulacra. Emma watches his many siblings descend from a carriage to visit:

> Mr and Mrs Willmot with their three eldest Daughters first appeared—Emma began to tremble—. Robert, Richard, Ralph, and Rodolphus followed—Emma turned pale—. Their two youngest Girls were lifted from the Coach—Emma sunk breathless on a Sopha. (*J*, p. 35)

When Emma demands that Mrs Willmot tell her how the rest of her family does, "particularly your eldest son", Mrs Willmot replies:

> "Our children are all extremely well but at present most of them from home. Amy is with my sister Clayton. Sam at Eton. David with his Uncle John. Jem and Will at Winchester. Kitty at Queens Square. Ned with his Grandmother. Hetty and Patty in a convent at Brussells. Edgar at college, Peter at Nurse, and all the rest (except the nine here) at home." (*J*, p. 36)

Emma in response to this news retires to her room to cry for the rest of her life. Austen "crams in" (to use Virginia Woolf's phrase) an enormous amount of detail into a small narrative space and, like 'The adventures of Mr Harley', at the expense of what one might expect to be the emotional centre of the tale, in this case the feelings of the characters for each other.

The genesis of such excessive and stalling listing is the same magnifying element, that love of the minute, that marks out Austen's fiction. It is the same characteristic that leads Austen in her letters to complain of her own minuteness, as she details one by one the company that she has met when visiting Godmersham. That Austen goes on to write *Emma*'s Miss Bates reveals an affectionate sympathy with non-selection. 'Edgar & Emma' also acknowledges sympathetically the desire to list: it is understandable that Edgar is no more important to his mother than Sam, David, Jem and Will etc. But while for a mother all children may be loved equally, Austen was aware that a novelist, as much as a lover, must be able to choose.

'Emma & Edgar' is one of only four chaptered fictions in Austen's juvenilia. All four of the chaptered novels are included in *Volume the First* and three of the four are placed by Austen at the beginning of the volume. All three of these opening works could be described as fiction in search of its protagonists. All three resist their framing titles. The five chapters of 'Frederic & Elfrida' have a carefully organized chiastic architecture, in which the relationship between the eponymous pair begins and ends the novel, but largely disappears in the three central chapters which are occupied by the engagements of Elfrida's friend Charlotte (Chapter 3) and their mutual acquaintance Rebecca Fitzroy (Chapters 2 and 4). By the end of this brief novel and at the point of their betrothal, Frederic and Elfrida have grown old. The couple are the superstructure – the title, starting point and conclusion – to a fiction that interests itself in others. The subject of 'Edgar & Emma', as we have seen, is Edgar's absence, while Emma herself only turns up in the second chapter of this three-chapter novel. Jack in 'Jack & Alice' similarly does not materialize, as "he never did anything worth mentioning" and then is reported as having died (*J*, p. 27).

Among these early chaptered novels, 'Jack & Alice' is the most overt critique of wandering, episodic fiction. It has a narrative structure of nestling inset tales: Lady Williams tells Alice of her "Life and adventures", to be interrupted by an encounter with Lucy who tells of her "Life and adventures". While Alice goes on to offer herself in marriage to Charles Adams in Pammydiddle, Lucy is being proposed to by a duke in Bath, then to be murdered by the "malvolent Sukey" [*sic*] (*J*, p. 30). Taken further than 'Frederic & Elfrida', chapters seem to propose to the young Austen an abrupt and digressive shifting between characters that is very different from her mature writing. Once more, one of Austen's later warnings to Anna of "too frequent a change from one set of people to another" seems prefigured in the satire of the juvenilia (*L*, p. 281).

'The beautifull Cassandra' is structurally different, as well as physically separated, from the other chaptered fictions in the juvenilia and is one of its most enigmatic pieces. The narrative is tightly focused on one character and has a very time-limited focus of seven hours in a day, with each chapter containing some specific action. The actions across the chapters are linked mainly by chronology and there is a dreamy surrealism to these unfolding chapters, as the sixteen-year-old Cassandra heads off from the family home to make her fortune. This involves walking past various persons with a curtsey or a blush, but also committing at least one act of violence, when she knocks down the pastry-cook. She refuses to pay for six ices she devours and when unable to pay for a coach fare she places her bonnet on the coachman's head, with unspecified force. The deliberate rebelliousness of the beautiful Cassandra is confirmed and nullified in a rather touching last chapter when, returning home, Cassandra is pressed safely to her mother's bosom. The novel takes pleasure in unladylike behaviour and as such captures something of the free-spirited heroines to come.

While it is true that the plot of 'The beautifull Cassandra' is simple structurally and in terms of action, this does not preclude it demonstrating a sophisticated piece of thinking about the novel form. Contraction is its foundational act of rebellion. Austen reduces "a novel" to twelve chapters, each containing an action as small as walking past someone in the street. This tale so vividly captures Austen thinking about the novel in the tiniest of units: small events, small time frame, tiny chapters. This is Austen shrinking the novel back to its most contained and constricted dimensions, and musing on what such dimensions can nevertheless hold.

## Little Habitations: Economies of Space

Austen's squeezing of narrative into diminutive text is re-enacted thematically across her teenage writing, as she squeezes characters into and out of exceptionally constricted spaces. The minute proportions of one chapter of 'The beautifull Cassandra' exemplifies this confluence of formal and thematic compression. While Austen squeezes her chapter into one sentence, a character inhabits a space that is far too small for her:

> CHAPTER THE 10TH
>
> Cassandra was next accosted by her freind the Widow, who squeezing out her little Head thro' her less window, asked her how she did? Cassandra curtseyed and went on.
>
> CHAPTER THE 11TH
>
> (*J*, pp. 55–6)

The point may be that the beautiful Cassandra's friend is so impoverished that she inhabits the smallest, cheapest room in a little house. But to have a window smaller than one's head is unusual. Austen creates a comedy of littleness to accompany her narrative diminishments and once again this generates verbal play with scale. The Widow while making herself physically smaller, becomes larger, lexically expanding into the "wi**n**dow" that she squeezes out of, while "little" has to fit (impossibly) through "less". Ultimately, the Widow's massive efforts bear negligible narrative yield, as Cassandra passes on.

Austen's writing on the "little" was significantly fostered by eighteenth-century satire, in particular the mock-heroic tradition. Austen's performance in Fielding's early eighteenth-century burlesque *Tom Thumb* in the family theatricals at Steventon is an apposite emblem of Austen's comic interest in the greatly small. She seems to have enjoyed the common satirical expansion "little diminutive" (used memorably by Sterne in *Tristram Shandy*).[50] Margaret Lesley uses the tautology twice of her new mother-in-law in 'Lesley Castle': "there is something so extremely unmajestic in her little diminutive figure, as to render her in comparison with the elegant height of Matilda and Myself, an insignificant Dwarf" (*J*, p. 157, also p. 174). Even at the end of her writing life, Austen was determined to include a bathetically named Capt: Little (again great and small) as one of the few subscribers to the circulating library at Sanditon, as surrounding text seems to have been written to accommodate him. The immediately preceding account of Mrs Whitby "sitting in the little inner parlour" is revised to "sitting in her inner room" (*S*, b2-18).

[50] Laurence Sterne, *The Life and Opinions of Tristram Shandy, Gentleman* eds. Melvyn New and Joan New; with an introductory essay by Christopher Ricks; and an introduction and notes by Melvyn New (London: Penguin Books, 1997; first published, 1759–67), p. 85. This is the description of Dr Slop's pony.

Brigid Brophy has suggested subtle, personal reasons for Austen's radical contractions in the juvenilia. Brophy identifies across Austen's work a psychological response to the downsizing of the family from the moneyed grandeur of her mother's ancestry in particular. Thus, Brophy sees the declining fortunes of the Austen family as underlying both the narrative compression of Austen's 'The History of England' and her repeated return in the published novels to small domestic spaces.[51] Austen's adult life was affected by a series of largely unwanted domestic moves, until she finally settled in Chawton, a house in which, according to her niece Caroline, some bedrooms were "very small" and "*none* very large", with a garden at least in which "you did not feel cramped for room".[52] The experiences of the Dashwoods, Fanny Price and the Elliots, who all have to re-accommodate themselves in relatively cramped conditions, do seem strikingly personal, given this context. In the teenage, pre-Chawton writing, Brophy sees Austen's interest in narrative contraction as exemplifying more of a generational consciousness of diminishing circumstances.[53] But this early fiction also has an explicit interest in tiny homes, endorsing an interpretation of Austen's consciousness of a life of downward mobility. Austen reduces habitable spaces to their furthest extremes in the juvenilia, much as she does the writing spaces her early stories inhabit. Whatever the causes for Austen's interest in this, there is an early correlation between stylistic conception and subject matter that pertains to Austen's mature writing life.

Samuel Beckett thought that Austen "had much to teach him", when reading *Sense and Sensibility* in 1935.[54] What might he have thought had he read 'Love and Freindship', where Austen envisages a scene comparable with *Endgame* or *Play* over a hundred years before Beckett was born?[55] While Beckett has characters in these two plays live in dustbins and urns, Austen blithely narrates the home of Gustavus and Philander in 'Love and Freindship' as the basket on the back of a stage-coach (*J*, p. 137). The basket does not have the same mortal connotations as Beckett's unusual residences, and the characters' residence there is not as necessarily long

[51] Brigid Brophy, 'Jane Austen and the Stuarts', in *Critical Essays on Jane Austen*, ed. B. C. Southam (London: Routledge & Kegan Paul, 1968), pp. 21–38, p. 31.

[52] Ibid., p. 28. Brophy quotes Caroline Austen's *My Aunt Jane Austen: a Memoir*, written in 1867 and published first in 1952.

[53] Ibid., p. 30.

[54] James Knowlson, *Damned to Fame: the Life of Samuel Beckett* (London: Bloomsbury, 1996), p. 203.

[55] There no record that Beckett did read 'Love and Freindship', though it was first published in 1922.

chapter, as well as my third, identifies narrative constraint as contributing to Austen's developments in depicting the mind in action, in free indirect discourse.

The third chapter, on dialogue, identifies a relatively unknown speech category, free direct speech, as an innovative force in Austen's fiction, which to date has not been fully grasped. Free direct speech occurs when direct speech is presented without framing clauses. Remarkably, given how little Austen says about her own fiction, she refers to this feature of her writing, describing missing "said he"s or "said she"s, in one of her letters to Cassandra about *Pride and Prejudice* (*L*, p. 210; 29 January 1813). The omission of speech attribution opens up aspects of Austen's thinking about the novel's relationship with drama, as speech is left unmediated by a narrator. On the other hand, Austen acknowledges that she is content to risk the reader's confusion or uncertainty in a manner that is inimical to drama, but, as I shall argue, is germane to the presentation of thought. Free direct speech contributes, in other words, to Austen's famed development of free *indirect* discourse. Free direct speech is itself a much neglected literary form, virtually unknown in comparison with its indirect relation. My claims for the innovatory nature of free direct discourse in Austen's novels have implications, therefore, that extend far beyond her fiction.

It would be difficult to overstate the significance of free indirect discourse in the history of the novel. It has even been described as the novel's identifiable form *per se*, as much as fourteen lines signify the form of a sonnet.[64] Free indirect discourse occurs when a narrative voice merges with, or seems to adopt, the voice of a character. The delivered speech is 'free' from a narratorial report as to the person speaking. In other words, there is no attribution. The technique transformed fiction by facilitating a subtle depiction of character consciousness, as narrative can move unobtrusively into the viewpoint of a character. This book shows how Austen's instincts for narrative concision interact with her interest in character consciousness. This can be demonstrated by reference to a last historical appreciation of Austen's skills in fictional economy.

Austen's best-known narrative omissions are her proposal scenes. In 1917 Reginald Farrer described them as "notorious", yet demonstrative of

[64] Frances Ferguson, 'Jane Austen, *Emma*, and the Impact of Form', in *Reading for Form*, eds. Susan J. Wolfson and Marshall Brown (Seattle and London: University of Washington Press, 2006; first published in 2000 as a special issue of the *Modern Language Quarterly*), pp. 231–55, pp. 233–4.

an intense "concentration" that makes Austen among the "greatest writers".[65] Jane Austen knew that the largest, the most significant things in life require, artistically, the smallest space:

> In the supreme moments, in point of fact, humanity becomes inarticulate, and thus no longer gives material for art. Jane Austen, knowing this, is too honest to forge us false coin of phrases, and too much an artist to pad out her lines with asterisks and dashes and ejaculations. She accepts the condition, asks her reader to accept it also, and contents herself with dealing with the emotions on either side of the crucial outbreak. It is notorious how she avoids detail in her proposal-scenes; certainly not from 'ladylike' cowardice, nor from any incapacity, but merely in her artist's certainty that the epical instants of life are not to be adequately expressed in words. 'What did she say? Just what she should, of course; a lady always does.' Jane Austen, with whimsical gaiety of candour, here lays down her position once for all, and frankly tells her reader that there are matters into which neither he nor she can decently pry.[66]

Such a pulling back from explicit romantic expression has garnered much critical attention and has been deemed a matter of tact, modesty and disinterest, as well as a creative instinct that silence says it best.

This is the longer scene from *Emma*, which Farrer uses to exemplify his point:

> What did she say?—Just what she ought, of course. A lady always does. —She said enough to show **there need not be despair**—and to invite him to say more himself. **He *had* despaired** at one period; he had received such an injunction to caution and silence, as for the time crushed every hope;—she had begun by refusing to hear him. —The change had perhaps been somewhat sudden;—her proposal of taking another turn, her renewing the conversation which she had just put an end to, might be a little extraordinary!—She felt its inconsistency; but Mr. Knightley was so obliging as to put up with it, and seek no farther explanation. (*E*, p. 470)

Austen does not, in fact, content herself with dealing with "emotions on either side" of an elision. Rather, this passage from *Emma* narrates the conversation that has been suppressed. The emphatic "He *had* despaired"

[65] Reginald Farrer, 'Jane Austen, *ob.* July 18, 1817', *Quarterly Review* (July 1917), in *Jane Austen: the Critical Heritage,* vol. 2, p. 253. "This elimination of the author is only part of the intense concentration which the greatest writers develop in their subject. [...] It is at this point that all living writers (with the exception of Rhoda Broughton) fail. They are telling stories [...] with an eye to their audience and to themselves and their own pet notions, telling them, that is, objectively, not subjectively, and piling up masses of detail and explanation in order to obscure the inner lack of any completed identity between the author and his matter" (p. 249).

[66] Ibid., pp. 252–3.

gives the intonation of Knightley replying to Emma, picking up on what retrospectively seem to be her own terms "there need not be despair". The summary of the narrator thus carries with it the sounds of a conversation that we have been led to believe is not there. Why does Austen, after ostensibly avoiding narrative description in such a pronounced way, go on to repeat in miniature the scene that has only just been summarized? What is the purpose of this elision that turns out to be barely that?

The scene is apophatic, as expression is negated only to be expressed. Frequently in Austen's fiction a declaration of non-expressibility brings with it an amplificatory effect in which Austen's interest in capturing the mind in motion is strongly implicated. Apophasis in this scene creates a sweetly comic irony, as such a significant matter cannot lie hidden. Austen allows the couple their privacy by not giving us their words directly, nor attributing any speech to them at all. Rather conversation is intimated in the indirect discourse that follows, which then flows into Emma's thoughts. Ultimately, a much more private space than even the declarations of two lovers is revealed: the subjective mind. Austen's use of free indirect discourse had a suppleness and subtlety as yet unprecedented in English fiction. In what follows, I suggest that Austen's instinct for stylistic contraction promoted it.

CHAPTER I

# *Structure*
## *Selection, Connection and the Picturesque*

### Introduction

Contraction was crucial to Austen's final preparation of *Pride and Prejudice* for publication. The novel, originally composed in 1796–7 as *First Impressions*, most likely underwent significant rewriting sometime between 1811 and 1812 before it was published on 28 January 1813.[1] The process of excision, that was evidently a major part of this rewriting, remained at the forefront of Austen's thoughts when she at last saw the three precious volumes in January:

> The 2[d] vol. is shorter than I c[d] wish—but the difference is not so much in reality as in look, there being a larger proportion of Narrative in that part. I have lopt & cropt so successfully however that I imagine it must be rather shorter than S. & S. altogether. (*L*, p. 210)

The difference between the lengths of the volumes of *Pride and Prejudice* in its first edition is certainly marked: the first volume has 307 pages, the second 239 and the third 323. But Austen, in defence of this outcome, redistributes her structural economy, positing the larger part of narrative to be in the shortest volume of the book. In *Northanger Abbey*, Henry Tilney alludes with disparagement to the mechanistic predictability of Gothic publications "in three duodecimo volumes, two hundred and seventy-six pages in each" (p. 114). One wonders whether this particular line was composed after Austen had seen her own work in print. Austen's comment on the distribution of her narrative across the component parts of the book raises some questions, to be returned to later in this chapter, as to the character of the "Narrative" in the second volume and why that volume comes out so short.

[1] I follow here Kathryn Sutherland's account of the chronology of the composition of Austen's novels, in 'Chronology of Composition and Publication', in *Jane Austen in Context*, ed. Janet Todd (Cambridge: Cambridge University Press, 2005), pp. 12–22. As Sutherland notes, R. W. Chapman pointed out that the action of *Pride and Prejudice* coheres with the calendars for 1811–12, in his 'Chronology of *Pride and Prejudice*' (p. 17).

As we have seen, the editing and shortening of *Pride and Prejudice* also came to Cassandra's mind when she prepared, possibly shortly after her sister's death in 1817, the memorandum of the dates of composition of her sister's six novels:

> First Impressions begun in Oct 1796
> Finished in Augt 1797. Publishd
> afterwards, with alterations & contractions
> under the Title of Pride & Prejudice.[2]

The reduction of *Pride and Prejudice* was obviously a memorable aspect of its reshaping for Cassandra Austen, at least four years after its publication, and it remains a tantalizing enigma to readers of Jane Austen. Does the novel in any way show the traces of that excised material? Did Austen cut out discrete sections (as Cassandra's phrasing might suggest) or did the text undergo a process of small tweaks? And why did that which was rejected deserve such a fate when generations of readers would relish and pore over Austen's every word?

D. A. Miller has described Austen's style – and indeed that style as the apotheosis of style – as originating with the "cut". He combines his sense of Austen's gender neutrality with her self-evisceration from the text. But the origins of his metaphor lie in the common vocabulary of Austen appreciation. Austen's style is "precise", "concise", "incisive": "We also know", Miller writes, "that, however trenchantly this Style may deal with characters, its first object has been itself, manifestly the result of rigorous selection, exclusion, reduction."[3] Austen's rigorous process of "selection, exclusion, reduction" may indeed be something 'we know', observed most frequently in her descriptive omissions and evasions of broader socio-historical reference. But Austen's actual process of selection and reduction when composing her novels still remains largely abstracted, viewed inevitably through the resulting precise style of the six published works. Miller's own account of the "cut" governing Austen's fiction is provocatively metaphorical and only vaguely literal.

I think that there is more to be said about Austen's development of the cut as a defining compositional practice of her fiction. Austen's early fiction, as well as her comments on reading and writing more generally in her letters, provide a full and coherent sense of her strongly held views on the shape of fiction and amount to an explicit commentary on the processes of

[2] See note 4 in Introduction.

[3] D. A. Miller, *Jane Austen, or The Secret of Style* (Princeton, NJ, and Oxford: Princeton University Press, 2003), p. 34.

"selection, exclusion, reduction" by which she transformed formal expectations for the English novel. This coherently, if disparately, voiced literary criticism by Austen intersects with a formalism that was emerging in novel criticism of the period. Austen's prose enacted a new aesthetic appreciation of the novel. There is a preoccupation with the subjects of length, prolixity and successiveness across Austen's writing, often brought into focus through the comparative genres of history and writing on travel and the picturesque. Furthermore, the principle of connection marks out Austen's narrative theory, also drawing on the picturesque, but as an aesthetic that, paradoxically, eschews description.

*Pride and Prejudice* remains a touchstone throughout this chapter. In this novel there are traces of Austen working hard to achieve the formal aesthetic that is one important aspect of the novel's brilliance. *Pride and Prejudice* is an experiment in brevity, a work of contraction, as striking, in some ways, as some of the miniature juvenile works and it displays, as well as comments on, a connectedness that governs its narrative principles. William Deresiewicz has said that Austen's commentary on *Pride and Prejudice* "gives no support to the theory that it involved anything other than shortening and tightening".[4] But we should not assume that "shortening and tightening" cannot be a form of major revision, which may signal an important rethinking of what a novel might be.

## Jane Austen and the Question of Length

In the few reviews that appeared in her lifetime, Austen's fiction is picked out from a background of books that can bore. The very first published review of Austen's fiction – the *Critical Review*'s appraisal of *Sense and Sensibility* in February 1812 – was attentive to how the author of the novel had got its length just right, so as not to tire its readers: "the conclusion [is] such as the reader must wish it should be, and the whole is just long enough to interest without fatiguing".[5] Walter Scott's much-cited review of *Emma* opens with a much-less cited account of yawning. Scott tells a tale about a boatswain on a ship bound for India, whose glory consists in winning the competition to complete the *Memoirs of Clegg the Clergyman*, an "unutterably stupid" work of fiction that had baffled the dullest of readers.

[4] William Deresiewicz, *Jane Austen and the Romantic Poets* (New York: Columbia University Press, 2004), p. 11.

[5] Unsigned review, *Critical Review* (February 1812), in B. C. Southam (ed.), *Jane Austen: the Critical Heritage* (London: Routledge & Kegan Paul, 1968), vol. 1, p. 35. Further references to *Jane Austen: the Critical Heritage* are by volume number.

Even "the worst novel ever written", writes Scott "will find some gentle reader content to yawn over it", pointing out the insatiable demand for fiction alongside more overtly serious and prestigious forms of reading matter. By opening his review in this way he creates a context in which Austen's novels, written with "spirit and originality", serve as a counter-example.[6]

Accounts of the dullness of fiction were often as reiterative as the novels they criticized. In her early fiction Austen took a contrary stance. In 'Catharine, or the Bower', she defends long novels against those who found them too tiring to get through. In *Northanger Abbey*, she seems to delight in Catherine Morland's desire to read *The Mysteries of Udolpho* for the rest of her life and criticizes those who find novels "insipid" by convention (*NA*, p. 30). Yet Austen's own fiction sought to fend off the protracted, even as she defended it. In her private criticism, Austen could admire aspects of Laetitia Matilda Hawkins's novel *Rosanne*, but describe the narration as "tedious";[7] and in the first biographical account of Austen, Henry Austen describes his sister as liberating herself from the prolixity and 'tediousness' of Samuel Richardson whom the family repeatedly stress as her favourite novelist.[8] It was "Richardson's power of creating, and preserving the consistency of his characters" that Austen appreciated, according to Henry Austen. However, it is much more difficult to untangle Richardson's characters from his style of writing than this account suggests, as their psychological processes depend on detail. It is also not clearly delineated whether Henry's comment on "the errors of [Richardson's] prolix style and tedious narrative" is his sister's judgement or his own. The subject of Richardson's prolixity had in fact become a subject of renewed debate in the early 1800s, when interest in Richardson's fiction was revitalized by means of Anna Barbauld's edition of Richardson's *Correspondence* and its accompanying biographical and critical essay.

As an admirer of Richardson, Austen is likely to have known Barbauld's *Correspondence* and allusions to it have been found in her work. Claude Rawson was the first to notice a correlation between Henry Tilney's disparagement of the use of the word "nice" in *Northanger Abbey* and a letter from Lady Bradshaigh to Richardson on "sentimental", which Austen could only

[6] Walter Scott, unsigned review of *Emma*, *Quarterly Review* (1815, issued March 1816), in *Jane Austen: the Critical Heritage*, vol. 1, pp. 58, 63.

[7] This is Laetitia Matilda Hawkins's novel *Rosanne; or, a Father's Labour Lost* which Austen writes to Anna Lefroy as being "much as you describe it; very good and clever, but tedious" (*L*, p. 301; possibly late February–early March, 1815).

[8] Henry Austen, 'Biographical Notice of the Author' (1818), in James Edward Austen-Leigh, *A Memoir of Jane Austen and Other Family Recollections*, ed. with an introduction and notes by Kathryn Sutherland (Oxford: Oxford University Press, 2002), p. 141.

have encountered in Barbauld's edition.[9] Jocelyn Harris has argued that Barbauld brought Austen back to reading Richardson such that Richardson becomes a pervasive influence in the writing of *Sense and Sensibility, Pride and Prejudice* and *Mansfield Park*. Harris also speculates as to whether Barbauld's edition influenced Austen away from the epistolary form,[10] as its introductory essay contains the earliest known analysis in English of different modes of narration.[11] In her prefatory 'Life of Samuel Richardson, with Remarks on his Writings', Barbauld addresses the subject of Richardson's prolixity and is ambivalent as to whether the justifications for such a style outweigh its tediousness. Of *Clarissa,* she writes that "[t]he first volumes are somewhat tedious, from the prolixity incident to letter-writing, and require a persevering reader to get through them". However, "the circumstantial manner" of Richardson's writing did make readers fully know and be invested in his characters.[12] The contrived nature of the plots put in place by Lovelace to keep Clarissa confined are sometimes "tedious", but the "wit of Lovelace, and the sprightliness of Miss Howe, prevent monotony" (vol. 1, p. xciii).

The relationship between Austen and Richardson is a tantalizing one, wedding together the most prolix and most precise of authors. While Barbauld wrote of *Sir Charles Grandison* in 1804, "It is the fault of Richardson that he never knew when to have done with a character",[13] Julia Kavanagh, in one of the earliest detailed accounts of Austen's style and structure, wrote by contrast, "Miss Austen added another [power] equally rare – she knew where to stop." Kavanagh incisively drew attention to what

[9] C. J. Rawson, '"Nice" and "Sentimental": a Parallel between *Northanger Abbey* and Richardson's *Correspondence*', *Notes & Queries*, 11, 5 (1964), 180.

[10] Jocelyn Harris, *Jane Austen's Art of Memory* (Cambridge: Cambridge University Press, 1989), pp. 44–5; and 'Anna Letitia Barbauld: Jane Austen's Unseen Interlocutor', in *Anna Letitia Barbauld: New Perspectives*, eds. William McCarthy and Olivia Murphy (Lewisburg, PA: Bucknell University Press, 2014), pp. 240–1. Claudia Johnson also writes of Barbauld as seeming to have been "a formative influence" on Jane Austen, in '"Let Me Make the Novels of a Country": Barbauld's *The British Novelists* (1810/1820)', *NOVEL: a Forum on Fiction*, 34, 2 (2001), 163–79, p. 175.

[11] William McCarthy, *Anna Letitia Barbauld: Voice of the Enlightenment* (Baltimore: The Johns Hopkins University Press, 2008), p. 425. See also, Catherine E. Moore, '"Ladies … Taking the Pen in Hand": Mrs. Barbauld's Criticism of Eighteenth-Century Women Novelists', in *Fetter'd or Free? British Women Novelists, 1670–1815*, eds. Mary Anne Schofield and Cecilia Macheski (Athens: Ohio University Press, 1986), pp. 383–97, p. 387.

[12] Anna Letitia Barbauld, *The Correspondence of Samuel Richardson* […] *Selected from the Original Manuscripts* […] *to Which Are Prefixed, a Biographical Account of That Author, and Observations on His Writings* (London: Richard Phillips, 1804), vol. 1, p. lxxxii. Further references to this edition are provided in the text.

[13] Barbauld exemplifies by means of Clementina: "Clementina would have been dismissed with dignity after her refusal of Sir Charles; instead of which, he resumes her story in the last volumes, brings her to England, a step little consistent with the delicacy of her character, nor necessary to any event", *Correspondence of Samuel Richardson*, vol. 1, p. cxxi.

Austen *shared* with prolix writers such as Richardson, or here Scudery: "she must have exercised great judgment, or possessed great tact, since her very qualities are those that lead to minuteness".[14] Austen's repeated claims in her letters for loving "particulars" suggest that Richardson's "minute particulars" may, in fact, have held for her a considerable attraction.

When Barbauld went on to prepare a ground-breaking fifty-volume edition of *British Novelists* for publication in 1810, she repeated verbatim much of her introduction to the *Correspondence of Samuel Richardson* in his prefatory biography. Interestingly, when the introduction to the *Correspondence* took a direction inappropriate for the purposes of the *British Novelists* she added the following sentence:

> It is a truth which cannot be denied, that the works of Richardson are not found to be so attractive to the present generation as they were to the past; the young and idle are deterred from reading him by his prolixity, and the defects of his style are become more prominent from the greater attention which has been paid to that part of composition by modern writers.[15]

This addition is made to round off this preface in *British Novelists*; none-theless Barbauld chose to stress categorically, six years later, how out of favour prolixity had become. Barbauld's *British Novelists* was published at the point when Austen was probably revising *Sense and Sensibility* and possibly *Pride and Prejudice* for publication, lopping and cropping *Pride and Prejudice* at least. Whatever Austen's view on Richardson's minute-ness, her compositional tastes were in sympathy with this generational shift, as she applied herself with *Pride and Prejudice* to making a longer work shorter, something that Richardson found very hard to manage.

At the end of *Belinda* – a novel that Austen praises by name in *Northanger Abbey* (p. 31) – Maria Edgeworth also muses on prolixity with reference to Richardson. Austen may have been struck by her shared interest in narrative elasticity. The contemporary interest in the amount of detail fiction should contain was such that even fictional characters feel the need to discuss it:

> 'O, that would be cutting matters too short,' said Mrs Margaret Delacour. 'I am of the old school, and though I could dispense with the

[14] Julia Kavanagh, 'Miss Austen's Six Novels' (1862), in *Jane Austen: the Critical Heritage*, vol. 1, p. 177. Kavanagh writes that Scudery's "prolixity was the result of a delicate and subtle mind, and that prolixity ruined her, for it made her well-nigh unreadable".

[15] Anna Letitia Barbauld, *The British Novelists; with an Essay; and Prefaces, Biographical and Critical, by Mrs Barbauld* (London: F. C. and J. Rivington, et al., 1810), vol. 1, p. xlvi. Further references to this edition are provided in the text. The text of *British Novelists* here departs from *Correspondence of Samuel Richardson*, vol. 1, p. cxlviii.

description of miss Harriet Byron's worked chairs and fine china [in *Sir Charles Grandison*], yet I own, I like to hear something of the preparation for a marriage, as well as of the mere wedding. I like to hear *how* people become happy in a rational manner, better than to be told in the huddled style of an old fairy tale — *and so they were all married, and they lived very happily all the rest of their days.*'

'We are not in much danger of hearing such an account of modern marriages,' said lady Delacour. 'But how shall I please you all? Some people cry, 'Tell me every thing' others say, that, 'Le secret d'ennuyer est celui de tout dire.'

'Something must be left to the imagination. Positively I will not describe wedding dresses, or a procession to church.'[16]

*Sir Charles Grandison* was notoriously long, stretching an already six-volume novel to seven, according to Anna Barbauld. Indeed, he could have lost "a good part of the sixth" volume with its descriptions of marriage preparations: "dress, and parade, and furniture" (*Correspendence of Samuel Richardson*, vol. 1, p. cxxxiii). By contrast, Lady Delacour's statement "Positively I will not describe wedding-dresses, or a procession to church" reads as a rule for writing conclusions that Austen adopted.

In the 1810s when Austen published her fiction, the novel's average length was starting to consolidate at three volumes.[17] Fiction by this date rarely strayed to the length of Richardson's. While two- and three-volume forms were equally prevalent during the 1800s, the four-volume format could occasionally exceed or match its three-volume competitor in a given year.[18] From the 1800s to the 1810s there is a small drop in the percentage of novels published in four volumes and above, but then in the 1820s the percentage of novels published in four volumes and above more than halved, falling to 10.9 per cent.[19]

Austen's taste was in tune with the prevailing disinclination for longer forms, but it was in contrast to other novelists she admired. When her father originally sent out *First Impressions* for publication in 1797 he described the work as "comprised in three volumes, about the length of Miss Burney's

[16] Maria Edgeworth, *Belinda*, ed. Kathryn J. Kirkpatrick (Oxford: Oxford University Press, 1994; first published 1801 in 3 vols.), p. 477.

[17] Peter Garside, 'The English Novel in the Romantic Era: Consolidation and Dispersal', in *The English Novel 1770–1829: A Bibliographical Survey of Prose Fiction Published in the British Isles*; *vol. II: 1800–1829*, ed. Peter Garside, Rainer Schöwerling; with the assistance of Christopher Skelton-Foord and Karin Wünsche; general eds. Peter Garside, James Raven, and Rainer Schöwerling (Oxford: Oxford University Press, 2000), p. 91.

[18] Ibid., p. 90. In 1801 there were more four-volume novels than three and in 1809 the same number of each were published.

[19] Ibid., p. 91. See Table 8, 'Volume Structure of New Novels, 1800–1829'.

Evelina". Using the measure of *Evelina*, by the time *Pride and Prejudice* was published it had been 'lopped and cropped' by about a quarter of its length.[20] Burney's work, by contrast, expanded from the three volumes of *Evelina* to the five volumes apiece of her next three novels. Austen's fiction also lengthened out in terms of words, though not volumes, from *Sense and Sensibility* to *Emma*, but then reduced quite considerably in her posthumously published novels, both of which she described in a letter as "short".[21]

Austen's letters tell us how she could critique protracted fiction, even that of Burney, an author whom she much admired. In a postscript to a letter written to Cassandra in 1796, Austen writes:

> Give my Love to Mary Harrison, & tell her I wish whenever she is attached to a young Man, some <u>respectable</u> Dr Marchmont may keep them apart for five Volumes. (*L*, p. 9; 5 September 1796)

There is something pointed in that specificity of *five* volumes, as if a plot contrivance sustained for such a length is excessive. If this is so, her views coincided with Anna Barbauld's who would sum up *Camilla*: "This work is somewhat too much protracted" (*British Novelists*, vol. 38, p. vii). One early reviewer of Austen, writing in 1823, distinguished Austen's fiction from the five-volume distresses of Burney's: "The hero and the heroine – the lover and the beloved – fall out and in, and out again, through the whole five volumes – do *they* always know, or *even* care to understand why?"[22]

Austen laughed out loud at another novel's tiresome length. When Anna Austen stayed with her aunts and grandmother at Chawton for three months, between June and September 1812, she borrowed Rachel Hunter's four-volume novel *Lady Maclairn, the Victim of Villany* [*sic*] from the circulating library. When she returned home, Anna, apparently in the persona of Mrs Hunter, sent to her aunt some thread papers (strips of folded paper in which to hold skeins of threads) illustrated with scenes from the novel, to which Austen replied:

> Miss Jane Austen's tears have flowed over each sweet sketch in such a way as would do Mrs Hunter's heart good to see; if Mrs Hunter could understand

20 Marilyn Butler, 'Disregarded Designs: Jane Austen's Sense of the Volume', in *Jane Austen in a Social Context*, ed. David Monaghan (London: Macmillan, 1981; first published in 'The Jane Austen Society Report for the Year 1978'), pp. 49–65, p. 52.

21 "I have a something ready for Publication, [...]. It is short, about the length of Catherine." (*L*, p. 348; 13 March 1817, to Fanny Knight). This is *Persuasion* and 'Catherine', "put upon the Shelve", is *Northanger Abbey*.

22 Unsigned review of the *Life and Adventures of Peter Wilkins*, in *Retrospective Review* (no month, 1823), in *Jane Austen: the Critical Heritage*, vol. 1, p. 107.

> all Miss Jane Austen's interest in the subject she would certainly have the kindness to publish at least 4 vols more about the Flint family, & especially would give many fresh particulars on that part of it which Mrs H. has hitherto handled too briefly; viz, the history of Mary Flint's marriage with Howard.
>
> Miss Jane Austen cannot close this small epitome of the miniature abridgment of her thanks & admiration without expressing her sincere hope that Mrs Hunter is provided at Norwich with a more safe conveyance to London than Alton can now boast, as the Car of Falkenstein which was the pride of that Town was overturned within the last 10 days. (*L*, pp. 203–4; possibly between 29–31 October 1812)

The family record of this episode stresses the extensiveness of Hunter's novel. Later in life, Anna remembered the novel as "an exceedingly lengthy affair".[23] Fanny Caroline Lefroy, Anna's daughter, described *Lady Maclairn* as the "voluminous and most tiresome and prosy novel the Aunt and Neice had been reading and laughing over. It was in 8 vols and the tears of the heroine were ever flowing".[24] Apropos of such length, Deirdre Le Faye has speculated that the Alton circulating library had rebound Hunter's four-volume novel to twice its actual size.[25] Libraries lent out sets by the volume and the breaking of volumes would have allowed more readers to enjoy popular novels. Whatever the case, Austen's ridicule of this novel's length has conserved it in an expanded form, stretched beyond the normal bounds of fiction of the day, making it longer even than Richardson's.

The joke between Austen and Anna about their reading of *Lady Maclairn* plays out in a number of dimensions. That Anna has chosen to present her aunt with images from the lengthy novel within the constricted space of thread papers may itself be a comment on size, in so palpably diminishing Tarefield Hall and other scenes. It is the same miniaturizing instinct that led aunt and niece to collaborate on transforming *Sir Charles Grandison* from seven volumes to a tiny five-act play. "The Car of Falkenstein" that Austen refers to in the same letter about *Lady Maclairn* was itself from a "mock heroic story" written by Anna and encouraged by Austen.[26] The receipt of the thread papers prompts Austen, in response, to wish

[23] Anna Lefroy, 'Recollections of Aunt Jane' (1864), in *A Memoir of Jane Austen and Other Family Recollections*, p. 159.

[24] Quoted by Deirdre Le Faye, in *L*, p. 417, note 6.

[25] Deirdre Le Faye, 'Jane Austen and Mrs Hunter's Novel', *Notes and Queries*, 32, 3 (1985), 335–6.

[26] Caroline Austen, *My Aunt Jane Austen: A Memoir* (1867), in *A Memoir of Jane Austen and Other Family Recollections*, p. 172. See Deirdre Le Faye, *Jane Austen: a Family Record* (Cambridge: Cambridge University Press, 2nd ed., 2004; first published 1989), p. 191.

comically that the novel be much increased in size (expanding from either four to eight volumes or eight to twelve), while her own language becomes possessed by a satirical form of otiose expansion, as she describes her own letter as "this small epitome of the miniature abridgment of her thanks & admiration". Austen mimics the prolix, playing again with paradoxes of size, her thanks becoming increasingly tautologous as she deems them minute.

Austen's response to *Lady Maclairn* was not merely to mock. Isobel Grundy has noted that aspects of Lydia Serge's elopement in the later volumes of *Lady Maclairn* bear comparison with the narrative of Austen's Lydia in *Pride and Prejudice*, which Austen was revising for publication in late 1812.[27] *Mansfield Park*, the work that Austen would then turn to, also has striking plot affiliations with *Lady Maclairn*.[28] Rather than "containing story within story", as Fanny Caroline Lefroy described Rachel Hunter's novel,[29] the narrative of Fanny Price in *Mansfield Park* combines the love story of Rachel Cowley, who becomes romantically attached to one of her adopted siblings, with the plight of the "oppressed orphan" Mary Howard (which is largely narrated by Rachel) who is forced to live under the tyrannical regime of a vindictive aunt.[30] It is the story of Mary's parents, in a novel of embedded tales and proliferating characters and settings, to which Austen specifically points. *Lady Maclairn* is also notable reading matter in advance of the composition of *Mansfield Park* given its pervasive, if elusive, engagement with subject of slavery.[31] Rachel Cowley feels that Mary Howard's situation in her aunt's English household is comparable to a slave's, while the novel has established at its outset (in what turns out to be a 113 page-long prelude), Rachel's birth and early years in Jamaica as the daughter of a slave-owner: this is a context and history that become more present as the novel's inset narratives unfold.[32]

[27] Isobel Grundy, 'Jane Austen and Literary Traditions', *The Cambridge Companion to Jane Austen*, eds. Edward Copeland and Juliet McMaster (Cambridge: Cambridge University Press, 1997), pp. 189–210, p. 203, p. 209 note 41.

[28] In Austen's February 1813 letter to Cassandra on the receipt of *Pride and Prejudice*, she turns immediately from her comment on 'lopping & cropping' to discussing her plans for *Mansfield Park*.

[29] Quoted in Le Faye, 'Jane Austen and Mrs Hunter's Novel', p. 336.

[30] Rachel Hunter, *Lady Maclairn, the Victim of Villany. A Novel* (London: for W. Earle and J. W. Hucklebridge, 1806 in 4 vols.), vol. 1, p. 216.

[31] In her essay 'Rachel Hunter and the Victims of Slavery', Isobel Grundy describes *Lady Maclairn* as "hard to categorise" (p. 27) in its position towards slavery: "as an epistolary novel, [it] offers by definition a range of conflicting views on every topic. But the slavery issue, which is woven into its fabric, is woven there in division and discrepancy" (p. 34); in *Women's Writing*, 1, 1 (1994), pp. 25–34, pp. 27, 34.

[32] Grundy points to the contradiction that Rachel seeks to bring about Mary's "emancipation", but not those of her own slaves in Jamaica, in 'Rachel Hunter and the Victims of Slavery', p. 31.

Austen retains the West Indian foundations for her own English country house novel, but conceivably, having recently read *Lady Maclairn*, radically redacts this model, to be far more elusive still.

When Austen wished that Mrs Hunter would "publish at least 4 vols more about the Flint family, & especially [...] the history of Mary Flint's marriage with Howard", she was in fact in dialogue with Rachel Hunter's own consciousness of insufficiency in providing information about her characters, "I could fill volumes with the praises and blessings still given to this matchless pair".[33] *Lady Maclairn*, in spite of its length, often acknowledges what needs to be passed over. Austen's alertness to bathetic claims of conciseness prompts her to exaggerate a desire for even more volumes. But, in terms of her own compositional practice, she was able to pinpoint artistic opportunities in the compression of the most protracted and diffuse of stories.

## Selection and History

Although Henry Austen claimed that his sister did not rank any work of Henry Fielding's as high as Richardson's, in formal terms Austen's novels have arguably more in common with Fielding's than Richardson's. In *Tom Jones*, Fielding refers often to the need to select and omit, and distinguishes himself from the "painful and voluminous historian".[34] Fielding may have had in mind actual historians, who, as Catherine Morland says, are "at so much trouble in filling great volumes" (*NA*, p. 110), or he may have been alluding to fictional historians, most specifically his rival, the voluminous Richardson.[35] Austen was also self-conscious about narrative selection and her plotting of *Emma* bears comparison with the skillful withholding of information for which *Tom Jones* was so famed.[36] Like Fielding, Austen used

[33] *Lady Maclairn, the Victim of Villany*, vol. 1, p. 280. By contrast, Austen writes of a letter from Richard Buller: "I was afraid he would oppress me by his felicity & his love for his Wife, but this is not the case; he calls her simply Anna without any angelic embellishments, for which I respect & wish him happy" (*L*, pp. 58–9; 8–9 November 1800).

[34] Henry Fielding, *The History of Tom Jones, a Foundling*, eds. John Bender and Simon Stern, with an introduction by John Bender (Oxford: Oxford University Press, 1996; first published, 1749 in 6 vols.), p. 67.

[35] See Anne Toner, *Ellipsis in English Literature: Signs of Omission* (Cambridge: Cambridge University Press, 2015), pp. 65–6.

[36] Anna Barbauld's praise for *Tom Jones* could have been written about *Emma*: "The peculiar beauty of the plot consists in this; that though the author's secret is impenetrable, the discovery is artfully prepared by a number of circumstances, not attended to at the time, and by obscure hints thrown out, which, when the reader looks back upon them, are found to agree exactly with the concealed event" (*British Novelists*, vol. 18, p. xx).

history as a foil to fiction. By placing 'Frederic & Elfrida' as the first piece in *Volume the First*, Austen playfully alludes to her own work as a 'History of England', where the tale of the Saxon Elfrida is inevitably found at its opening.[37] Austen adopted the role of historian in 'The History of England', composed in 1791, to parody "real, solemn history" (*NA*, p. 109). This comic redaction of the imposingly massive reduces the lives of English kings and queens to a mere thirty-three pages of manuscript and thirteen short biographies.

Oliver Goldsmith's 1771 *The History of England, from the Earliest Times to the Death of George II* was the primary source for Austen's 'The History of England', and Austen extensively annotated her copy.[38] Austen would also come to own a copy of David Hume's *The History of England*, originally published between 1754 and 1762. In the preface to his 1771 *History of England*, Goldsmith acknowledges that his four-volume work is an "abridgement" from the works of "Rapin, Carte, Smollett and Hume", his "aim being not to add to our present stock of history, but to contract it".[39] Following the success of his four-volume *History*, Goldsmith published in 1774 an even more successful *History*, an abridged, one-volume duodecimo text, the "abridgement of an abridgement".[40] Austen followed in the wake of Goldsmith's abridgements by abbreviating his *History ad absurdum* (a "small epitome of the miniature abridgement" as she would write of *Lady Maclairn*). In *Northanger Abbey*, Jane Austen may have satirized the praise heaped on the "nine-hundredth abridger of the History of England" (p. 31) in contrast to the work of the novelist, but it was by being an abridger herself that she learnt a significant part of her art of fiction.

Austen's historian in her 'The History of England' is comically exasperated by detail. She describes herself as "a partial, prejudiced, and ignorant Historian" (*J*, p. 176), where "partial" means "biased [...] in a person's favour" (here Mary Queen of Scots) but also carries the sense of "involving a part of something rather than the whole [...] incomplete".[41] Most often, she can't be bothered to give a full account of her subject. Of the Earl of Essex, she silently extracts from Goldsmith to make a comic construction

[37] See for instance, Goldsmith's account in *The History of England, from the Earliest Times to the Death of George II*, 4 vols. (London: for T. Davies; Becket and De Hondt; and T. Cadell, 1771), vol. 1, chapter 4.

[38] See Peter Sabor's transcription of these annotations as 'Appendix B' to *Juvenilia*, pp. 316–51.

[39] Goldsmith, *The History of England*, vol. 1, p. vi.

[40] The phrase is Christopher Kent's, who provides a summary of the publishing history of Goldsmith's Histories, in 'Learning History with, and from, Jane Austen', in *Jane Austen's Beginnings: the Juvenilia and Lady Susan*, ed. J. David Grey; foreword, Margaret Drabble (Ann Arbor, MI: UMI Research Press, 1989), pp. 59–72, p. 63.

[41] *OED*, definitions II 4b and I 2a.

of the memorably particular ("clapped his hand on his Sword") and vague bluff ("many other services to his Country"):

> **It would be endless to recount** the misfortunes of this noble and gallant Earl. It is sufficient to say that he was beheaded on the 25th of Febry, after having been Lord Leuitenant of Ireland, after having clapped his hand on his Sword, and after performing many other services to his Country. (p. 186)

The detestable characters in England during the reign of Charles the 1st "would make too long a list to be written or read", so the history only mentions the "leaders of the Gang" (p. 188). Sometimes details fail to materialize due to ignorance ("it is not in my power to inform the Reader who was his [Henry the 4th's] Wife"), or, in the case of Henry the 8th, because she does not wish to take the "trouble of writing what I do not perfectly recollect" and which the reader most likely already knows (p. 177, p. 180). Her history's ostentatious bias also demotes documentary completeness. Recounting the backstory of more than thirty years of civil strife is troublesome and irrelevant. Of Henry the 6th she says:

> I suppose you know all about the Wars between him and the Duke of York who was of the right side; if you do not, you had better read some other History, **for I shall not be very diffuse in this**, meaning by it only to vent my Spleen *against*, and shew my Hatred *to* all those people whose parties or principles do not suit with mine, and **not to give information**. (p. 178)

Austen's partiality has been read as a critique of Goldsmith's tendency to attempt historical evenhandedness.[42] But partiality has a practical dimension too. Events in the reign of Charles the 1st are described as "too numerous for my pen", and only then justified as "uninteresting" (or, in first draft, "tedious") (p. 188). The historian's declarations of omission escalate in this her final biography of Charles the 1st, where details are denied three times. The omissive nature of ending is indicated here, as the author's purpose has been completed and her comically limited energies spent. 'The History of England' ends with detail surrendering to triumphant prejudice:

> **As therefore it is not my intention to give any particular account of the distresses into which this King was involved through the misconduct and Cruelty of his Parliament**, I shall satisfy myself with vindicating him from the Reproach of Arbitrary and tyrannical Government with which he has often been Charged. This, I feel, is not difficult to be done, for with

[42] Peter Sabor, 'Jane Austen: Satirical Historian', in *Swift's Travels: Eighteenth-Century British Satire and Its Legacy*, eds. Nicholas Hudson and Aaron Santesso (Cambridge: Cambridge University Press, 2008), pp. 217–32.

> one argument I am certain of satisfying every sensible and well disposed person whose opinions have been properly guided by a good Education—and this Argument is that he was a **Stuart**.[43]
>
> FINIS (pp. 188–9)

This quotation, in its closing excision of distresses is a comic foreshadowing of Austen's famous elision with which she starts to bring *Mansfield Park* to its end, at the beginning of its last chapter:

> Let other pens dwell on guilt and misery. I quit such odious subjects as soon as I can, impatient to restore every body, not greatly in fault themselves, to tolerable comfort, and to have done with all the rest. (p. 533)

In both works, Austen compensates for narrative deletion by turning with 'satisfaction' to something else: "I shall satisfy myself with vindicating him […] I am certain of satisfying every sensible and well disposed person" (*J*); "My Fanny indeed at this very time, I have the satisfaction of knowing, must have been happy in spite of every thing" (*MP*, p. 533).

The omissions in 'The History of England' acknowledge the enormous amount of matter a historian has to handle.[44] But history and fiction are intertwined. She compares Lord Essex and Elizabeth to characters in Charlotte Smith's *Emmeline*, the narrative design and length of which Austen reflects upon in 'Catharine, or the Bower', a work composed within a year of 'The History of England'. In 'The History of England', Austen's incipient preferences as a novelist are evident. Austen selects a particular story based around a pair of female characters – Mary and Elizabeth – so that the overall shaping of her 'History' has a strong narrative focus. The attention to these two women prefigures Catherine Morland's concern with the exclusion of women from history, one part of a larger criticism of historical writing:[45]

> I read it a little as a duty, but it tells me nothing that does not either vex or weary me. The quarrels of popes and kings, with wars or pestilences, in every page; the men all so good for nothing, and hardly any women at

[43] The emboldening of 'Stuart' follows the Cambridge edition of the *Juvenilia* to indicate Austen's emphasis of the word.

[44] However, the formal self-consciousness in 'The History of England' is comparable with that in Austen's letter writing. Letter writing, taking the form of domestic history, shares an observance of diurnal or sequential events.

[45] This criticism of history's exclusion of women has received considerable attention. For example, Antoinette Burton, '"Invention Is What Delights Me": Jane Austen's Remaking of "English" History', in *Jane Austen and Discourses of Feminism*, ed. Devoney Looser (Basingstoke, Hampshire: Macmillan Press, 1995), pp. 35–50; and Devoney Looser, *British Women Writers and the Writing of History, 1670–1820* (Baltimore and London: The Johns Hopkins University Press, 2000), pp. 198–203.

> all—it is very tiresome: and yet I often think it odd that it should be so dull, for a great deal of it must be invention. The speeches that are put into the heroes' mouths, their thoughts and designs—the chief of all this must be invention, and invention is what delights me in other books.
>
> [...]
>
> If people like to read their books, it is all very well, but to be at so much trouble in filling great volumes, which, as I used to think, nobody would willingly ever look into, to be labouring only for the torment of little boys and girls, always struck me as a hard fate; and though I know it is all very right and necessary, I have often wondered at the person's courage that could sit down on purpose to do it. (*NA*, pp. 110–1)

Catherine describes a formal dissatisfaction with history that resonates with the complaints made in 'The History of England', that is, its capacity to be "endless", "too long," "too numerous", "uninteresting". Catherine testifies to history writing as being "very tiresome", "so dull", "labouring", making her "weary". There is also a bibliographical dimension to this criticism, as history repeats itself "in every page", "filling great volumes".[46]

Satires on successiveness elsewhere in the juvenilia allude to history. This is the case in 'Sir William Mountague', subtitled 'an unfinished performance' (probably written in 1788) which is a critique of narrative repetition. Mountague is a something of a sentimental Henry the 8th: in the space of five pages, he manages to fall in love seven times and commits murder. The work makes courtly allusions through its surnames, Percival and Arundel, the first of which recurs in 'Catharine, or the Bower'.[47] 'Sir William Mountague' and the piece that follows it, 'Memoirs of Mr Clifford', another 'unfinished tale—', are the only works by

[46] Brigid Brophy contends that Austen's 'The History of England' satirizes "ill-thought-out literary construction". Austen was "to castigate random story-telling [...] with a randomness equal to the randomness she was criticizing" ('Jane Austen and the Stuarts', in *Critical Essays on Jane Austen*, ed. B. C. Southam (London: Routledge & Kegan Paul, 1968), pp. 21–38, pp. 22–3). As Christopher Kent has pointed out, Austen's history isn't quite as random as Brophy contends ('Learning History with, and from, Jane Austen', p. 67). Devoney Looser has described how 'The History of England' "deconstructs historical material and then reconstructs it in a fictional mold [...] For Austen, truthfulness ('telling it like it is') requires a skilled author of instructive fiction" (*British Women Writers*, p. 190). It seems to me that the deconstruction of historical writing in 'The History of England' and in *Northanger Abbey* is as much a recognition of the similarity of historical construction to fictional construction, as it is of difference.

[47] Catharine's aunt, so averse to her niece's romantic attachments, has her name changed from Peterson to Percival, as if to allude to the ditched and outraged Lady Percival of 'Sir William Mountague'. Kathryn Sutherland argues that this revision to the manuscript, along with others including the revision of the title 'Kitty, or the Bower' to 'Catharine, or the Bower', were made by the teenage James Edward Austen-Leigh, with his aunt's permission. 'From Kitty to Catharine: James Edward Austen's Hand in *Volume the Third*', *The Review of English Studies*, 66 (2014), 124–43.

Jane Austen to close with the etcetera of a sequence of dots. This punctuation in 'Sir William Mountague' expresses the ongoing pattern of indiscriminate amatory exchange "as he hoped to have, by his acquaintance with her Ladyship, free access to Miss Wentworth........" (*J*, p. 49) and the eight-dot ellipsis serves as a narrative mirror to the opening familial genealogy where appear eight generations of the Mountague line:

> Sir William Mountague was the son of Sir Henry Mountague, who was the son of Sir John Mountague, a descendant of Sir Christopher Mountague, who was the nephew of Sir Edward Mountague, whose ancestor was Sir James Mountague a near relation of Sir Robert Mountague, who inherited the Title and Estate from Sir Frederic Mountague. (p. 47)

The interrelated forms of genealogy and history writing are the most chronological and successive of genres. While the Bertram sisters in *Mansfield Park* are proud of knowing "the chronological order of the kings of England, with the dates of their accession, and most of the principal events of their reigns!", probably from a book like Goldsmith's abridged *History* (*MP*, p. 21), the narrator of *Mansfield Park* firmly "chooses to "abstain from dates" (p. 544), as does 'The History of England' in which Austen declares, "There will be very few Dates in this History" (*J*, p. 176). The genealogy at the opening of *Persuasion* is, in its narrative function, anti-successive, in articulating the stalled genealogy of Sir Walter, without a male heir, upon which plight the narrative dwells.

Catherine Morland's criticisms of historical writing are only half the story, however, as Austen has Eleanor Tilney sensibly defend it. Austen informed herself of new developments in historical writing, describing Robert Henry's *The History of Great Britain* (1771) in a letter to Martha Lloyd. There were two novelties to Henry's *History*. The first was his inclusion of much more than Catherine Morland's "popes and kings [...] wars or pestilences". Innovatively, he designated space for the history of culture, arts and manners, arguing that it is impossible to form just ideas of the past without going beyond major events of national disharmony.[48] But Austen singles out Henry's other innovation: the organization of history not by chronology but by themes:

> I am reading Henry's History of England, which I will repeat to you in any manner you may prefer, either in a loose, disultary, unconnected strain, or dividing my recital as the Historian divides it himself, into seven parts,

[48] Robert Henry, *The History of Great Britain, from the First Invasion of It by the Romans under Julius Caesar. Written on a New Plan* (London: printed for the author, 1771), vol. 1, pp. vi–vii.

> The Civil & Military—Religion—Constitution—Learning & Learned Men—Arts & Sciences—Commerce Coins & Shipping—& Manners; (*L*, pp. 61–2; 12–13 November 1800)

Austen takes the time to spell out for Martha the organization of this history and she suggests that to recount a history *other* than according to Henry's thematic divisions is to narrate in a manner that is "loose, disultary, unconnected".[49] The terms "disultary" and "unconnected" are pejorative words for Austen in her criticisms of fiction.

Austen was evidently consulting David Hume's *History of England, under the House of Tudor*, as well as Goldsmith, when composing her own 'History of England'.[50] Austen may have criticized history for its tediousness, but Hume made the same complaint of literature. His *History* of the Tudors closes with criticism of the protracted in literature, in a critique of Spenser:

> Yet does the perusal of his [Spenser's] work become so tedious, that one never finishes it from the mere pleasure which it affords: It soon becomes a kind of task-reading; and it requires some effort and resolution to carry us on to the end of his long performance. [...] The **tediousness** of continued allegory [...] has also contributed to render the *Fairy Queen* **peculiarly tiresome**; not to mention **the too great frequency of its descriptions**, and the languor of its stanza. [...] **Several writers of late have amused themselves with copying the stile of Spencer; and no imitation has been so indifferent as not to bear a great resemblance of the original: His manner is so peculiar, that it is almost impossible not to transfer some of it into the copy.**
>
> FINIS[51]

Hume throws down the gauntlet for Austen. At the period when she was reading Goldsmith and Hume intensively, she chooses in 'Catharine, or

[49] But Austen is also likely to have been alert to the contradictions in Henry's general preface, claiming to be selective and comprehensive.

[50] There is evidence for this in Austen's vindication of Mary Queen of Scots. Austen echoes Hume's terms rather than Goldsmith's and seems to answer Hume directly. Austen writes of the queen: "she had been accused of several **crimes** during the time of her reigning in Scotland, of which I now most seriously do assure my Reader that she was entirely innocent; having never been guilty of anything more than **Imprudencies** into which she was betrayed by the openness of her Heart, her Youth, and her Education" (*J*, p. 185), while Hume asks of Mary Queen of Scots, "whether we admit them to be **imprudences or crimes,** as the result of an inexplicable, tho' not uncommon, inconstancy in the human mind, of the frailty of our nature, or of the violence of passion, and of the influence which situations, and sometimes momentary incidents, have on persons". *The History of England, under the House of Tudor*, 2 vols. (London: for A. Millar, 1759), vol. 2, p. 622.

[51] Ibid., vol. 2, pp. 738–9.

the Bower' to select *The Faerie Queene*'s bower of bliss for her narrative's setting, in another contracted homage to the long.[52] Hume's account of Spenser's "tediousness" and "the too great frequency of his descriptions" becomes an explicit discussion about contemporary fiction in 'Catharine, or the Bower', as Austen asks, by means of Charlotte Smith, what it means to be "tired" of a novel and why one might choose to skip its "descriptions".

## *Northanger Abbey*: Form in the Early Fiction

'The History of England', 'Catharine, or the Bower' and *Northanger Abbey* are closely entwined compositions. 'Catharine, or the Bower' and 'The History of England' have proximate composition dates and share precise fictional and historical references.[53] *Northanger Abbey* reworks passages from both. All three works have a preoccupation with length and form.[54]

The composition history of *Northanger Abbey* is complex. Austen probably began to write the novel in 1798, with the title *Susan*, finishing it the following year. She revised it in late 1802 and in the spring it was purchased by the publisher Benjamin Crosby. After an interlude of fourteen years in which the novel was left unpublished, Henry Austen bought back the manuscript in 1816 and Austen went on to revise it in the year before her death. Narelle Shaw has dated parts of *Northanger Abbey* containing free indirect discourse, which occurs most often in the second volume, to the later period of revision.[55] Explicit discussions of length, which predominate in the first volume, have their genesis in one of the earlier periods of composition, I would suggest, given the evidence of their prevalence elsewhere in Austen's early fiction.

In defending the novel in *Northanger Abbey*, Austen compares it with other genres:

> And while the abilities of the nine-hundredth abridger of the History of England, or of the man who collects and publishes in a volume some dozen lines of Milton, Pope, and Prior, with a paper from the Spectator, and a chapter from Sterne, are eulogized by a thousand pens,—there seems

[52] Clara Tuite, *Romantic Austen: Sexual Politics and the Literary Canon* (Cambridge: Cambridge University Press, 2002), pp. 42–3.

[53] Clara Tuite describes the works' shared interest in Elizabethan history specifically, in ibid., pp. 39–49.

[54] For instance, the young Catherine Morland, who objects to "books of information" (*NA*, p. 7), remains close to the feelings of Austen's earlier narrator, who in composing 'The History of England' disdains to "give information" (*J*, p. 178).

[55] Narelle Shaw, 'Free Indirect Speech and Jane Austen's 1816 Revision of *Northanger Abbey*', *SEL* 30, 4 (1990), 591–601, p. 593.

> almost a general wish of decrying the capacity and undervaluing the labour of the novelist, and of slighting the performances which have only genius, wit, and taste to recommend them. "I am no novel-reader—I seldom look into novels—[...]" Now, had the same young lady been engaged with a volume of the Spectator, instead of such a work, how proudly would she have produced the book, and told its name; though the chances must be against her being occupied by any part of that voluminous publication, of which either the matter or manner would not disgust a young person of taste: (p. 31)

The "labour" of the novelist lies between works characterized, on the one hand, by the single volume – the abridgement and the anthology – and, on the other hand, the "voluminous" periodical publication. The novel should be valued for being a serious and extensive form: it involves "labour", "the most thorough knowledge of human nature" and a supple inclusiveness by embracing nature in its "varieties" (p. 31). But the novel is positioned favourably in relation to the "voluminous", a critique that is echoed when Catherine wonders at historians "filling great volumes". Furthermore, Austen situates the novel between works that are formally discontinuous: the abridgement, the anthology and the periodical. Value is given to fiction for being cohesive and sustained.

In *Northanger Abbey*, Austen reuses the discussion of novels' length in the unpublished 'Catharine, or the Bower', by replicating the opposition between a heroine who enjoys lengthy fiction and foils who don't. Camilla Stanley bemoans that Charlotte Smith's "Ethelinde is so long". Catharine's reply that "if a book is well written, I always find it too short" is echoed by the later Catherine Morland in her enthusiasm for *The Mysteries of Udolpho*: "Oh! I am delighted with the book! I should like to spend my whole life in reading it (*NA*, p. 33)."[56] The Thorpe siblings, like Camilla who gets "tired [of a well-written book] before it is finished", can't "get through" long works of reputation. John Thorpe has read barely the first few pages of *Camilla*: "I took up the first volume once, and looked it over, but I soon found it would not do [...] I was sure I should never be able to get through it" (*NA*, p. 43). Isabella finds *Sir Charles Grandison* unreadable on the basis of her friend Miss Andrews not being able to "get through the first volume" (*NA*, p. 35).

[56] Anne Henry Ehrenpreis discusses 'Catharine, or the Bower' as a source text for *Northanger Abbey*, in particular for the longer discussion of Gothic fiction between Isabella and Catherine Morland from which this extract is taken. Ehrenpreis draws attention to similarities between *Ethelinde* and 'Catharine, or the Bower' but does not discuss the common interest in novelistic length; in '*Northanger Abbey*: Jane Austen and Charlotte Smith', *Nineteenth-Century Fiction*, 25, 3 (1970), 343–8.

Austen based her discussion of the length of *Ethelinde* on a passage about authorship in *Ethelinde* itself. There, the aspiring novelist Clarinthia Ludford boasts about being Richardsonian even though, when asked by Ethelinde how many volumes her novel is to be, she discloses that she can barely stretch it out to two: "But you know now 'tis the fashion to have little books, with a wide margin, and a vast deal of white paper."[57] Smith ridicules such a paucity of writing within a five-volume work. Jane Austen alights on this passage in 'Catharine, or the Bower' to have her characters debate Smith's own choice as to length. The passage is then rewritten and published, eventually, in a short two-volume work, the form that Smith disparaged. In 'Catharine, or the Bower' and in *Northanger Abbey*, Austen ridicules the reader who dislikes Smith or Richardson or Burney *because* of their length. Yet in *Northanger Abbey* Austen defends specific books for which there is evidence to suggest that she queried the value of their duration. She does so too in a novel that does not replicate the length that she ostensibly champions. Catherine may wish to read *The Mysteries of Udolpho* forever, but Austen gave her own reader barely half the length of Radcliffe's four volumes. Such restraint need not be a dumbing down for a Camilla Stanley or John Thorpe, but an independent aesthetic judgement on the organization and sustainability of plot, as well as a shrewd awareness regarding a more widespread readability.

Austen imitates another source text behind *Northanger Abbey*, Charlotte Lennox's 1752 *The Female Quixote.* The quixotic behaviour of Lennox's Arabella is fostered by the "voluminous Romances" of the seventeenth century which her servant is barely able to carry.[58] Walter Scott described how Richardson, no less, liberated fiction from such "protracted" and "wearisome performances" as the seventeenth-century romance: "[i]t requires a reader to be in some degree acquainted with the huge folios of inanity, over which our ancestors yawned themselves to sleep, ere he can estimate the delight they must have experienced from this unexpected return to truth and nature".[59] The yawning readers whom Scott again conjures up when reviewing Austen suggest how in his view her fiction was another leap away from the protracted. Lennox was keen to point out the

[57] Charlotte Smith, *Ethelinde, or the Recluse of the Lake*, ed. Stuart Curran (London: Pickering & Chatto, 2005; first published 1789 in 5 vols.), p. 143.

[58] Charlotte Lennox, *The Female Quixote, or The Adventures of Arabella*, ed. Margaret Dalziel; with an introduction by Margaret Anne Doody; chronology and appendix by Duncan Isles (Oxford: Oxford University Press, 1989; first published 1752 in 2 vols.), p. 49.

[59] Walter Scott, *Sir Walter Scott on Novelists and Fiction*, ed. Ioan Williams (London: Routledge & Kegan Paul, 1968), pp. 21–2.

horror of length in *The Female Quixote*, while giving Arabella credit for her extraordinary capacity to apply herself to such massive works, but in a slim two volumes like *Northanger Abbey* and with noticeably abbreviated paragraph and chapter lengths.

Austen also underlines formal contraction thematically and discursively. "How were Mr. Allen's succession-houses worked?" asks General Tilney of Catherine, boasting of his wealth in owning hothouses of varied temperatures through which plants could be moved. "Mr. Allen had only one small hot-house" replies Catherine (*NA*, p. 183).[60] There is a formal metaphor about successiveness here that works its way through Austen's fiction. The extent of the General's gardens takes a dizzyingly imaginative hold of Catherine: "The walls seemed countless in number, endless in length; a village of hot-houses seemed to arise among them, and a whole parish to be at work within the inclosure" (p. 182). The General's grounds are large, but Catherine's response is to fictionalize them into impossible and imposing lengths. Gothic fiction has repeatedly expansive and generative associations for her. Catherine is surprised in looking at a portrait of Mrs Tilney that multiple generations are not summoned into view:

> Catherine had depended upon meeting with features, air, complexion that should be the very counterpart, the very image, if not of Henry's, of Eleanor's;—the only portraits of which she had been in the habit of thinking, bearing always an equal resemblance of mother and child. A face once taken was taken for generations. But here she was obliged to look and consider and study for a likeness. (p. 196)

Catherine is obliged to study one image on its own terms, seeking to find "a" likeness. Catherine's oblique reference to a new Gothic work that is to come out of London generates anxieties for Eleanor (according to Henry's interpretation) of a rioting mob of three thousand. Catherine's susceptibility to quantitative exaggeration is indicated in her catchphrase "ten thousand times" (pp. 86, 93). Henry Tilney refers to fiction's propensity to the spawning of simulacra, in the form of "Julias and Louisas" (p. 108). Finally, towards the novel's end, Austen's narrator points out how in the world of fiction, the conclusion of a heroine's tale can necessitate protraction in the scene ("a long train" and "three [...] and-four behind her") and in the telling ("may well delight to dwell"):

> A heroine returning, at the close of her career, to her native village, in all the triumph of recovered reputation, and all the dignity of a countess,

[60] See B. C. Southam, 'General Tilney's Hot-Houses: Some Recent Jane Austen Studies and Texts', *Ariel* 2 (1971), 52–62, p. 60.

> with a **long train** of noble relations in their several phaetons, and **three** waiting-maids in a travelling chaise-**and-four**, behind her, is an event on which the pen of the contriver **may well delight to dwell;** it gives credit to every conclusion, and the author must share in the glory she so liberally bestows. (pp. 240–1)

Catherine's story is different: the ordinariness of her circumstances (her disgrace, her association with "one hot-house" as opposed to a "succession") is posited by contraction, rather than length. Similar to the self-reflexive ending of *Belinda*, the narrator considers the twin prospects of narrative protraction and curtailment:

> But my affair is widely different; I bring back my heroine to her home in solitude and disgrace; and **no sweet elation of spirits can lead me into minuteness**. [...] **Swiftly therefore** shall her post-boy drive through the village, amid the gaze of Sunday groups, and **speedy** shall be her descent from it. (p. 241)

From the outset of Austen's fiction, Austen's succinct world is one premised on, and reverberating with, redundancy. This, as Deidre Lynch has shown, occurs prominently in the iterations of ordinary life.[61] In *Northanger Abbey*, the banalities of Mrs Allen and Isabella are alluded to but not replicated: "repeated so often" (p. 14), "felt and lamented, at least three times a day" (p. 38), "spoken more than once" (p. 88), the "third repetition" and then "fourth" (p. 246). Austen points out fiction's similar propensity to repetitive iteration, in an attempt to alleviate the tedium of everyday life, but which also ultimately reproduces it, in protracted narration.

Henry's exchangeable "Julias and Louisas" are adumbrated in the world of the characters, in the anonymous "long string of passing ladies" (p. 74), against which Catherine is singled out. Alex Woloch has described how Austen's fiction sees the emergence of the singular protagonist, a characterization that will ultimately create room for the exploration of an individual psychology.[62] Austen's rejection of "minuteness" at the end of *Northanger Abbey* repeats the terms by which alternative life stories have earlier been expelled from the novel in the form of the inset tale:

> This brief account of the family is intended to supersede the necessity of a long and **minute** detail from Mrs. Thorpe herself, of her past adventures

[61] Deidre Shauna Lynch, *The Economy of Character: Novels, Market Culture, and the Business of Inner Meaning* (Chicago and London: University of Chicago Press, 1998).

[62] Alex Woloch, *The One vs. the Many: Minor Characters and the Space of the Protagonist in the Novel* (Princeton, NJ and Oxford: Princeton University Press, 2003).

> and sufferings, which might otherwise be expected to occupy the **three or four** following chapters; in which the worthlessness of lords and attornies might be set forth, and conversations, which had passed twenty years before, be **minutely** repeated. (p. 27)

Omission of rival narratives proves the foundation for the emergence and growth of a singular, prominent character, but the omission is equally about the shortening of the book. In the manner of the juvenile volumes, *Northanger Abbey* envisages its own publication from within, as the spinning out of alternative adventures is conceived of in quantifiable and bibliographical terms "three or four" chapters.[63] Singularity does not only pertain to person, but also to plot. In *Pride and Prejudice*, the sequence of picturesque scenes that Elizabeth Bennet encounters on her way to the Peak District is explicitly suppressed for one view only. It is Pemberley that is "all":

> It is not the object of this work to give a description of Derbyshire, nor of any of the remarkable places through which their route thither lay; Oxford, Blenheim, Warwick, Kenelworth, Birmingham, &c. are sufficiently known. A small part of Derbyshire is all the present concern. (*P&P*, p. 266)

*One* hot-house stands metonymically for Austen's social preference in *Northanger Abbey* to have an ordinary heroine, but more broadly for Austen's literary technique, which will pinpoint the singular.

Chapter 14 of the first volume of *Northanger Abbey* serves as a compendium of formal matters engaged with elsewhere in the novel. This is the conversation concerning matters of culture and taste that takes place between Catherine and the Tilneys as they walk out "round Beechen Cliff" and that ranges across fiction, language use and dictionaries, history, drawing and the picturesque. In almost every case, the subject of proliferation is alluded to and contested.

Austen seems to have had *Camilla* in mind when composing chapter 14. She refers to the "natural folly in a beautiful girl", a commonly identified allusion to Indiana Lynmere. From the outset, the narrative protractions of a *Camilla* are invoked:

> The Tilneys called for her at the appointed time; and no new difficulty arising, no sudden recollection, no unexpected summons, no impertinent

[63] More than any other of Austen's published novels, *Northanger Abbey* is self-conscious about being a book, with a high density of references to bibliographical features: pages, chapters, volumes.

> intrusion to disconcert their measures, my heroine was most unnaturally able to fulfil her engagement, though it was made with the hero himself. They determined on walking round Beechen Cliff, that noble hill, whose beautiful verdure and hanging coppice render it so striking an object from almost every opening in Bath. (*NA*, p. 107)

Catherine does not have "some respectable D[r] Marchmont" to "keep them apart for five Volumes" (*L*, p. 9). A fulfilled engagement, and thus rejection of extended form, significantly permits the enjoyment of a picturesque scene. This discursive engagement with structure, so as to issue in a singular view, bears comparison with Elizabeth's journey to the Peak District in which, likewise, negated narrative options result in the picturesque image of Pemberley.

In chapter 14, selection and specificity are privileged over the voluminous. The "hundreds and hundreds" of novels that Henry claims to have read with their indistinguishable "Julias and Louisas" are narrowed down to a specific simile, evoking a single work: "I want an appropriate simile;—as far as your friend Emily herself left poor Valancourt when she went with her aunt to Italy" (p. 108). The "mob of three thousand men" that Eleanor imagines are whittled down to "three duodecimo volumes" (p. 114). The ubiquitous word "nice" complains Henry, "does for **every thing**", when once it was used more selectively "to express neatness, propriety, delicacy, or refinement" (p. 109). Catherine dislikes histories in which quarrel**s** of pope**s** and king**s**, war**s** and pestilence**s** are repeated "in **every** page". When the characters turn to talk about the picturesque, Henry is as abundant in his knowledge as he is in his reading of novels:

> He talked of fore-grounds, distances, and second distances—side-screens and perspectives—lights and shades;—and Catherine was so hopeful a scholar, that when they gained the top of Beechen Cliff, she voluntarily rejected the whole city of Bath, as unworthy to make part of a landscape. (p. 113)

While satirizing the jargon of the picturesque, as well as Catherine's enthusiastic decimation of "the whole city of Bath", this conversation endorses the messages purveyed throughout this chapter in favour of discrimination amidst proliferation. Catherine has an instinct for selection which is juxtaposed with her propensity to proliferate the terrors of the Gothic. Catherine comes to embody the two propensities that Austen the letter writer tried to manage in herself: the love, and the management, of the multiplying minute.

## Connection and the New Formalism

Prolixity in itself is not inimical to cohesive narrative structures, but an uncontrolled permissiveness of detail is. Austen privileged careful narrative integration and was definite in her disapprobation of the "unconnected".

In November 1798, Austen wrote to Cassandra about their neighbour Egerton Brydges's novel *Arthur Fitz-Albini*: "There is very little story, and what there is told in a strange, **unconnected** way. There are many characters introduced, apparently merely to be delineated" (*L*, p. 23; 25 November 1798). Austen's dislike of characters extraneous to plot is repeated throughout her criticism of fiction and in it. In *Northanger Abbey* the narrator draws attention to how "the rules of composition forbid the introduction of a character **not connected** with my fable" (p. 260). Contemporary reviews singled out this compositional feature of Austen's writing. The *Critical Review* noticed of *Pride and Prejudice* that all its characters were essential to its plot: "There is not one person in the drama with whom we could readily dispense."[64] The reviewer in the *Gentleman's Magazine* commented on something similar in *Emma*: the reader never "loses sight of a single individual till the completion of the work".[65] In 1917, Reginald Farrer, praising the coherence of Austen's characters to her plots, described the irrelevance of Margaret Dashwood in *Sense and Sensibility* as a sign of the novitiate status of her first published novel.[66]

In writing of *Pride and Prejudice*, Austen refers to the inclusion of extraneous material, rather than characters, joking with Cassandra about the need for:

> something **unconnected** with the story; an Essay on Writing, a critique on Walter Scott, or the history of Buonaparté — […] — I doubt your quite agreeing with me here — I know your starched Notions. (*L*, p. 212; 4 February 1813)

This claim that Cassandra could not abide disconnected passages in fiction is consistent with Austen's much later account to Anna Austen of Cassandra's disapproval of "desultory novels".

> Your Aunt C. does not like desultory novels, & is rather fearful yours will be too much so, that there will be too frequent a change from one set of people to another, & that circumstances will be sometimes introduced

[64] Unsigned review, *Critical Review* (March 1813), in *Jane Austen: the Critical Heritage*, vol. 1, p. 47.

[65] Unsigned notice, *Gentleman's Magazine* (September 1816), in *Jane Austen: the Critical Heritage*, vol. 1, p. 72.

[66] Reginald Farrer, 'Jane Austen, *ob.* July 18, 1817', *Quarterly Review* (July 1917), in *Jane Austen: the Critical Heritage*, vol. 2, p. 258–9.

> of apparent consequence, which will lead to nothing.—It will not be so great an objection to me, if it does. I allow much more Latitude than She does—& think Nature & Spirit cover many sins of a wandering story—and People in general do not care so much about it—for your comfort. (*L*, p. 281; 10–18 August 1814)

Cassandra held strong views on this subject, but while more lenient, Austen nonetheless states the undesirability of a wandering story, with its "sins". Austen had long before described history writing *not* organized around specific areas or topics, as "loose, disultary [*sic*], unconnected". Desultory comes from the Latin *desultorius* meaning, literally, "belonging to a vaulter": "Skipping about, jumping or flitting from one thing to another" (*OED* 1), as indeed a reader might.

Cassandra's dislike of "too frequent a change from one set of people to another" turns up again in Austen's satirical 'Plan of a Novel, according to hints from various quarters'. This satirical plan, probably composed in May 1816, offers a sustained critique of the episodic novel of which Cassandra, and Austen herself, evidently disapproved.

> From this outset, the Story will proceed, & contain a **striking variety of adventures**. Heroine & her Father never above a fortnight together in one place, [...] no sooner settled in one Country of Europe than they are necessitated to quit it & retire to another—always making new acquaintance, & always obliged to leave them.—This will of course exhibit a **wide variety of Characters**—but there will be no mixture; **the scene will be for ever shifting from one Set of People to another**. (*LM*, pp. 227–8)

Austen's repetition of the phrase "from one set of people to another" from her letter to Anna suggests that it has become a principle of fiction that has taken on a set form from sustained use. That Anne Elliot had not wanted the change to Uppercross "to learn that a removal from one set of people to another [...] will often include a total change of conversation, opinion, and idea" is indicative of her author's knowledge as a writer of plot. (*P*, p. 45)

Austen keyed into her 'Plan of a Novel' the sources for particular ideas, whether her niece Fanny Knight, Mary Cooke or Mrs Pearse of Chilton-Lodge. Next to the passage I have just cited, just in front of "fortnight", is keyed the annotation "Many Critics". This is the only "hint" to have emerged from more than one source. The specificity of fortnight argues against this length of time being the specific advice or preference of "many critics". Rather, Austen sets herself against a common model in fiction of the time, in which protagonists are on the move. As she wrote to Anna of such wandering: "People in general do not care so much about it."

The best-known contributor to the satire of 'Plan of a Novel' was James Stanier Clarke, the Prince Regent's librarian. Austen met Clarke in November 1815 when he showed her around Carlton House and gave her to understand that she might dedicate a future work to the Prince Regent. The 'Plan of a Novel' repeats almost verbatim Clarke's suggestions from his letter to her, written around December 21st. In this letter to Austen, Clarke suggested that she might compose an episodic novel based on a character who was very like himself:

> Do let us have an English Clergyman after your fancy—much novelty may be introduced—shew dear Madam what good would be done if Tythes were taken away entirely, and describe him burying his own mother— as I did [...]. Carry your Clergyman to Sea as the Friend of some distinguished Naval Character about a Court—you can then bring foreward like Le Sage many interesting Scenes of Character and Interest. (*L*, p. 320; possibly 21 December 1815)

Austen's polite reply to this and a subsequent letter from Clarke urging the composition of a "Historical Romance" was that "I must keep to my own style & go on in my own Way" (*L*, p. 326; 1 April 1816). In private, she gave vent to her amusement and irritation in 'Plan of a Novel', the putative first volume of which satirizes an inset backstory, akin to the dismissal of Mrs Allen's adventures in the first volume of *Northanger Abbey*:

> The Father to be induced, at his Daughter's earnest request, to relate to her the past events of his Life. This Narrative will reach through the greatest part of the 1.[st] vol. — as besides all the circumstances of his attachment to her Mother & their Marriage, it will comprehend his going to sea as Chaplain to a distinguished Naval Character about the Court, his going afterwards to Court himself, which introduced him to a great variety of Characters & involved him in many interesting situations, concluding with his opinion of the Benefits to result from Tythes being done away, & his having buried his own Mother [...]. (*LM*, pp. 226–7)

Unconnected events, extraneous characters and detached set pieces are again satirized. Whether it be an essay on Buonaparté or a rant about tythes, the inclusion of a detachable "opinion" piece was an anathema.

Austen raised the subject again in December, joking with her nephew James Edward about artificially lengthening their novels by inserting something extraneous, namely Uncle Henry's sermons. This, Austen suggests, would be in the manner of Walter Scott's *The Antiquary*, but she also evokes the persistently interrupted narrative *Tristram Shandy*, where the author does indeed include one of his sermons to be read aloud by a character:

> Uncle Henry writes very superior Sermons.—You & I must try to get hold of one or two, & put them into our Novels;—it would be a fine help to a volume; & we could make our Heroine read it aloud of a Sunday Evening, just as well as Isabella Wardour in the Antiquary, is made to read the History of the Hartz Demon in the ruins of St Ruth—tho' I beleive, upon recollection, Lovell is the Reader. (*L*, p. 337; 16–17 December 1816)

*The Antiquary* had been published seven months before Austen wrote this letter. While Austen isn't quite criticizing Scott, she is not complimentary about his narrative design either, in that she compares the inset tale of 'The Fortunes of Martin Waldeck' (on encountering the Hartz demon) to the inclusion of "one or two" of Uncle Henry's sermons into her *or* Henry's novel in an imprecise and indiscriminate way.

Austen's mind continued to turn on the grafting of extraneous material into fiction, as she continued in her letter:

> By the bye, my dear Edward, I am quite concerned for the loss your Mother mentions in her Letter; two Chapters & a half to be missing is monstrous! It is well that I have not been at Steventon lately, & therefore cannot be suspected of purloining them;— two strong twigs & a half towards a Nest of my own, would have been something.—I do not think however that any theft of that sort would be really very useful to me. What should I do with your strong, manly, spirited Sketches, full of Variety & Glow?—How could I possibly join them on to the little bit (two Inches wide) of Ivory on which I work with so fine a Brush, as produces little effect after much labour? (*L*, p. 337)

Both images of the nest and the ivory emerge out of the letter's fuller context. Austen first contemplates the writing of fiction as allowing the integration of variant, heterogeneous, strands of material. But on reflection this will not do. It is specifically the impossibility of grafting other material onto her fiction that prompts the metaphor of ivory. The container metaphor of the nest is replaced by the surface metaphor of ivory because of the nest's potential to absorb and accrete. What defines Austen's fiction is impermeability, irreversibility and a constricted shape. But these are definitions specifically adopted as a rejection of the idea of miscellaneous addition.

How could James Stanier Clarke have got it so wrong? How could he, having taken as much pleasure in Austen's writing as he claims, have misunderstood her style so dreadfully (*L*, p. 309; 16 November 1815)? He did after all grasp in part what is distinctive about Austen's fiction: "there is so much nature—and excellent description of Character in every thing you describe" (*L*, p. 320; possibly 21 December 1815). His allusion to

Alain-René Le Sage, on the other hand, shows that he had no grasp of Austen's aims for form. Le Sage, like Tobias Smollett with whom he was frequently compared, adopted a narrative style that was episodic and disjunctive. There are few authors so antipathetic to Austen's privileging of narrative cohesiveness, nor to the prominent formalist criticism that was emerging in the 1810s. Jane Austen was not alone in her strong preference for narrative connection.

Anna Barbauld's fifty-volume edition of *British Novelists* is a landmark publication. It was the first authoritative collection of British novels published in a high-quality format, accompanied by an impressive opening essay 'On the Origin and Progress of Novel-Writing', as well as introductory prefaces to each of her twenty-one chosen authors.[67] It transformed the reputation of the novel[68] and promoted a novelistic canon that was inclusive and diverse,[69] including a significant number of women writers and living authors.[70] It seems unlikely that such a publication could have escaped a novel enthusiast, such as Austen, not least given her seemingly close attention to Barbauld's edition of Richardson's *Correspondence*. Jocelyn Harris describes Barbauld as Jane Austen's "unseen interlocutor". Equally, Jane Austen can be conjured up as Barbauld's ideal novelist. Austen's fiction endorses so many of Barbauld's judgments about the novel: its purpose, value, and aesthetics. Kathryn Sutherland claims that "*British Novelists* provides a history and textual authority for the kind of fiction Austen writes: novels in which seriousness and standards of truth to life are promoted."[71] Barbauld's collection also advocated specific standards of formal organization.[72]

[67] Claudia Johnson describes 'On the Origin and Progress of Novel-Writing' as "one of the most important essays on prose fiction written in the nineteenth century", '"Let Me Make the Novels of a Country"', p. 167. On the relationship between Barbauld's *British Novelists* and earlier collections of novels, see Michael Gamer, 'A Select Collection: Barbauld, Scott, and the Rise of the (Reprinted) Novel', in *Recognizing the Romantic Novel: New Histories of British Fiction, 1780–1830*, eds. Jillian Heydt-Stevenson and Charlotte Sussman (Liverpool: Liverpool University Press, 2008), pp. 155–91.

[68] Michael Gamer comments on how the "first edition in 1810 arguably laid the intellectual groundwork for the novel's ascent to cultural dominance during the Regency", in 'A Select Collection', p. 179.

[69] Johnson, '"Let Me Make the Novels of a Country"'.

[70] Kathryn Sutherland, *Jane Austen's Textual Lives: from Aeschylus to Bollywood* (Oxford: Oxford University Press, 2005), p. 219.

[71] Ibid., p. 219.

[72] Olivia Murphy has suggested that Austen's sympathies would have been in tune with Barbauld's canon of women writers; *Jane Austen the Reader: the Artist as Critic* (Basingstoke: Palgrave Macmillan, 2013), pp. 20–3, p. 25.

Amidst all of the analyses of the connections between Barbauld's and Austen's writing, the significance of their shared formal insistence has not been much elaborated upon. Claudia Johnson has noted Barbauld's disapproval of "episodic and digressive plots" describing how Barbauld includes only one novel by Smollett in her *British Novelists*.[73] Harris notices Barbauld's praise for the "unity" of *Clarissa* and *Grandison* compared to the "detached episodes" in Fielding's fiction. Fielding's interpolated stories were commonly criticized in the eighteenth century as flaws in his art and, according to Barbauld, they were "thrown in like make-weights, to increase the bulk of the volume" (*British Novelists*, vol. 1, pp. xxxvii–viii). Harris sees Austen as repeating such a structural criticism when she apparently wished for *Pride and Prejudice* "to be stretched out [...] with [...] something unconnected with the story".[74] Austen also repeats this disparagement of make-weights, in her suggestion to James Edward Austen that they use one of Uncle Henry's sermons to pad out a volume (*L*, p. 337).

A major part of Barbauld's contribution to the standing of the novel consists in her formal evaluations.[75] The novel is to be appreciated not just as a purveyor of affect, of entertainment or of moral instruction, but it must be judged architecturally by "the ordonnance of the plan" (*British Novelists*, vol. 1, p. 3). Austen's prevalent formal term "connect" rings across Barbauld's critical writing. Barbauld was doing nothing new when she praised the 'connectedness' of Fielding's plot, but the use of "well connected" as a repeated criterion of endorsement, across a range of authors, was.[76] Sterne, Le Sage and Smollett are judged unfavourably because of their detached, unplanned narratives:

> In this work of Le Sage [*Gil Blas*], like some of Smollet's [*sic*], the hero of the piece excites little interest, and it rather exhibits a series of separate adventures, slightly linked together, than a chain of events concurring in one plan to the production of the catastrophe, like the *Tom Jones* of Fielding. The scenes of his *Diable Boiteux* are still more slightly linked together. (*British Novelists*, vol. 1, p. 19)

Smollett's *Roderick Random* is later compared with *Gil Blas*, having "little or nothing of regular plot, and no interest is excited for the hero, whose name serves to string together a number of adventures" (*British Novelists*, vol. 30, p. 5).

[73] Johnson, '"Let Me Make the Novels of a Country"', p. 173.

[74] Harris, *Jane Austen's Art of Memory*, pp. 43–4.

[75] See Catherine E. Moore, '"Ladies ... Taking the Pen in Hand"' and Anne Toner, 'Anna Barbauld on Fictional Form in *The British Novelists* (1810)', *Eighteenth-Century Fiction*, 24, 2 (2011–12), 171–93.

[76] See for instance, Clara Reeve's *The Old English Baron* (vol. 22, p. i), Frances Brooke's *Lady Julia Mandeville* (vol. 27, p. i), and Henry MacKenzie's *Julia de Rubigné* (vol. 29, p. iii).

Barbauld's dislike of the disconnected is a fully theorized position. A novel is *not* personal memoir, nor is it a tour, but a singular and complete construction whose success, in part, is distinct from the real:

> real life is a kind of chance-medley, consisting of many **unconnected** scenes. [...] it is a fault in *his* [the author's] composition if every circumstance does not answer the reasonable expectations of the reader. But in real life our reasonable expectations are often disappointed; **many incidents occur which are like "passages that lead to nothing,"** and characters occasionally turn out quite different from what our fond expectations have led us to expect. (*British Novelists*, vol. 1, pp. 55–6)

In her 1814 letter to her niece Anna, Austen uses the same words to express her fear that in Anna's novel "circumstances will be sometimes introduced of apparent consequence, **which will lead to nothing**". (*L*, p. 281). The shared phrasing here was not especially common. Charlotte Smith, like Barbauld, quoted Thomas Gray's description of "passages that lead to nothing" in *Desmond*, in its original, literal sense to describe the corridors in a house.[77] Austen's and Barbauld's shared use of the phrase as a rejection of irrelevant detail in fiction suggests the confluence in their thinking and even Austen's direct allusion.

## Barbauld, Austen and the Narratological Picturesque

Barbauld reiterates that a novel is a distinct construction and not a work of discursive prose in a fictional disguise. In doing so, she repeatedly censures the vogue for passing off scenic tours as 'novels'.

Picking out Thomas Amory's *The Memoirs of Several Ladies* (1756) for its unconnected style – "the intervals between description and adventure are filled up with learned conversations on abstruse points of divinity" – she described its influence in spreading "that taste for lake and mountain scenery which has since been so prevalent" (*British Novelists*, vol. 1, pp. 39–40). The work does not have a place in the *British Novelists*. Frances Brooke's *The History of Emily Montague* is criticized for having a story that "serves but as a thread to connect a great deal of beautiful description of the manners and scenery of Canada, which country the author had visited" (vol. 27, p. i). Of Smollett's *Humphry Clinker* Barbauld writes: "There is very little of plot [...]. It is carried on in letters, and is rather a frame for remarks on Bath, London, &c. than a regular

[77] Charlotte Smith, *Desmond, a Novel* (London: for G. G. J. and J. Robinson, 1792 in 3 vols.), vol. 2, p. 204.

story" (vol. 30, p. xvi). The latter part "might be entitled with some propriety A Tour into Scotland" and more generally "[t]he reader is often put in mind of *The Bath Guide*, which has suggested several of his remarks and descriptions" (p. xvii). Of Charlotte Smith, Barbauld writes:

> [...] there is much beauty in the descriptive scenery, which Mrs. Smith was one of the first to introduce. Descriptions, of whatever beauty, are but little attended to in a novel of high interest, particularly if introduced, as they often are, during a period of anxious suspense for the hero or heroine. (*British Novelists*, vol. 36, pp. vi–vii)

While the 'picturesque' was approvingly applied to descriptive poetry introduced to longer works as an embellishment,[78] in Barbauld's account, the picturesque is a most ambivalent embellishment to a novel. Indeed, Barbauld dismisses 'description' from the best fiction. Description can be an elegant form of "variety", but only in a work that does not aim at anything powerful like "deep pathos" or "strength". Mrs Radcliffe's fiction is replete with descriptive passages to which novel-readers may be inattentive: "There are beauties in Mrs. Radcliffe's volumes, which would perhaps have more effect if our curiosity were less excited – for her descriptions are rich and picturesque" (vol. 43, p. vii). Ten years earlier, Austen had suggested some similar distinction between description and event (and preference for the latter) when she wrote to Cassandra about a letter from their brother Frank: "The rest of the letter, according to the present fashionable stile of Composition, is cheifly Descriptive; of his Promotion he knows nothing, & of Prizes he is guiltless" (*L*, p. 54; 1 November 1800).

Yet Barbauld deployed picturesque theory herself as a means of articulating the organization of the best prose fiction. A picturesque narrative containing intermittent topographical description obstructs successful novel composition. But the "picturesque" understood as a skillfully organized topography proves a rewarding analogy for the most successful narrative construction. This is the narratological picturesque. It is the means by which Barbauld describes *Clarissa* as an exemplary novel in its perfect design and containment of plot. This description appears in the introductory essay to Richardson's *Correspondence* and is repeated in the preface to Richardson in the first volume of *British Novelists*. Barbauld describes the experience of reading *Clarissa* as an encounter with a picturesque scene:

[78] Richard Payne Knight describes how the word 'picturesque' enters the vocabulary of criticism to describe narration or description that "shows every event or object distinctly, as if represented in a picture"; *An Analytical Inquiry into the Principles of Taste* (London: for T. Payne and J. White, 1805), p. 151. Hugh Blair selects Thomson, Parnell and Milton as English poets successful in "Picturesque Description", *Lectures on Rhetoric and Belles Lettres* (London: W. Strahan; T. Cadell; and W. Creech in Edinburgh, 1783), vol. 2, pp. 371–76, p. 372.

> The plot, as we have seen, is simple, and no under-plots interfere with the main design. No digressions, no episodes. It is wonderful that without these helps of common writers, he could support a work of such length. With Clarissa it begins,—with Clarissa it ends. We do not come upon unexpected adventures and wonderful recognitions, by quick turns and surprises: we see her fate from afar, as it were through a long avenue, the gradual approach to which, without ever losing sight of the object, has more of simplicity and grandeur than the most cunning labyrinth that can be contrived by art. In the approach to the modern country-seat, we are made to catch transiently a side-view of it through an opening of the trees, or to burst upon it from a sudden turning in the road; but the old mansion stood full in the eye of the traveller, as he drew near it, contemplating its turrets, which grew larger and more distinct every step that he advanced; and leisurely filling his eye and his imagination with still increasing ideas of its magnificence. (*Correspondence of Samuel Richardson*, vol. 1, pp. lxxxiii–iv)

This vision of *Clarissa* coheres with Barbauld's dismissal of the digressive and episodic elsewhere. Descriptive passages are not endorsed by a picturesque narratology in which the unity of a novel has to be grasped conceptually in its entirety, in the manner of the picturesque composition. Barbauld imagines the experience of reading *Clarissa* as akin to moving through a landscape, which is the novel itself, and she values the 'simple' above the labyrinthine, a consistency of visual focus, rather than "quick turns and surprises" or 'transient' and oblique views of the novel's or its protagonist's fate and end.

The passage is closely aligned with theories of the picturesque. William Gilpin proselytized the envisioning of landscape as a successfully composed picture. The concept of narrative unity, in which as Barbauld puts it, "no under-plots interfere with the main design", is consistent with the fundamental tenet of picturesque theory that privileges the apprehension of a gestalt or whole. When Elizabeth Bennet embarks on her trip to the Peak District, Austen alludes to the first four sections of Gilpin's *Observations, Relative Chiefly to Picturesque Beauty, Made in the Year 1772, on Several Parts of England, Particularly the Mountains and Lakes of Cumberland and Westmoreland* (1786). At the end of this fourth section, Gilpin writes of Hagley Hall in Worcestershire with organizational concerns in mind:

> The plan of Hagley, (if there be any) is so confused, that it is impossible to describe it. There is no coherency of parts. One scene is tacked to another; and any one might be removed, without the least injury to the rest.
>
> A work of art, (be it what it may, house, picture, book, or garden,) however beautiful in it's *underparts*, loses half it's value, if the *general scope* of it be

> not obvious to conception. Even the wild scene of nature, however pleasing in itself, is still more pleasing, if the eye is able to combine it into a whole.[79]

In Gilpin's and Barbauld's writing, "underparts" (Gilpin) or "under-plots" (Barbauld) are rejected for "the general scope" (Gilpin) or the "main design" (Barbauld). In 'On Landscape Painting, a Poem', Gilpin evokes the strict Aristotelean unity that governs a tragedy as comparable to the rules to which landscape painters must abide: "all that obtrudes / On the chief theme, how beautiful soe'er / Seen as a *part*, disgusts us in the *whole*".[80]

Barbauld's writing on *Clarissa* resonates with this core picturesque emphasis on the singular view.[81] But in its detail it comes strikingly close to the writing of Uvedale Price in his *Essay on the Picturesque*, first published in 1794. When Price and his neighbour and fellow picturesque theorist Richard Payne Knight were writing, the fashion for landscape gardening was at its height. Price's *Essay on the Picturesque* challenged the ubiquitous landscaping trends of Capability Brown. Barbauld's description of *Clarissa* is especially close to Price's discussion of the 'avenue', sacrificed by Brown for the derided 'belt', a circle of trees spaced around a property. Price writes on this in terms that Barbauld's description of *Clarissa* closely echoes:

> [The belt] has, indeed, all the sameness and formality of the avenue, to which it has succeeded, without any of its **simple grandeur**; for though in an avenue **you see the same objects from beginning to end**, and in the belt a new set every twenty yards, yet each successive part of this insipid circle is so like the preceding, that though really different, the difference is scarcely felt; and there is nothing that so dulls, and at the same time so irritates the mind, as perpetual change without variety.[82]

The "long avenue", with its perspectival merits, becomes for Barbauld a simile for the construction of *Clarissa*, with Price's "simple grandeur" emphasized by Barbauld's hendiadys, "simplicity and grandeur":

[79] William Gilpin, *Observations, Relative Chiefly to Picturesque Beauty, Made in the Year 1772, on Several Parts of England; Particularly the Mountains and Lakes of Cumberland, and Westmoreland* (London: for R. Blamire, 1786), vol. 1, p. 57–8.

[80] William Gilpin, *Three Essays: On Picturesque Beauty; on Picturesque Travel; and on Sketching Landscape: to Which Is Added a Poem, on Landscape Painting* (London: for R. Blamire, 1792), p. 7.

[81] Richard Payne Knight's poem *The Landscape. A Didactic Poem* of 1795 refers to the "best approach" to a "beauteous scene" as one in which "nought occurs to [...] bring the Landscape piecemeal to the eyes"; *The Landscape, a Didactic Poem*, 2nd ed. (London: by W. Bulmer and Co., 1795), p. 13.

[82] Uvedale Price, *An Essay on the Picturesque, as Compared with the Sublime and the Beautiful; and, on the Use of Studying Pictures, for the Purpose of Improving Real Landscape [...] A New Edition, with Considerable Additions* (London: for J. Robson, 1796), p. 270.

> we see her fate from afar, as it were through a long avenue, the **gradual approach** to which, **without ever losing sight of the object**, has more of **simplicity and grandeur** than the most cunning labyrinth that can be contrived by art. (Barbauld, *Correspondence of Samuel Richardson*, vol. 1, p. lxxxiii.)

More generally, Price advocates the inherent "intricacy" of the natural landscape, but in this section of the *Essay on the Picturesque* the avenue is defended for its straight line. The belt offers multiple perspectives, but only in a monotonous and predicable way. Instead, Price dwells on the long, gradual view that the avenue gives:

> The avenue has a most striking effect, from the very circumstance of its being strait; no other figure can give that image of a grand gothic aisle with its natural columns and vaulted roof, whose general mass **fills the eye,** while the particular parts insensibly steal from it **in a long gradation of perspective**.[83]

For Barbauld it is the fate of Clarissa herself that is seen in a "gradual approach", "leisurely **filling his [the traveller's] eye**".

It is in *Mansfield Park*, of course, that Fanny Price mourns the loss of avenues in the face of modern landscape improvement, by quoting William Cowper: "Ye fallen avenues, once more I mourn your fate unmerited" (*MP*, p. 66). Fanny laments the lost avenue in the course of a conversation where Mr Rushworth, who is planning improvements at Sotherton, wishes for the approach to his own Elizabethan house to be altered in the manner of a friend's estate which has changed beyond recognition: "[y]ou see the house in the most surprising manner" (p. 62). Henry Austen testified to his sister's early attachment to Gilpin's picturesque writing.[84] Austen's thinking on the picturesque has often been identified as closely in sympathy with the writing of Uvedale Price.[85] This is most overt in *Mansfield Park*, in Fanny Price's telling surname,[86] her defence of the avenue and the traditional view of the landscape she espouses in the face of the fashion for Humphry Repton's improvements.

[83] Ibid., pp. 270–1.

[84] Henry Austen, 'Biographical Notice of the Author' (1818), in *A Memoir of Jane Austen and Other Family Recollections*, pp. 140–1.

[85] For instance, Jill Heydt-Stevenson, 'Liberty, Connection, and Tyranny: the Novels of Jane Austen and the Aesthetic Movement of the Picturesque', in *Lessons of Romanticism: a Critical Companion*, eds. Thomas Pfau and Robert F. Gleckner (Durham, NC: Duke University Press, 1998), p. 261; Peter Knox-Shaw, *Jane Austen and the Enlightenment* (Cambridge: Cambridge University Press, 2004), p. 73; and Nigel Everett, *The Tory View of Landscape* (New Haven, CT, and London: The Paul Mellon Centre for Studies in British Art by Yale University Press, 1994), p. 194.

[86] Everett, *The Tory View of Landscape*, p. 188.

Uvedale Price repeatedly emphasized the principle of "connection". The greatest "defect" in the present system of landscape improvement "is want of connection—a passion for making everything distinct and separate".[87] Connection, as a range of commentators have pointed out, has aesthetic, ethical and social implications.[88] Jill Heydt-Stevenson has described how Rushworth's enthusiastic comments on improvement suggest the disconnecting of a house from its past, from its natural landscape and from its surrounding community.[89] This is in contrast to the well-managed estates in Austen's fiction, most notably Donwell Abbey and Pemberley. Donwell Abbey embraces a view of the Abbey-Mill Farm in an inclusive, organic aesthetic as Alistair Duckworth has pointed out,[90] in contrast, say, to Maria Bertram's relief at the distance of the church from Sotherton. According to Peter Knox-Shaw, Pemberley demonstrates "the principle of connectedness both in its landscape and in the field of social relations" by being the location of Darcy's meeting with the Gardiners.[91] Barbauld was not the only novel critic emphasizing the singular view. In another collection of novels published in 1810, William Mudford wrote of Smollett's narratives: "it was less easy to connect them together in such a manner as should shew a regular coherency of parts and a simultaneous tendency of the whole, to produce one general effect".[92] This is interchangeable with Price's view of unsuccessful landscapes and paintings: "the eye, instead of reposing on one broad, connected whole, is stopt and harassed by little disunited, discordant parts".[93]

Price himself explicitly rejected connection as a defining attribute of literary composition. He distinguished between painting and writing, believing that written compositions *can* tolerate detached elements, whether they be episodes, scenes or stanzas. It was not possible in "the progress of a work of any length" that everyone can "retain the connection of the different parts, and their dependence on each other".[94] Barbauld answers Price directly on this account when she praises Richardson for

[87] Price, *An Essay on the Picturesque*, p. 261.

[88] On this, see Everett, *The Tory View of Landscape*, especially chapter 3, 'The Mansion and the Landscape'.

[89] Heydt-Stevenson, 'Liberty, Connection, and Tyranny', p. 264.

[90] Alistair M. Duckworth, *The Improvement of the Estate: a Study of Jane Austen's Novels* (Baltimore and London: The Johns Hopkins University Press, 1971), p. 175; and Everett, *The Tory View of Landscape*, p. 195.

[91] Knox-Shaw, *Jane Austen and the Enlightenment*, p. 96.

[92] William Mudford, *The British Novelists; Comprising Every Work of Acknowledged Merit Which is Usually Classed Under the Denomination of Novels* (London, 1810–16), vol. 2, p. ii.

[93] Price, *An Essay on the Picturesque*, pp. 160–1.

[94] Ibid., p. 185.

eschewing digressions and episodes, remarking how nevertheless "he could support a work **of such length**." As a knowledgeable admirer of the picturesque *and* of Richardson, Austen may well have been struck by Barbauld's fusing of the two in her account of reading *Clarissa*. *Pride and Prejudice* gives the best evidence for Austen's interest in the narratological picturesque, influenced by Gilpin, Price and Barbauld, and the efforts she took towards realizing that aesthetic.

## Picturesque Form in *Pride and Prejudice*

Barbauld's analogy between reading a book and moving through a landscape was one that had been developed by Austen herself, most overtly in 'Catharine, or the Bower'. Austen too had been reflecting on the relationship between narrative organization and a picturesque tour.

Let us look at the conversation between Catharine and Camilla Stanley in its larger context. Camilla Stanley's discussion of reading is a prelude to an account of a journey that she is undertaking:

> "Oh! I do not know anything about *that*—but it [*Emmeline*] is better in *everything*—Besides, Ethelinde is so long—" "That is a very common Objection I beleive, said Kitty, but for my own part, if a book is well written, I always find it too short."
>
> "So do I, only I get tired of it before it is finished." "But did not you find the story of Ethelinde very interesting? And the Descriptions of Grasmere, are not they Beautiful?" "Oh! I missed them all, because I was in such a hurry to know the end of it— Then from an easy transition she added, We are going to the Lakes this Autumn, and I am quite Mad with Joy [...]". (*J*, pp. 249–50)

Camilla goes on to describe this trip to the Lake District and how she and her family will stop either at Matlock or Scarborough on the way, which prompts Kitty's surprise:

> "You intend then to into Yorkshire?"
>
> "I beleive not—indeed I know nothing of the Route, for I never trouble myself about such things—. I only know that we are to go from Derbyshire to Matlock and Scarborough, but to which of them first, I neither know nor care." (*J*, p. 250)

Camilla has no interest in location. She is ignorant that Matlock is in Derbyshire and Scarborough in Yorkshire, and that Scarborough is situated, far north of Matlock, on the other side of the country to the Lakes. As Catharine concludes of Camilla: "She appeared to be shamefully ignorant as to the Geography of England" (*J*, p. 251).

Austen has her characters comment upon the descriptive passages in *Ethelinde* about Grasmere, which Austen then adapts into a literal journey to the Lakes within the story, which becomes in consequence an analogy for the process of reading. The hinge for this figurative process is the phrase "from an easy transition". The "easy transition" that Camilla makes from reading to travelling is the association with her own imminent trip to the Lake District, but the "easy transition" has a textual dimension, signalling the common analogy between a book and a journey, familiar in the English novel from Fielding at least. In *Joseph Andrews*, Fielding creates an extended parallel between the chapters in his novel and stages on a journey.[95] Unlike Fielding's readers who are advised to use those stages to "consider of what he hath seen in the Parts he hath already past through", Camilla is only focused on an end. She is entirely ignorant of her route to the Lake District, because she thinks solely of the fashionable events she will attend and the clothes she will wear when she reaches her destinations. Similarly, she reads only for an ending, skipping Charlotte Smith's celebrated landscapes, the valuable and rewarding sights she encounters en route, "because I was in such a hurry to know the end".

Not only did Austen return to this passage of 'Catharine, or the Bower' in *Northanger Abbey* when thinking about length (see above pp. 47–8), but she returned to it much more directly in *Pride and Prejudice*. When Elizabeth Bennet is invited to join the Gardiners on their tour to the Lakes, Elizabeth seems to respond directly to Camilla Stanley. While Camilla says of her trip to the Lake District, "indeed **I know nothing of the Route**, for I never trouble myself about such things", Elizabeth cries out to her aunt with little direct motivation: "**We *will* know where we have gone—we *will* recollect what we have seen.** Lakes, mountains, and rivers, shall not be jumbled together" (*P&P*, pp. 174–5). A. Walton Litz even suspected that this passage of *Pride and Prejudice* originated in the earlier draft *First Impressions*, not because of its similarity to 'Catharine' in particular, but because of the closeness of its tone to that of the juvenilia.[96] Elizabeth voices the implicit narratorial criticism in 'Catharine, or the Bower' of the lazy, inattentive traveller.

[95] Henry Fielding, *The History of the Adventures of Joseph Andrews and of His Friend Mr Abraham Adams; and, an Apology for the Life of Mrs Shamela Andrews*, ed. Douglas Brooks-Davies; revised with a new introduction by Thomas Keymer (Oxford: Oxford University Press, 1999; *Joseph Andrews* first published, 1742 in 2 vols.), p. 76.

[96] A. Walton Litz, 'The Picturesque in *Pride and Prejudice*', *Persuasions*, 1 (1979), 13–15, 20–4.

Furthermore, like 'Catharine, or the Bower', in *Pride and Prejudice* Austen also fuses travelling with the experience of narrative. Once Elizabeth has embarked on her northern tour, to Derbyshire rather than the Lakes as it turns out, the narrator of *Pride and Prejudice* also turns explicitly to novelistic form. The tour evokes narrative reflection:

> It is not the object of this work to give a description of Derbyshire, nor of any of the remarkable places through which their route thither lay; Oxford, Blenheim, Warwick, Kenelworth, Birmingham, &c. are sufficiently known. A small part of Derbyshire is all the present concern. To the little town of Lambton, the scene of Mrs. Gardiner's former residence, and where she had lately learned that some acquaintance still remained, they bent their steps, after having seen all the principal wonders of the country; and within five miles of Lambton, Elizabeth found from her aunt, that Pemberley was situated. (*P&P*, p. 266)

*Pride and Prejudice* echoes 'Catharine', but in a manner that is in tension with the delight expressed by Elizabeth (and indeed Catharine) for topographical reflection. While Camilla states plainly that she passed over "the Descriptions of Grasmere" when reading *Ethelinde*, here it is Austen's narrator who states that she eschews a "description of Derbyshire". Camilla Stanley is reprimanded in Elizabeth Bennet's injunction to careful recollection of place, but Austen has also, to some extent, conceded to Camilla's reading habits. Austen makes evident in *Pride and Prejudice* the value of keeping one particular end in sight.

Instead of depicting "Oxford, Blenheim, Warwick, Kenelworth, Birmingham, &c.", the narrative, by means of this negation, locates itself within Derbyshire and specifically to the area where "Pemberley was situated". The chapter that follows, which is the opening of the third volume, begins with an extended account of Elizabeth's approach towards and view of Pemberley:

> Chapter 1
>
> Elizabeth, as they drove along, watched for the first appearance of Pemberley Woods with some perturbation; and when at length they turned in at the lodge, her spirits were in a high flutter.
>
> The park was very large, and contained great variety of ground. They entered it in one of its lowest points, and drove for some time through a beautiful wood, stretching out over a wide extent.
>
> Elizabeth's mind was too full for conversation, but she saw and admired every remarkable spot and point of view. They gradually ascended for half a mile, and then found themselves at the top of a considerable eminence, where the wood ceased, and the eye was instantly caught by Pemberley

> House, situated on the opposite side of a valley, into which the road with some abruptness wound. It was a large, handsome, stone building, standing well on rising ground, and backed by a ridge of high woody hills;—and in front, a stream of some natural importance was swelled into greater, but without any artificial appearance. Its banks were neither formal, nor falsely adorned. Elizabeth was delighted. She had never seen a place for which nature had done more, or where natural beauty had been so little counteracted by an awkward taste. (*P&P*, p. 271)

Austen's interest in picturesque description is signalled as Elizabeth surveys Pemberley, as much as Gilpin does Blenheim and Chatsworth, attending to Pemberley in its surrounds rather than the details of the house itself. The description of Pemberley is also an endorsement of the narratological picturesque that privileges a larger whole over smaller descriptive scenes. Austen has just made explicit a narrative purpose in excluding one sort of landscape description (that of a journey through multiple locations), and does so to replace it with another landscape description (that of Darcy's house and grounds). The attention to Pemberley tells us of Elizabeth's amazement, of Austen's interest in picturesque description, but it also tells us about the composition of the novel as a whole and its privileging of the sustained single view.

Jane Austen, like Anna Barbauld, saw the relevance of picturesque design for narratological thinking. That is not to say that Austen is explicitly evoking Barbauld in her account of Pemberley. There are differences between Barbauld's description of the old mansion that is *Clarissa* and Austen's description of Pemberley. Barbauld dislikes a house bursting upon a viewer's eye, while the language of abruptness is present in Elizabeth's first sighting of Pemberley. This preference may reflect Austen's indebtedness to Gilpin[97] and indeed Uvedale Price's stressing of the "abrupt" over a "uniform smoothness".[98] Nevertheless, both Barbauld and Austen linger on the sustained rather than transitory view of a country seat, both dwell on the approach to the house as 'gradual' ("the gradual approach" [Barbauld], "they gradually ascended" [Austen]), and both explicitly reject the "artificial" (Austen) and "contrived" (Barbauld) in the admired landscape.

More significantly, Barbauld described the experience of reading *Clarissa* as one in which the reader never loses "sight of the object", until "the old mansion stood full in the eye of the traveller, as he drew near it, contemplating its turrets, which grew larger and more distinct every step that he advanced, and leisurely filling his eye and his imagination with

97 Knox-Shaw, *Jane Austen and the Enlightenment*, p. 83.

98 Price, *An Essay on the Picturesque*, p. 23.

still increasing ideas of its magnificence". Similarly, in the larger scale of *Pride and Prejudice* we never lose sight of the work's object, the courtship of Elizabeth and Darcy that culminates in the manifestation of Darcy's house. We neither lose sight of that object, by distracting descriptions of towns or counties, nor by interpolated stories that absorb the reader's attention, or allow her to skip and interrupt narrative continuity. Alistair Duckworth has described Elizabeth's journey through Pemberley's grounds and into the house as spatially recapitulating her associations with Darcy.[99] Elizabeth's apprehension of Pemberley also recapitulates the narratological argument that immediately precedes it.

The first sighting of Rosings is in stark contrast to this first one of Pemberley. Elizabeth first sees Rosings from Mr Collins's garden:

> Here, leading the way through **every walk and cross walk**, and scarcely allowing them an interval to utter the praises he asked for, **every view** was pointed out with a **minuteness which left beauty entirely behind. He could number the fields in every direction, and could tell how many trees there were in the most distant clump. But of all the views which his** garden, or which the county, or the kingdom, could boast, none were to be compared with the prospect of Rosings, afforded by an opening in the trees that bordered the park nearly opposite the front of his house. It was a handsome modern building, well situated on rising ground. (*P&P*, pp. 177–8)

Mr Collins does not have the art of judicious selection: "every walk and cross walk", "every view", "a minuteness which left beauty behind", "number", "how many". Mr Collins is himself metonymically the crowded, fussy approach to Rosings.[100] Like Barbauld, Austen seems to have been influenced by Uvedale Price when composing these approaches. Although Rosings has in common with Pemberley the qualities of a modern house situated on rising ground, that reference to a "clump" is damning, certainly for any admirer of Price. Uvedale Price's description of the clump as characterized by "sameness and insipidity" transfers to its admirer Collins, and "the stubborn clump" to its presumable owner, Lady Catherine de Bourgh. Pemberley is "backed by a ridge of high woody hills", Rosings surrounded by clumps. Price writes:

> Natural groups, being formed by trees of different ages and sizes, and at different distances from each other, often too of a mixture of timber trees with thorns, hollies, and others of inferior growth, are full of variety in

[99] Duckworth, *The Improvement of the Estate*, p. 125.

[100] This is something like what Litz describes as a "moral picturesque" which he argues Austen develops; see 'The Picturesque in *Pride and Prejudice*'.

> their outlines; and from the same causes, no two groups are exactly alike. But clumps, from the trees being generally of the same age and growth, planted nearly at the same distance in a circular form, and from each tree being equally pressed by his neighbour, are as like each other as so many puddings turned out of one common mould.[101]

Collins's arboreal knowledge is one of quantification. His admiration for trees that "are as like each other as so many puddings turned out of one common mould" says a good deal too for his view of the interchangeability of women.

The presence of the picturesque across Austen's fiction has been the subject of much analysis. In *Pride and Prejudice*, Elizabeth Bennet shows her knowledge of Gilpin when she brilliantly compares the Bingley sisters and Darcy to a group of cows: "The picturesque would be spoilt by admitting a fourth. Good bye" (*P&P*, p. 58). Less has been said, however, about Austen's turn to Pemberley by allusion to Gilpin's *Observations, Relative Chiefly to Picturesque Beauty.* When she writes that the route to "Oxford, Blenheim, Warwick, Kenelworth, Birmingham, &c. are sufficiently known", that knowledge may be firsthand or by means of Gilpin's celebrated account. Why does Austen refer at all to a route that is "sufficiently known"?

First, it is important to consider more fully Austen's deployment of the contractive technique of apophasis here. Apophasis – the subject of the next chapter – draws attention to that which it claims to pass over. Austen's narrator, in declaring that she *will not* describe the places through which the party travelled, does indeed do so, listing with accuracy a particular route. Austen makes it explicit, first through Elizabeth's rebuttal of inattentive travelling and then through the narrator's rhetorical dexterity, that there is no vagueness in her own conceptions of topographical space and the world her characters inhabit. Austen even flatters her readers into attentiveness, suggesting their own recall of the route. In these ways, Austen endorses the mindfulness of careful observation, but nonetheless that which is observed is carefully subordinated to a singular novelistic purpose. Austen's chosen form of fiction will not allow attention to every stage of a journey to distract from the coherence of its shape. The narrator eschews Gilpin's descriptive style.

The allusion to Gilpin's 1772 *Observations* is also a mark of indebtedness. Austen's tour replicates as well as subverts the tour mapped out by

[101] Price, *An Essay on the Picturesque*, pp. 267–8.

Gilpin. Gilpin describes in the sixth section the "romantic scenes" of the Lake District as "the principal inducement to this tour". The same romantic scenes were the principal inducement for Elizabeth Bennet to agree to tour with the Gardiners. Austen cannot allow Elizabeth to think that she is going to Derbyshire because this would prompt the accusation that she agreed to go there specifically to see Pemberley and perhaps Darcy himself.[102] The inevitable geographical sequencing that Gilpin lays down is thus challenged by the intervention of chance in *Pride and Prejudice*, as Elizabeth's route to the Lakes is deflected. Austen proposes a tour such as Gilpin's only to narrate its unsuitability and to disassociate her novel from touristic writing as written by Gilpin or Charlotte Smith, by Tobias Smollett or Frances Brooke.

The point at which the Gardiners cease to follow the route of the *Observations* is when their road takes them to Derbyshire rather than further north to the Lakes. But it is also the point, as noted above, where Gilpin visits Hagley, where he disparages any "work of art" in which "one scene is tacked to another; and any one might be removed, without the least injury to the rest". This concluding intertextual statement makes the point that is being articulated by Austen at the very moment at which Gilpin's *Observations* are alluded to. There is a paradox to Gilpin's writing in that while valuing within his books the well-shaped scene, the very genre of picturesque writing which he establishes is in its essence loose and successive. Early on in the 1772 *Observations*, Gilpin apologizes for his own "tedious" and "unconnected" style:

> Travelling continually among rocks, and mountains; hills, and vallies; and remarking upon them, he feared might be tedious: and therefore, when any observations, anecdote, or history, grew naturally from his subject, he was glad to take advantage of it; [...] If any of these digressions however should appear forced—out of place—or unconnected with the subject; for *them* he wishes to apologize.[103]

In the fifth section, following on from where Austen departs from Gilpin, there is a greater sense of hasty successiveness as he aims to reach the Lakes: "The country we now traversed, may be called a kind of **connecting thread**: itself of an uncharacterized species, striking us with no determined features".[104] The "uncharacterized" species of country that

[102] These were the sorts of criticisms that Richardson's Pamela had to contend with.

[103] Gilpin, *Observations, Relative Chiefly to Picturesque Beauty*, vol. 1, pp. xx–xxi.

[104] Ibid., vol. 1, p. 74.

Gilpin feels obliged to acknowledge is equivalent to the empty space of the "&c" at the end of Austen's "Oxford, Blenheim, Warwick, Kenelworth, Birmingham, &c". Barbauld criticized stories that serve "but as a **thread** to connect a great deal of beautiful description of [...] manners and scenery". Yet while Austen swerves away from Gilpin's route to the Lakes though starting out on it, the tour within *Pride and Prejudice* does in fact follow Gilpin to his end, as the second volume of his *Observations* concludes in Derbyshire. The tour in *Pride and Prejudice* departs from the picturesque model but also provides a contraction of it, ending in the same place as Gilpin. Austen, however, rigorously suppresses any narrative that could strike us as having "no determined features".

Does the attention given to the tour's exclusion suggest anything of Austen's excisions in their most literal sense? On publication, Austen was concerned about the shortness of volume two, but was reassured of "there being a larger proportion of Narrative in that part", an assertion that is difficult to measure out in terms of narrative event. The trip to Hunsford occurs in volume two, with the rejection of Darcy, but volume three contains arguably more incident. Austen, of course, was able to assess the "proportion of Narrative" in constituent parts of the book by knowing what she may have come to deem *non*-narrative material in the process of editing or rewriting. Remember that in this part of the novel, which registers a closeness to her teenage writings, Elizabeth commits herself to remembering where she will have been when she undertakes this tour, but the novel, in its published form, does not carry through this promise. If it was the case that Austen had originally delineated more of Elizabeth's and the Gardiners' trip, then Austen's apophatic negation is, in fact, the trace of that which it partly suppresses.

Mary Poovey has described what she calls Austen's "non-referential aesthetic" in *Pride and Prejudice* as including moments where reference is made to something in the novel that does not occur. In volume three, chapter 18, Elizabeth refers to a "resolution" of thanking Darcy for his "kindness to Lydia" (*P&P*, p. 422). This seems to refer back to chapter 16, where Elizabeth does indeed thank Darcy for his kindness, but also refers back to another time when Elizabeth learnt of Darcy's kindness and longed to "acknowledge [...] how gratefully I feel it" (*P&P*, pp. 405–6). But when we go back to that scene in chapter 3, there is no such resolution. Poovey transforms an absent textual origin into a larger argument about the 1797 Bank Restriction Act, which disrupted any essential connection between paper money and gold. Paper money no longer obligated the Bank of England to redeem money in gold, thus limiting money to a "*merely* representational" function.[105] More prosaically, Elizabeth's missing resolution may have been scratched out as extraneous given its later appearance.[106]

We know that in revising *Pride and Prejudice*, Jane Austen was committed to cutting. The unevenness between the novel's volume lengths may testify to this contraction, as Austen's concern about the shortness of volume two is associatively linked in her letter with her thoughts about lopping and cropping. There are other formal unevenesses in the novel. *Pride and Prejudice* has the greatest contrast among the novels in its length of volumes, but also in length of chapters.[107] Jane Austen's joke in her letter to Cassandra about *Pride and Prejudice* needing "a long chapter" has added significance when we realize that she is composing the shortest chapters of her mature work. The opening chapter of *Pride and Prejudice* is startlingly short in comparison with her other novels, but also with contemporary fiction that she admired.[108] Here we witness the construction of a narrative unit with quite tangible miniaturization, concentrating the reading eye both vertically and horizontally, with its brief lines of dialogue. Four chapters in the opening volume of *Pride and Prejudice* have these minute dimensions.

It is impossible to know whether the shortness of these chapters came about at the late stage of 'lopping and cropping' or by preceding design. As Edd Winfield Parks, for one, has noted, chapters in the first volume can seem suddenly foreshortened: chapter 20 ends quite abruptly in the middle of a conversation, after Mr Collins's speech to Mrs Bennet following Elizabeth's rejection of his proposal, with no attempt at rounding off.[109] On the other hand, the positioning of her very short chapters at the beginning of the novel creates a uniform impression of what she describes as her

[105] Mary Poovey, 'From Politics to Silence: Jane Austen's Nonreferential Aesthetic', in *A Companion to Jane Austen*, eds. Claudia L. Johnson and Clara Tuite (Oxford: Wiley-Blackwell, 2009), pp. 251–60, p. 257.

[106] This would, in fact, reinforce the analogy with the Bank Restriction Act, as the original referent would be purposely deleted.

[107] The chapter lengths in *Mansfield Park* are different in being remarkably consistent throughout the novel's entirety, perhaps fitting for a work whose protagonist is also steady and reflective. By the time that Austen writes *Persuasion*, she is using the internal divisions of the book to construct a delicate symmetry across its two volumes, which are also remarkably close to each other in length. This is not to say that Austen progressed steadily towards symmetrical forms of narrative division: *Emma* shows more of the structural variations of *Pride and Prejudice*.

[108] By contrast to *Pride and Prejudice*'s 857 words, Edgeworth's *Belinda* opens with a chapter of 4,483 words; Burney's *Camilla*, 2,869 words; and *Cecilia*, 1,880 words. Even Elizabeth Inchbald's *A Simple Story* has an opening chapter of just over a thousand words. Of Austen's mature works, it is only *Pride and Prejudice* that contains chapters that fall below one thousand words.

[109] Edd Winfield Parks, 'Jane Austen's Lure of the Next Chapter', *Nineteenth-Century Fiction*, 7, 1 (1952), 56–60, and on this chapter in *Pride and Prejudice* in particular, p. 60.

'epigrammatism'. It is not just that the novel opens with her most famous epigrammatic utterance – "It is a truth universally acknowledged [...]" – but it opens with a very noticeable succinctness of form: a blazon of brevity. Excision is indistinguishable from innovation in *Pride and Prejudice*, a novel whose raw, even experimental quality is part of its energy. The rejection of description at the end of volume two narrates Austen's vision of her novel. *Pride and Prejudice* also provides clues as to the process by which she enacted it.

## The Reception of Austen's Form and the Fiction of Walter Scott

George Henry Lewes gave the wrong impression when he said that "scarcely any one has insisted on Miss Austen's construction" in contrast with the ubiquity of praise for Fielding's.[110] What praise there was of Austen, pre-1860, embraced the design of her plots.

Both the *Critical Review* notice of *Pride and Prejudice* and the *Gentleman's Magazine*'s of *Emma* state that all characters were essential to plot (see above p. 53). Walter Scott, in the 1816 *Quarterly* review of *Emma* made the same point about Austen's skillful integration of character within plot. This is in contrast to older adventure fiction where "violent changes of time, of place, and of circumstances, hurry him [the protagonist] forward from one scene to another, and his adventures will usually be found **only connected with each other** because they have happened to the same individual".[111] Austen is not compared with Fielding. Rather, she replaces Fielding as a writer whose form is antithetical to the unconnected, the type of fiction associated frequently with Smollett and Le Sage.

Other reviews of *Emma*, like Scott's, used Aristotelian terminology. A notice in the *British Critic* read: "In few novels is the unity of place preserved."[112] The *Gentleman's Magazine* commented likewise: "The unities of time and place are well preserved."[113] In 1821, Richard Whately compared Austen's plots favourably with those structured around "unconnected events". Whately praises Austen's "compactness of plan":

[110] George Henry Lewes, 'A Word about *Tom Jones*', in *Jane Austen: the Critical Heritage*, vol. 1, p. 175.
[111] Walter Scott, review of *Emma*, in *Jane Austen: the Critical Heritage*, vol. 1, p. 61.
[112] Unsigned notice, *British Critic* (July 1816), *Jane Austen: the Critical Heritage*, vol. 1, p. 71.
[113] Unsigned notice, *Gentleman's Magazine* (September 1816), *Jane Austen: the Critical Heritage*, vol. 1, p. 72.

> Her [Austen's] fables appear to us to be, in their own way, nearly faultless; they do not consist (like those of some of the writers who have attempted this kind of common-life novel writing) **of a string of unconnected events** which have little or no bearing on one main plot, and are introduced evidently for the sole purpose of bringing in characters and conversations; but have all that **compactness of plan** and **unity of action** which is generally produced by a sacrifice of probability: yet they have little or nothing that is not probable; [...] the final catastrophe is scarcely every clearly foreseen from the beginning, and very often comes, upon the generality of readers at least, quite unexpected. We know not whether Miss Austin [*sic*] ever had access to the precepts of Aristotle; but there are few, if any, writers of fiction who have illustrated them more successfully.[114]

This emphasis on Aristotelian principles signals how seriously Austen's novels are being appraised as art, facilitated by the broader shift in criticism that promoted the novel's value according to aesthetic criteria. The dramatic power of Austen lay not just in her facility with dialogue, but in her ability to apply the long-established dramatic means of plot construction to a narrative form that was often perceived to be unwieldy and accretive.

William Galperin has described a contrary view, however. Galperin argues that reviews of Austen's *Emma* testify to a tension in her work between plot and a disruptive interest in "everyday particularity", or the 'real'.[115] *Emma*, in fact, of all of Austen's fiction emblematizes this tension, as Miss Bates's and Mr Woodhouse's "preoccupation with detail effectively recapitulates the work of Austen's real overall in bringing the narrative of *Emma* to a grinding halt".[116] Galperin connects Austen's plots with theories of the picturesque, using Walter Scott's review of *Emma* in part to do so. Taking Richard Payne Knight's writing on aesthetics as a primary source, Galperin's view of the picturesque is of a regulatory ideology, to which Austen was both "responsive but also opposed":[117] "the prevalence of picturesque theory in Austen's writings may also reflect a certain anxiety or dissatisfaction with some of the picturesque's more sinister operations".[118] By this Galperin refers to the partiality of the picturesque, its class interests and illiberal containment of "opposition, possibility, and novelty".[119]

[114] Richard Whately, unsigned review of *Northanger Abbey* and *Persuasion*, *Quarterly Review* (January 1821), *Jane Austen: the Critical Heritage*, vol. 1, pp. 95–6.

[115] Galperin comments that "in virtually all the reviews of *Emma* [...] the "interest" generated by plot and theme is almost always subordinated to the interest given to everyday particularity in the novel", in William H. Galperin, *The Historical Austen* (Philadelphia: University of Pennsylvania Press, 2003), p. 68.

[116] Ibid., pp. 67–8.

[117] Ibid., p. 46.

[118] Ibid., p. 53.

[119] Ibid.

The politics of the picturesque have long been debated: in its various formulations, it has been identified as both politically conservative and liberal, containing and liberating. On the one hand, the picturesque signifies hegemony, control and arrest,[120] on the other, roughness, irregularity and abrupt variation.[121] For Austen to declare herself a "partial" and highly selective historian in her 'History of England' is indeed to limit her narrative to the sphere of her own prejudices, but in doing so she attends to a closer range of interest, in favour of individuals within a socially minoritized group (women). Galperin is less interested in apportioning the unappealing implications of the picturesque to particular theorists, or to Austen herself, than to establishing a paradigm between a regulatory mechanism in Austen's fiction (the picturesque) and something that transgresses and opposes that (the real).

My own readings in this chapter endorse Galperin's suggestions in many ways, but with a different emphasis. I have suggested that Austen's containment of plot is indeed indebted to picturesque theory and that in her most personal writings she engages head-on with the tension between regulation and something more expansive that threatens to transgress that regulation. However, to what extent a highlighting of that detail has to be disruptive or anti-picturesque is more difficult to determine, not least because in picturesque theory, "variety" is so strongly endorsed.[122] Galperin's attention is on the 'real', suggesting, by analogy, that the selective emphasis of her fiction, the "picturesque", is more artificial and contrived. I would stress, by contrast, the originality of Austen's picturesque narratology as a technique of formal design.[123] I would also suggest that Walter Scott deemed the disruptive potential of Austen's fiction to be

[120] Alan Liu, *Wordsworth: the Sense of History* (Stanford, CA: Stanford University Press, 1989). The picturesque is a means of "social control" (p. 90); picturesque guidebooks and theory "project an arrest […] disciplinary in force" (p. 95).

[121] Sidney K. Robinson, *Inquiry into the Picturesque* (Chicago and London: University of Chicago Press, 1991), pp. 1–30, pp. 25–6.

[122] Austen's claim that *Pride and Prejudice* "wants shade […] anything that would form a contrast" is an allusion to the picturesque (*L*, p. 212). Gilpin emphasizes in *Three Essays* how "*[v]ariety* too is equally necessary in his composition: so is *contrast.* […] One uniform light, or one uniform shade produces no effect" (p. 20).

[123] As Marilyn Butler has pointed out: "Naturalness and verisimilitude, qualities which relate the world of the novel to the actual world, are critical terms to conjure with before 1830; unity, which takes the novel to be self-sufficient, is not"; 'Disregarded Designs: Austen's Sense of the Volume', p. 50. Cynthia Wall's book, *Grammars of Approach*, was published as this book was going to press. There she too argues that Austen's narrative stragegy is shaped by the picturesque. Free indirect discourse is "the psycholiterary equivalent of the approach" (p. 217) and is one part of Austen's "narrative picturesque". Cynthia Wall, *Grammars of Approach: Landscape, Narrative and the Linguistic Picturesque* (Chicago and London: University of Chicago Press, 2019).

negligible. While Galperin reads Scott's review of *Emma* as an effort to fend off the 'real' and to defend realism from "troublesome complications" that diverge from plot,[124] it seems to me that Scott noticeably steps back from acknowledging any such disruptiveness in Austen's fiction, because he had gone much further than Austen in embracing it.

In his review of *Emma*, Walter Scott quotes a long conversation from chapter 12 in the first volume, largely between Mr Woodhouse and Isabella about their respective physicians. Scott praises "[t]he author's knowledge of the world, and the peculiar tact with which she presents characters that the reader cannot fail to recognize [...]. The subjects are not often elegant [...] but they are finished up to nature, and with a precision which delights the reader".[125] But after quoting this substantial passage Scott does appear to display ambivalence regarding Austen's style:

> Perhaps the reader may collect from the preceding specimen both the merits and faults of the author. The former consists much in the force of a narrative conducted with much neatness and point, and a quiet yet comic dialogue, in which the characters of the speakers evolve themselves with dramatic effect. The faults, on the contrary, arise from the minute detail which the author's plan comprehends. Characters of folly or simplicity, such as those of old Woodhouse and Miss Bates, are ridiculous when first presented, but if too often brought forward or too long dwelt upon, their prosing is apt to become as tiresome in fiction as in real society.[126]

In the wake of Austen's merits, Scott's listing of Austen's faults becomes confusing. Austen's "faults [...] arise from the minute detail which the author's plan comprehends", but it is not clear whether Austen ever quite commits these faults, as Scott phrases his critique through a conditional: "Characters of folly or simplicity, such as those of old Woodhouse and Miss Bates, are ridiculous when first presented, but if too often brought forward or too long dwelt upon, their prosing is apt to become as tiresome in fiction as in real society." Scott, as Galperin points out, immediately turns Austen's fiction into a landscape improved along picturesque principles, bearing the "same relation" to sensational fiction "that cornfields and cottages and meadows bear to the highly adorned grounds of a show mansion, or the rugged sublimities of a mountain landscape". Thus, in Galperin's analysis, Scott almost recognizes the 'real', but tries to marginalize its disruptive yield.

[124] Galperin, *The Historical Austen*, p. 68.

[125] Scott, review of *Emma*, in *Jane Austen: the Critical Heritage*, vol. 1, p. 67.

[126] Ibid., pp. 67–8.

When Scott wrote the review of *Emma*, his third novel, *The Antiquary*, was almost ready for the press.[127] This was the novel that Austen herself used as an example of heterogeneous composition in writing to her nephew. Jonathan Oldbuck, the antiquary, is the title character, although he could hardly be called the hero and has little share in the plot.[128] Oldbuck is a character of an explicitly "prosing" nature, discoursing profusely on his favourite topics. In the nineteenth chapter, Lovel, the more conventional hero of the work, curses the antiquary for his tiresome digressions:

> it is inconceivable how often, in the course of that short walk, Lovel, exhausted by the unceasing prosing of his worthy companion, mentally bestowed on the devil, or any one else that would have rid him hearing more of them, all the orders and disorders of architecture which had been invented or combined from the building of Solomon's temple downwards.[129]

In this chapter, Scott dramatizes the formal dangers to the progression of plot in the "strife of narrators", as Oldbuck, Sir Arthur Wardour and the Reverend Dr Blattergowl, who is similarly and more than once described as "prosing", seek to find ascendancy in the conversation.[130]

Not only that, Miss Oldbuck, the antiquary's sister, is similarly prone to detail. In chapter 9, Oldbuck ironically chastises her for her verbosity, only to digress on the subject of succinctness:

> "Sister Grizzel, this is abominable," interrupted Oldbuck; "I vow to Heaven ye might have raised the ghosts of every abbot of Trotcosey since the days of Waldimir, in the time you have been detailing the introduction to this single spectre—Learn to be succinct in your narrative—Imitate the concise style of old Aubrey, an experienced ghost-seer, who entered his memoranda on these subjects in a terse business-like manner, *exempli gratia* — 'At Cirencester, 5$^{th}$ March, 1670, was an apparition — Being demanded whether good spirit or bad, made no answer, but instantly disappeared with a curious perfume, and a melodious twang.'—*Vide* his Miscellanies, p. eightieth, as well as I can remember, and near the middle of the page."[131]

There is an association from the very first chapter of *The Antiquary* between Jonathan Oldbuck and forms of delay. Oldbuck seems to have

[127] Peter Sabor, '"Finished up to Nature": Walter Scott's Review of *Emma*', *Persuasions*, 13 (1991), 88–99, p. 90.

[128] John Wilson Croker makes this point in his review of *The Antiquary*, *Quarterly Review* (April 1816), in *Walter Scott: the Critical Heritage*, ed. John O. Hayden (London: Routledge & Kegan Paul, 1970), p. 101.

[129] Walter Scott, *The Antiquary*, ed. David Hewitt (Edinburgh: Edinburgh University Press, 1995; first published 1816 in 3 vols.), p. 148.

[130] Ibid., pp. 149, 274.

[131] Ibid., p. 71.

been written deliberately to test narrative form. As John Wilson Croker pointed out, Oldbuck is reminiscent of the Baron of Bradwardine in *Waverley*,[132] a character who attracted much attention, good and ill, standing out as an eccentric caricature as in the fiction of Smollett.[133] The *British Critic* praised Scott's characterization in *Waverley*, noting that the characters "relieve one another with so much art, that the reader will not find himself wearied even with the pedantic jargon of the old baron of Bradwardine."[134] Scott resurrects the pedantic jargon of Bradwardine in *Waverley* in Jonathan Oldbuck in *The Antiquary*, but takes much further its wearying effect.

In light of all of this, does not Scott's criticism of the faults of *Emma* seem inflected by his own current authorial interests? His faint indictment of Austen through a conditional may well be an acknowledgement of the success of Austen's economics of detail – the manner in which Austen reins in what threatens to divert – while he had decided to address this most important of narrative balances by increasing the prosing that ostensibly impedes narrative, for comic and analytical gain. It would have been inconceivable for Scott *not* to imagine that his own antiquary was likely to be found fault with. Indeed he was found fault with, in the same terms that Scott used hypothetically of Austen, verbatim. Scott commented on how the "**prosing** [of Mr Woodhouse and Miss Bates] is apt to become as **tiresome** in fiction as in real society". The *Monthly Review* writes of taking leave of the antiquary: "condemning him as a **tiresome** companion in his inveterate habit of **prosing**, he allows him all the merits of a good and amiable man".[135]

There is no doubt that Miss Bates proves a test case in Austen's published fiction for the store that Austen set by the value of the connected and the concise. Some readers have found her prosings tediously unnecessary, others brilliantly real. But Austen takes care to make Miss Bates's chatter subtly revealing of plot for those who are attentive and ingenious enough to listen, such that even Austen's extraneous proves to be integrated. In a manner reaching back to her juvenile work 'The Mystery', in

[132] John Wilson Croker, review of *The Antiquary*, *Walter Scott: the Critical Heritage*, p. 101.

[133] For example, Francis Jeffrey, review of *Waverley*, *Edinburgh Review* (November 1814), in *Walter Scott: the Critical Heritage*, p. 82.

[134] Unsigned review of *Waverley*, *British Critic* (August 1814), in *Walter Scott: the Critical Heritage*, p. 69.

[135] Unsigned review of *The Antiquary*, *Monthly Review, or Literary Journal*, 82 (January 1817), 38–52, p. 51. The attention given to the minute and prosing continues as a subject of interest in Scott's criticism, as in his *Lives* of Reeve, Defoe and Richardson, in *Lives of the Novelists. Sir Walter Scott: On Novelists and Fiction*, ed. Ioan Williams.

which there is a contrastive ratio between excessive talk and the comically elliptical, in *Emma* Austen weighs detail against restraint in her characterization. Not only is Miss Bates shadowed by her taciturn niece, Jane Fairfax, but Mr Knightley "who had nothing of ceremony about him, was offering by his **short, decided** answers, an amusing contrast to the **protracted** apologies and civil hesitations of the other" (*E*, p. 60). In other words, the compositional tension between the minute and the concise, on which Austen had reflected for much of her writing life, inflects the dramatic scene of *Emma*. Austen reprised this interest in *Sanditon* where verbose characters are multiplied. But what plans, and what restraints, she had in mind for its minuteness of detail we will never know.

CHAPTER 2

# *Language*
## *Apophatic Austen (Not Saying Things and Saying So)*

### Introduction

For all of Jane Austen's reputed silences, she is quite commonly not at all silent about what she omits. Rather, she makes conspicuous that which she chooses not to dwell on, even telling her reader what she is not going to tell them. This fusion of evasion and disclosure is a core narrative practice for Austen.

For instance, Austen is famously *not* silent about the slave trade. *Mansfield Park* seems to narrate its own formal strategies with Fanny reporting how she raised the topic of the slave trade with her uncle but that the topic was swallowed in silence. It is undoubtedly the case that Edmund voices the wish of so many of Austen's readers that such a "question would be followed up by others". But instead the room, Fanny and then the narrator fall silent on the topic, in any explicit sense. That the subject is reported rather than dramatized makes the scene doubly reflective on the subject of disclosure and negation:

> "But I do talk to him more than I used. I am sure I do. Did not you hear me ask him about the slave-trade last night?"
>
> "I did—and was in hopes the question would be followed up by others. It would have pleased your uncle to be inquired of farther."
>
> "And I longed to do it—but there was such a dead silence! And while my cousins were sitting by without speaking a word, or seeming at all interested in the subject, I did not like—I thought it would appear as if I wanted to set myself off at their expense, by shewing a curiosity and pleasure in his information which he must wish his own daughters to feel." (*MP*, pp. 231–2)

The reasons for the "dead silence" in the Bertram circle are left enigmatically unexplained and the silence brings forward a potential disquiet or anxiety about the topic for the family ("without […] **seeming** at all interested in the subject").[1]

[1] Edward Said referred to "that very odd combination of casualness and stress" by which Austen refers to Antigua, in 'Jane Austen and Empire', in *Culture and Imperialism* (London: Chatto & Windus, 1993), p. 106. This could describe the rhetorical figure of apophasis.

Mary Poovey's sense of Austen's "non-referential aesthetic" allows Austen "simultaneously to register and to deflect attention away from historical realities".[2] Poovey describes systems of foreclosure, blocking and curtailment, by which Austen raises and submerges topics that may have been fraught for her contemporary audience: in *Pride and Prejudice*, these are matters of military, economic and epistemological uncertainty. One dimension to the reference to the slave trade in *Mansfield Park* is plausibly to acknowledge the anxiety that Austen, as described by Poovey, often seeks to assuage. This is the anxiety of an audience – fictional and actual – exposed to the possibility of a discussion of the most serious political and moral concern. Austen dramatizes that anxiety more overtly in the Bristol-born Mrs Elton who bristles at what she believes to be a reference to the slave trade (*E*, p. 325). Whatever one might conclude of the Bertrams' and Austen's own views on the issue of the slave trade – views which have been so extensively debated in response to this passage – Austen with her famed precision and economy invites attention to the subject, with the result that slavery has been understood by many as the defining topos of the novel, illuminating, among other things, Fanny's and women's social subordination.[3]

Austen's other most famed narrative evasion occurs in the conclusions to her love plots. Austen, the keenly dramatic writer, often refrains from uniting her lovers through dialogue. In all of her novels, she brings her readers to the moment of romantic denouement and then summarizes and contracts. Such instances invert the sequence of reference followed by negation described above. The reference to the slave trade in *Mansfield Park* is literally followed by silence in the dramatic scene and the possibly ominous appearance of the militia in *Pride and Prejudice* results in their comic expulsion to the gaieties of Brighton. By contrast, in her love scenes, Austen destabilizes the referential capacity of her text ("What did she say?" asks the narrator of Emma's response to Knightley) but in doing so gives voice to what she begins by passing over. That is, Austen negates disclosure in order to narrate:

> She spoke then, on being so entreated.—**What did she say**?—Just what she ought, of course. A lady always does.—She said enough to show there need not be despair—and to invite him to say more himself. (*E*, p. 470)

[2] Mary Poovey, 'From Politics to Silence: Jane Austen's Nonreferential Aesthetic', in *A Companion to Jane Austen*, eds. Claudia L. Johnson and Clara Tuite (Oxford: Wiley-Blackwell, 2009), pp. 251–60, p. 252.

[3] For an overview, see Rajeswari Sunder Rajan, 'Critical Responses, Recent', in *Jane Austen in Context*, ed. Janet Todd (Cambridge: Cambridge University Press, 2005), pp. 101–10, especially pp. 105–7.

> **I purposely abstain from dates** on this occasion, that every one may be at liberty to fix their own, aware that the cure of unconquerable passions, and the transfer of unchanging attachments, must vary much as to time in different people.—I only intreat every body to believe that **exactly at the time when it was quite natural that it should be so**, and not a week earlier, Edmund did cease to care about Miss Crawford, and became as anxious to marry Fanny, as Fanny herself could desire. (*MP*, p. 544)

Such romantic evasions have been celebrated for their tact, as Austen leaves her lovers to themselves in a charged intimate moment, not to be accessed by readers, nor the narrator, in spite of the generic familiarity of a concluding love scene.[4] Austen deploys a structural paradox in this affective economy, conveying intimacy and the deeply personal by means of the universal and curtailed. All of these examples go some way to exemplifying Mary Augusta Ward's suggestive praise of Austen's style, in intimating the expansiveness of "that self-restraint, that concentration, which is the **larger** half of style".[5]

Referential paradox is a key to understanding the economy of Austen's prose style. More than that, I would suggest, referential paradox – the dynamic of denying and disclosing – galvanized Austen's stylistic thinking. Henry Austen described his sister as from an early age "sensible to the charms of style, and enthusiastic in the cultivation of her own language".[6] In this chapter I aim to show how across Austen's work, a single rhetorical figure demonstrates how style (how we say things) *provoked* her thinking, even about thought itself. The figure is apophasis, which occurs when a speaker *tells* what they claim to be *not* telling. Outside of the rhetorical tradition, apophasis is a term used from the late nineteenth century in the theological sense of apophatic or negative theology, by which God is known only by what he is not. The sublime possibilities of apophasis are not irrelevant to Jane Austen's writing, as we shall see. But Austen's foundational interest in apophasis is as it occurs in ordinary language. It is there in the everyday phrase "not to mention", where an obvious paradox

4 The evasions in the proposal scenes have been described as "epitaphic and sibylline" [...] recognizing "the opacities of language" by Laura Dabundo in 'Jane Austen's Opacities', *Jane Austen and Mary Shelley and Their Sisters*, ed. Laura Dabundo (Lanham, MD: University Press of America, 2000), pp. 53–60, p. 58. Marvin Mudrick writes that Austen "is steadily wary, she must keep her distance from the threat of contact, above all from the ultimate commitment of sex. It is no accident that whenever social maneuvering ceases and lovers much come face to face in a moment of love, Jane Austen makes a joke – as with Emma"; *Jane Austen: Irony as Defense and Discovery* (Princeton, NJ: Princeton University Press, 1952), p. 30.

5 Mary Augusta Ward, 'Style and Miss Austen', *Macmillan's Magazine*, 51 (December 1884), p. 91.

6 Henry Austen, 'Biographical Notice of the Author' (1818), in James Edward Austen-Leigh, *A Memoir of Jane Austen and Other Family Recollections* (Oxford: Oxford University Press, 2002), p. 137.

occurs as a speaker inevitably goes on to mention that which he or she claims to avoid. Austen employs the figure repeatedly.

Austen recognized the contradictions of apophasis, and the figure in its bluntest forms is burlesqued in her juvenilia, both for an essential disingenuousness and also for its formulaic nature. The apophasis reveals much about Austen's thinking regarding routinely contracted language in clichés and epigrams. Austen scrutinizes apophasis intensely in her first three published novels and, as I shall argue, progressively recuperates and transforms its bathetic nature. In fact, I would propose an evolution to Austen's writing of silence by means of this figure. Apophasis plays a key role in shaping her development of free indirect discourse, where speech is similarly both denied and disclosed. Apophasis – the claim that something is unexpressed or even inexpressible – seems instrumental in Austen's development of the representation of the mind.

## Apophasis: From Irony to Ethics

Apophasis in the rhetorical tradition is the means "whereby an Oratour seems to wa[i]ve what he would plainly insinuate".[7] This is the common definition of apophasis in the eighteenth century, following Nathan Bailey's much reprinted *Universal Etymological English Dictionary* of 1721. It is a definition repeated, for instance, in Thomas Sheridan's *A General Dictionary of the English Language* of 1780 and its later editions.[8] Charles Bland in his 1706 *Rhetorick* gives the following example of apophasis: "I *say nothing of your Roguery, your Vices and your Ill Manners*; but if I should, they are known to the whole World".[9]

The rhetorical figure of apophasis is closely related to a number of other figures, most particularly paralipsis (known also as paralepsis or paraleipsis, or in its Latin name, *occupatio*).[10] The distinction between apophasis and paralipsis is fine. While the apophasis *denies* what it

[7] Nathan Bailey, *An Universal Etymological English Dictionary* (London: for E. Bell, J. Darby, A. Bettesworth, F. Fayram, J. Pemberton, 1721). Bailey's *Dictionary* went into twenty-eight editions before 1800. See R. C. Alston, *A Bibliography of the English Language from the Invention of Printing to the Year 1800* (Ilkley: Janus Press, 1974), vol. 5, pp. 16–22.

[8] Thomas Sheridan, *A General Dictionary of the English Language* (London: [by William Strahan] for J. Dodsley; C. Dilly; and J. Wilkie, 1780). Likewise, the same definition of apophasis occurs in *A New English Dictionary. Containing a Brief and Clear Explication of Most Words in the English Language* (Glasgow: for Charles Hutcheson, 1759).

[9] Charles Bland, *The Art of Rhetorick, as to Elocution; Explain'd: and Familiarly Adapted to the Capacityes of School-boys, by Way of Question and Answer* (London: for S. Sturton, 1706), p. 49.

[10] Other related figures include cataphasis and parasiopesis.

does in fact declare, the paralipsis *claims to pass by* what it declares.[11] The narrowness of this distinction meant that the two figures were often acknowledged as near identical in eighteenth-century grammars and guides to rhetoric. John Smith, in *The Mystery of Rhetorick Unveiled*, first published in 1657 and reprinted in the early eighteenth century, claimed that the two figures are "the same in the Matter and Sence".[12] The common terms of definition across other grammars and rhetorics often made the figures indistinguishable. The characteristic of 'omission' often serves to define both apophasis and paralipsis.[13] Apophasis is the term I will adopt for a number of reasons, but especially because the *denial* of expression is the effect that I most commonly explore in Austen's writing.[14]

So what are the uses of such a "pretended Omission"?[15] John Ward, writing on oratory in 1759, called on the second-century rhetoric of Hermogenes to explain the uses of such fake silences. Paralepsis (in this case) is used "either when things are small, but yet necessary to be mentioned; or well known, and need not be enlarged on; or ungrateful, and therefore should be introduced with caution, and not set in too strong a light".[16] In this much-repeated account, the apophasis is a means of discourse management, regulating scale and maintaining equilibrium: it

[11] See, for instance, J. Green, *A Short Grammar, or Rudiments of the Latin tongue* (London, 1759): "*Apophasis*, or a denying, which cries I do not say, when at the same time it doth: and *Paraleipsis*, or Praeterition, which cries I let it pass when at the same time it mentions" (p. 62).

[12] John Smith, *The Mystery of Rhetorick Unveiled* (London: for R. Wilkin, B. Tooke, D. Midwinter, B. Cowse and G. Mortlock, 1721), p. 124. Smith writes that the figures may only differ "in the manner of speaking" (p. 124) and seems to understand the difference in speaking as the Preterition or Paralipsis not necessarily inflecting irony. Smith's work ran to ten editions from 1657 to 1721 (Alston, *A Bibliography*, vol. 6, pp. 16–17). I refer to the tenth and last printed edition. On the closeness of the paraleipsis and apophasis, see also John Shaw, *A Methodical English Grammar* [...] *To Which Is Subjoined, an Epitome of Rhetoric*. The Fourth Edition, Carefully Revised, Corrected, and Improved (London: for W. Richardson; and J. Prescott, Manchester, 1793), p. 252.

[13] Anne Fisher's popular *A Practical New Grammar* [...] *The Seventh Edition Enlarged, and Much Improved* (Newcastle: for Thomas Slack, 1762) includes the paralepsis but not the apophasis, defining the former as "a pretended Omission of some Things purely to make an Advantage by reciting them, and implies a Design upon the Hearers" (p. 125). Thomas Gibbons includes the apophasis but not the paralepsis, describing it as "a Figure by which an Orator pretends to conceal or omit what he really and in fact declares", in *Rhetoric; or, a View of Its Principal Tropes and Figures, in Their Origin and Powers* (London: by J. and W. Oliver, 1767), p. 157.

[14] Furthermore, apophasis is the favoured term in the popular dictionaries with which I began this section. Neither Bailey nor Sheridan list paralepsis or its variants. Samuel Johnson also prefers apophasis in *A Dictionary of the English Language* (London: by W. Strahan, for J. and P. Knaptor; T. and T. Longman; C. Hitch and L. Hawes; A. Millar; and R. and J. Dodsley, 1755).

[15] Fisher, *A Practical New Grammar*, p. 125.

[16] John Ward, *A System of Oratory, Delivered in a Course of Lectures Publicly Read at Gresham College, London: to Which Is Prefixed an Inaugural Oration* (London: for John Ward, 1759), vol. 2, p. 84.

deflects protests about the small, while fencing in the expansive. The apophasis also serves as a rhetorical legerdemain, minimizing the impact of sensitive material. Like the parenthesis, the apophasis allows for the inclusion of material that is nevertheless held in abeyance. Other eighteenth-century writers on language recognized the subterfuge or even spitefulness to which such figures could be put: "[i]t is a sly way of speaking or making a *Reflection* upon a Person".[17] In this last respect, especially, apophatic language is a perennial and very current political strategy.[18]

Whether Austen would have been familiar with the apophasis specifically from the rhetorical tradition is uncertain. Austen's father taught Latin to pupils within the household,[19] and there is no reason to think that Austen would not have been knowledgeable herself about the formal tradition of rhetorical tropes.[20] What is certain is that from a very young age, Austen recognized and targeted the apophasis, providing her own textbook examples. At the earliest stages of her writing career, she recognized its slyness and she exploited its comic potential.

Austen's interest in the apophasis is evident in one of the earliest pieces in *Volume the First*. This is in 'Jack & Alice', composed probably in 1790 when Austen was about fourteen. In this story, the young Alice Johnson, like the rest of her family, is a drunk. After asking Lady Williams to tell her life story, Alice takes exception to Lady Williams's suggestion that a Mrs Watkins had too red a complexion. Alice, who is under the influence, evidently feels that this is a personal insinuation and, after losing her temper, becomes violent.

A few days later, Lady Williams generously wishes to resume her life story, but does so by using increasingly explicit apophatic language, here marked in bold:

> "I have as yet forborn my dear Alice to continue the narrative of my Life from **an unwillingness of recalling to your Memory** a scene which (since it reflects on you rather disgrace than credit) had **better be forgot than remembered**."

[17] Bland, *The Art of Rhetorick*, p. 50. Stefano Guazzo writes of speakers who employ *occupatio* as able to "say the most spiteful Things their Malice can invent", in *The Art of Conversation* (London: for J. Brett, 1738), p. 53.

[18] Donald Trump received media attention for his use of the paralipsis during the 2015–16 presidential campaign. For a discussion of the uses of apophatic language in recent American politics more broadly, see Richard Benjamin Crosby, 'Mitt Romney's Paralipsis: (Un)Veiling Jesus in "Faith in America"', *Rhetoric Review*, 32, 2 (2013), 119–36.

[19] See Ingrid Tieken-Boon van Ostade, *In Search of Jane Austen: the Language of the Letters* (Oxford: Oxford University Press, 2014), p. 110.

[20] Margaret Anne Doody asserts Austen's knowledge of rhetorical figures in 'Turns of Speech and Figures of Mind', *A Companion to Jane Austen*, eds. Johnson and Tuite, pp. 165–84, p. 165.

> Alice had already begun to colour up and was beginning to speak, when her Ladyship perceiving her displeasure continued thus.
>
> "I am afraid my dear Girl that I have offended you by what I have just said; **I assure you I do not mean to distress you by a retrospection of what cannot now be helped**; considering all things I do not think you so much to blame as many People do; for **when a person is in Liquor, there is no answering for what they may do**."
>
> "Madam, this is not to be borne, I insist—"
>
> "My dear Girl dont vex yourself about the matter [...] I will now pursue my story; **but I must insist upon not giving you any description of Mrs. Watkins**; it would only be reviving old stories and as you never saw her, **it can be nothing to you, if her forehead was too high, her eyes were too small, or if she had too much colour**." (*J*, p. 21)

This passage is extremely comic in its escalation of insults, as Austen turns up the volume on the possible intentionality of Lady Williams's slurs. At the beginning of this exchange it is conceivable that Lady Williams is simply deaf to the contradictions of her own speech: she unintentionally touches on a sore point while really wishing to avoid it. But increasingly, such putative insensitivity seems to give way to something much more malicious. Lady Williams makes sure to be explicit about Alice's boozy behaviour, while denying that she will refer at all to what happened. Finally, she reiterates, in crisply articulated detail (note the concluding monosyllables: "was too high, her eyes were too small, or if she had too much"), the originally offensive topic by insisting upon never doing so, and concludes with a triumphant use of the most inflammatory word of all: "colour". This is apophasis in its most bald and outrageous form.

Jane Austen must have been delighted by the inbuilt irony of the figure of apophasis. Apophasis, it was repeatedly pointed out in the rhetorical tradition, was a figure of irony, "whereby we deny that we say or do, that which we especially say or do".[21] Samuel Johnson, whom Austen so admired, added to Nathan Bailey's standard description of the apophasis when compiling his *Dictionary*: it is used by an orator "speaking ironically".[22] Marvin Mudrick's famed account of Austen's impulse for irony, her "compulsion and genius [...] to look only for incongruity",[23] is in part borne out by the way that she pinpointed this figure for its contradictions. Austen's fiction will go on in many subtle ways to hone in

[21] This is Smith on apophasis as a "kind of an Irony", *The Mystery of Rhetorick*, p. 123. See also Bland, *The Art of Rhetorick*, p. 49, and *A New English Dictionary* (under 'paralipsis').

[22] Johnson, *A Dictionary of the English Language*, under 'apophasis'.

[23] Mudrick, *Jane Austen*, p. 2.

on the frictions that occur between what is said and what may be meant. Even in the burlesque of 'Jack & Alice', the interpretative range Austen gives the apophasis raises questions about language and its ethics that will prevail throughout her fiction. The figure exposes an easy slippage between semantic insensitivity on the part of the user (not hearing the contradictions in one's own language) and a behavioural invidiousness. As a speech act, the apophasis is conventionally infelicitous in that it contradicts its own ostensible purpose for emphasis.[24] A speaker's awareness of that infelicity can be moot, which in turn acts as a key to apprehending their psychology and motivation.

Lucy Steele is one inheritor of Lady Williams's apophatic language. In a letter to Elinor, Lucy both blames and 'says nothing' of her sister's culpability in betraying the secret of her engagement to Edward to Fanny Dashwood, bringing down upon Lucy and Edward the wrath of the Ferrars: "Poor Anne was much to blame for what she did, but she did it for the best, **so I say nothing**" (*S&S*, p. 315). As Lucy has written this, she has not even the excuse of direct speech for this poorly phrased exposure of her rancour towards her sister. The apophasis is a double-edged tool of politeness. A speaker may be aware, if only subliminally, of the indecorousness of blame and incrimination, while apophasis facilitates its (partial) expression.

But is what Lucy expresses here unambiguous rancour? In fact, the figure of apophasis encapsulates Lucy's dilemma, caught as she is between the desire for people to know of her engagement (to warn off competitors such as Elinor on the one hand, but more largely to let the marriage have some chance of taking place) and the need for it to remain a secret, hoping that events will prove propitious for her full acceptance by Edward's family. The contradictions of the apophasis – telling while claiming not to tell – neatly sum up Lucy's role within the plot, as her secrets, selectively disclosed, generate a major narrative strand of tensions and distress for the novel's protagonist. Lucy's use of the apophasis above may expose her capacity for spite, but may also reveal something more private and complicated about her own ambivalence regarding her sister's disclosure. Far from eviscerating narrative content by means of denial, apophatic language carries complex possibilities of tone and motivation.

[24] J. L. Austin, *How to Do Things with Words: The William James Lectures Delivered at Harvard University in 1955*, 2nd edition, eds. J. O. Urmson and Marina Sbisà (Oxford and New York: Oxford University Press, 1975; first published 1962).

## Apophasis and Elegance

The rhetorical tradition provides other insights into why Austen may have been interested in the figure of apophasis. Thomas Gibbons's *Rhetoric; or a View of Its Principal Tropes and Figures* was published in 1767 and it has been noted especially for its stylistic emphasis and for its thoroughness.[25] Gibbons's account of the apophasis provides a sustained sense of how the apophasis was being appreciated in the second half of the eighteenth century. In particular, Gibbons seems taken with the elegance of the figure and gives new attention to its *affective* power. Elegance had been associated with the apophasis before, but in conjunction with, or alongside, its irony.[26] The apophasis could operate *sotto voce* as well as *fortissimo.* Charles Bland described how the paralepsis can occur "when we say *we pass* a Thing over, which yet we take *Notice* of with *Elegancy* and *Queintness*".[27] The term "queintness" is interesting. When Bland was writing in 1706, "quaint" (its more modern spelling) had the sense of "wise, clever, ingenious" (*OED*, 1b) or "elegant" and "refined" (*OED*, 5), thus reinforcing the elegancy that Bland has already noted. But "queintness" also suggested "cunning, crafty, given to scheming or plotting" (*OED*, 1a) thus conserving an echo of that inherent slyness to apophatic language, even when operating gracefully.

Thomas Gibbons, by contrast, makes no mention at all of irony in respect to the apophasis, nor of any sly, incongruous or unpleasant motivation to its usage.[28] Instead, he first dwells upon the apophasis as "delicate, striking, and persuasive" (p. 161), before going on to describe more fully its role in the conveyance of "sentiment". The apophasis, writes Gibbons, is a figure of affective economy that allows a more direct route to a reader's apprehension and emotive response:

> By this Figure we may **crowd** abundance of sentiment into a small compass, and arm our discourses as with an invincible strength, by collecting and **compacting** our ideas; and how much is such a method to be preferred to a tedious and minute detail of circumstances, which grows languid upon the hearer by a weak and subtil diffusion?[29]

[25] Michael G. Moran, ed., *Eighteenth-Century British and American Rhetorics and Rhetoricians: Critical Studies and Sources* (Westport, CT, and London: Greenwood Press, 1994), pp. 96–7.

[26] See Smith, *The Mystery of Rhetorick*, p. 123, on preterition.

[27] Bland, *The Art of Rhetorick*, pp. 49–50.

[28] The only exception to this is when he repeats the common uses of the apophasis listed by Hermogenes: "I have somewhere found it observed concerning the *Apophasis*, that it is principally used on the following occasions [...] when things are [...] ungrateful, and therefore should be introduced with caution"; Gibbons, *Rhetoric; or, a View of Its Principal Tropes and Figures*, p. 162.

[29] Ibid., p. 161.

This was a manner of writing that Austen would have wholeheartedly endorsed. We know her explicit subordination of "tedious and minute detail of circumstances", to a more compact style (see Chapter 1). The plenitude that may exist within "a small compass" resonates with Austen's description of her own work as "the little bit (two Inches wide) of Ivory". Gibbons's description of the apophasis prefigures critical accounts of Austen's writing, such as Roger Gard's comments on the reticence of the narrator in describing Emma's response to Knightley's proposal: this is "inspired brevity [...] we need no more than this to be appropriately moved. More reference or description [...] would negate the whole piercing effect".[30] In one of her proposal scenes, Austen even manages literally to provide a "crowd" in the small, ostensibly unheeded space of an apophatic negation:

> And there, as they slowly paced the gradual ascent, **heedless of every group** around them, **seeing neither sauntering politicians, bustling house-keepers, flirting girls, nor nursery-maids and children,** they could indulge in those retrospections and acknowledgements, and especially in those explanations of what had directly preceded the present moment, which were so poignant and so ceaseless in interest. (*P*, pp. 261–2)

Here that which is denied in the dramatic scene (what is apparently unseen by the couple) is nonetheless delivered in the narrative. I will be returning to this example later in this chapter.

Gibbons, elaborating upon Hermogenes's account of the uses of apophasis, reflects on the influence that efficiency and compression can bring: "the very caution with which we employ the *Apophasis*, may give it a **speedier passage into the soul**, and ensure and augment its influence over the person to whom it is directed". This would also have appealed to Austen, the writer who sought not only to entertain but also to deliver moral example without tedious didacticism. This is Gibbons again on the apophasis:

> While they [our audience] hear us saying, *We omit such and such things,* or *we shall not touch upon them*, or *we shall not mention them*, we appear to them as if we thought the things which we pretend to wave were light and inconsiderable; when, to their astonishment (and astonishment will always be attended with a strong impression) they are evidently very weighty and momentous. Arguments delivered in this unexpected manner, fall like accidental fire from heaven, which strikes much more powerfully than the regular **expanded** lusters of the day.[31]

[30] Roger Gard, *Jane Austen's Novels: the Art of Clarity* (New Haven, CT, and London: Yale University Press, 1992), p. 20.

[31] Gibbons, *Rhetoric; or, a View of Its Principal Tropes and Figures*, p. 162.

This passage resonates with the end of *Mansfield Park* when Austen dispenses quickly with Maria Bertram and Henry Crawford's adultery to concentrate on the more happy event of the betrothal of Fanny and Edmund:

> Let other pens dwell on guilt and misery. I quit such odious subjects as soon as I can, impatient to restore every body, not greatly in fault themselves, to tolerable comfort, and to have done with all the rest. (*MP*, p. 533)

It is important to be precise about rhetorical terms here, as Austen uses the paralipsis, claiming to pass over rather than omit "odious subjects" entirely. The narrator is not to be implicated at this serious moment in the ironies of outright contradiction. Yet the common contradictions of paralipsis and apophasis pertain, as the narrator does in fact "dwell" on the subject that is ostensibly rejected, with the hard-hitting emphasis of not only "guilt" but "misery", and the "odious" nature of the adultery plot that dispels it from the narrative.

## Apophasis and *The Loiterer*

Austen's formative interest in the apophasis developed in the 1790s, the years when she was composing her juvenilia. Further to any possible direct exposure to the rhetorical tradition, her eldest brother James's student publication *The Loiterer* brought Austen into close contact with the figure in one of its earliest issues.

While at Oxford, James Austen set up a weekly periodical, starting in January 1789 and ending in March 1790. James was the principal writer, but there were other contributors from among his circle at Oxford. These included his younger brother Henry, and possibly in the ninth issue, in a satirical letter sent by a female reader named 'Sophia Sentiment', his thirteen-year-old sister Jane.[32] The evidence as to Jane's authorship of *Loiterer* 9 is convincing though unprovable, but either way, Jane Austen must have known her brothers' publishing venture intimately. The periodical would doubtless have been read and much discussed in the Austen household. Austen was already writing her own fiction at this time, and *The Loiterer* may have influenced her or she may well have influenced the composition of *The Loiterer*.[33]

[32] Peter Sabor provides a summary of the debate regarding the attribution of Sophia Sentiment's letter to Jane Austen, in appendix D, *Juvenilia*, pp. 356–61.

[33] Olivia Murphy rightly challenges any assumption that Austen's development as a writer was "the product of her brothers' nurturing influence"; *Jane Austen the Reader: the Artist as Critic* (Basingstoke: Palgrave Macmillan, 2013), p. 7.

The second issue of the periodical is a case in point. *Loiterer* 2 bears comparison with many of Austen's interests. Its subject is the minimal adherence between language and truth. The issue begins in a sharply satirical style, as the writer seems to endorse the banishment of "that absurd custom" of using language to express ideas. Instead it is proposed that "Language be entitled the Art of concealing our Ideas".[34] The ethical implications of such satire culminate in the essay's closing section, which imagines a modern gazette printing the actual, self-interested views of those in political and religious authority. The source for this idea is acknowledged as Madame de Genlis's *Le Palais de Verité* where "all who entered its walls were obliged to speak their real thoughts without being themselves sensible that they did so".[35] One such figure *The Loiterer* imagines is a minster opening the budget in the House of Commons by announcing his dislike of finance, but especially so having overspent the country's revenue by giving his friends massive pensions. In the central part of the *Loiterer* essay, by contrast, dissembling is considered more sympathetically as a form of basic politeness and even compassion in "the common intercourse of life".[36]

Apophasis introduces this part of the discussion:

> [...] **I shall say nothing** of the numerous tribes, whose situation authorises and in some measure obliges them to a continual breach of veracity; (**such as** foreign ministers, ladies' maids, lawyers, and physicians; to which list I may also add lovers and their mistresses, who can claim so many precedents in favour of this practice, that they may be said to lie by prescriptive right) and only consider how little attention we all of us pay to truth in the common intercourse of life.[37]

The essay is here, and elsewhere, comically self-conscious of its own forms of concealment. Later, the conventional apophasis "not to mention" introduces the subject of writers and thus compounds the implicit questioning of *Loiterer* 2's own truth status: "not to mention Poets, who have always claimed exemption from her [Truth's] rules; even plain scribblers of prose pay so little regard to her laws".[38] Linguistic self-consciousness is signalled at the very start of *Loiterer* 2 in its claim for

[34] James Austen [ed], *The Loiterer, A Periodical work, in Two Volumes. First Published at Oxford in the Years 1789 and 1790* (printed for the author, 1790); *A Facsimile Reproduction*, ed. with an introduction by Li-Ping Geng (Ann Arbor, MI: Scholars' Facsimiles & Reprints, 2000); *Loiterer* 2, Saturday 7 February 1789, p. 4.

[35] Ibid., pp. 6–7.

[36] Ibid., p. 4.

[37] Ibid.

[38] Ibid., p. 5.

superior knowledge of the *Ars Rhetorica*. The visibility of the apophasis in the last inset quotation consists in flamboyant listing: not one, but a string of nouns contradict the speaker's claim of silence ("I shall say nothing of [...] foreign ministers, ladies' maids, lawyers, and physicians; [...] lovers and their mistresses"). The apophasis thus functions to implicate its speaker in that which he criticizes: not telling the truth. Indeed, dissembling is introduced, through this figure, as a familiar conversational event. The apophasis ushers in a discussion of benign deception, leading the reader from the large-scale dissembling of foreign ministers to lovers to common, domestic untruths. We dissemble, according to *Loiterer* 2, for the purposes of basic civility:

> When my friend Jack Saunter enters my room on a fine day, and catches me with my hat in my hand, and one glove on, just ready to enjoy my morning's walk; he would have a strange opinion of my politeness, did I not meet him with a smile, entreat him to sit down, and express myself so wonderfully happy in his company, that one would imagine I thought myself obliged to him for depriving me of my favourite amusement; and my old acquaintance Capt. Prolix would think me a brute did I not express myself highly delighted with the account of the battle of Bunker's Hill, though he well knows I have not heard it on the most moderate computation less than two hundred times—[39]

The ideas expressed in *Loiterer* 2 echo through Austen's fiction: "Seldom, very seldom," says the narrator of *Emma* pragmatically, "does complete truth belong to any human disclosure; seldom can it happen that something is not a little disguised or a little mistaken" (*E*, p. 470). But *Loiterer* 2 seems most overtly present in *Sense and Sensibility*, which was itself first drafted in the 1790s though not published until 1811. Marianne Dashwood, who prides herself on being "sincere" rather than "deceitful", would have as little time for Captain Prolix, as she has for the prosy Mrs Jennings or Sir John Middleton (*S&S*, p. 57) and much narrative attention is given to Marianne's inability to conciliate herself politely to such persons. "Where is Marianne?" asks Sir John, "Has she run away because we are come? I see her instrument is open." (p. 122). For Marianne, "it was impossible [...] to say what she did not feel", in what is another version of *The Loiterer*'s imagining of transparent minds. But such an idealistic commitment to veracity is not condoned, as the sentence continues "and upon Elinor therefore the whole task of telling lies when politeness required it, always fell" (p. 141). Li-Ping Geng makes a similar connection between

[39] Ibid., pp. 4–5.

this issue of *The Loiterer* and *Sense and Sensibility*, as we are required by the intricacies of life "to tell white lies with well-measured tactfulness".[40]

*The Loiterer*'s imitation of Madame de Genlis's *Le Palais de Verité*, where the tutelary genius makes characters "speak their real thoughts without being themselves sensible that they did so", is also suggestive in relation to *Sense and Sensibility*'s employment of free indirect discourse. James Austen imagines what it would be like if we could see into people's minds, in a social sphere where we conventionally dissemble. Jane Austen imagines the same. While Marianne aspires to a transparency between speech and feeling, Elinor, the character who is least available through her speech alone, is the character whose mind is most available through the narrative genius of inner speech. Unlike James Austen's fictional politicians who find themselves unintentionally disclosing their inner thoughts first in public meetings and then in the public testimony of the newspaper, Jane Austen uses the similarly publicly circulated form of the novel to allow private reflections to be expressed. The very chapter in which Elinor "lies" for politeness ends with her articulating "her real thoughts". The Miss Steeles have been talking of Edward Ferrars:

> Elinor heard all this with attention and surprise. "And who was this uncle? Where did he live? How came they acquainted?" She wished very much to have the subject continued, though she did not chuse to join in it herself; but nothing more of it was said [...]. (*S&S*, p. 145)

The use of speech marks with indirect speech here makes for a moment of uncertainty as Elinor's thoughts seem spontaneously to erupt into the dramatized public domain, but then are confirmed as concealed and hidden, through the past tense (indicating an indirect rather than direct mode) and the narrative elaboration that Elinor chose not to disclose her feelings or her curiosity. Elinor dissembles, but her "real thoughts" and the veracity of her situation are spoken aloud for the reader.

## Apophasis and Inexpressibility

While apophasis provided Austen with a means of thinking about the dynamics between withholding and telling, it also provided her with a means of scrutinizing the very possibilities of expression. Let us take another example of apophasis from Austen's juvenilia. This example

[40] Li-Ping Geng, '*The Loiterer* and Jane Austen's Literary Identity', *Eighteenth-Century Fiction*, 13, 4 (2001), 579–92, p. 591.

occurs in the fifth and last of the letters in 'A Collection of Letters', written in 1792 and included in *Volume the Second* where Austen mimics, as she does throughout the teenage writing, the hyperbole of contemporary fiction. Henrietta Harlton writes to her friend of a conversation she has had with Lady Scudamore who tells her that Tom Musgrove is in love with her. The following quotation is Lady Scudamore speaking, as reported in Henrietta's letter:

> "Inshort my Love it was the work of some hours for me to persuade the poor despairing Youth that you had really a preference for him; but when at last he could no longer deny the force of my arguments, or discredit what I told him, **his transports, his Raptures, his Extacies are beyond my power to describe**."
>
> "Oh! the dear Creature, cried I, how passionately he loves me!" (*J*, p. 213)

Austen understood expressions of non-expressibility as apophatic. Lady Scudamore's use of three increasingly dramatic nouns – "transports", "Raptures", "Extacies" – has the effect of making Musgrove seem insincere and certainly ridiculous. But the triplet also ostentatiously undermines her statement that the qualities of his reaction "are beyond my power to describe". In fact, Lady Scudamore describes that reaction thrice over in the specificity of the nouns she chooses, as well as by accumulation. That Austen perceived the undescribable to be apophatic is spelt out in her last work, as Sir Edward Denham in *Sanditon* employs "all the usual Phrases [...] **descriptive of [...] <u>undescribable</u>** Emotions" (*S*, b2-30).

To state that an emotional experience is beyond the power of words to describe is a commonplace of the late eighteenth century, emerging out of the traditions of the sublime and the sentimental. Indeed, Sir Edward Denham is descanting on the sublimities of the sea and the seashore, in this instance. However, the nature of Austen's relationship to indescribability is far from being satirical only. James Thompson, for one, has pointed to Austen's admissions of inexpressibility as an index of her Romanticism, amounting to a poetic consciousness of the limits of language, akin to Wordsworth's.[41] Laura Dabundo has stated similarly that moments "where language fails" in Austen are Wordsworthian and Romantic.[42] *Mansfield Park* is the text in which Austen most often deploys inexpressibility tropes and where they are most commonly delivered by

[41] James Thompson, *Between Self and World: the Novels of Jane Austen* (University Park: Pennsylvania State University Press, 1988); chapter 3, 'Limits of Language'.

[42] Dabundo, 'Jane Austen's Opacities', p. 58.

or used in relation to the reticent heroine, Fanny, whose claim to "feel much more than I can possibly express" (*MP*, p. 304) is repeated in variant forms. William Deresiewicz has argued that as a consequence of reading Romantic poetry and especially Wordsworth, Austen's fiction from *Mansfield Park* on reveals a much greater interest in interiority.[43] It is conceivable that Austen rethought indescribability in the light of this poetic instruction. Thompson suggests that Austen's consciousness of the "limits of language" is part of "larger, more pervasive trends toward interiorization and privatization".[44]

Austen's interest in interiorization can be denied by no one and she certainly harnessed tropes of inexpressibility as a means of saying something about Fanny Price's vexed inner world. Irrespective of the influence of Wordsworth, however, there is evidence to suggest that Fanny's Price's repeated inability to express herself comes out of Austen's long-standing interest in apophatic constructions and her interest in the ironies that accompany declarations of non-expression. The division between Fanny's repeated claims that language fails her and the narrator's private articulation of them through free indirect discourse, is, in fact, an apophatic construction of denial and delivery. Austen's route to ineffability was shaped by means of a trope that, in a great part of her work, signalled cliché and burlesque.

The apophasis is a remarkably efficient figure of speech. By the very act of denying expression that which is denied *is* expressed. The denial intensifies the object described and thus proves descriptive. The declaration that feelings are beyond expression becomes, paradoxically then, the most affective and efficient way of expressing them. Ironically, this attempt to express the ineffable nature of an individual human response becomes reified and reiterated in the form of cliché. This was as much the case when Austen began to write as when she was composing Sir Edward Denham in 1817. In the year that Austen wrote 'A Collection of Letters', 1792, Lady Scudamore's modest expression – "beyond my power to describe" – is one that recurs in novels published by Charlotte Smith, Robert Bage, and the anonymous author of *The Child of Providence*, at least.[45] James Thompson says that

[43] William Deresiewicz, *Jane Austen and the Romantic Poets* (New York: Columbia University Press, 2004), pp. 54–5.

[44] Thompson, *Between Self and World*, p. 79.

[45] Charlotte Smith, *Desmond, a Novel* (London: for G. G. J. and J. Robinson, 1792 in 3 vols.), vol. 3, p. 57; Robert Bage, *Man as He Is. A Novel* (London, 1792 in 4 vols.), vol. 1, p. 174; [Anon.], *The Child of Providence: a Novel* (London: for William Lane, at the Minerva Press, 1792 in 4 vols.), vol. 2, p. 120. It recurs identically in 'A Collection of Letters', Bage's *Man as He Is* and in *The Child of Providence*. Smith uses another common, near identical formulation: "My dear Bethel, I expect your next letter with impatience, that is beyond the power of words to describe".

"it will not do simply to assert that this figure [of inexpressibility] is a cliché when found in lesser writers, but important in Austen and Wordsworth".[46] But to expand the list of Wordsworth and Austen by including other writers such as Burney and Radcliffe (as does Thompson), or Bage and Smith, does not address the problem of whether we should understand Fanny Price's frequent claims of inexpressibility as cliché or not. In *Pride and Prejudice*, Austen dramatizes, more than once, cliché as a means of refining and sharpening Elizabeth's thought. There is reason to suggest that this was a process familiar to Austen's own working with language.

Austen was familiar with the apophasis as a cliché of romance. Lady Scudamore's rapturous apophasis parodies the hyperbole of romance fiction. Austen imitates in this case, and in the fifth letter of 'A Collection of Letters' more broadly, Charlotte Lennox's *The Female Quixote*, itself a romantic burlesque. Austen re-read *The Female Quixote* (first published in 1752) with admiration in 1807, and was likely to have read it much earlier.[47] Lennox, as described in the previous chapter, parodied romances that were famous for their interminable lengths. Apophasis acted as a comic form of compression that conveyed nonetheless the repetitive delays of the source text. Austen would have enjoyed Lennox closing an episode with a flamboyant apophasis as follows:

> Nothing very remarkable happen'd during this Journey, **so we shall not trouble our Readers with** several small Mistakes of *Arabella*'s, **such as** her supposing a neat Country Girl who was riding behind a Man, to be some Lady or Princess in Disguise, forc'd away by a Lover she hated, and intreating Mr. *Glanville* to attempt her Rescue; which occasion'd some little Debate between her and Sir *Charles*, who could not be persuaded to believe it was as she said, and forbid his Son to meddle in other People's Affairs. Several of these Sort of Mistakes, as we said before, **we omit**, and will therefore if our Reader pleases, bring our Heroine **without further Delay** to *London*.[48]

The fifth letter of 'A Collection of Letters' echoes the fantastically absurd story of *The Female Quixote*'s Sir George, as he tells Arabella and a circle of friends of his life and adventures, imitating the ridiculous stories that Arabella adores. Lady Scudamore's description,

[46] Thompson, *Between Self and World*, p. 94.

[47] "'Alphonsine' did not do [...] and we changed it for the 'Female Quixotte', which now makes our evening amusement; to me a very high one, as I find the work quite equal to what I remembered it." (*L*, p. 120; 7–8 January 1807), to Cassandra Austen. Austen refers to Mme de Genlis's, *Alphonsine; ou La Tendresse maternelle* (1806).

[48] Charlotte Lennox, *The Female Quixote, or The Adventures of Arabella*, ed. Margaret Dalziel; with an introduction by Margaret Anne Doody; chronology and appendix by Duncan Isles (Oxford: Oxford University Press, 1989; first published, 1752 in 2 vols.), p. 331.

> his transports, his Raptures, his Extacies are beyond my power to describe

with its triple emphasis within a structure of non-expression, recalls Sir George's description of seeing the eyes of his first love Dorothea:

> **But what Words shall I find to express the Wonder, the Astonishment, and Rapture,** which the Sight of those bright Stars inspired me with? The Flames which darted from those glorious Orbs, cast such a dazzling Splendor upon a Sight too weak to bear a Radiance so unusual, that, stepping back a few Paces, I contemplated at a Distance, that Brightness, which began already to kindle a consuming Fire in my Soul.
>
> Bless me! interrupted Sir *Charles*, confounded at so pompous a Description; who could this be?
>
> The pretty Milk-maid, *Dolly Acorn*, replied Mr. *Glanville* gravely: Did you never see her, Sir, when you was at your Seat, at —? She used often to bring Cream to my Lady.[49]

Tom Musgrove understands as much as Sir George, that by the laws of romance he must propose his own death with due pomposity in order to display his fidelity to the distant beloved (*J*, p. 211). 'A Collection of Letters' similarly ends in domestic bathos soon after Lady Scudamore has declared Tom's "transports", "Raptures" and "Extacies". After two further manuscript pages Henrietta signs off her letter, being called by her aunt "to come and make the pies" (*J*, p. 214).[50] This may be a sign of the "stinginess and oddness" of Henrietta's uncle and aunt.[51] But it also marks the inevitable intrusion of domestic and linguistic reality (pies not raptures, acorn and cream rather than consuming fire) in the imaginary life of a Quixote. These are consumables rather than consummation.

That which is beyond expression is noted by the young Austen as a formula of the romance tradition. Later in life, Austen was unusually forthright on the subject of formulaic language when advising her niece Anna on the writing of her novel. When it comes to Anna's use of the phrase "vortex of dissipation" Austen does not hold back:

> Devereux Forester's being ruined by his Vanity is extremely good; but I wish you would not let him plunge into a "vortex of Dissipation". I do not object to the Thing, but **I cannot bear the expression**; it is such thorough novel slang—and so old, that I dare say Adam met with it in the first novel he opened. (*L*, p. 289; 28 September 1814)

[49] Ibid., p. 214.

[50] 'A Collection of Letters', in *Volume the Second*, ms, p. 236. Lady Scudamore announces Charles's raptures on p. 234.

[51] This is Peter Sabor's view in *Juvenilia*, p. 476, note 68.

But it is not accurate to say that Austen hated jargon whatever.[52] The first three of Austen's novels – *Northanger Abbey*, *Sense and Sensibility*, and *Pride and Prejudice* – are all extended meditations upon the value of popular language, whether it be fashionable and novelistic or more generally commonplace. All three of these early novels are intensely curious about the value of clichés, to the extent that, in each of them, characters explicitly debate the worth of fashionable words or phrases. When Austen employs Henry Tilney to put pressure on words of popular discourse, "amazingly" and "nice", it remains unresolved whether Catherine, who uses these words, or Henry, who pedantically criticizes them, is more in the right (*NA*, pp. 108–9). In *Sense and Sensibility*, Marianne deplores "jargon", yet Willoughby seems to be at his most genuine when able to express himself through the "common" and "hackneyed". Mrs Gardiner, in *Pride and Prejudice*, corrects Elizabeth's language to raise questions about the communicative potential of a cliché.

In *The Economy of Character*, Deidre Lynch describes how Austen embraces free indirect discourse as a retreat from the rattling commonplaces of the every day, while acknowledging the commonplace as an integral part of the private mind. Easy utterances can obstruct a reader's sense that characters can be more than their words, but they also convey that very sense, as Anne Elliot (to take Lynch's example) turns her mind to the weather, that most conventional of topics, as a means of expressing her emotional disturbance on the sight of Captain Wentworth from the Bath confectioner's, Molland's.[53] In this instance, cliché is a deflection from, or buffer to, emotional truth. Elsewhere, Austen speculates as to how the iteration of cliché *is* truth, often of the most intense and emotional kind. In this context, Austen was reluctant to leave alone expressions of unsayability. While Austen often exposed the duplicity of such claims, she also probed what might be true about them. When Willoughby professes, "what I felt is—in the common phrase, not to be expressed" (*S&S*, p. 368), Elinor, at least, is convinced by him.

What is it, asks Austen again and again, that can make a "common phrase" routine and banal, as well as interesting and true? Austen reworks the same question, in near identical terms, from among her earliest to her last fiction. In *The Watsons*, Mr Howard, though "chatting on the

[52] Donald D. Stone, 'Sense and Semantics in Jane Austen', *Nineteenth-Century Fiction*, 25, 1 (1970), 31–50.

[53] Deidre Lynch, *The Economy of Character: Novels, Market Culture, and the Business of Inner Meaning* (Chicago and London: University of Chicago Press, 1998), p. 236.

dynamic between Willoughby and Elinor, a dynamic played out in direct speech with relatively few interventions by the narrator, is a principal focus for Austen. Elinor's sympathy towards Willoughby varies dramatically over the course of their interview ("softened", "hardening", "softened again"), but Elinor is herself conscious, as much as Elizabeth Bennet is, of the charm and influence of spoken voice and "manner". However, in reprimanding herself for being sway to unreasonable influence in responding to Willoughby, Elinor's juxtaposition of his "uncommon attraction" with his "still ardent love for Marianne" is surprising. Elinor simply accepts his love for Marianne as fact, as much as she accepts the more easily verifiable facts of his "person", his attractiveness and manner.

The Willoughby exculpation scene stands as a test case within the novel of its core epistemological questions regarding the knowability of other people. By believing unambiguously in Willoughby's "still ardent love for Marianne", we may speculate as to whether Elinor has here been duped, as Laura Mooneyham believes: "Willoughby's rationalizations are so patently false that Elinor should have remained unswayed".[57] But there is some possible narratorial endorsement as to the truth of Willoughby's testimony, something beyond interpersonal influence. We are told of Willoughby "rousing himself from a reverie at least equally painful" (p. 375), though even this narratorial comment is ambiguous, possibly reflecting Elinor's viewpoint and also failing to say why exactly Willoughby's reverie might be "painful". (Could this be guilt in the fact of his own mendacity as much as the pain of lost love?) How far anyone can believe Willoughby is left pointedly uncertain.

Willoughby becomes most impassioned in his expression of pain, in this chapter, when he narrates having received Marianne's first letter in London. Until then, he has been bent on telling a narrative with a doggedly objective, self-scrutinizing honesty. But in describing the receipt of that letter, his language takes on a more fragmentary, spontaneous quality, reliving, it seems, the pain of that moment. But this speech highlights as well as deepens the uncertainty about Willoughby's moral and emotional character, for as he becomes more vehement, he becomes more banal, reaching for language that he acknowledges is "common" and "hackneyed". Willoughby's redemption seems to hang on the conventionality of his language, beginning with a familiar expression of inexpressibility:

[57] Laura G. Mooneyham, *Romance, Language and Education in Jane Austen's Novels* (Basingstoke: Macmillan, 1988), p. 43.

> "When the first of her's reached me, (as it immediately did, for I was in town the whole time,) what I felt is—**in the common phrase, not to be expressed;** in a more simple one—perhaps too simple to raise any emotion—my feelings were very, very painful.—Every line, every word was—**in the hackneyed metaphor** which their dear writer, were she here, **would forbid**—a dagger to my heart. To know that Marianne was in town was—**in the same language—a thunderbolt**.—Thunderbolts and daggers!—what a reproof would she have given me!—her taste, her opinions—I believe they are better known to me than my own,—and I am sure they are dearer."
>
> Elinor's heart, which had undergone many changes in the course of this extraordinary conversation, was now softened again; (pp. 368–9)

The staccato nature of this speech may suggest something like an authentic provisionality or immediacy to Willoughby's narration of retrieved "feelings". The dashes at least at the start, suggest a spoken disfluency that unusually for Austen's punctuation (and for punctuation in general) works against syntactic sense. Willoughby's fluency seems to disintegrate as he becomes self-conscious about his choice of words. The dashes go on to mark out, however, a more schematic divide between his registers. Another dash after "in the common phrase" would create a clearly organized parenthetic commentary of "common phrase", "hackneyed metaphor", "the same language". It is entirely feasible that any putative missing dash is a printing house error or an error transcribed from Austen's own manuscript. As it stands, however, Willoughby's early disjointedness compounds the effect of a man at first struggling to find the right vocabulary before he reconciles himself to the wrong one.

However much Willoughby's words are "in the common phrase" they are dizzyingly difficult to decipher. From the outset we encounter paradox. At the moment when Willoughby claims to "open my whole heart" (itself a cliché) to Elinor (p. 361), that is when he shows a sensitivity and complexity that mitigates the callousness of his behaviour, his language is at its most blatantly predictable. Liberating himself from playing the stereotype of the heartless rake of sentimental fiction who abandons his lover, Willoughby's language becomes stereotypical. Willoughby proves himself to be non-conventional when he is most linguistically conventional, most convincing at his most clichéd. Marianne's detestation of jargon presses upon Willoughby as he speaks with Elinor and, comically we might say, he finds himself resorting to an inappropriate language (in Marianne's view) for his plight. Yet by speaking in clichés, he is freeing himself from a role that she in part has projected upon him. To be hackneyed is a relief. On the other hand, Willoughby's language should surely prompt scepticism and dissent. Is the language of the thunderbolt and the dagger – the staginess of Willoughby's confession – in any way persuasive? Does this passage, rather than displaying the complexity of Willoughby, tell us of his insincerity or his banality? Willoughby, as much as Marianne, is caught in a trap of conventionality. He struggles against and surrenders to a preformed language, and whether this surrender is a triumph or failure, Austen holds brilliantly in the balance.

Willoughby's first instinct in describing this traumatic recognition of Marianne in London is to reach for the short cut of inexpressibility: "what I felt is—in the common phrase, not to be expressed", which he acknowledges to be inadequate. In this first published work, as well as her last work, *Sanditon*, inexpressibility is specifically designated as "common" ("common phrase", "common place"). Austen's interest, across her work, in how "common" language might signify is particularly in evidence in *Sense and Sensibility*. Indeed, Willoughby's recognition of the commonality of his language is an overt trigger to a debate that the novel has already intensely pursued. Variations of "common" saturate *Sense and Sensibility*, in relation to language in particular, and the novel seems in one dimension to fend off the commonplace, represented by the Middleton circle. Lady Middleton fancied the Dashwood sisters "satirical: perhaps without exactly knowing what it was to be satirical; but *that* did not signify. It was censure in common use, and easily given" (p. 280). She herself "had nothing to say for herself beyond the most common-place inquiry or remark" (p. 36). Mrs Jennings engages in "common-place raillery" (p. 40). Marianne, of course, is the commonplace's antagonist *par excellence*, as she castigates Sir John for his "**common-place phrase**", disparaging his use of dead metaphor, however much she is fond of "dead leaves":

> "That is an expression, Sir John," said Marianne, warmly, "which I particularly dislike. I abhor every **common-place phrase** by which wit is intended; and 'setting one's cap at a man,' or 'making a conquest,' are the most odious of all. Their tendency is gross and illiberal; and if their construction could ever be deemed clever, time has long ago destroyed all its ingenuity." (p. 53)

That Sir John's phrases are "illiberal" impolitely makes the point that his language is "ill-bred, ungentlemanly, [...] vulgar, rude" (*OED*, def. 1) or, if Marianne herself has considered her own use of language far enough, "not free or generous in giving; stingy" (*OED*, def. 3), which borders on the outrageously rude, given his generosity to her family. The "common" is repeatedly positioned against the romantic, expressive manner adopted by Marianne:

> I have been too much at my ease, too happy, too frank. I have erred against every **common-place notion** of decorum; I have been open and sincere where I ought to have been reserved, spiritless, dull, and deceitful: —had I talked only of the weather and the roads, and had I spoken only once in ten minutes, this reproach would have been spared. (p. 57)

What makes Willoughby so attractive to Marianne may be perceived through the viewpoint of Elinor and Mrs Dashwood: on his first appearance it is noted that his "person [...] was **uncommonly** handsome" and "received additional charms from his voice and expression" (p. 50). The same observation about the uncommonness of his person recurs to Elinor almost verbatim following his Cleveland visit.

What significance are we to give then to Willoughby's descent to a language that is expressly designated as "common"? Why is that Austen has him present his "feelings" as inexpressible in this formulaic way? The heightened fervour of this section of chapter 8 allows Willoughby's distress in receiving Marianne's letter to mirror, whether faintly or with a grim irony, Marianne's distress in receiving his. Marianne's silent scream ("covering her face with her handkerchief, almost screamed with agony" [p. 208]) is a shocking and extreme emblem of the myriad codes of silence and self-censorship with which the novel is preoccupied. More routinely, Willoughby's apophatic language repeats Marianne's own conventional apophatic formulation in her second note to him: "**I cannot express my disappointment** in having missed you the day before yesterday, **nor my astonishment** at not having received any answer to a note which I sent you above a week ago" (p. 213). Apophasis proves to be central to Marianne's own predicament in both longing for originality and being inevitably thwarted in that wish. Apophasis as denied or negated speech is figurative of Marianne's suffering, as it undermines her ideal of speaking openly, transparently and without restriction. Elinor even identifies Marianne's relationship with Willoughby as apophatic, puzzling about it as a "strange" denial that nonetheless strongly connotes: "But for this strange kind of secrecy maintained by them relative to their engagement, which in fact concealed nothing at all, she could not account" (p. 83).

Willoughby's inability to speak out of cliché is a concentrated form of the commonly perceived paradigm of *Sense and Sensibility* which describes the blindness of Marianne to her own stereotypical behaviour. In thinking that she avoids the predictable, she lives her life along well-travelled sentimental routes. Her story, as a betrayed sentimental heroine, is as "worn and hackneyed" as the language she purports to hate. Not only that, Austen veers Marianne perhaps closest to an awareness of the bathetic replication that inevitably occurs on straining for exceptionality, on the very subject of inexpressibility:

> "It is very true," said Marianne, "that admiration of landscape scenery is become **a mere jargon.** Every body pretends to feel and tries to describe with the taste and elegance of him who first defined what picturesque beauty was. I detest **jargon of every kind**, and sometimes I have kept my feelings to myself, because I could find no language to describe them in but what was **worn and hackneyed out of all sense and meaning**." (pp. 112–13)

"I detest jargon of every kind" is voiced with something of the vehemence with which the older Austen "cannot bear" novel slang. But Austen has Marianne deliver a cliché in the act of eschewing it. To be without language in the face of a landscape is as "worn and hackneyed" a response as one can have. Marianne identifies the picturesque as presenting linguistic snares that must be avoided, but avoidance seems not an option, as the picturesque provided a prevalent language for a "common", however sublimely felt, experience. It is significant that in this passage Austen deflects attention from apophasis as a sublime feeling (to feel oneself without words) to examine it as a linguistic condition. Similarly, with respect to Willoughby, Austen quickly slides our attention from the experience of inexpressibility to its expression.

Unlike when Willoughby declares himself unable to find a language with which to express his feelings, Marianne proves unself-conscious about the sentiment that she voices, seeming to remain oblivious to the irony. Marianne's dullness to irony is insisted upon in the extended discussion of the picturesque from which this passage is taken. Precipitating Marianne's dismissal of "jargon" is Edward's rejection of the picturesque. Edward speaks to Marianne:

> "I dare say it is a picturesque one [country] too, because you admire it; I can easily believe it to be full of rocks and promontories, grey moss and brush wood, but these are all lost on me. I know nothing of the picturesque."
>
> "I am afraid it is but too true," said Marianne; "but why should you boast of it?"

> "I suspect," said Elinor, "that to avoid one kind of affectation, Edward here falls into another. Because he believes many people pretend to more admiration of the beauties of nature than they really feel, and is disgusted with such pretensions, he affects greater indifference and less discrimination in viewing them himself than he possesses. He is fastidious and will have an affectation of his own." (p. 112)

That Marianne needs such a translation takes one aback, when Edward is able to refer so fluently and extensively to writings on the picturesque, in a discussion of the subject extending considerably beyond that which is quoted here. This contradiction is evident even in this last picturesque checklist, all of which allude to Gilpin.[58] All reinforce the apophatic irony of Edward's "I know nothing of the picturesque" which Elinor goes on to spell out.

It is possible that Marianne's dislike of claims for inexpressibility is on Willoughby's mind when he stumbles over "the common phrase, not to be expressed". But his clichés become more apparent "in the hackneyed metaphor which their dear writer, were she here, would forbid—a dagger to my heart [...] in the same language—a thunderbolt.—Thunderbolts and daggers!—what a reproof would she have given me!". Nonetheless, the semantic core of Willoughby's testimony remains every one of these "hackneyed" and "common" phrases. How is it, again we may ask, that "Elinor's heart [...] now softened again"? One answer is the affection that Willoughby expresses outright for Marianne ("her taste, her opinions—I believe they are better known to me than my own,—and I am sure they are dearer"). But also, it seems that the very self-consciousness, and the instinct to rephrase and repair, lend much weight to sincerity. When Willoughby reformulates "the common phrase, not to be expressed, in a more simple one—perhaps too simple to raise any emotion—my feelings were very, very painful", the slippage from hyperbole to simplicity plays out the novel's titular debate between a language of sensibility and one of sense. Janine Barchas has written about the use of "very" in *Emma*, noting its contribution to a language that is "deliberately ordinary, subdued, and unpretentious", noting adroitly that "words such as *very* humanize".[59]

[58] In the passage cited here alone, Edward's terms suggest Gilpin, *Three Essays*, "brushwood" (p. 8); *An Essay upon Prints*, "the grey moss upon the ruin" (p. 41); *Observations on the River Wye*, "promontory of rock" (p. 24). *Three Essays: On Picturesque Beauty; on Picturesque Travel; and on Sketching Landscape: to Which is Added a Poem, on Landscape Painting* (London: for R. Blamire, 1792); *An Essay upon Prints; Containing Remarks upon the Principles of Picturesque Beauty* (London: J. Robson, 1768); *Observations on the River Wye, and Several Parts of South Wales, &c. Relative Chiefly to Picturesque Beauty* (London: for R. Blamire, 1782).

[59] Janine Barchas, 'Very Austen: Accounting for the Language of *Emma*', *Nineteenth-Century Literature*, 62, 3 (2007), 303–38, p. 322.

In Willoughby's concern that his language might be too simple "to raise any emotion" (itself interesting in that he is conscious of how his language impacts), Willoughby may raise emotion, with the simple ordinariness of his rephrasing. Likewise, Willoughby acknowledges hyperbole as a form of "common" language, the recognition of which does something to humanize him from both an "uncommon" Romantic paragon and a rake, capable of the "blackest art" (p. 215).

It is perhaps little surprise that Austen reveals such an interest in apophatic structures in *Sense and Sensibility*, which is composed around a paradigm of two sisters who embody an antithesis of telling and concealment. This is an antithesis that Marianne herself narrates and also, paradoxically, reverses: "We have neither of us any thing to tell; you, because you communicate, and I, because I conceal nothing" (p. 193). Marianne's late negation ("nothing") facilitates a syntactical tension in suggesting first that Elinor communicates and that she, Marianne, conceals (both verbs capable of being understood in an intransitive sense), before "nothing" concludes her sense and changes the verbs to transitive forms. The neat structural opposition between the sisters is complicated by Austen placing inside it a sentence that contradicts the one that Marianne speaks: on one side, concealment thwarting a character who prides herself on telling everything (Marianne) and, on the other, a frankness being permitted to a character who tells little (Elinor). What Marianne keeps private from the public realm is occluded also from the narrative, what Elinor keeps private is often disclosed, through the revelatory medium of free indirect discourse. Free indirect discourse is a response, an innovative compensatory tactic in a work that insists, especially through the case of Willoughby and the insensitivities of Marianne to her sister, on the difficulty of accessing what another feels. Eric Lindstrom has described in relation to *Sense and Sensibility* "the bracingly different starting coordinates of omniscient transparency and epistemological opacity".[60] Free indirect form, as I shall go on to argue more fully in relation to *Mansfield Park*, redirects the apophatic paradox that so interested Austen (not telling and telling at the same time) into a narrative solution to such opacity.

In a novel so concerned with the apophatic, even the narrator of *Sense and Sensibility* deploys apophasis in a highly visible form, when describing,

[60] Eric Lindstrom, '*Sense and Sensibility* and Suffering; or, Wittgenstein's Marianne?', *ELH*, 80, 4 (2013), 1067–91, p. 1072.

towards the end of the novel, the future relationship between Edward Ferrars and Colonel Brandon:

> **It would be needless to say, that the gentlemen advanced in the good opinion of each other, as they advanced in each other's acquaintance, for it could not be otherwise.** Their resemblance in good principles and good sense, in disposition and manner of thinking, would probably have been sufficient to unite them in friendship, without any other attraction; but their being in love with two sisters and two sisters fond of each other, made that mutual regard inevitable and immediate, which might otherwise have waited the effect of time and judgment. (p. 419)

Within her own narrative, Austen rarely uses such baldly apophatic contradictions. *Persuasion* is one exception where apophasis slyly slips in a statement that annihilates Elizabeth Elliot's moral character:

> and Anne——but it would be an insult to the nature of Anne's felicity, to draw any comparison between it and her sister's; the origin of one all selfish vanity, of the other all generous attachment. (*P*, p. 201)

In *Sense and Sensibility*, the narrator's apophasis is an act of formal contraction that works to bring the story to a close, to tie up its ends. But in its unusual visibility in this first published work – expanding so lengthily that which it suppresses – it stands as a clue, or perhaps as a first step, to the other apophatic contractive techniques that Austen is inclined to adopt at the ends of her novels, to summarize and close off elements of her plot.

Apophasis is a rhetorical figure of condensation that often promotes expansion. Willoughby's claim that he cannot express what he feels brings about an attempt to express those feelings nonetheless: "in a more simple one—perhaps too simple to raise any emotion—my feelings were very, very painful". The doubled "very" here, then, is only part of a larger amplification. Janine Barchas has pointed out that "so many *verys* may, in fact, force us to rethink Austen's economy of language".[61] This is also the case with apophasis. The paralipsis as the 1759 *New English Dictionary* puts it is "a figure in Rhetorick, wherein that thing seems to be **let pass**, which nevertheless is designed to be insisted on **at large**."[62] As such, the apophasis is remarkably suited to Austen's restrained enjoyment of the minute, as discussed in the last chapter. Free indirect discourse, as many local instances will testify, is also an amplification of that which is designated as denied. The more reticient heroines, Elinor and Fanny Price, are particularly instructive in this dynamic.

[61] Barchas, 'Very Austen', p. 308.
[62] *A New English Dictionary*, under 'paralipsis'.

## Epigrammatism

The compositional chronology of Austen's first two published novels is difficult to disentangle. They have a genesis that evolved to some significant degree in tandem. One part of their intertwinedness is a shared preoccupation with the valency of common language, including the apophatic. In *Sense and Sensibility*, this interest in common language takes, in the main, a sombre form, as an accommodation with linguistic commonality is reached in part by castigating Marianne's commitment to the exceptional. From the first, famously epigrammatic, sentence, *Pride and Prejudice* embraces forms of communal expression in a comic mode.

Jane Austen coined the term "Epigrammatism" for the "general stile" of *Pride and Prejudice*.[63] Jocelyn Harris has compared Austen's comment with Anna Barbauld's observation that Richardson "did not possess that 'terseness or dignity, which is necessary to give brilliancy to moral maxims and observations'", suggesting Austen's adoption of a contrastingly compact written style.[64] When Reuben Brower describes stretches of *Pride and Prejudice* as "Pope without couplets", Austen's wit is viewed as equivalent to the formal condensations of this most famously epigrammatic poet.[65] In Austen's own letter, epigrammatism is presented quite generally as a matter of form. "Epigrammatism" is contrasted with that which is "stretched out", "long" and "unconnected". But what Austen meant by this contrast, and what she meant by "**general** stile", is difficult to pin down. No-one could contend that every sentence of *Pride and Prejudice* is epigrammatic. The "general stile" seems to suggest a mood of concision and pointedness, and may even embrace the structure of the work, as I have discussed in the last chapter. Janet Todd places the epigrammatic in a coherent conceptual pair with minimalism, referring to Austen's "epigrammatic minimal style".[66] Epigrammatism, however, is a teasing word, itself "stretched out" and not especially minimalistic. Is it, we may ask, itself a piece of "solemn, specious nonsense"? Austen's coinage of "Epigrammatism" suggests that subtle, witty burgeoning that so often accompanies her writing on the minute: the tiny always takes up more space than one would imagine.

[63] Jane Austen is the first of only two entries for 'epigrammatism' in *OED*.

[64] Jocelyn Harris, *Jane Austen's Art of Memory* (Cambridge: Cambridge University Press, 1989), p. 44.

[65] Reuben A. Brower, 'Light and Bright and Sparkling: Irony and Fiction in *Pride and Prejudice*', in *Jane Austen: a Collection of Critical Essays*, ed. Ian Watt (Englewood Cliffs, NJ: Prentice-Hall, 1963), pp. 62–75, p. 62.

[66] Janet Todd, *The Cambridge Introduction to Jane Austen* (Cambridge: Cambridge University Press, 2006), p. 60.

For D. A. Miller, in his essay 'Austen's Attitude', the epigram is "the elemental unit of Austen's prose", the "grace, economy, intelligence, authority" of which excludes (Miller himself and by implication other readers). This early formulation of what would become Austen's 'Absolute style' in Miller's later work *Jane Austen, or The Secret of Style* characterizes the epigram as "boast[ing] what [...] I might have thought was **beyond any language** to enjoy: complete confident mastery of what it has to say".[67] The apophasis is antithetical to the epigram by this definition, even though it can share "the compactness of its contours".[68] The epigram masters language, while the apophasis flaunts its credentials to being "beyond" language and delights in the deflation of linguistic control.

Miller contends that the epigram is a form of speech that lacks evident provenance and audience:

> By whom epigram is spoken is no less obscure than to whom it speaks – or at any rate, epigram always assumes far broader authority than any mere individual can possibly enjoy. Invidiously free of idiosyncrasy, it issues, in Elizabeth Bennet's words, with "all the eclat of a proverb". Yet, a proverb having by definition surrendered its claim to eclat at the moment it becomes proverbial [...] Elizabeth's formulation is paradoxical, espousing both the contradiction and the cruelty inherent in a folk wisdom of which folk are made to feel their ignorance. In terrible alliance with the most peremptory expressions of collective authority (besides proverb: commandment, judgment, inscription), epigram proposes excluding me from my entire community.[69]

Miller collapses the distinction between epigram and proverb – both are expressions of "collective authority" – and in doing so he takes his cue from Elizabeth. But Elizabeth may be distinguishing between the epigrammatic and proverbial in a more historical manner than Miller's reading takes account of. There is certainly a puzzling incompatibility between the dazzle of éclat and the familiarity of proverb. But in the larger context of Elizabeth's barb at Darcy – "unless we expect to say something that will amaze the whole room, and be handed down to posterity with all the eclat of a proverb" (*P&P*, p. 103) – time and "posterity" mediate this difference, as that which initially amazes must inevitably be transformed into something more familiar. While Miller makes proverb synonymous with epigram at the moment of iteration, thus making both proverb and epigram the antagonists of community rather

[67] D. A. Miller, 'Austen's Attitude', *The Yale Journal of Criticism: Interpretation in the Humanities*, 8, 1 (1995), 1–5, p. 2.

[68] Ibid., p. 3.

[69] Ibid.

than community's voice, Elizabeth seems to hand over imagined words to "posterity", a communal usage which applauds, if dulls, them.

This confusion between epigram and proverb seems very much to the point in *Pride and Prejudice*. Concise utterances that have a ring of familiarity, quotability or universality about them, run from the epigram to the proverbial to the cliché, and such uses frequently slide into each other. Elizabeth's "handed down to posterity with all the eclat of a proverb" is a variation of Marianne's historical linguistics, as she says of "commonplace" phrases such as "setting one's cap at a man," or "making a conquest", "if their construction could ever be deemed clever, time has long ago destroyed all its ingenuity" (*S&S*, p. 53). The insights of both familiar proverb and tedious commonplace are likely to have begun life with some "eclat". Furthermore, the exact point where wit becomes banality must be hard to determine: part of Elizabeth's jibe is that that which they think may "amaze" may inevitably be more predictable than they would like. The first line of *Pride and Prejudice* best makes this point. The sentence is sententious and bathetic, witty and truistic, impersonal and familiar. It is as imitative of Dr Johnson as it is of Mrs Bennet, it rings of conversational cliché and communal wisdom, and yet it speaks in the anonymous voice of the ironist. This absence of clear provenance endorses Miller's sense that "by whom epigram is spoken is no less obscure than to whom it speaks", but it is not only epigram that is speaking in this particular sentence. The bravura opening to *Pride and Prejudice*, so persistently described as epigrammatic and aphoristic,[70] signals that a single utterance, even an epigrammatic one, may have many, even conflicting, registers.

Elizabeth is one of *Pride and Prejudice*'s most witty and epigrammatic speakers, but why of all of Austen's characters is she is the one who is chastised for using hackneyed language? Mrs Gardiner, like the older Austen writing to Anna about "vortex of dissipation", extracts and queries Elizabeth's expression. Elizabeth complains:

> "It does not often happen that the interference of friends will persuade a young man of independent fortune to think no more of a girl, whom he was violently in love with only a few days before."
>
> "But that expression of 'violently in love' is so hackneyed, so doubtful, so indefinite, that it gives me very little idea. It is as often applied to feelings which arise from an half hour's acquaintance, as to a real, strong attachment. Pray, how *violent was* Mr. Bingley's love?"

[70] To take two examples, respectively, Peter Sabor, 'Preface', in *The Cambridge Companion to Emma*, ed. Peter Sabor (Cambridge: Cambridge University Press, 2015), pp. xi–xiv, p. xi; William Deresiewicz, 'Community and Cognition in *Pride and Prejudice*', *ELH*, 64, 2 (1997), 503–35, p. 503.

> "I never saw a more promising inclination. He was growing quite inattentive to other people, and wholly engrossed by her. Every time they met, it was more decided and remarkable. At his own ball he offended two or three young ladies, by not asking them to dance, and I spoke to him twice myself, without receiving an answer. Could there be finer symptoms? Is not general incivility the very essence of love?" (*P&P*, pp. 159–60)

Mrs Gardiner's linguistic care prompts her to refine the term 'hackneyed' to two other terms "doubtful" and "indefinite" ("what", writes Christopher Ricks, "as a metaphor, could be more hackneyed than *hackneyed*?").[71] Mrs Gardiner's assiduousness about phrasing encourages Elizabeth to be likewise more careful in presenting her evidence. Her response is three short evaluative sentences:

> I never saw a more promising inclination.
>
> He was growing quite inattentive to other people, and wholly engrossed by her.
>
> Every time they met, it was more decided and remarkable. (p. 160)

This leads to a more playful analysis that concludes with a pithy observation, indeed, an epigram: "Is not general incivility the very essence of love?" Rather than cliché representing an inevitable decay of language, Elizabeth's use of a hackneyed phrase prompts thought and proves the genesis of wit.

Mrs Gardiner's question clears the ground for the narration's return to the phrase at the novel's denouement, to be used in relation to Darcy: "he expressed himself on the occasion as sensibly and as warmly as a man violently in love can be supposed to do" (pp. 406–7). There is an emotional economy here between the exceptional circumstance in which Darcy finds himself and the narratorial choice of a phrase already established as "hackneyed" to describe him. Perhaps, as with Willoughby (on a generous interpretation), only the most evident of expressions serves for the most extreme of emotional circumstances. This is a mild teasing of Darcy. The seemingly exceptional figure is reduced to the common plight of the emotions. Furthermore, as has often been pointed out, the phrase "violently in love" is suggested first by Mr Collins: "nothing remains for me but to assure you in the most animated language of the violence of my affection" (p. 119). Love is the great leveller and Darcy is explicitly linked here with Elizabeth, Collins and Bingley (whom Elizabeth describes), with Collins and Bingley both being highly prone to conventional utterances.

[71] Christopher Ricks, 'Clichés', in *The Force of Poetry* (Oxford: Clarendon Press, 1984), pp. 356–68, p. 356.

It is the extraordinary feat of *Pride and Prejudice* that its originality, its wit and "sparkling" qualities, emerge from a social setting repeatedly emphasized as being dull and repetitive. The novel's charm and power come in a significant degree from the vivification of cliché that both expresses and transforms the ordinary repetitive world it depicts. The Bingley sisters "repeated three or four times" (p. 38) and "repeatedly asked" (p. 96). Lady Lucas yawns at Mrs Bennet's "repetition of delights" (p. 112), Mr Collins "repeated his apologies" (and a great deal more, p. 82) and we hear from Mrs Bennet and Lydia the "constant repinings at the dulness of every thing" (p. 263). Austen could not "bear" the repetition of novelistic slang. Nor can Elizabeth understand how "Lady Catherine could bear" the obsequious repetitions of Collins and "echo" of Sir William Lucas (p. 184). How can we put up with, then, a novel that itself ostentatiously repeats?

Not only is "violently in love" circulated among a cross-section of characters, so too is "the happiest of men". Again the phrase travels along a sequence of three characters, this time Collins/Jane/Elizabeth with Mr Collins as the originator of both. The narrator chooses to summarize Mr Collins's proposal to Charlotte to imitate his own linguistic efficiencies: "he earnestly entreated her to **name the day that was to make him the happiest of men**" (p. 137). The predictable language that he deploys (like "amiable Charlotte" and "humble abode") is further ossified by its casual narrative repetition in relation to him: "the day would be fixed **that was to make him the happiest of men**" (p. 158). This formula of betrothal can be unearthed in Austen's early novel 'The Three Sisters', where the young Austen exposes it, in her opening sentence, as a romantic cliché for what is vitriolic spite: "I **am the happiest creature** in the World, for I have just received an offer of marriage from Mr Watts [...] How I will triumph over the Duttons!" (*J*, p. 74). Yet in *Pride and Prejudice*, the phrase can also be Jane's:

> Jane could have no reserves from Elizabeth, where confidence would give pleasure; and instantly embracing her, acknowledged, with the liveliest emotion, that **she was the happiest creature in the world**. (*P&P*, p. 384)

Does this phrase from the reflective Jane whisper something critical of her originality, or does "the liveliest emotion" nullify that option? Yet again the phrase is used in Elizabeth's letter to Mrs Gardiner, no less, following her own engagement:

> I am the happiest creature in the world. **Perhaps other people have said so before, but not one with such justice.** I am happier even than Jane; she only smiles, I laugh. (p. 424)

*Pride and Prejudice* endorses Christopher Ricks's view that "[o]ne serious and various way you may resist a cliché's propensity to bypass reflection is by using the cliché self-reflexively, with a sense of how the very words of a particular cliché have some relation to what makes it a cliché".[72] Elizabeth does not illuminate cliché through wordplay, but always through reflection and expansion, in a much more comfortable version of Willoughby's self-consciousness about the "common phrase". Cliché is endorsed but with a direction to scrutinize the terms that it proposes. This is why Austen tends to provide small but knowing intensifiers or modifiers to her more familiar expressions.

The repetitions of *Pride and Prejudice* tell us about how our language weaves us together. Mary offers "threadbare morality" (p. 67); Wickham renders interesting the most "threadbare topics" (p. 85); and Elizabeth is queried about a particular phrase of hers that is threadbare (*OED*'s definition 2b of threadbare is "hackneyed"). But when Elizabeth declares herself "the happiest creature in the world", the cliché, like "violently in love", prompts originality. Banality turns to reflection issuing in an epigrammatic summation: "she only smiles, I laugh" (p. 424). In one sense, this confirms D. A. Miller's opinion that the epigram is divided from the communal. It is the power of a superlative utterance that separates Elizabeth from the repetitive strains that are the backdrop to her brilliance. Part of Elizabeth's individuation from other characters, as she emerges as the central consciousness in *Pride and Prejudice*, is her capacity to think about language, which, as much as character, travels from flat to round. Yet Austen seems keen in *Pride and Prejudice* to keep the epigrammatic and the hackneyed as close relations of each other, as she makes the dynamic process of circulation, decay, repetition and revivification so evident. In her own correspondence Austen was keenly aware of how language uses a writer or speaker, as much as the other way round:

> Benjamin Portal is here. How charming that is!—I do not exactly know why, but the phrase followed so naturally that I could not help putting it down.—[…] —I have got your Cloak home, which is quite delightful!—as delightful at least as half the circumstances which are called so.—I do not know what is the matter with me to day, but I cannot write quietly; I am always wandering away into some exclamation or other. – (*L*, pp. 46–7; 11 June 1799)

Apophatic expressions of non-expression take the same route as other clichés in *Pride and Prejudice*. They begin by being associated with Collins: "You will find her manners beyond any thing I can describe" (p. 119) he says of Lady Catherine. At one point, the narration mimes his expressions

[72] Ricks, 'Clichés', p. 361.

of speechlessness, when Collins reflects on the intimacy between Rosings and Hunsford: "Words were insufficient for the elevation of his feelings; and he was obliged to walk about the room, while Elizabeth tried to unite civility and truth in a few short sentences" (p. 239). In an excellently indeterminate speech act, Austen leaves it unresolved whether Collins speaks apophatically ("Words are insufficient for the elevation of my feelings!") reported in free indirect discourse, or whether the narrative summarizes his speechlessness in his own idiom. It is also unclear whether Elizabeth herself is mimicking Collins or speaking conventionally when she thanks Charlotte Lucas for taking on the burden of listening to Mr Collins: '"It keeps him in good humour," said she, "and I am more obliged to you than I can express"' (p. 136).

The process of self-revaluation that Elizabeth undergoes in response to Darcy's proposal, can be traced through apophatic expressions. When Darcy first proposes to Elizabeth, the narrator tells us that, "Elizabeth's astonishment was beyond expression. She stared, coloured, doubted, and was silent" (p. 211). Expression is denied so as to express Elizabeth's astonishment in comically superlative measure. However, in the process of reading Darcy's letters, similar phrases are reworked to reflect a more subtle ratiocinative process that starts to unfold in response to Darcy and that emerges through the narration:

> **Her feelings as she read were scarcely to be defined.** With amazement did she first understand that he believed any apology to be in his power; and stedfastly was she persuaded that he could have no explanation to give, which a just sense of shame would not conceal. With a strong prejudice against every thing he might say, she began his account of what had happened at Netherfield. (p. 226)

That Elizabeth's astonishment in the proposal scene is "beyond expression" is comically dramatic. Attention is drawn to a physiological rather than a consciousness-orientated response: she "stared, coloured, doubted, and was silent". However, when reading Darcy's letter, the adverb "scarcely" in "scarcely to be defined" shows the attempt at expression that the narrator takes on, to reveal Elizabeth's thoughts and emotions: "With amazement did she first understand [...] stedfastly was she persuaded [...] With a strong prejudice." This process continues, with the narrator diluting once again the apophasis – diluting the denial of expression – to something that articulates the struggle involved in defining: "But when this subject was succeeded by his account of Mr. Wickham [...] her feelings were yet more acutely painful and more difficult of definition. Astonishment, apprehension, and even horror, oppressed her" (pp. 226–7).

Chapters 12 and 13 of the second volume of *Pride and Prejudice* must be among the least epigrammatic of the book. Chapter 12 comprises Darcy's letter of explanation and is the second longest chapter of the novel. Chapter 13 contains Elizabeth's repetitious reading of Darcy's letter. She turns over the words that she reads in an atmosphere of increasingly thoughtful evaluation. Tellingly, when apophasis is later used in the novel in relation to Elizabeth (even possibly by Elizabeth in free indirect discourse), it is carefully modified by the adverb "indeed":

> She dreaded seeing Wickham again [...] The comfort to *her*, of the regiment's approaching removal, was **indeed beyond expression**. (p. 246)

This repeats the sentiment less obliquely voiced by Elizabeth in her letter to Mrs Gardiner: "Perhaps other people have said so before, but not one with such justice". Austen is able, with the utmost economy, to make evident the thinking mind by a single adverb. It is perhaps little surprise that Elizabeth becomes so adept at thinking through the truth in truisms, being an expert observer of phatic language, reprimanding Darcy while dancing for his failures in formulaic conversation, his refusal to follow verbally the required moves that he carries out with his feet.

Samuel Johnson's last example of 'epigram' in his *Dictionary* is John Gay's: "I writ/An *epigram* that boasts more truth than wit". Elizabeth Bennet is a character gifted for her wit. Her talent for the epigrammatic is one that probes the truths that pertain in routine utterances. Geoffrey Hartman's sense that Romantic lyric emerged out of the epigram, as wit is "liberated" into something more simple, serves as an analogy for the plot trajectory of Elizabeth, whose wit and point are seen to become more qualified and meditative, largely through the education of her feelings for Darcy.[73] These words could also describe the development from *Pride and Prejudice* to *Mansfield Park*, in which Austen's interest in probing that which lies, apparently, beyond expression becomes a primary focus of characterization and plot.

## Incapable of Expressing in *Mansfield Park*

Austen was not done with apophasis. On the contrary, *Mansfield Park* approaches the subject head-on. In the early stages of her writing, Austen seemed less interested in the *experience* of inexpressibility, than in the bind of expressing it meaningfully. *Sense and Sensibility* and *Pride and Prejudice*

[73] Geoffrey H. Hartman, 'Wordsworth, Inscriptions, and Romantic Nature Poetry', in *Beyond Formalism. Literary Essays 1958–1970* (New Haven, CT, and London: Yale University Press, 1970), pp. 206–30, p. 219.

reach towards a thoughtful accommodation of apophasis as part of ordinary, truistic language. In *Mansfield Park*, Austen seems more inclined to investigate the possible validity of statements of inexpressibility in terms of psychological response. This perpetuates Austen's interest in the verbalizing of an emotional state, but it involves a much fuller narrative participation in the contradictions of apophasis.

Apophasis is given an entirely new prominence in the language of Fanny Price. Fanny is often linked with Elinor Dashwood and especially Anne Elliot, as reticent heroines. But Elinor and Anne are different from Fanny as they do not frequently claim to be without words. Fanny is persistently conscious of what she is not saying or what she is not able to say:

> I feel much more than I can possibly express. (*MP*, p. 304)

The narrator summarizes Fanny's sense of her own inexpressibility:

> Fanny's feelings on the occasion were such as she believed herself incapable of expressing. (p. 18)

But the narrative also tells us, with simple factuality, that Fanny's feelings *are* inexpressible:

> her delight [in the horse that Edmund gave to her [...]] and the addition it was ever receiving in the consideration of that kindness from which her pleasure sprung, was **beyond all her words to express**. (p. 43)

For Fanny, a quiet *tête-à-tête* with Lady Bertram is "unspeakably welcome" (p. 40). Her anxiety for Edmund on the return of Sir Thomas from Antigua is "**indescribable**", though others were able to give "vent to their feelings of vexation" (p. 207). Fanny has "not words strong enough to satisfy her own humility" (p. 307). To be with William would be an "unspeakable indulgence" (p. 326), while to be with Henry Crawford precipitates repeated verbal anxieties:

> Your kindness to William makes me more obliged to you **than words can express**; but I do not want, I cannot bear, I must not listen to such— (p. 349)

Fanny is also unable to find words in the presence of Edmund and Sir Thomas.

In *Pride and Prejudice*, Collins's language is mirrored by other characters both in similarly phatic and in more meaningful ways. In *Mansfield Park*, the language of unsayability enacts a more schematic division of characters along moral grounds. After Fanny, the characters who most frequently draw attention to what they don't say are the Crawfords. In a letter to Fanny, Mary falls back on the clichés of non-expression to be charming, but also to absolve herself of the effort of trying to get at some more substantive communication for Fanny, anxious for news from her old friends:[74]

> it is impossible to put an hundredth part of my great mind on paper, so I will abstain altogether, and leave you to guess what you like. (p. 482)

Mary's 'abstaining' is noticeably close to the narrator's choice to "abstain" from dates, though without any compensatory revelation of content. Mary is elsewhere an eviscerating narrator when she talks of the trip to Sotherton to Edmund: "There we went, and there we came home again; and what was done there is not to be told". But in Mary's mouth, abstention from detail is insidious, deliberately, in this instance, evoking censorship and innuendo (rather than, for instance, shame or pity). This is the passage in full:

> "you know Henry to be such a capital improver, that you cannot possibly engage in any thing of the sort at Thornton Lacey, without accepting his help. Only think how useful he was at Sotherton! Only think what grand things were produced there by our all going with him one hot day in August to drive about the grounds, and see his genius take fire. There we went, and there we came home again; and **what was done there is not to be told**!"
>
> Fanny's eyes were turned on Crawford for a moment with an expression more than grave, even reproachful; but on catching his were instantly withdrawn. With something of consciousness he shook his head at his sister, and laughingly replied, "I cannot say there was much done at Sotherton; but it was a hot day, and we were all walking after each other and bewildered." (pp. 284–5)

This innuendo of Mary's verges on the scandalous and, with its focus on heat, it is potentially combustible. What was done at Sotherton? Mary means something by it. Fanny infers something from it. Henry is conscious of it and tries to laugh it off. What is the "genius" that takes fire? Henry's intellectual or creative power, his natural inclinations or in a more obsolete sense of "genius", his "appetite"?[75] Henry himself uses innuendo and non-referential language to insinuate himself with Fanny: he "was so abounding in the *deepest interest*, in *twofold motives*, in *views and wishes more than could be told*, that Fanny could not have remained insensible of his drift, had she been able to attend" (pp. 347–8). Or when visiting her

[74] For a comparison of Mary's and Fanny's claims for impeded speech, see also Thompson, *Between Self and World*, p. 93.

[75] These are respectively *OED* definitions 9; 6a (*Obs.* last recorded usage, 1781); and 1b: "a person's appetite", only recorded use is 1607, Jonson *Volpone*.

in Portsmouth, he presses upon her his personal wish for another summer and autumn at Mansfield, "infinitely superior to the last. As animated, as diversified, as social—but with circumstances of superiority undescribable" (pp. 470–1).

As with so much else, inexpressibility proves a means of contrasting Fanny and Mary, the rivals for the affections of Edmund Bertram. At one point, Mary says of Edmund:

> "I honour him beyond expression." And she looked around as if longing to tell him so. (p. 319)

This is brilliantly ambivalent. We encounter the possibility of Mary's sincere admiration of Edmund. She uses apophasis as an impetuous gesture of affection. But the narrator strongly hints at thoughtlessness, even a form of insincerity in the overt contradiction between words and action, in a character who is often reckless in the way she uses language.[76] This is the same irony out of which Austen composes some of her best comedy. What Mary says is not much different from Mrs Bennet's:

> "Well, Lizzy," said Mrs Bennet one day, "what is your opinion *now* of this sad business of Jane's? For my part, I am determined never to speak of it again to anybody. I told my sister Philips so the other day." (*P&P*, p. 252)

But in Mary's case, it is the narrator who suggests the irony, rather than Mary being obtuse to a verbalized contradiction and in doing so, the narration probes the complexities of Mary's psychology.

I have been pointing out how forms of scepticism or of self-consciousness tend to accompany Austen's apophatic utterances in her fiction: whether in irony (Lady Williams or Mary Crawford) or in self-conscious amplification and repair (Willoughby) or adverbial modification (Elizabeth). What is it that prevents us from seeing Fanny's conventional phrases of inexpressibility as problematic or contradictory? The most obvious answer is that they are true to Fanny. *Mansfield Park* permits non-expressibility as the just and awkward expression of Fanny's youth and sensitivity, of her sensibility and vulnerability. But that we can know that such expressions are true to Fanny depends upon the narrative taking on and sharing the burden of expression that Fanny feels herself unequal to. Although Fanny says that she can't express what she feels, the narrator will tend to express

[76] An example is Mary's disrespect towards the clergy in the presence of Edmund. She fails to consider that as second son this may be his destined profession (pp. 101–2).

it for her, dramatizing the conscientious work of Fanny's mind. This is an intensification of what we see with Elizabeth turning over the letter from Darcy. It is well established that Fanny is more available to the reader through free indirect discourse in *Mansfield Park* than Elizabeth is in *Pride and Prejudice*. The more extensive development of free indirect discourse in this novel is especially pertinent to Fanny's character as tongue-tied and intensely feeling. But to be tongue-tied and intensely feeling is also pertinent to apophasis. Apophatic phrases are frequently in Fanny's mouth, while its structure of denial and expression serves as a technical hinge for the free movement of the mind.

We see this vividly occur in a passage where the narrator describes why it is that Fanny is so often silent. This is when she learns that she is to return to her family in Portsmouth:

> though never a great talker, she [Fanny] was always more inclined to silence when feeling most strongly. At the moment she could only thank and accept. Afterwards, when familiarized with the visions of enjoyment so suddenly opened, she could speak more largely to William and Edmund of what she felt; **but still there were emotions of tenderness that could not be clothed in words—The remembrance of all her earliest pleasures, and of what she had suffered in being torn from them, came over her with renewed strength, and it seemed as if to be at home again, would heal every pain that had since grown out of the separation. To be in the centre of such a circle, loved by so many, and more loved by all than she had ever been before, to feel affection without fear or restraint, to feel herself the equal of those who surrounded her, to be at peace from all mention of the Crawfords, safe from every look which could be fancied a reproach on their account!—This was a prospect to be dwelt on with a fondness that could be but half acknowledged.** (pp. 426–7)

The narrator claims that there were existing in Fanny, "emotions of tenderness that could not be clothed in words" and yet immediately goes on to clothe in words those very emotions. There is an increasing emotional intensity in this passage that is strongly suggestive of Fanny's own voice. Parallelism and repetition convey the growing "strength" of Fanny's feelings and the circling of her thoughts; the final exclamation, her own palpable relief: "To be in the centre of such a circle, **loved** by so many [...] **loved** by all [...] **to feel** affection [...] **to feel** herself the equal [...] **to be** at **peace** [...] **safe** [...] !". The free indirect discourse is part of an apophatic construction. The constituent parts of apophasis are layered between the *denial* of expression in dialogue and the narration's subsequent expression of that which has been denied: "but still there were emotions of tenderness that **could not be clothed** in words—**The remembrance of all her earliest pleasures** [...]".[77]

Nevertheless, at the end of this passage the narrator continues to insist that Fanny dwelt on this prospect of domestic happiness with a fondness that could be but "half acknowledged". Are the feelings that have been clothed in words, then, a full acknowledgement of Fanny's fondness to which we are privy or do they still remain only a half-acknowledgement of it? Is it that we, like William and Edmund, will only ever know a part of what she feels? This is irresolvable. Free indirect discourse (by being free of attribution as well as being indirectly reported) disallows any absolute knowledge as to whether the words expressed are to be understood as quoted in any sense or whether they are to be understood only as an approximation. Akin to the apophasis, then, free indirect discourse also manages, in its very essence, to be both expression and its denial.[78]

## Apophasis and Triple Emphasis

Henry Crawford tells Fanny of his success in securing her brother William's promotion in the navy with palpable enthusiasm:

> The post was late this morning, but there has not been since, a moment's delay. **How impatient, how anxious, how wild I have been on the subject, I will not attempt to describe;** (p. 346)

Much narrative drama lies in how we judge Henry Crawford in this section of the novel, where he seems close to being recuperated by his love for Fanny and the novel seriously entertains the possibility of their marriage. Austen makes Henry's apophasis likewise equivocal at this point. The giddy excitement Henry expresses in being able to promote the interests of William Price may testify endearingly to the intensity of his feelings. Like his sister Mary, he uses apophasis as a spontaneous means of expressing his affection. At the same time, and certainly in retrospect, the

[77] James Thompson has discussed this passage as exemplifying Austen's commitment to inexpressibility. "Inexpressibility [...] is more commonly invoked in Austen's novels when emotion is carefully examined". However, our interpretations differ as Thompson believes that the passage "is narrated entirely by an external authority; because Austen does not use free indirect discourse here, we can see none of Fanny's thoughts directly, but only in their indirect presentation by a highly protective narrator"; Thompson, *Between Self and World*, pp. 95–6.

[78] This doubleness – of speaking and not speaking – also chimes with two distinct theories of free indirect discourse: the "dual voice" theory in which "voice" is apprehended in free indirect discourse and the "unspeakability" of free indirect discourse (or represented speech and thought) as maintained by Ann Banfield, in *Unspeakable Sentences: Narration and Representation in the Language of Fiction* (London: Routledge & Kegan Paul, 1982).

phrasing is itself perhaps worryingly "wild" and illogical. This is a character who later reveals himself to have a culpable absence of self-command.

Henry Crawford has a lot in common with Willoughby. He is a morally equivocal character in *Mansfield Park*, who seems genuinely to fall in love with the heroine. Tom Musgrove, from 'A Collection of Letters', is a prototype for both, expressing love in a manner that the narrative asks us to question. There is a more specific link between Tom Musgrove and Henry Crawford in the parallel between Crawford's apophatic phrasing and that of Lady Scudamore's when speaking of Tom, composed by Austen over twenty years earlier:

> his transports, his Raptures, his Extacies are beyond my power to describe.

Like Lady Scudamore, Henry Crawford uses an emotionally accumulative triplet – impatient, anxious, wild – which perfectly describes the impatience and anxiety that he deems beyond expression. In both cases – even more so with the personal quality of Henry's adjectives – the claim to inexpressibility is deflated. It is through this particular stylistic recurrence of the triplet that I hope to show further the evolution of the apophasis in Austen's fiction into a means of accessing an unspoken consciousness.

The language of non-expression very often precipitates a compensatory listing, as in attempting to articulate the sublime. In this example from *The Mysteries of Udolpho*, St Aubert experiences the Pyrenees silently, but the narrator presents a tripartite somatic response:

> The serenity and clearness of the air in these high regions were particularly delightful to the travellers; it seemed to inspire them with a finer spirit, and diffused an indescribable complacency over their minds. **They had no words to express the sublime emotions** they felt. **A solemn expression** characterized the feelings of St. Aubert; **tears often came to his eyes**, and **he frequently walked away from his companions**.[79]

When Austen provides somatic gestures in the place of speech, she does so with a condensed efficiency, rather than with such a lingering attention to bodily detail. We have seen this in *Pride and Prejudice* where Elizabeth's "astonishment was beyond expression. She **stared, coloured, doubted, and was silent**" (p. 211). In *Northanger Abbey*, Austen comically accelerates Catherine's response to the manuscript she imagines, or hopes, to be a mouldering document equivalent to those found in Gothic novels.

[79] Ann Radcliffe, *The Mysteries of Udolpho*, ed. Bonamy Dobrée; with an introduction and notes by Terry Castle (Oxford: Oxford University Press, 1998; first published 1794 in 4 vols.), p. 43.

Catherine's physical reaction is as quick and predictable as her assumptions: "her feelings at that moment were **indescribable. Her heart fluttered, her knees trembled, and her cheeks grew pale**" (*NA*, p. 174).

If we return to the passages in *Pride and Prejudice* that involve Elizabeth's meditations on Darcy's letter, the language of non-expression is again seen to prompt a tripartite response. Here the triplet expands to suggest a more ruminative response on Elizabeth's part. When Darcy gives Elizabeth his letter, the narrator summarizes the workings of Elizabeth's mind, through the parallelism of a foregrounded adverb or adverbial phrase:

> Her feelings as she read **were scarcely to be defined**. (1) **With amazement did she first understand** that he believed any apology to be in his power; and (2) **stedfastly was she persuaded** that he could have no explanation to give, which a just sense of shame would not conceal. (3) **With a strong prejudice against every thing he might say, she began** his account of what had happened at Netherfield. (*P&P*, p. 226; with numerical additions)

As the problem of defining her feelings becomes more acute, the narrator again turns to a triple iteration:

> her feelings were yet more acutely painful and more difficult of definition. **Astonishment, apprehension, and even horror**, oppressed her. She wished to discredit it entirely, repeatedly exclaiming, "This must be false! This cannot be! This must be the grossest falsehood!"—and when she had gone through the whole letter, though scarcely knowing any thing of the last page or two, put it hastily away, protesting that she would not regard it, that she would never look in it again. (pp. 226–7)

What seems important at this point in *Pride and Prejudice* is the emergence of a ratiocinative process, as Elizabeth has to confront her prejudices. In this second example, the content of the triplet summarizes and abstracts Elizabeth's response ("even" strongly suggests that external summary, along with the abstract nouns), while in its repetition it reflects the emotional disturbance and intensity that Elizabeth experiences. Austen keeps Elizabeth's feelings abstracted while intimating something of their effect upon her. Elizabeth's thoughts result here in her own direct speech, as she exclaims: "This must be false! This cannot be! This must be the grossest falsehood!" The value given to processes of thought in *Pride and Prejudice*, above impressions or prejudices, contributes here to the resistance to expressions of inexpressibility ("scarcely to be defined", "difficult of definition").

Remarkably close to this last passage from *Pride and Prejudice* is the conclusion to the expedition to Box Hill in *Emma*, where Emma departs alone for home, having thoughtlessly humiliated Miss Bates and having been reprimanded by Mr Knightley. Again we meet a heroine who has been shocked out of her complacencies. Again the heroine's process of thought is constructed first by reflecting upon whether her feelings *can* be expressed, followed by the employment of a triplet which starts to express them:

> **She was vexed beyond what could have been expressed**—almost beyond what she could conceal. **Never had she felt so agitated, mortified, grieved, at any circumstance in her life. She was most forcibly struck. The truth of his representation there was no denying. She felt it at her heart. How could she have been so brutal, so cruel to Miss Bates!** (*E*, p. 409)

While the two passages are almost identical in some respects, there are subtle differences in presenting inner states. First of all, in *Emma*, Austen permits apophasis: Emma is "vexed beyond what could have been expressed", even if her vexation has some visible manifestation. Austen allows, in other words, as she does in *Mansfield Park*, inexpressibility to be a viable state, but only for it to be contradicted immediately by a passage of increasingly vivid internal reflection. The summary quality of the triplet in *Pride and Prejudice* ("Astonishment, apprehension, and even horror oppressed her") is modulated. The shift from abstract nouns to adjectives, from a passive construction to an active one (with an explicit reference to what Emma "felt"), makes Emma more involved in an unfolding sequence of emotions: "Never had she felt so agitated, mortified, grieved, at any circumstance in her life", within which there are possible intimations of Emma's own verbalization in an indirect form ("mortified", "in her life"). The passage repeats the trajectory towards exclamation, but this is an inner exclamation, in the form of free indirect discourse: "How could she have been so brutal, so cruel to Miss Bates!"

The emotional extravagance of Lady Scudamore's tricolon, "transports [...] Raptures [...] Extacies", and to a lesser degree Henry Crawford's "impatient, anxious, wild" are transformed when relocated from direct speech into narration. In the narrative passages quoted above, the emotive triplet that accompanies difficult expression is not so much hyperbole, rather it is a means of scrutinizing and articulating acute inner states. The differences between the passages from *Pride and Prejudice* and *Emma* do not need to be understood necessarily as exemplifying an evolutionary paradigm. Austen had her reasons for presenting each passage as she does. However, by the time that she composes *Emma*, free indirect discourse plays a much more extensive part in her writing. In both novels, the triplet serves as a bridge between the narrator's view and the heroine's, but in *Emma* its formulation works much more to bring together the character's and narrator's viewpoints, anticipating and even invoking the free indirect discourse into which the passage develops.

In free indirect discourse, Austen finds a middle way between absurd or indulgent attempts to vocalize extreme emotion and a reliance upon cliché to avoid the effort of expression. Austen endorses moments of inexpressibility in human experience, but encourages inner scrutiny to accompany them. While free indirect discourse contradicts the inexpressible, it also enforces it, as expression remains private and internal, and also removed, in the indirect form, from direct presentation of speech or thought. The comic contradictions of the early fiction are transformed into a complex narrative strategy that voices and leaves unvoiced at one and the same time. Apophasis, with its paradoxical claim for expressing that which is not expressed, provided Austen with a structure to speak of silence and yet intimate something beyond.

## Peripheral Vision: The Ending of *Persuasion*

Triplets are a stylistic feature of Jane Austen's writing that are associated with her admiration for Samuel Johnson.[80] A trajectory prevails in accounts of Austen's prose style, in which her prose moves from eighteenth-century cadences, largely associated with Johnson, to something more associative and modern, although it is important to stress, as does Norman Page, that there are variant styles in evidence over the chronology of her writing.[81] Page takes the example of *Persuasion* where Austen's modernistic "experiments with dramatic syntax" reveal nonetheless the influence of Johnson.[82]

[80] On *oratio trimembris* in Austen's fiction, see Knud Sorensen, 'Johnsonese in *Northanger Abbey*: a Note on Jane Austen's Style', *English Studies*, 50 (1969), 390–97. Also Norman Page, *The Language of Jane Austen* (Oxford: Basil Blackwell, 1972), p. 93, and Freya Johnston, 'Johnson and Austen', in *Samuel Johnson after 300 Years*, eds. Greg Clingham and Philip Smallwood (Cambridge: Cambridge University Press, 2009), pp. 225–45, p. 228. On Johnson's parallelism, including the triplet, see W. K. Wimsatt, *The Prose Style of Samuel Johnson* (New Haven, CT: Yale University Press, 1941).

[81] Page, *The Language of Jane Austen*, p. 91, and Sorensen, 'Johnsonese in *Northanger Abbey*', p. 396.

[82] Page, *The Language of Jane Austen*, pp. 99, 100.

The passage that Page singles out to demonstrate this is the reunion of Anne and Wentworth at the end of the novel, which we have already encountered:

> There they returned again into the past, more exquisitely happy, perhaps, in their re-union, than when it had been first projected; more tender, more tried, more fixed in a knowledge of each other's character, truth, and attachment; more equal to act, more justified in acting. **And there, as they slowly paced the gradual ascent, heedless of every group around them, seeing neither sauntering politicians, bustling house-keepers, flirting girls, nor nursery-maids and children, they could indulge in those retrospections and acknowledgments, and especially in those explanations of what had directly preceded the present moment, which were so poignant and so ceaseless in interest.** (*P*, pp. 261–2)

Page describes Austen's style here as belonging both to the eighteenth and the nineteenth centuries, with the careful balances of the second, emboldened, sentence evoking Johnson, but Johnson composed with an affective rather than rational sense of climax.[83] The same may also be said for the triplet, as Austen elsewhere in *Persuasion*, creates webs of triple amplifications for the purpose of depicting the fragmentary, accumulative process of emergent thoughts and feelings.[84] In other words, Austen's more lyric, associative and emotional style, emerged not away from the Johnsonian sentence, but with it.

Adela Pinch points to Jonathan Swift's street scenes as another eighteenth-century precedent for Anne and Wentworth's reconciliatory walk.[85] Furthermore, this moving account in which the love plot culminates, is apophatic. Austen's list, "**heedless** of every group around them, **seeing neither** sauntering politicians, bustling house-keepers, flirting girls, nor nursery-maids and children", is very close to *The Loiterer*'s, "**I shall say nothing** of the numerous tribes, whose situation authorises and in some

[83] Ibid., p. 101.

[84] I have here in mind, the scene where Anne realizes that Wentworth still loves her: "(1) Her happiness was from within. (2) Her eyes were bright, and (3) her cheeks glowed,—but she knew nothing about it. She was thinking only of the last half hour, and as they passed to their seats, her mind took a hasty range over it. (1) His choice of subjects, (2) his expressions, and still more (3) his manner and look, had been such as she could see in only one light. (1) His opinion of Louisa Musgrove's inferiority, an opinion which he had seemed solicitous to give, (2) his wonder at Captain Benwick, (3) his feelings as to a first, strong attachment,—sentences begun which he could not finish—(4) his half averted eyes, and more than half expressive glance,—all, all declared that he had a heart returning to her at least; that (1) anger, (2) resentment, (3) avoidance, were no more; and that they were succeeded, not merely by (1) friendship and (2) regard, but by the (3) tenderness of the past; yes, some share of the tenderness of the past" (pp. 201–2; with numerical additions).

[85] Adela Pinch, *Strange Fits of Passion: Epistemologies of Emotion, Hume to Austen* (Stanford, CA: Stanford University Press, 1996), pp. 149, 156.

measure obliges them to a continual breach of veracity; (**such as** foreign ministers, ladies' maids, lawyers, and physicians; to which list I may also add lovers and their mistresses [...]". Both lists travel identically from public life and politicians to lovers and the domestic scene. To deliver the psychological state of heedlessness by means of an apophasis, transforms an arch form of rhetorical irony into a psychological state of absorption. Freya Johnston has pointed to Johnson's own pleasure in the paralipsis in his life of Richard Savage, where the figure allows Johnson to dwell on Savage's writing though he claims not to. What Johnston describes as a "simultaneously inclusive and exclusive [...] sensibility"[86] is delicately dramatized by Austen, as the exclusive, constricted gaze of the lovers opens up, momentarily, to a larger scene.

The figure of apophasis conveys brilliantly a state of consciousness between noticing and not noticing, inattentive to, but mildly aware of. With equal subtlety, the figures that emerge in the half-sight of Anne and Wentworth are coyly germane to themselves, from the separate and gendered public and domestic concerns of "politicians" and "house-keepers", to flirting, and to the consequential nursery-maids and children. Whether these specific figures register with Anne or Wentworth is unresolved, but beyond them, a vaster scene emblematic of larger generational patterns are figured in a subordinated space. More optimistically than the novel's last outward gesture to future war, Austen places Wentworth and Anne's romance within a larger frame that is only obliquely visible. While that which the couple are heedless of is grammatically subordinated to their own self-absorption, the crowd that exists alongside them is paratactically figured, existing in a disconnected, associative relation. This apophasis, in its ordering, in its more universal gaze and with its psychological insights, is as "poignant" as the particular memories they turn over.

The contradictions of speaking and remaining silent fascinated Austen through her fiction. Bharat Tandon has associated Anne Elliot with another rhetorical figure associated with silence, the aposiopesis, where a sentence breaks off, unfinished: "As befits a character who starts the novel living under erasure, as 'nothing' [...] Anne becomes identified with the blank dash '—': a notation of absence, of aposiopesis, of being prematurely cut off at twenty-seven".[87] In classical rhetoric, the aposiopesis and the

[86] Freya Johnston, *Samuel Johnson and the Art of Sinking 1709–1791* (Oxford: Oxford University Press, 2005), p. 179.

[87] Bharat Tandon, *Jane Austen and the Morality of Conversation* (London: Anthem Press, 2003), p. 233.

apophasis are often closely linked. Austen chooses, in *Persuasion*, when chastising Elizabeth, to entwine them:

> Very, very happy were both Elizabeth and Anne Elliot as they walked in. Elizabeth, arm in arm with Miss Carteret, and looking on the broad back of the dowager Viscountess Dalrymple before her, had nothing to wish for which did not seem within her reach; and Anne——but it would be an insult to the nature of Anne's felicity, to draw any comparison between it and her sister's; the origin of one all selfish vanity, of the other all generous attachment. (*P*, p. 201)

It can be no coincidence that the dash of aposiopesis, where the narrator self-consciously disallows a sentence to reach completion, follows the self-satisfied limitations of Elizabeth who, gazing at the "broad back" of the dowager Viscountess Dalrymple, "had nothing to wish for which did not seem within her reach". While Elizabeth reaches for the back of the Dowager, Anne looks around for Wentworth, but "her eye could not reach him" (p. 202). The contracted space between Elizabeth and the limits of her worldly ambitions is contrasted with an eye that has a capacious desire for something more. But Austen in this extract does not allow aposiopesis to have the last word. Instead, the promise of omitting a comparison between the sisters is negated as the aposiopesis becomes apophatic with the narrator comparing the "selfish vanity" of one with the "generous attachment" of the other. Here we have two claims to non-expression, which, once again, prompt the reverse, a reaching to articulate at least something of that which is being denied.

The drive to articulate characterizes the plot of *Persuasion* more generally. During the first half of the novel, Anne is repeatedly passed over. But while the dramatic action of *Persuasion* suppresses Anne's self-expression, the narration facilitates self-expression through free indirect discourse and then through Anne's increasingly audible speaking voice. *Persuasion* is the shortest of Austen's novels and yet the one in which the protagonist's mind is most fully available. In this sense, *Persuasion* is the logical conclusion (as it turned out) of the technical developments from Austen's earliest published work, where the narrator increasingly takes on the burden of non-expression.

Anne says towards the end of the novel: "Men have had every advantage of us in telling their own story" (*P*, p. 255). *Persuasion* is a novel where a woman finds that voice. There is a noticeable contrast between Elizabeth Bennet of whom it is reported "[t]he comfort to *her*, of the regiment's approaching removal, **was indeed beyond expression**" (*P&P*, p. 246) and Anne Elliot on realizing that Wentworth has written to her: "The revolution which one instant had made in Anne, **was almost beyond expression**" (*P*, p. 257). The "indeed" of *Pride and Prejudice* gives credence to the conventional phrase whether or not it endorses its experiential content. In *Persuasion*, however, the "almost" of "almost beyond expression" characterizes most vividly, I believe, Austen's emergent philosophy. Expression *is* within our "reach" and to it we are accountable. In this respect, the work of free indirect discourse has been accomplished.

CHAPTER 3

# *Dialogue*
## *Austen's Missing Speakers and the Case for Free Direct Discourse*

### Introduction

"I do not write for such dull elves" has become a motto for Jane Austen's provocative brilliance. The words, written to Cassandra on the publication of *Pride and Prejudice*, have been reused by critics to illuminate the multiple facets of her writing that test her readers' skill and insightfulness. Reginald Farrer described Austen's demanding restraint: she "does not work 'for such dull elves' (as she says herself) as will not so far come to meet the author as to make out for themselves his conclusions and deductions".[1] And yet, as here, the phrase is commonly detached from its context. How strange it is, when there are so few comments by Austen about her own stylistic choices, that the immediate referent of this celebrated statement has been largely overlooked.

Austen's comment to Cassandra about *Pride and Prejudice* is specifically concerned with speech attribution, the he saids and she saids of dialogue. She writes:

> There are a few Typical errors—& a "said he" or a "said she" would sometimes make the Dialogue more immediately clear—but "I do not write for such dull Elves"
> "As have not a great deal of Ingenuity themselves."—(*L*, p. 210; 29 January 1813)

Austen's thoughts turn here from typical errors occurring in the printing house to what seems like concern about an authorial misjudgement regarding the amount of narratorial direction provided in passages of dialogue. Austen concludes her thought, however, by shifting responsibility

[1] Reginald Farrer, 'Jane Austen, *ob.* July 18, 1817', *Quarterly Review* (July 1917), in B. C. Southam (ed.), *Jane Austen: the Critical Heritage 1870–1940,* vol. 2 (London and New York: Routledge & Kegan Paul, 1987), pp. 248–9. Further references to *Jane Austen: the Critical Heritage* are by volume number. See too, Claudia L. Johnson, *Jane Austen's Cults and Cultures* (Chicago and London: University of Chicago Press, 2012), p. 3.

for the understanding of the text onto her readers. Austen had good reason for concern. The "typical errors" of the printing house included the misattribution of speeches, errors caused, at least in part, by Austen's failure to elaborate verbally in every case who was speaking. In the next letter that Austen writes to Cassandra, she dwells on the "greatest blunder" in *Pride and Prejudice* being an instance where "two speeches are made into one" (*L*, p. 212; 4 February 1813).[2] The passage that Austen is referring to is one in which Jane speaks some of Elizabeth's words, an error that was first recognized, if not resolved, in Bentley's 1833 edition. Nevertheless, in spite of this misunderstanding of her work, Austen defends stylistic economy above transparency in the presentation of dialogue, which is striking from an author lauded for the crisp distinctiveness of her characters' speech.

In this chapter, I contend that Austen's stripping away of speech attribution – the "said he" and "said she" of dialogue – is a significant stylistic feature of her fiction. In this letter to Cassandra, Austen explicitly grapples with the risks that she took in writing the dialogue of this novel, dialogue that would come to be celebrated in perpetuity. My purpose is to examine how Austen attends to the matter of speech attribution across her fiction and to demonstrate how important this seemingly small feature of the written text was to the shape, sound and semantics of her prose style. It is notable how many of the most innovative prose stylists have left some form of testimony as to their concerns about the problem of denoting speakers in passages of dialogue. Austen prefigures George Meredith, Henry James and Joseph Conrad, among others, in this matter. But Austen's decision to minimize speech attribution has further ramifications for the history of the novel. Her readiness to liberate direct speech from a narratorial frame bears a striking resemblance to her most famed narratorial innovation, the development of free indirect discourse.

Anne Waldron Neumann is one critic who has speculated as to whether Austen's letter actually refers to the use of free indirect discourse.[3] While I would endorse the instinct in making this connection, the context provided by the letters points to non-attributed *direct* speech. Much less well known than free indirect discourse, direct speech without a he said or a she said is free direct speech, which is a fundamental contributing element

[2] The relation between "Typical errors—& a 'said he' or a 'said she'" could be either associative or disassociated by virtue of the ampersand. The elaboration for Cassandra on the "greatest blunder", however, points to their connection.

[3] Anne Waldron Neumann, 'Characterization and Comment in *Pride and Prejudice*: Free Indirect Discourse and "Double-Voiced" Verbs of Speaking, Thinking, and Feeling', *Style*, 20, 3 (1986), 364–94, p. 369.

to Austen's development of representations of interiority. Austen's letter is an early acknowledgement of the stylistic thinking that resulted in free indirect discourse.[4]

## The Opening Chapter of *Pride and Prejudice*

There are several names for phrases in which a spoken utterance is assigned to a particular speaker. Terminology ranges from the *verbum dicendi* of classical grammar to *inquit* tags or speech tags, reporting clauses or attributive phrases. Most simply, as in Austen's shorthand, there is the "said he" or "said she" of conversational exchange.[5]

We encounter Austen's commitment to omitting speech tags in *Pride and Prejudice* in its very first chapter, in the celebrated conversation between Mr and Mrs Bennet about the letting of Netherfield. The chapter is unusual, even in Austen's fiction, for its high proportion of dialogue. After two aphoristic sentences from the narrator, the chapter is composed entirely of the Bennets' conversation, before returning to one paragraph of narration that closes the chapter. The conversation between Mr and Mrs Bennet consists of twenty-nine turns. There are only six attributions of speech and four of those attributions occur in quick succession at the opening of the dialogue, establishing the alternating pattern of only two speakers. Attribution then falls away and the reader depends on their emerging knowledge of the characters' opinions and the rhythm of the exchange to know who is speaking when.

From the outset, Austen refrains from elaboration as to vocal inflection, movement and setting, all of which could be developed within a reporting clause. Everything is to be implied in the words of the characters. Only one early attribution has an adverbial expansion:

> "Do not you want to know who has taken it?" cried his wife impatiently. (*P&P*, p. 3)

This one phrase of impatience and animated vocal manner does a great deal of work in setting up Mrs Bennet's character. This conversation is

[4] I develop in this chapter my essay, 'A "Said He" or a "Said She": Speech Attribution in Austen's Fiction', *Persuasions*, 34 (2012), 140–9. Stuart Burrows has also written on free direct discourse in Austen's fiction: 'The Privatization of Public Life: Free Direct Discourse in *Persuasion*', *The Prose of Romanticism*, ed. Yoon Sun Lee (February, 2017), *A Romantic Circles Praxis Volume*, http://www.rc.umd.edu/praxis/prose/praxis.2016.prose.burrows.html. This last essay's focus is not so much to define the speech category of 'free direct discourse' which Burrows describes as "a rare and critically neglected form" (para. 3); rather, Burrows provides a subtle account of characters speaking by proxy in *Persuasion*, as one character can provide a voice for another.

[5] The most extensive literary discussion of the uses of the *inquit* tag of which I am aware is Mark Lambert's book *Dickens and the Suspended Quotation* (New Haven, CT: Yale University Press, 1981).

one of the most famous in English literature and yet it is pared back to such an extreme that we have no idea where it occurs, whether the characters are inside or out, whether they sit or stand or whether they move as the conversation ensues.[6] Austen's minimalism, her eschewal of description, has been described from the earliest commentaries on her work.[7] In the opening to *Pride and Prejudice*, however, not only is Austen's minimalism evident in her refusal to elaborate on the setting in which she places her characters, on their personal appearance and demeanour, but it also extends to the omission of what are ostensibly essential narrative superstructures. He saids and she saids are almost ostentatiously absent from the novel's first chapter.

Norman Page is one critic who has commented on speech attribution in Austen's fiction in *Jane Austen's Language* and *Speech in the English Novel*. In the latter, in which he describes means of speech presentation available to authors, he writes that "some writers contrive to dispense with explicit indications [of direct speech] without dire results", citing the opening chapter of *Pride and Prejudice* as an example.[8] But, the results of non-attribution are far more replete and dramatic than this suggests. Non-attribution strips away detail, but it can also paradoxically supplement a scene, as in this exchange suggesting the close relations of a long-married couple whose intimate antagonism is best conveyed without mediation:

> "What is his name?"
> "Bingley."
> "Is he married or single?"
> "Oh! single, my dear, to be sure! A single man of large fortune; four or five thousand a year. What a fine thing for our girls!"
> "How so? how can it affect them?" (pp. 3–4)

The alarming marital conversation in the second chapter of *Sense and Sensibility*, between Fanny and John Dashwood, works similarly. John and Fanny Dashwood deliver much more lengthy speeches than the Bennets, and the narratorial framing of the chapter is greater, yet the central dialogue has relatively little attribution. This is a style that *Pride and Prejudice* intensifies and foregrounds.

[6] For a discussion of the absence of setting in Austen's fiction, see Andrew Elfenbein, 'Austen's Minimalism', in *The Cambridge Companion to Pride and Prejudice*, ed. Janet Todd (Cambridge: Cambridge University Press, 2013), pp. 109–21, pp. 109, 115.

[7] For example George Henry Lewes: "She [Austen] seldom describes anything, and is not felicitous when she attempts it"; 'The Novels of Jane Austen', *Blackwood's Edinburgh Magazine* (July 1859), in *Jane Austen: the Critical Heritage*, vol. 1, p. 157.

[8] Norman Page, *Speech in the English Novel*, 2nd ed. (Atlantic Highlands, N.J.: Humanities Press International, 1988; first published, 1973), p. 28.

Austen's commitment to unattributed speech, can be seen even more sharply if we compare the opening of *Pride and Prejudice* with the opening of a novel by one of Austen's favourite contemporary writers, Maria Edgeworth.[9] In many respects, Edgeworth's first chapter of *Patronage* (1814) is more grippingly dramatic than *Pride and Prejudice*, published the previous year. *Patronage* opens immediately onto tense dialogue which sets an evocative scene describing a storm and prefiguring a shipwreck. There is no narratorial preamble and Edgeworth uses reporting clauses in their briefest form:

> Chapter 1
>
> "How the wind is rising!" **said Rosamond**. – "God help the poor people at sea to night!"
>
> Her brother Godfrey smiled. – "One would think," **said he**, "that she had an argosy of lovers at sea, uninsured."
>
> "You, gentlemen," **replied Rosamond**, "imagine that ladies are always thinking of lovers".
>
> "Not always," **said Godfrey**, "only when they show themselves particularly disposed to humanity."
>
> "My humanity, on the present occasion, cannot be suspected," **said Rosamond**, "for you know, alas! that I have no lover at sea or land."
>
> "But a shipwreck might bless the lucky shore with some rich waif," **said Godfrey**.
>
> "Waifs and strays belong to the lady of the manor", **said Rosamond**, "and I have no claim to them."
>
> "My mother would, I dare say, make over her right to you," **said Godfrey**.
>
> "But that would do me no good," **said Rosamond**, "for here is Caroline, with superior claims of every sort, and with that most undisputed of all the rights of women – beauty."
>
> "True – but Caroline would never accept of stray hearts," **said Godfrey**. "See how her lip curls with pride at the bare imagination!"
>
> "Pride never curled Caroline's lip," **cried Rosamond** – "Besides, pride is very becoming to a woman. No woman can be good for much without it, can she, mother?"
>
> "Before you fly off, Rosamond, to my mother, as to an ally, whom you are sure I cannot resist," **said Godfrey**, "settle first, whether you mean to defend Caroline upon the ground of her having or not having pride."
>
> A fresh gust of wind rose at this moment, and Rosamond listened to it anxiously.[10]

[9] Austen names Edgeworth's *Belinda* in her praise of the novel in *Northanger Abbey* (p. 31). Not long after the publication of *Patronage*, Austen playfully flatters her aspiring-novelist niece Anna Austen in asserting that she will only like Anna's novels and those of Miss Edgeworth (*L*, p. 289).

[10] Maria Edgeworth, *Patronage*, introduction by John Mullan (London: Sort of Books, 2011; first published 1814 in 4 vols.), pp. 1–2.

Edgeworth may have felt the need to underline that it is Godfrey and Rosamund who continue to talk as other characters are revealed as assembled with them. Nevertheless the dialogue could be read without ambiguity with less narratorial support. Edgeworth was alert to the potentially distracting or interruptive aspect of reporting clauses as she keeps them spare, with only minimal variation in verb choice (in this extract, ten instances of "said", one "replied", one "cried"). Here attribution does little to distract the reader away from the speech being spoken. Indeed, this passage from *Patronage* raises the question as to how noticeable reporting clauses are.

Ford Madox Ford thought that such verbs of saying were not noticeable at all. The matter of the inclusion of reporting clauses in passages of dialogue was a subject on which he and Joseph Conrad disagreed when collaborating, at the beginning of the twentieth century. Conrad preferred to replace "he said" and "she said" with alternatives, such as "'answered Mr. Verloc' and the like":

> [Conrad] had one minute passion with regard to conversations: he could not bear the repetition of "he said's" and "she said's", and would spend agitated hours in chasing those locutions out of his or our pages [...] The writer [Ford himself] was less moved by this consideration, it seemed to him that you could employ the words 'he said' as often as you like, accepting them as being unnoticeable, like 'a', 'the', 'his,' 'her', or 'very'.[11]

To some degree Ford's point is true. An indefinite article "a" may not usually electrify, as "constancy" does Captain Wentworth, when heard spoken by Anne Elliot. William Empson, on the other hand, felt that even a "therefore" in a poem can be equivalent to a "bang on the nose".[12] One may not notice the repetition of "he saids" and "she saids" in the opening of *Patronage* if one accepts them as part of the furniture of the page. But for another kind of reader, every word *is* fundamentally noticeable, always carrying semantic, symbolic and acoustic significance. Even in this passage from Edgeworth's novel there is a discernible tempo to the reporting clauses within the quoted speech, returning as they do, after the first phrase or independent clause.[13]

[11] Ford Madox Ford, *Joseph Conrad: a Personal Remembrance* (London: Duckworth & Co., 1924), pp. 187–8.

[12] William Empson, 'Argufying in Poetry', in *Argufying: Essays on Literature and Culture*, ed. John Haffenden (London: Chatto & Windus, 1987; first published in *Listener*, 22 August, 1963), pp. 167–73, p. 170.

[13] Or to put it another way, a reporting clause only appears at the end of a speech turn, if that turn is short, consisting of a single independent clause.

Alan Palmer has written of a bias in narratology against the narrator and in favour of mimetic speech forms. This bias is expressed in terms used of the narrator, such as "interruption", "intrusion", "interference" or "distortion".[14] In passages of dialogue, however, surely speech tags can be reasonably described as "interruptive" appearing as they do in the midst of an ostensibly independent conversation, asking the reader to relocate from the dramatic presentation of speech. Dickens's extended interventions into the speech of his characters have even been described as expressing "hostility" towards their attractiveness.[15] That Austen comically overuses reporting clauses in her teenage writing reveals, at the very least, a consciousness as to their frequency and purpose, and the manner in which she was observing in contemporary fiction their interplay with the spoken.

## Speech Attribution and Satire

Austen's sensitivity to the repetitions of attributive clauses – that she saw and heard them as she read – is evident through their relative absence in her mature work, as in *Pride and Prejudice*, but perhaps more tellingly, by their excessive presence in her juvenilia.

In the following example from 'Love and Freindship', an early novel dated 1790, written when Austen was fifteen, some speech attribution is required, as more than two people speak. But while the event is mundane (someone is knocking at the door), the language of the characters is otiose, as they spell out with increasing redundancy that indeed someone is knocking at the door. The insistent speech attribution is implicated in that redundancy, marking out comically unnecessary speech:

> My Father started—"What noise is that," (said he.) "It sounds like a loud rapping at the Door"—(replied my Mother.) "it does indeed." (cried I.) "I am of your opinion; (said my Father) it certainly does appear to proceed from some uncommon violence exerted against our unoffending Door." "Yes (exclaimed I) I cannot help thinking it must be someone who knocks for Admittance." (*J*, p. 106)

Over the course of the eighteenth century, the practice of signaling attribution with brackets was on the wane, as inverted commas were standardized for the marking of speech.[16] Austen uses a high frequency of attributions in

[14] Alan Palmer, *Fictional Minds* (Lincoln and London: University of Nebraska Press, 2004), p. 57.

[15] Lambert, *Dickens and the Suspended Quotation*, p. 35.

[16] See John Lennard, *But I Digress: the Exploitation of Parentheses in English Printed Verse* (Oxford: Clarendon Press, 1991), p. 216.

'Love and Freindship' and gives them further visibility through the mannered presentation of brackets, used tautologically alongside the inverted commas. These teenage writings provide an interesting testimony to a moment when conventions in the presentation of speech were changing. Victorina González-Díaz has argued that the especially high proportion of bracketed attributions in Austen's early epistolary works suggests that she is associating them with sentimental fiction written in the letter form.[17] The multiple speech attributions in Austen's juvenilia are, in part, a critique of the first-person form, where characters have to record who is speaking and struggle to give a sense of spontaneity and the natural in reporting conversations they have had. But the performance of high sentiment is equally ridiculed, as is evident in Austen's choice of verb forms in this passage. With four different verbs within five closely spaced speech tags ("said", "replied", "cried", "exclaimed"), we encounter an excessively dramatic manner that varies with Austen's later published fiction.

As is common to novels of the eighteenth and early nineteenth centuries, Austen's mature works are fairly conservative in the range of verbs deployed and 'said' is the default or unmarked verb, although, as Mark Lambert has pointed out, for some writers of this period 'cried' competes with 'said' as the most prevalent verb of reporting.[18] In Frances Burney's *The Wanderer*, for instance, characters more often cry something than say it. Norman Page has concluded that in Austen's fiction "[t]he use of *cried* rather than *said* is generally reserved for the vulgar or disagreeable characters", and that the phrase "cried Mrs Norris" in *Mansfield Park* shows Austen departing from her usual lack of interest in vocal manner to suggest "a shrill and noisy officiousness".[19] However, it is, in fact, Fanny Price's speech that is most often accompanied with the verb 'cried' in *Mansfield Park*, in spite of her timidity and reserve. This alone says a great deal for the drama of Fanny Price and the subtlety in depicting her distress. A schematic account of verb choices, such as that given by Page, has some truth elsewhere in Austen's fiction. In *The Watsons*, Emma Watson's words are accompanied by means of only two verbs of saying: "said" and "replied". This is in contrast to other characters who cry, continue, ejaculate, whisper, observe, repeat, answer and add. A steadiness and, to some degree, a mystery is provided for Emma Watson by means of attributive equilibrium.

[17] Victorina González-Díaz, 'Round Brackets in Jane Austen', *English Text Construction*, 5, 2 (2012), 174–207, pp. 197–8.

[18] Lambert, *Dickens and the Suspended Quotation*, p. 17.

[19] Norman Page, *The Language of Jane Austen* (Oxford: Basil Blackwell, 1972), p. 143.

There seems little doubt that Austen even at a very early stage of her writing career was reflecting on this formal feature of her writing. The opening of 'Edgar & Emma' provides a revealing contrast with the opening of *Pride and Prejudice* in terms of speech attribution. The scenario bears comparison with the later novel, as in each a husband and "his Lady" bicker:

> "I cannot imagine," **said Sir Godfrey to his Lady**, "why we continue in such deplorable Lodgings as these [...]
> "I'm sure Sir Godfrey," **replied Lady Marlow** [....]
> "Nay my dear," **answered Sir Godfrey** [...]
> "My dear," **replied Lady Marlow** [...]
> As, after a few more speeches on both sides they could not determine which was the most to blame, they prudently laid aside the debate (*J*, pp. 33–4)

Here Austen deploys the rigidity of the attribution to heighten the starchiness of the exchange. As in the example from 'Love and Freindship', the varying of verbs seems to highlight the mechanical nature of providing attribution. Here, variation draws attention to sameness. In *Pride and Prejudice*, by contrast, narratorial attribution falls quickly away.

The use of attribution *within* direct speech does continue, however, in a quietly satirical vein in Austen's mature writing. Profuse inset reporting of others' speech is often a marker of class in literature of the period. In *Patronage*, Alfred Percy's description of a legal quarrel between farmers as "an infinite confusion of *said Is,* and *said hes*" suggests more than just the outlying of a case.[20] 'Said I' and 'said he' is particularly a trope of the comic servant: for instance, Radcliffe's loquacious Annette, who narrates scenes that her author chooses not to, or the brilliant narrative inventiveness of Dickens's Sam Weller.[21] While you would be unlikely to hear a "said she" or a "said he" from one of Austen's heroines, the satire of embedded attribution detaches from a particular class. Miss Bates's pleasure in relaying (and repeating) who said what, not only in conversations she has had, but also in conversations reported within those conversations, gestures towards that comic tradition.[22] But Sir Walter Elliot's tedious

[20] Edgeworth, *Patronage*, p. 246.

[21] Bruce Robbins has described the long history of the servant's "performance of narrative functions" in *The Servant's Hand: English Fiction from Below* (Durham and London: Duke University Press, 1993; first published, 1986), p. 92.

[22] In a single monologue, Miss Bates tells twice what Frank Churchill said (which we have already heard), what Mr Knightley said and what she said in return, but also what Patty said William Larkins had said Mrs Hodges said (*E*, pp. 256–8).

conversational recall transforms a chatty conveyance of news into the refrains of a class-inflected narcissism:

> 'In the name of heaven, who is that old fellow?' **said I**, to a friend of mine who was standing near, (Sir Basil Morley.) 'Old fellow!' **cried Sir Basil**, 'it is Admiral Baldwin. What do you take his age to be?' 'Sixty,' **said I**, 'or perhaps sixty-two.' 'Forty,' **replied Sir Basil**, 'forty, and no more.' Picture to yourselves my amazement; I shall not easily forget Admiral Baldwin. I never saw quite so wretched an example of what a sea-faring life can do; (*P*, p. 22)

Interestingly, embedded quoted speech within dialogue occurs frequently in Austen's first published novel, with Mrs Jennings, Mrs Palmer, Nancy Steele, John Dashwood and Robert Ferrars narrating what a he or she has said. The frequency of this speech characteristic decreases across the published novels, with Miss Bates standing out as an emphatic exception. With a subtle realism, when Miss Bates repeats what someone has said, she will do so slightly differently.[23] Miss Bates's characteristics as a voluble and interrupting narrator distinguish her from the novel's own narration, but even their smallest details convey the careful dramatic construction of her character.

## The Dramatic Model: Barbauld and Burney

By omitting speech attribution from direct speech, Austen optimized the dramatic quality of her dialogue. In the removal of narratorial intervention in this way, novelistic dialogue comes closer, in one respect, to the dramatic quality of the play.

Austen's talents as a dramatic writer have always been fundamental to the esteem in which her fiction has been held. Walter Scott, in his review of *Emma*, commented upon the "quiet yet comic dialogue, in which the characters of the speakers evolve themselves with dramatic effect".[24] According to George Henry Lewes, the relative absence of description in her novels is justified, or even accounted for, by her talent of characterization through dialogue:

[23] Austen subtly modifies Miss Bates's repetition of Frank Churchill's offer to fix her mother's spectacles (*E*, p. 256).

[24] Walter Scott, unsigned review of *Emma*, *Quarterly Review* (1815, issued March 1816), in *Jane Austen: the Critical Heritage*, vol. 1, p. 68.

> instead of *description*, the common and easy resource of novelists, she has the rare and difficult art of *dramatic presentation*: instead of telling us what her characters are, and what they feel, she presents the people, and they reveal themselves. In this she has never perhaps been surpassed, not even by Shakespeare himself.[25]

More recently, Paula Byrne has described Austen's "extraordinary gift for theatrical dialogue".[26] A key, if barely visible, aspect of Austen's dramatic power is the minimizing of speech attributions.

Reporting clauses can dissipate the energy of dialogue, as was soon acknowledged by innovators in fiction in the eighteenth century. Jean-François Marmontel articulated his disapproval of "the enervating repetition of the means of speaking" ("*lui dis-je, reprit-il, me répondit-elle*") in his essay 'Direct' in the *Encyclopédie* (1754). Such expressions are 'interruptions which curtail the vivacity of dialogue and make the style tedious when it should be the most animated', and Marmontel pinpoints the bind in which writers find themselves, having to avoid, on one side, confusion and, on the other, tediousness when apportioning speech to characters.[27] The solution that he alights upon is the use of a textual symbol to mark a change of speaker, a proposal he carried through by means of an extra full-stop in some of his tales published between 1755 and 1759.[28] The analogy with punctuation limits the semantic potential of the reporting clause, much like Ford Madox Ford's sense of its "unnoticeability".

There was another writer, contemporary with Marmontel, who may have had a direct impact on Austen's thinking about reporting clauses. That is Samuel Richardson. In *Sir Charles Grandison*, published 1753–4, which according to Austen family tradition was Jane Austen's most loved novel, Harriet Byron writes:

[25] Lewes, 'The Novels of Jane Austen', in *Jane Austen: the Critical Heritage*, vol. 1, p. 157. From the 1840s, at least, such comparisons between Austen and Shakespeare began to be made. Thomas Babington Macaulay had "no hesitation" in declaring Jane Austen as having "approached nearest to the manner of the great master [Shakespeare]"; unsigned article, 'The Diary and Letters of Mme D'Arblay', *Edinburgh Review* (January 1843), in *Jane Austen: the Critical Heritage*, vol. 1, p. 122.

[26] Paula Byrne, *Jane Austen and the Theatre* (London: Hambledon and London, 2002), p. xi.

[27] Jean-François Marmontel, 'Direct' (1754), in *Encyclopédie, ou dictionnaire raisonné des sciences, des arts et des métiers, etc.*, eds. Denis Diderot and Jean le Rond d'Alembert, (1751–72). Available at University of Chicago: ARTFL Encyclopédie Project (Autumn 2017 Edition), Robert Morrissey (ed.), http://encyclopedie.uchicago.edu/.

[28] See Vivienne Mylne, 'The Punctuation of Dialogue in Eighteenth-Century French and English Fiction', *The Library*, 1 (1979), 43–61, p. 50.

> By the way, Lucy, you are fond of plays; and it is come into my head, that, to avoid all *says-I's* and *says-she's*, I will henceforth, in all dialogues, write names in the margin:[29]

Harriet Byron doesn't elaborate on why she (and Richardson) wished to avoid "says-I's" and "says-she's". However, epistolary fiction made the issue of repetitiveness even more vexed. In novels written in letters, there is no illusion of narratorial invisibility in the writing of dialogue, as reporting clauses characterize the letter writer as much as the conversations they are ostensibly transcribing. By adopting the form of a play text, the internal writer weakens their association with the act of narration, while Richardson is able, simultaneously, to deepen it, suggesting the essential dramatization that occurs in the recollection of speech. More generally, Richardson may have been attracted to the inclusion of theatrical layouts in his fiction because he aspired to a dramatic style in composing his novels. The epistolary novel is an extended form of conversation between writers, with each letter written in the characters' distinguishable voice. This necessary dramatic element to the epistolary novel was powerfully expressed in the early nineteenth century by Anna Barbauld in her analysis of Richardson's fiction.

In her account of different modes of narration, Barbauld examined the narrative or epic style (third-person narration) alongside memoirs and the epistolary mode, assessing the relative merits and disadvantages of each. The epistolary novel, according to Barbauld, was essentially flawed by its improbability (*Correspondence*, vol. 1, p. xxvii). Barbauld also pointed out the problems of protagonist narrators transcribing conversations, which "supposes a memory more exact than is generally found" (p. xxvii). Austen had made this very point in her juvenilia. More positively, Barbauld describes the epistolary form as a "natural" way of telling a story and "[i]t makes the whole work dramatic, since all the characters speak in their own persons" (p. xxvi–vii). For a work to be dramatic is the keystone of Barbauld's sense of a novel's success. The author of the narrative mode will fail, by contrast, if he does not attend sufficiently to the "dramatic" and in this Frances Burney is exemplary:

> But his narration will not be lively, except he frequently drops himself, and runs into dialogue: all good writers therefore have thrown as much as possible of the dramatic into their narrative. Mad. d'Arblay has done this so successfully, that we have as clear an idea, not only of the sentiments, but the manner of expression of her different personages, as if we took it from the scenes in a play. (pp. xxiii–iv)

[29] Samuel Richardson, *The History of Sir Charles Grandison*, ed. and with an introduction by Jocelyn Harris (London: Oxford University Press, 1972; first published 1753–4 in 7 vols.), vol. 1, p. 273.

Barbauld's argument regarding the importance of dialogue and the dramatic style is another point of contact with Austen's own intuitions and practice.

Austen is likely to have endorsed Barbauld's appreciation of Burney's play-like dialogue. In fact, Caroline Austen attests this from hearing her aunt read aloud. Her Aunt Jane took up "a volume of Evelina and read a few pages of Mr. Smith and the Brangtons [*sic*] and I thought it was like a play".[30] It is well documented that reading novels aloud was an important pastime in the Austen household, and it was an activity that Austen excelled at. Austen herself had a strong sense of her characters' voices, complaining of her mother's "too rapid" reading of *Pride and Prejudice*: "—& tho' she perfectly understands the Characters herself, she cannot speak as they ought" (*L*, p. 211; 4 February 1813). But in *Evelina*, Burney gave her readers overt instructions as to how many of her characters should sound. It is surely telling that it was Mr Smith and the Branghtons that Caroline Austen remembers Austen reading as if from a play, as these are characters depicted through exaggerated verbal mannerisms: solecism, colloquialism and slang. Austen did not rely to the same extent as Burney on the overt collision of socially disparate word choices by the protagonist and her foils. Austen's comedy by contrast occurs in "low relief", with an "unemphatic treatment of idiosyncrasy" as Mary Lascelles put it,[31] while Burney's talent for mimicry was seen as detrimental to her fiction. This is Horace Walpole's view:

> The great fault is that the authoress is so afraid of not making all her *dramatis personae* set in character, that she never lets them say a syllable but what is to mark their character, which is very unnatural.[32]

Burney's desire to make written speech indicate character did, however, allow her to develop dramatic writing beyond the use of idiolectal mannerism alone.

The distinctive nature of Burney's speakers meant that she was frequently able to portray their conversations using free direct speech. On the whole, Burney is careful to attribute who is speaking in passages of dialogue with multiple speakers, but she often does this by allowing the *Ma Foi*'s and other affected Gallicisms of Mme Duval and the aggressive

[30] Caroline Austen, *My Aunt Jane Austen: A Memoir* (1867), in James Edward Austen-Leigh, *A Memoir of Jane Austen and Other Family Recollections* (Oxford: Oxford University Press, 2002), p. 174.

[31] Mary Lascelles, *Jane Austen and Her Art* (Oxford: Oxford University Press, 1939), p. 95. Lascelles points to syntax and phrasing, rather than vocabulary, as distinguishing between Austen's characters.

[32] Quoted in ibid., p. 98.

nautical language of Captain Mirvan to serve the same role as speech tags.[33] We might feel that the comic energy of their speech breaks free of Evelina's composing hand, but Burney is keeping a firm grip on the dramatic specificity of each character. Austen sometimes allows vulgarity to speak for itself, even if only momentarily, as in Mrs Jennings's prying as to Colonel Brandon's private business:

> But how came the hand to discompose you so much, if it was only a letter of business? Come, come, this wo'nt do, Colonel; so let us hear the truth of it. (*S&S*, p. 75)

The query is undoubtedly Mrs Jennings's (as a later turn in conversation confirms), but this is largely identified as such, by the characteristic impertinence of the enquiry, rather than any ostentatious idiolect.

Austen's restraint with mannerism brings us to a paradox with respect to the general use of he saids and she saids. The principle of non-attribution cultivates the dramatic mode by making dialogue immediate and vivid by being unmediated. But non-attribution can also undermine the dramatic mode by denying elaboration as to a character's verbal manner. Interestingly, in the theatricals in *Mansfield Park*, the narrator mirrors the theatrical preoccupation, as Austen's prose becomes unusually expansive with respect to "tone", "posture" and "voice":

> "By Jove! This won't do"—**cried Tom, throwing himself into a chair with a hearty laugh**. "To be sure, my dear mother, your anxiety—I was unlucky there."
>
> "What is the matter?" **asked her ladyship in the heavy tone of one half roused**,—"I was not asleep."
>
> "Oh! dear, no ma'am—nobody suspected you—Well Edmund," **he continued, returning to the former subject, posture, and voice, as soon as Lady Bertram began to nod again**— (*MP*, p. 148)

In this instance, the narrator provides stage directions by means of expanded attributions. More usually, such performative instructions are absent.

Austen takes free direct speech to a further extreme than Burney. She refrains from even providing attributions of speech for speakers who are not so distinctive. In such cases, the lack of attribution is equivalent to a dramatist entirely failing to record who speaks a line. There are cases

[33] For example, in vol. 1, letter XVI, attribution falls away with the antagonistic exchanges of Duval and Mirvan. Another example is in vol. 1, letter XX, where the affected speech of Lovel occasions the only unattributed utterances. Frances Burney, *Evelina, or, the History of a Young Lady's Entrance into the World*, ed. Margaret Anne Doody (London: Penguin, 1994; first published, 1778 in 3 vols.), pp. 65–7, pp. 89–90.

in Austen's fiction where the speaker in a conversation is unidentifiable. While in a play text from this time, this is unthinkable, in fiction, the risk can have positive consequences. These consequences will bring us closer to the evolution of free indirect discourse.

## Varieties of Attribution

Before turning to such moments when speech is left entirely without provenance, it is important to underline that Austen does not adopt non-attribution as an absolute rule. As in the last example, from *Mansfield Park*, speech tags expand according to their given context.

Variety is a basic principle in Austen's writing of dialogue. Even in the opening chapter of *Pride and Prejudice*, Mr Bennet's first response to his wife is in the indirect rather than direct mode, before the passage settles into alternating direct speech:

> "My dear Mr Bennet," said his lady to him one day, "have you heard that Netherfield Park is let at last?"
>
> Mr Bennet replied that he had not.

Mr Bennet's indirect response is one way in which Austen seeks to dispel, from the outset, dialogic monotony and to deny any implicit promise that we have a verbatim report of what is spoken. This becomes an important aspect of Austen's mature dialogue. It is a trait in her writing of conversations, for example, that she summarizes the opening of a conversation, marking out that we have access to only a part of it. The interplay between direct and indirect speech has characterological subtleties, as Mr Bennet's quiet will is established in that opening indirectness. Austen grasped these subtleties early on in her fiction and pursued them with careful nuance as her fiction progressed. This is best exemplified early on in *Mansfield Park* where Edmund converses with the child Fanny in direct speech with Fanny replying indirectly. Austen manages to convey Fanny's timid self-effacement by the mode in which her speech is reported, rather than persistent attributive explanation. Note the conventional use of speech marks both for the direct and indirect mode of speech, and the interplay of speakers without separate lines of print for each of their utterances:

> It was William whom she talked of most and wanted most to see. [...] "William did not like she should come away—he had told her he should miss her very much indeed." "But William will write to you, I dare say." "Yes, he had promised he would, but he had told *her* to write first." (*MP*, p. 17)

Similarly, variations between attributed and non-attributed speech can be exceptionally revealing. In *Sense and Sensibility*, the simple attribution 'said Elinor' is frequently used as ballast and pause in conversations with her more excitable mother and sister. Towards the end of the novel, Elinor tries to ask Edward casually about his supposed recent marriage to Lucy Steele: "I meant," said Elinor, taking up some work from the table, "to inquire after Mrs. *Edward* Ferrars" (*S&S*, p. 407). Here, the expanded speech attribution conveys in its content, in Elinor's business with her work, a visible attempt at self-concealment. The attribution also conveys rhythmically, and with pertinent disguise, how Elinor struggles to get the words out. In many cases, as in this, free direct style is evidently not appropriate. In contrast to the minimal attribution of the conversation between the Bennets in the opening chapter of *Pride and Prejudice*, in the scene in which Darcy first proposes to Elizabeth there is a strikingly high level of attribution. In a conversation of seventeen turns, fifteen are attributed.

> "You take an eager interest in that gentleman's concerns," said Darcy in a less tranquil tone, and with a heightened colour.
>
> "Who that knows what his misfortunes have been, can help feeling an interest in him?"
>
> "His misfortunes!" repeated Darcy contemptuously; "yes, his misfortunes have been great indeed."
>
> "And of your infliction," cried Elizabeth with energy. "You have reduced him to his present state of poverty, comparative poverty." (*P&P*, p. 214)

Here attribution works not necessarily to keep the reader informed as to who is speaking. Rather the intruding voice conveyed in the reporting clause captures and constructs the distance and anxious formality between the speakers.

In *Mansfield Park*, 'said he' subtly conveys a terrible blow for Fanny, signalling as it does, the return of a barrier between her and Edmund after a brief spell of intimate conversation without even narratorial intrusion. In this example, as in the opening of *Pride and Prejudice*, Austen uses free direct style to capture intimacy, but here a sequestered, almost magical moment of intimacy, hovering on the romantic:

> "I like to hear your enthusiasm, Fanny. It is a lovely night, and they are much to be pitied who have not been taught to feel in some degree as you do—who have not at least been given a taste for nature in early life. They lose a great deal."
>
> "*You* taught me to think and feel on the subject, cousin."
>
> "I had a very apt scholar. There's Arcturus looking very bright."

> "Yes, and the bear. I wish I could see Cassiopeia."
> "We must go out on the lawn for that. Should you be afraid?"
> "Not in the least. It is a great while since we have had any star-gazing."
> "Yes, I do not know how it has happened." The glee began. "We will stay till this is finished, Fanny," **said he**, turning his back on the window; (*MP*, p. 132)

After seven non-attributed utterances, the narrator intervenes with "said he", marking, with a decisive finality, the close of the characters' tête-à-tête, as Edmund is distracted back to the glee and to Mary. A simple "said he" carries the intrusive inflections of a third person, a narrator who had previously been dispelled. The phrase also conveys the perlocutionary effect of Edmund's speech on Fanny – its distancing of her – even though it ("said he") is beyond her ears, within narrative description.

## Free Direct Speech and *Pride and Prejudice*'s Blunders

Marmontel pondered the difficulty of avoiding ambiguity when omitting speech tags, but other writers have deliberately cultivated obscurity by means of this economy. In their discussion of free direct speech in *Style in Fiction*, Geoffrey Leech and Mick Short give an example from Hemingway's fiction:

> Hemingway is fond of omitting the reporting clause. In *A Clean, Well-Lighted Place* he uses this choice to portray the quick to-and-fro of the conversation between the two waiters:
>
> > 'He's drunk now,' he said.
> > 'He's drunk every night.'
> > 'What did he want to kill himself for?'
> > 'How should I know.'
> > 'How did he do it?'
> > 'He hung himself with a rope.'
> > 'Who cut him down?'
>
> In fact this is only a portion of some twenty-eight lines of FDS [free direct speech] between the initial direct speech and the next narrative sentence. Without the introductory clauses specifying which waiter says what, it becomes difficult to remember which waiter is which, so that confusion is gradually produced in the reader's mind. Indeed, one critic, David Lodge, has argued that this is precisely the point of Hemingway's story.[34]

[34] Geoffrey Leech and Mick Short, *Style in Fiction: a Linguistic Introduction to English Fictional Prose*, 2nd ed. (Harlow: Pearson Education Limited, 2007; first edition published 1981), pp. 258–9.

George Meredith was criticized for creating obscurity by failing to mark his speakers.[35] Removing conversational tags from passages of direct speech was one way of constructing a sense of the fragmentary, fleeting and spontaneous nature of conversation, deliberately at the expense of narratorial explication. In his social comedies, Evelyn Waugh made definitive conversational attribution impossible.[36]

Jane Austen may at first sight seem unlikely company for such pioneers of dialogic obscurity. On the contrary, commentators have pinpointed the individuality of her speakers. W. F. Pollock writing in 1860, for example, celebrated the skillfulness of Austen's dialogue in this respect (with an implicit comparison with a writer such as Burney):

> there are no catch words or phrases perpetually recurring from the same person; yet we recognise as soon as spoken the truthful individuality of everything that is made to fall from each speaker.[37]

Yet, in many places in Austen's fiction, the counter-view should pertain. David Lodge's conclusion that Hemingway deliberately makes things difficult for his readers by omitting speech tags is likewise applicable to Jane Austen, who explicitly justifies a decision to refrain from making her dialogue "more immediately clear". The printers' errors in *Pride and Prejudice* make the difficulty of following unattributed dialogue evident. It simply is not the case, as Thomas Henry Lister maintained in 1830, that "[e]very thing that is said, however short and simple, belongs peculiarly to the person by whom it is uttered, and is indicative of their situation, or turn of mind."[38] Rather, on a number of occasions speech hovers unresolvedly between variant possible sources.

Austen described *Pride and Prejudice*'s "greatest blunder" as an instance where "two speeches are made into one". Austen is specific about where this "blunder" occurs, encouraging Cassandra to have a look: "The greatest blunder in the Printing that I have met with is in Page 220—Vol. 3" (*L*, p. 212). This is chapter 12 of the third volume of the novel, when Jane Bennet, speaking privately with Elizabeth, denies an attachment to Bingley on his return to Netherfield. The dialogue as it appears in

[35] Unsigned review, *Saturday Review* (15 November 1879), in Ioan Williams (ed.), *George Meredith: the Critical Heritage* (London: Routledge & Kegan Paul, 1971), p. 221.

[36] Bronwen E. Thomas discusses this in 'Multiparty Talk in the Novel: the Distribution of Tea and Talk in a Scene from Evelyn Waugh's *Black Mischief*', *Poetics Today*, 23, 4 (2002), 657–84.

[37] W. F. Pollock, 'British Novelists – Richardson, Miss Austen, Scott', *Fraser's Magazine* (January 1860), in *Jane Austen: the Critical Heritage*, vol. 1, pp. 169.

[38] Thomas Henry Lister, unsigned review of *Women as They Are* by Mrs Catherine Gore (July 1830), in *Jane Austen: the Critical Heritage*, vol. 1, p. 114.

all editions published within the years of Austen's lifetime (first and second editions, 1813; third edition, 1817),[39] is as follows. I have added the implied attributions in square brackets (see Illustration 3.1 for the first printed edition):

> "It has been a very agreeable day," said Miss Bennet to Elizabeth. "The party seemed so well selected, so suitable one with the other. I hope we may often meet again."
>
> Elizabeth smiled.
>
> [JANE] "Lizzy, you must not do so. You must not suspect me. It mortifies me. I assure you that I have now learnt to enjoy his conversation as an agreeable and sensible young man, without having a wish beyond it. [...]"
>
> [ELIZABETH] "You are very cruel," said her sister, "you will not let me smile, and are provoking me to it every moment."
>
> [JANE] **"How hard it is in some cases to be believed! And how impossible in others!"**
>
> [ELIZABETH] **"But why should you wish to persuade me that I feel more than I acknowledge?"**
>
> [JANE] **"That is a question which I hardly know how to answer. We all love to instruct, though we can teach only what is not worth knowing. Forgive me; and if you persist in indifference, do not make *me* your confidante."**[40]

The dialogue seems to go awry when Elizabeth queries why she is being persuaded that she feels more than she acknowledges. The conversation makes more sense, therefore, when corrected as follows:

> [JANE] "Lizzy, you must not do so. You must not suspect me. It mortifies me. I assure you that I have now learnt to enjoy his conversation as an agreeable and sensible young man, without having a wish beyond it. [...]"
>
> [ELIZABETH] "You are very cruel," said her sister, "you will not let me smile, and are provoking me to it every moment."
>
> [JANE] **"How hard it is in some cases to be believed!"**
>
> [ELIZABETH] **"And how impossible in others!"**
>
> [JANE] **"But why should you wish to persuade me that I feel more than I acknowledge?"**
>
> [ELIZABETH] **"That is a question which I hardly know how to answer [...]"** (*P&P*, pp. 379–80; attribution in brackets added)

[39] Austen seems to have had no involvement in the publication of these subsequent editions, having sold the copyright to Thomas Egerton, the publisher. See David Gilson, *A Bibliography of Jane Austen. New Introduction and Corrections by the Author* (Winchester: St Paul's Bibliographies, 1997), p. 27. It is uncertain whether the third edition was issued before or after Austen's death (pp. 41–2).

[40] Jane Austen, *Pride and Prejudice: a Novel* (London: T. Egerton, 1813), vol. 3, pp. 220–1.

( 220 )

one with the other. I hope we may often meet again."

Elizabeth smiled.

"Lizzy, you must not do so. You must not suspect me. It mortifies me. I assure you that I have now learnt to enjoy his conversation as an agreeable and sensible young man, without having a wish beyond it. I am perfectly satisfied from what his manners now are, that he never had any design of engaging my affection. It is only that he is blessed with greater sweetness of address, and a stronger desire of generally pleasing than any other man."

"You are very cruel," said her sister, "you will not let me smile, and are provoking me to it every moment."

"How hard it is in some cases to be believed! And how impossible in others!"

"But why should you wish to persuade

suade

( 221 )

suade me that I feel more than I acknowledge?"

"That is a question which I hardly know how to answer. We all love to instruct, though we can teach only what is not worth knowing. Forgive me; and if you persist in indifference, do not make *me* your confidante."

CHAP-

Illustration 3.1 Jane Austen, *Pride and Prejudice: a Novel* (London: T. Egerton, 1813), vol. 3, pp. 220–1. By permission of the Syndics of Cambridge University Library. Keynes.K.1.10-12

With the speech redistributed, Elizabeth playfully echoes Jane's phrasing to assert that it is impossible to believe her detachment from Bingley.

But without the evidence of Austen's letter that "*two* speeches are made into one", the dialogue can be reorganized otherwise, to make equally good sense. R. W. Chapman pointed out that "the first attempt at correction was in one of Bentley's editions, in which these two sentences ["*How hard it is in some cases to be believed!*" / "*And how impossible in others!*"] and the next (to *acknowledge*) are all given to Jane", to read as follows (attribution in brackets added)[41]:

[41] *Pride and Prejudice*, in *The Novels of Jane Austen*, ed. R. W. Chapman, 3rd ed. (Oxford: Oxford University Press, 1932 [1st ed., 1923]), p. 395.

[JANE] **"How hard it is in some cases to be believed! And how impossible in others! But why should you wish to persuade me that I feel more than I acknowledge?"**

[ELIZABETH] **"That is a question which I hardly know how to answer [...]"**

Here Jane would acknowledge her inability to convince her sister of what she does not wish to be convinced: "how impossible in others!". If this reading were correct, then three speeches (rather than two) would have erroneously been made into one. What this variant reading shows, however, is that the dialogue on its own is not absolutely identifiable as one character's.

The original error in *Pride and Prejudice,* the making of two speeches into one, was caused in no small part by the lack of speech attribution. Instead of speech tags, Austen's printed dialogue relies on *alinéa* or the use of a new line for separate turns in dialogue, a convention that developed in the printing of novelistic dialogue in the mid-eighteenth century. That Austen would have had expectations that her dialogue would be conventionally presented with a new line for each speaker is evident from the teenage manuscript notebooks. There, where Austen presents her fiction as within the conventions of print, she allows herself generous white space for distinguishing speakers as Illustration 3.2 from 'Jack & Alice' in *Volume the First* demonstrates. This use of *alinéa* continues with some few exceptions into *Volume the Third* (see Illustration 3.3 from 'Catharine, or the Bower').

However, the cancelled chapters of *Persuasion* are more like what Austen would have submitted to her printers.[42] In *The Watsons*, the cancelled chapters of *Persuasion*, and *Sanditon*, speakers tend to share the same manuscript line when there is sufficient space. Dialogue is indicated by quotation marks, and a dash also sometimes marks the separation of speakers. Both *Persuasion* and *Sanditon* demonstrate on single pages this small variation in marking dialogue (for *Persuasion*, see Illustration 3.4).[43] When reading dialogue in these manuscripts – or indeed in print, where speeches are not given distinctive lines of their own[44] – without the aid of

[42] Sutherland, *Jane Austen's Textual Lives: from Aeschylus to Bollywood* (Oxford: Oxford University Press, 2005), p. 155.

[43] This occurs in the manuscript of *Persuasion*, p. 31 and *Sanditon*, b2-2.

[44] For instance in the dialogue in *Mansfield Park* between Edmund and the young Fanny which alternates between direct and indirect speech. See above, p. 145.

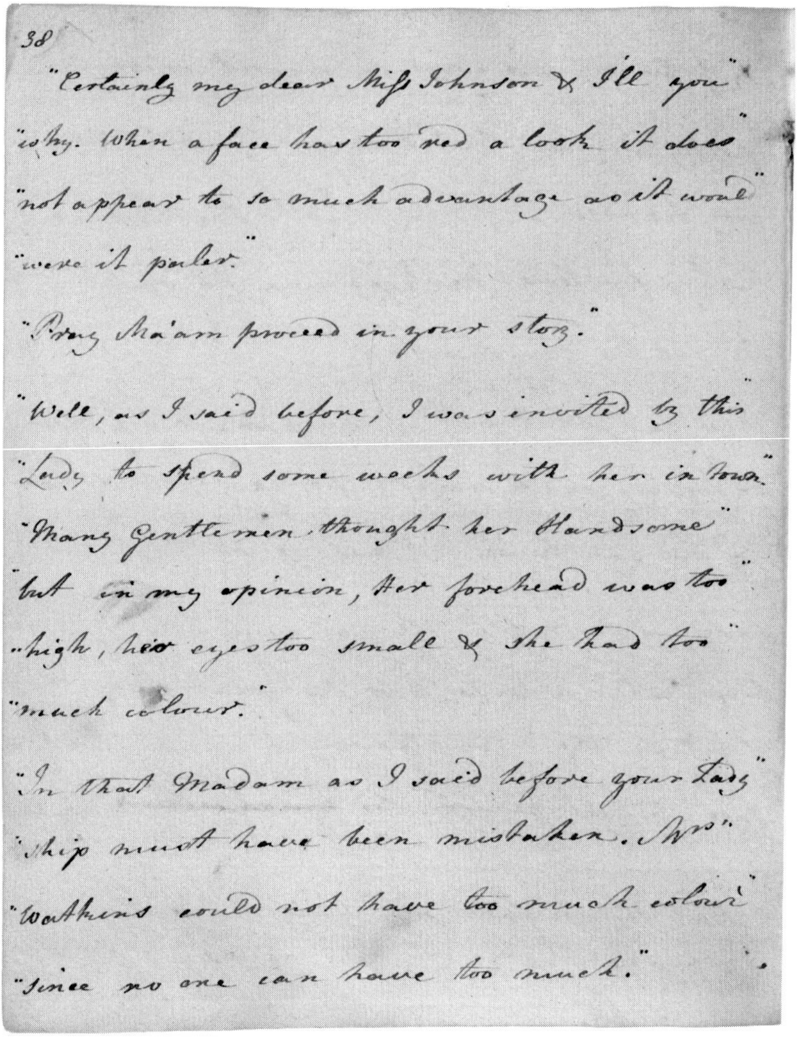

38

"Certainly my dear Miss Johnson & I'll you"
"why. When a face has too red a look it does"
"not appear to so much advantage as it would"
"were it paler."

"Pray Ma'am proceed in your story."

"Well, as I said before, I was invited by this"
"Lady to spend some weeks with her in town."
"Many Gentlemen thought her Handsome"
"but in my opinion, Her forehead was too"
"high, her eyes too small & she had too"
"much colour."

"In that Madam as I said before your Lady"
"ship must have been mistaken. Mrs"
"Watkins could not have too much colour"
"since no one can have too much."

Illustration 3.2 Jane Austen, 'Jack & Alice', in *Volume the First*, p. 38. By permission of the Bodleian Libraries, The University of Oxford. MS.Don.e.7

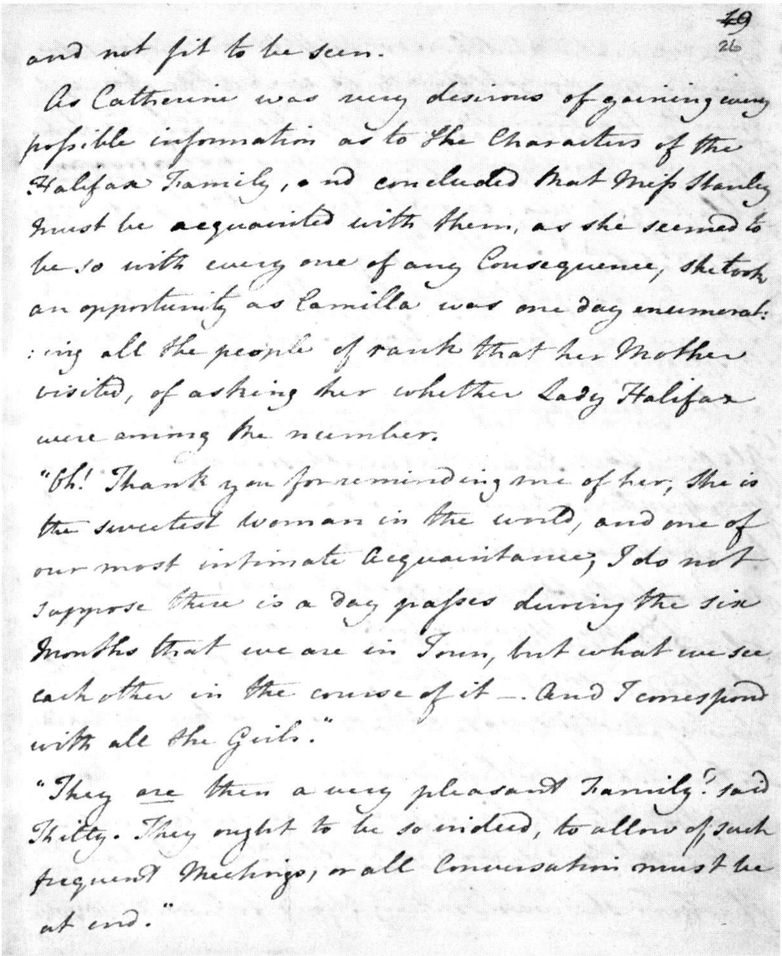

~~49~~ 26

and not fit to be seen.

As Catherine was very desirous of gaining every possible information as to the Characters of the Halifax Family, and concluded that Miss Stanley must be acquainted with them, as she seemed to be so with every one of any Consequence, she took an opportunity as Camilla was one day enumerat:ing all the people of rank that her Mother visited, of asking her whether Lady Halifax were among the number.

"Oh! Thank you for reminding me of her; She is the sweetest woman in the world, and one of our most intimate Acquaintance; I do not suppose there is a day passes during the six Months that we are in Town, but what we see each other in the course of it—. And I correspond with all the Girls."

"They *are* then a very pleasant Family? said Kitty. They ought to be so indeed, to allow of such frequent Meetings, or all Conversation must be at end."

Illustration 3.3 Jane Austen, 'Catharine, or the Bower', in *Volume the Third*, p. 49. By permission of the British Library Board, London. Add.MS.65381

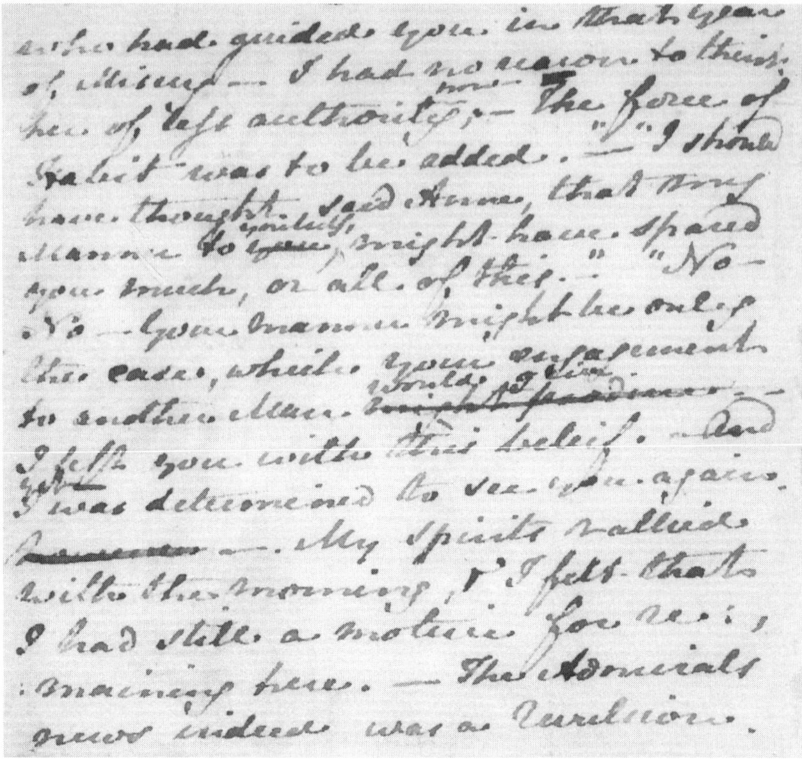
who had guided you in that year of misery. — I had no reason to think her of less authority now. — The force of habit was to be added. — "I should have thought, said Anne, that my manner to yourself might have spared you much, or all of this." "No — No — your manner might be only the ease, which your engagement to another Man would give. — I left you with this belief. — And yet I was determined to see you again. — My spirits rallied with the morning, & I felt that I had still a motive for remaining here. — The Admiral's news indeed was a revulsion.

Illustration 3.4 Jane Austen, the cancelled chapters of *Persuasion*, p. 31. By permission of the British Library Board, London. MS. Egerton 3038

white space or attribution, one does feel close to the repartee of the characters, as speech alternates with such immediacy between them. The page from the manuscript of *Persuasion* shown in Illustration 3.4, in contrast to the examples from Austen's earlier writing, may show how it could have been possible for a compositor to have lapsed in following who was speaking when.[45]

[45] Was William Gifford including speech attribution when he wrote to John Murray of *Pride and Prejudice* that "'tis very good – wretchedly printed in some places, & so pointed as to be unintelligible"? Quoted in Kathryn Sutherland, 'Jane Austen's Dealings with John Murray and His Firm', *The Review of English Studies*, 64 (2012), 105–26, p. 121.

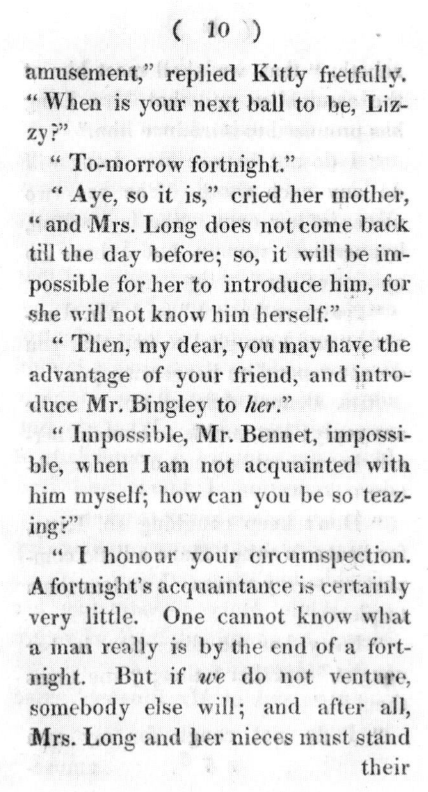

( 10 )

amusement," replied Kitty fretfully. "When is your next ball to be, Lizzy?"

"To-morrow fortnight."

"Aye, so it is," cried her mother, "and Mrs. Long does not come back till the day before; so, it will be impossible for her to introduce him, for she will not know him herself."

"Then, my dear, you may have the advantage of your friend, and introduce Mr. Bingley to *her*."

"Impossible, Mr. Bennet, impossible, when I am not acquainted with him myself; how can you be so teazing?"

"I honour your circumspection. A fortnight's acquaintance is certainly very little. One cannot know what a man really is by the end of a fortnight. But if *we* do not venture, somebody else will; and after all, Mrs. Long and her nieces must stand their

Illustration 3.5 Jane Austen, *Pride and Prejudice: a Novel* (London: T. Egerton, 1813), vol. 1, p. 10. By permission of the Syndics of Cambridge University Library. Keynes.K.1.10-12

There is, in fact, another passage of dialogue in *Pride and Prejudice* that most likely combines two speeches into one. Again this is due to the failure of attribution. In the second chapter of the novel, as it reads in the first edition, Kitty asks Elizabeth when her next ball will be in the following dialogue (see Illustration 3.5 for the first edition):

> Mrs. Bennet deigned not to make any reply; but unable to contain herself, began scolding one of her daughters.
>
> "Don't keep coughing so, Kitty, for heaven's sake! Have a little compassion on my nerves. You tear them to pieces."

> "Kitty has no discretion in her coughs," said her father; "she times them ill."
>
> **"I do not cough for my own amusement," replied Kitty fretfully. "When is your next ball to be, Lizzy?"**
>
> "To-morrow fortnight."
>
> "Aye, so it is," cried her mother.[46]

R. W. Chapman was the first editor to query the attribution:

> *'When is your next ball to be, Lizzy?'* is given to Kitty by all editions. But why should Kitty ask what she must have known? And why should she call it 'your ball'? The speech is of course Mr. Bennet's. In *A* it begins a line, and the printer merely failed to indent the first word.[47]

E. M. Forster's praise of Chapman's discovery – "It is a tiny point, yet how it stirs the pools of complacency!" – revels in the revitalization of Austen's discourse by such attentive reading.[48] Chapman's emendation is most likely correct and it has been generally accepted ever since. By looking further at absent speech attributions in Austen's fiction, the pools of complacency are stirred even further as one realizes that the provenance of a particular speech can occasionally be insoluble.

## Unattributed Speech – Unidentifiable Speakers

When Austen writes to Cassandra, "There are a few Typical errors—& a "said he" or a "said she" would sometimes make the Dialogue more immediately clear—" she asserts that lack of clarity occurs "sometimes" and indeed it is possible to discover other instances of attributive ambiguity in *Pride and Prejudice*, unconnected with any printing error. For instance, in the following conversation at Netherfield when the Bingley circle are discussing the Bennet sisters:

> "I am afraid, Mr. Darcy," observed Miss Bingley, in a half whisper, "that this adventure has rather affected your admiration of her fine eyes."
>
> "Not at all," he replied; "they were brightened by the exercise."—A short pause followed this speech, and Mrs. Hurst began again.
>
> "I have an excessive regard for Jane Bennet, she is really a very sweet girl, and I wish with all my heart she were well settled. But with such

[46] Austen, *Pride and Prejudice* (1813), vol. 1, pp. 9–10.

[47] *Pride and Prejudice*, ed. Chapman, p. 391. '*A*' refers to the 1813 edition of *Pride and Prejudice*.

[48] E. M. Forster, from a review of the Clarendon edition of the novels edited by R. W. Chapman, *Nation and Athanaeum* (5 January 1924), in *Jane Austen: the Critical Heritage*, vol. 2, p. 280.

> a father and mother, and such low connections, I am afraid there is no chance of it."
>
> **"I think I have heard you say, that their uncle is an attorney in Meryton."**
>
> "Yes; and they have another, who lives somewhere near Cheapside."
>
> "That is capital," added her sister, and they both laughed heartily.
>
> "If they had uncles enough to fill *all* Cheapside," cried Bingley, "it would not make them one jot less agreeable." (*P&P*, pp. 39–40)

Who speaks the highlighted line? The most likely answer is Caroline Bingley, egging her sister on to snobbish revelations. It is Miss Bingley who, the narrator tells us, leads the derogatory discussion of the Bennets. The conversation began eight turns earlier with Miss Bingley and Mrs Hurst exchanging similarly spiteful remarks. Darcy has only entered the discussion because he has been directly addressed. However, on the basis of Austen's general practice of alternating speakers, the last speaker continues to hold the floor until we are positively told otherwise, in which case it is a curious Darcy who prompts further discussion of the Bennet girls. An elfish debate may then ensue. Would Darcy voice such vulgar curiosity? He has made crasser comments to date in the novel. Perhaps more persuasively, the narrator would have been sure to tell us if this was Darcy, as it would be a noteworthy glimpse into his interest in Elizabeth. Austen may wish us to use our ingenuity to decide who speaks these words, but ultimately, whatever decision we come to, the provenance in *absolute* terms is insoluble.

Subsequent attribution in this case does not help. If Darcy speaks the unattributed line then the subsequent tag "'That is capital' added her sister" would inform us that Miss Bingley 'added' to Mrs Hurst's revelation of an uncle in Cheapside. However, if it is Caroline who says "I think I have heard you say, that their uncle is an attorney in Meryton", then the subsequent "added her sister" could confirm this attribution, suggesting that Carline Bingley 'adds' to her own previous comment regarding the other uncle in Meryton. In this case, "added her sister" is a retrospective attribution.

Retrospective attribution is a common feature of Austen's extended dialogues. For instance in *Sense and Sensibility*:

> "We have heard Sir John admire it [Norland] excessively," said Lucy, who seemed to think some apology necessary for the freedom of her sister.
>
> "I think every one *must* admire it," replied Elinor, "who ever saw the place; though it is not to be supposed that any one can estimate its beauties as we do."

> **"And had you a great many smart beaux there? I suppose you have not so many in this part of the world; for my part, I think they are a vast addition always."**
>
> "But why should you think,' said Lucy, looking ashamed of her sister, "that there are not as many genteel young men in Devonshire as Sussex?" (*S&S*, p. 142)

Here, any underlying rule of alternating speakers in dialogue is undermined when a late "said Lucy" confirms her sister as the speaker of the preceding highlighted utterance. At this early stage of acquaintance with the Steeles, at which point Anne is not immediately recognizable as the more unguarded and foolish, one cannot identify which sister speaks about 'beaux' without narrative guidance.

At other times, a subsequent tag eliminates a supposed contributor as the speaker of the previous words and we may have to revise our first apprehension of the order of speakers in a scene. When Mrs Bennet and her two youngest girls discuss the departure of the militia regiment from Meryton to Brighton, one may be a little surprised at having to re-attribute the hyperbolic desire for sea-bathing from a young Kitty to Mrs Bennet whose silliness is thereby confirmed:

> "If one could but go to Brighton!" observed Mrs. Bennet.
>
> "Oh, yes!—if one could but go to Brighton! But papa is so disagreeable."
>
> **"A little sea-bathing would set me up for ever."**
>
> "And my aunt Philips is sure it would do *me* a great deal of good," added Kitty. (*P&P*, p. 254)

In the example of the Bingley circle from *Pride and Prejudice*, by contrast, 'added her sister' confirms nothing. Instead, "I think I have heard you say, that their uncle is an attorney in Meryton" proves to be discourse freed from attribution, including attributive reconstruction. This, then, is free direct speech in its freest sense, entirely liberated from a specific speaker. This is a viable technique in Austen's fiction, as other lines have the power to perplex in terms of attribution. In *Sense and Sensibility*, for example, in a discussion between Elinor, Marianne and Willoughby about the character of Colonel Brandon, the speaker of the following highlighted line is undetermined:

> "That he is patronized by *you*," replied Willoughby, "is certainly in his favour; but as for the esteem of the others, it is a reproach in itself. Who would submit to the indignity of being approved by such women as Lady Middleton and Mrs. Jennings, that could command the indifference of any body else?"
>
> "But perhaps the abuse of such people as yourself and Marianne, will make amends for the regard of Lady Middleton and her mother. If their

> praise is censure, your censure may be praise, for they are not more undiscerning, than you are prejudiced and unjust."
>
> **"In defence of your protegé you can even be saucy."**
>
> "My protegé, as you call him, is a sensible man; and sense will always have attractions for me. Yes, Marianne, even in a man between thirty and forty." (*S&S*, p. 60)

Does this line reveal the sudden familiarity of Willoughby with Elinor or the spirited interjection of Marianne? Willoughby could hold the floor as the previous speaker, but Elinor's subsequent address to Marianne could act equally as a form of retrospective attribution.

Another example occurs in *Mansfield Park*. In the early part of the first volume Austen includes a three-way conversation between Mary, Henry Crawford and Mrs Grant in which there is no narratorial reporting clause following the first turn in the conversation. Impressively, twenty-two turns in a conversation between three people are shaped by means of one initial "said he". Up until the midway point when Mrs Grant enters the conversation, there has been no explicit acknowledgement that she is even present. Speakers enter and leave conversation without any narratorial direction, allowing the following highlighted attribution to remain unconfirmed. The first speaker in this quotation, by alteration from the opening of the conversation, must be Henry Crawford:

> "But Miss Bertram does not care three straws for him [Mr. Rushworth]; *that* is your opinion of your intimate friend. *I* do not subscribe to it. I am sure Miss Bertram is very much attached to Mr. Rushworth. I could see it in her eyes, when he was mentioned. I think too well of Miss Bertram to suppose she would ever give her hand without her heart."
>
> "Mary, how shall we manage him?"
>
> "We must leave him to himself I believe. Talking does no good. He will be taken in at last."
>
> "But I would not have him *taken in*, I would not have him duped; I would have it all fair and honourable."
>
> "Oh! dear—Let him stand his chance and be taken in. It will do just as well. Every body is taken in at some period or other."
>
> **"Not always in marriage, dear Mary."**
>
> "In marriage especially. With all due respect to such of the present company as chance to be married, my dear Mrs. Grant, there is not one in a hundred of either sex, who is not taken in when they marry." (*MP*, p. 53)

The sentiment most likely suggests that Mrs Grant is the speaker and the turns preceding this quotation are hers. Nonetheless, it is possible that Henry speaks here, to support his provocative stance regarding the sincerity of Maria's attachment to Rushworth. The following address to "my dear Mrs Grant" may be made then by Mary apologetically rather than responsively. My point is that without narratorial attribution there is no way of distinguishing *definitively* between Henry Crawford and Mrs Grant at this point.

To what extent then does accurate attribution matter? In *Pride and Prejudice*, "I think I have heard you say, that their uncle is an attorney in Meryton" is an utterance for which we can come to no certain conclusion. Of course somebody within the fictional world is deemed to have said it, most likely Caroline or Darcy, but once those two possibilities are accepted, Bingley too could be a plausible candidate. In a play text or a film adaption, one character above another would have to be selected. Within the reading text, however, we encounter a type of free-roaming curiosity about the Bennet sisters, that to some extent the reader must share and that is unnecessary, in Austen's view, to associate sharply with an individual. In *Mansfield Park,* the disembodied interjection, with its rational and gently moralizing tone, "Not always in marriage, dear Mary" voices the position of scepticism that the reader is encouraged to take towards Mary throughout the novel. This unattributed utterance, spoken either by the very different characters of Henry Crawford or Mrs Grant, is infused with the larger narratorial stance towards Mary Crawford.

Meir Sternberg has asserted the "direct speech fallacy".[49] Sternberg's claim is that direct speech shares the same perspectival framing as indirect forms of speech.[50] Indirect speech is essentially ambiguous as one is uncertain whether the discourse is that of the reporter or the reportee.[51] While direct speech gives the illusion of being a verbatim transcript, distortion occurs because utterances are not absolutely reproducible.[52] Direct speech, writes Sternberg, can reveal a "balance between mimetic representation and functional communication [...] according to the global ends of the frame".[53]

[49] Meir Sternberg, 'Point of View and the Indirections of Direct Speech', *Language and Style*, 15 (1982), 67–117, p. 68.

[50] Ibid., p. 77.

[51] Ibid., p. 71.

[52] See also Meir Sternberg, 'Proteus in Quotation-Land: Mimesis and the Forms of Reported Discourse', *Poetics Today*, 3 (1982), 107–56, p. 152.

[53] Sternberg, 'Point of View and the Indirections of Direct Speech', p. 79.

Sternberg's interest in the framing of discourse sheds light on the work of reporting clauses. Even the sparest of reporting frames, we may add, can be fundamental in terms of insinuating another point of view. One of the longest dialogues in *Emma* with one of the lowest attribution counts is a conversation between Emma and Knightley, which has thirty-one turns marked by only seven attributions. In these minimal reporting clauses, narratorial attention is subtly weighted towards Knightley rather than Emma. By the elaboration of "coolly", "rather displeased", "warmly" and, finally, "with a degree of vexation", Knightley's speech is probed by a narrator who subordinates his words to a reporting clause and surreptitiously facilitates his declared feelings at the novel's conclusion.[54] Adverbially, Emma once merely laughs (*E*, pp. 156–62).

However, it is often radically unframed discourse that provides a strong sense of the "global ends of the frame". That words cannot be fixed immediately to a single speaker quietly exposes a larger purpose to the utterance beyond any appreciation of that utterance typifying the language or sentiments of one particular character. The unattributed line of *Pride and Prejudice*, for example, displays the purpose of the passage in exposing the snobbery on the part of the Bingley circle. In *Mansfield Park*, the unattributed utterance works to undermine and reprimand Mary by forcing her to play her hand. In these respects, a larger narratorial purpose can be intuited at work in the dialogues of characters. But the "global ends of the frame" may be more global. By disallowing the strict attribution of speech to person, Austen also allows her dialogue modes of inter-personal exchange that have political dimensions. After all, unattributed dialogue is, by another name, free speech.

## Free Speech: Robert Bage and the Politics of *Pride and Prejudice*

One of the more intriguing works known to have been owned by Jane Austen is Robert Bage's politically radical novel *Hermsprong*. Of the twenty surviving books owned by her, four are works of English

[54] Direct speech is not grammatically subordinated to a reporting clause in the manner of indirect speech (he said that …). Instead, the attributing voice and speaking voice are juxtaposed (he said:). However, as Meir Sternberg has put it: "While indeed possibly independent in its original context – and while misleadingly retaining this independence forever in grammatical terms, regardless of its subsequent fortunes – the quoted speech-event is reduced in transmission to subordinate status in terms of point of view and communicative role"; Sternberg, 'Point of View and the Indirections of Direct Speech', pp. 69, 73.

fiction. Besides *Hermsprong*, these are Samuel Richardson's *Sir Charles Grandison*, Samuel Johnson's *Rasselas* and Frances Burney's *Camilla*.[55] It is fair to say that Johnson, Burney and Richardson – and these three particular works by them – held significant import for Austen. All three are named or directly alluded to in her fiction. Austen's relationship with Bage is more oblique. That her copy of *Hermsprong* survives need not necessarily imply that it had any particular significance for her: books can survive for a range of contingent reasons. However, many connections between *Hermsprong* and *Pride and Prejudice* have been identified.[56] It is also possible that Austen read *Hermsprong* in the year that she began to compose *Pride and Prejudice*. *Hermsprong* was published in 1796, tallying with Cassandra Austen's memory of the year of *Pride and Prejudice*'s genesis.

*Hermsprong* is one of the many novels of the period that contains the phrase "pride and prejudice", but there are more convincing resonances between them. One of the most noticeable similarities between *Hermsprong* and *Pride and Prejudice* is in the character of Maria Fluart – the spirited, arch and witty friend of the more demure Caroline Campinet – who bears considerable resemblance to Elizabeth Bennet. At one point, Maria preempts Elizabeth's chastisement of Darcy's absurdly exclusive definition of accomplished women.[57] The Sumelins are also noticeably similar to the Bennets. Bage dramatizes the domestic wrangles between a cynical husband and a garrulous, fretful, more intellectually limited wife, as well as their silly offspring. The conversation between the Sumelins on the elopement of their daughter Harriet (much like Lydia Bennet) elicits a Bennet-like exchange long before the Bennets ever saw print. The similarity is especially striking in Mr Sumelin's dour and ironical dealings with his wife:

> "Well, and for what is all this noise and pother, Mrs. Sumelin? Your daughter is gone to be married, that's all. I suppose you intended she should marry one day?"

[55] Gilson, *A Bibliography of Jane Austen*, pp. 431–46. This is excluding Austen's copy of the children's book *The History of Goody Two Shoes*. Austen's copy of *Hermsprong* is held in the Huntingdon Library, California. See, Anne Toner, 'Free Speech: Jane Austen, Robert Bage, and the Subversive Shapes of Dialogue', *Textus. English Studies in Italy*, 30, 3 (2017), 167–87, p. 174.

[56] Stuart Tave, 'Introduction' to the facsimile reprint of Robert Bage, *Hermsprong; or, Man as He Is Not*, edited, annotated, and with an introduction by Stuart Tave (University Park and London: Pennsylvania State University Press, 1982), pp. 1–2.

[57] Robert Bage, *Hermsprong; or, Man as He Is Not*, ed. Pamela Perkins (Peterborough, ON: Broadview Literary Texts, 2002; first published, 1796 in 3 vols.), pp. 212–3; *P&P*, p. 43.

> "But to marry so much beneath her, Mr. Sumelin,—and such a coxcomb."
>
> "As to his being a coxcomb, my dear, we must set that down as a circumstance in Harriet's favour; coxcombry being the most approved qualification of man, in the mind of woman [...]."[58]

*Hermsprong* is known for its aspirations to political freedom. The work also embraces a formal freedom in its presentation of dialogue, as this small extract demonstrates. Bage, like Austen, adopted a dramatic style, even occasionally switching to play-book layout when managing a conversation between multiple speakers. Bage writes dialogues freed from attribution, extending considerably beyond the lengths of Austen's. One occasion – when Maria Fluart teases her friend Caroline for her preference of Hermsprong in twenty-six unattributed and often quick-fire lines – is remarkably similar in style *and* subject to Elizabeth's teasing of Jane that occasioned her compositor's "blunder" as to who was speaking when.[59]

Marilyn Butler pinpointed Bage's use of dialogue as significant for Austen in another sense. Bage valued dialogue and gave it substantial content. He would thus "inaugurate one of the most interesting sub-species of the coming generation, the intellectual comedy of Maria Edgeworth, Jane Austen and Thomas Love Peacock".[60] This is in spite of what Butler saw as their profoundly divergent political sympathies. Butler's conservative Austen does not set out to overthrow peers of the realm, a result which Hermsprong – "a walking Rights of Man"[61] – collaterally effects. Butler's sense of Austen's political affiliations continues to be vigorously debated. Furthermore, Butler's separation between political message and dialogic influence may be disputed.

As Butler points out, Bage presents debates of ideological or political significance through conversation. This may be through open discussions about competing systems of government, political corruption, and the value and means of female education; or, more covertly through the workings of the romance plot. The longest unattributed dialogue in the novel is between the reprehensible aristocrat Lord Grondale and Maria Fluart. Grondale, while persecuting his daughter Caroline, is pursuing her friend, who at every stage outwits him. This conversation with its

[58] Bage, *Hermsprong*, ed. Perkins, p. 88.

[59] Ibid., pp. 234–6. Caroline calls Maria a "perverter of meanings" (p. 236), which Jane echoes in describing her sister as persuading her to more than she feels.

[60] Marilyn Butler, *Jane Austen and the War of Ideas* (Oxford: Clarendon Press, 1975), p. 86.

[61] This phrase is Kenneth R. Johnston's in *Unusual Suspects: Pitt's Reign of Alarm and the Lost Generation of the 1790s* (Oxford: Oxford University Press, 2013), p. 173.

amatory, teasing tone explicitly connects parental tyranny over daughters to the larger political sphere. This partly comic head-to-head between Miss Fluart and Lord Grondale consists in an astonishing sixty-five turns of dialogue with only one attribution. The conversation does not begin with an attribution – even this is implied – rather, the one single attribution signals a shift into greater formality on Lord Grondale's part and thus is a reminder (conveyed more explicitly by the narrator) of his status:

> "Miss Fluart," **said his lordship, increasing the solemnity of his tone**, "I fear Miss Campinet has not had in you so prudent a friend and monitor, as I had hoped."[62]

Earlier in the novel, Hermsprong is introduced from the following ironic perspective, as subverting "forms" of politeness:

> But he had faults; one for which it would be difficult to procure pardon in the court of politeness. It was a sort of secret contempt for politeness itself; or rather for its forms; forms so numerous and trifling, that they destroyed its essence. It was quite disagreeable to Mrs. Sumelin and Miss Harriet, to see them, that is to say, the bows, the smiles, and the graces, hurried over to-day, in order to address himself more particularly to Miss Campinet [...].[63]

In a sense, the removal of speech attribution is a removal of the bows and graces attendant upon dialogue. Non-attribution liberates speech from reminders of title and of person, and from authoritative glosses and prescriptions upon behaviour. This is something that Austen seems to have been alert to.

It is noticeable that in the course of *Pride and Prejudice*, Austen does not extensively dramatize Mr Collins in conversation with Lady Catherine or with Darcy. At the ball, Elizabeth watches Collins from a distance approaching Darcy and there "prefaced his speech with a solemn bow" (p. 109). Elizabeth is unable to hear what is spoken and the narrator eschews the descriptive work that would have to be done in conveying Collins's obsequiousness. When Elizabeth herself speaks with an imperious Lady Catherine there is little attribution to signify status or power outside of their respective roles in the conversation. Rather the dialogue between the two women is one in which Lady Catherine tries to assert "who I am" (p. 393), but the narrative voice does little to underpin her

[62] Bage, *Hermsprong*, ed. Perkins, p. 266.
[63] Ibid., pp. 208–9.

status or articulate the relationship between the two. The deference of Mrs Bennet's early role in the conversation is attested to by a reporting clause:

> "Yes, madam," **said Mrs Bennet, delighted to speak to a lady Catherine**. (p. 390)

But after this, attribution attenuates to highlight Elizabeth's fight for her own authority, status and rights in her own words:

> "[...]You are to understand, Miss Bennet, that I came here with the determined resolution of carrying my purpose; nor will I be dissuaded from it. I have not been used to submit to any person's whims. I have not been in the habit of brooking disappointment."
>
> "*That* will make your ladyship's situation at present more pitiable; but it will have no effect on *me*."
>
> "I will not be interrupted [...]." (p. 394)

As with Bage's fiction, such an attack on authority can be read as politically subversive in the terms of the day. Contrary to Butler, Helena Kelly more recently has described Elizabeth as "fundamentally, a radical" and the novel in which she appears "revolutionary".[64] While, in the end, Austen disallows unambiguous political messages to be drawn from her fiction, indeed to some degree like Bage, who could obscure ideology in comedy, she dramatizes a freedom of mind and purpose that is undoubtedly, and with immense subtlety, endorsed by the layout of her page.

Bage's dialogue accommodated, in innovatory ways, serious political ideas within the romantic plot. His fiction distanced dialogue from the philosophical tradition from which it at least in part emerges. The steady back and forth of attributions in *Rasselas* for instance – and Bage as well as Austen was indebted to Johnson[65] – signal a clearly designated viewpoint. It is not commonly pertinent for philosophical or moral positions to be delivered free of a clear sense of provenance and thus be subject to erroneous attribution. However, Bage privileged the dynamics of conversation in flow and the circulation of ideas, without a preconceived delineation of authority. The freedom of Austen's expression may have been political or it may have been more temperamental, as in Stuart Tave's view:

> In Bage the freer life is not the product of a doctrine that seems so often to make happiness in political novels so lugubrious, but it is a life of some

[64] Helena Kelly, *Jane Austen: the Secret Radical* (London: Icon Books, 2016), pp. 155, 139.

[65] Tave, 'Introduction', p. 1.

> wit and joy. Freedom really seems to offer a humane spirit and more interesting human beings. It offers an invitation to join in its community of liveliness. That was the sort of invitation Jane Austen could accept with pleasure [...].[66]

*Pride and Prejudice* has as its centre a character whose freedom of spirit did challenge at least in part the habits and expectations of traditional forms of authority. More widely across her fiction, Austen embraced the spirit and free flow of conversation in which non-attribution becomes a significant style for the presentation of a social, collective and equalizing experience.

## Unattributed Speech and "The General Voice"

If one participates in the sort of quick, lively dialogue that Austen wished to portray, it is common that the sentiments of individual participants are not always entirely individualized. Words seem to emerge from a group and precise attribution does not really matter. In *Persuasion*, Anne Elliot, playing the piano through her tears, overhears perhaps one of the Miss Musgroves, or is it one of the Miss Hayters, speaking to Wentworth about her. Even without this emotional barrier, the mood of a conversation is often more significant than who exactly said what. The subject of the discussion can, as we have seen, be more important than particular discussants. With a new intensity following *Pride and Prejudice*, there is a palpable trajectory in Austen's fiction towards the omission of attribution, so as to denote pluralized utterance or groups speaking in forms of unison.

One of many innovations with respect to the reporting of speech in *Mansfield Park* is an increasing depiction of a collective response. This is particularly evident in the group activities of the young people of the house during the theatricals, when quoted direct speech has attribution no more specific than its emergence from among groups of characters:

> "It was a hard case, upon my word;" and, "I do think you were very much to be pitied;" were the kind responses of listening sympathy. (*MP*, p. 144)

Either two specific people are responsible for these exact utterances or these are approximations of the sorts of things any number of the collected auditors might have said. The narrator does not tell us exactly. Instead, the reader's attention is drawn more to the dynamics of conversation, in this case to "listening sympathy", rather than any particular speaker.

66 Ibid., p. 12.

It is fascinating that in Austen's extant writing, the first use of a reporting clause marked a collective utterance.[67] This is in 'Frederic & Elfrida', in *Volume the First*, where, on meeting Rebecca, three characters (Charlotte, Frederic and Elfrida)

> all with one accord jumped up and exclaimed.
>
> "Lovely and too charming Fair one, notwithstanding your forbidding Squint, your greazy tresses and your swelling Back, which are more frightfull than imagination can paint or pen describe, I cannot refrain from expressing my raptures, at the engaging Qualities of your Mind." (*J*, p. 6)

The young Austen finds the notion of simultaneous utterance comic and perhaps she is commenting on what Lennard J. Davis complained about as the novel's "very poor range of mimetic possibilities to handle group linguistic behavior".[68] Austen herself goes on to attempt to rectify such a situation by experimenting with innovative forms of polyphony.

Collective utterance often continues to have a satirical purpose in the later fiction, against which the heroine's individuality is situated. Austen uses collective utterance to designate the interchangeability of individuals and indistinguishable sisters seem to have been a shaping idea for Austen, certainly by *The Watsons*: "he enquired after one of my daughters, but I do not know which. I suppose you know among yourselves" (*LM*, p. 114). I have already pointed to the temporary indistinguishability between the Steele sisters' speech in *Sense and Sensibility*, before retrospective attribution decides between them. In *Mansfield Park*, Austen flaunts her disinterest in the individuality of the young Bertram sisters by refusing to grant them any individual attribution as they criticize Fanny:

> **they thought her** prodigiously stupid, and for the first two or three weeks **were** continually bringing some fresh report of it into the drawing-room. "Dear Mamma, only think, my cousin cannot put the map of Europe together—or my cousin cannot tell the principal rivers in Russia—or she never heard of Asia Minor [...]
>
> "**My dear,"** their considerate aunt would reply; [...]
>
> "But, aunt, she is really so very ignorant!" [...]
>
> "Yes," **added the other**; "and of the Roman emperors" [...]
>
> "Very true, indeed, my dears, [...]" (*MP*, pp. 20–21)

Free direct speech emerges out of a collective feeling held by them both. Although a particular conversation comes into focus as Mrs Norris replies,

[67] This is on the basis of the current dating of the teenage writing.

[68] Lennard J. Davis, *Resisting Novels: Ideology and Fiction* (New York and London: Methuen, 1987), p. 180.

Austen clinches her disparagement with a non-referential "added the other". Other pairings whose direct speech is not individuated include Mrs Norris and Lady Bertram; the Musgrove sisters; Charles and Mary Musgrove. Beyond such pairings, there are larger groups who speak in unison. There is an example of this, in the early manuscript fragment *The Watsons*, where unattributed pluralized speech denotes the excited chatter of a group. This is what the narrator elsewhere calls "the general voice"(*LM*, p. 130):[69]

> [wheels] stopped beyond a doubt at the garden gate of the parsonage. "Who could it be? —it was certainly a postchaise. —Penelope was the only creature to be thought of. She might perhaps have met with some unexpected opportunity of returning." —A pause of suspense ensued. (*LM*, p. 126)

The direct quality of the speech – un-introduced and in speech marks – in combination with an indirect manner of speaking ("Who could it be?" rather than "Who can it be?") gives immediacy to an approximation of the language of a group in unison.

Kenneth L. Moler has examined "group voices" in Austen's fiction in the form of general public opinion. For Moler, group voices are central to the "economy of [Austen's] art",[70] as they provide a compensatory depth in the face of relative lack of description or direct authorial commentary. Thus group voices help to give "the impression of presenting a fully fleshed-out world."[71] Moler compares two instances of Highbury voicing which share a recognizable style "in the repetitiveness and unsophisticated structures of sentences". First, Highbury comments on Frank Churchill's letter:

> There was not a dissentient voice on the subject, either when Mrs. Perry drank tea with Mrs. and Miss Bates, or when Mrs. and Miss Bates returned the visit. Now was the time for Mr. Frank Churchill to come among them; and the hope strengthened when it was understood that he had written to his new mother on the occasion. For a few days every morning visit in Highbury included some mention of the handsome letter Mrs. Weston had received. **"I suppose you have heard of the handsome letter Mr. Frank Churchill had written to Mrs. Weston? I understand it was a very handsome letter,**

[69] There is one notable instance of free direct speech used in a dialogue in *The Watsons*: an unattributed line ("We had two dances more.") hanging between Emma, Mrs Edwards and Miss Edwards (*LM*, p. 109).

[70] Kenneth L. Moler, '"Group Voices" in Jane Austen's Narration', *Persuasions*, 13 (1991), 7–12, p. 12. I am grateful to Hatsuyo Shimazaki for originally bringing this essay to my attention.

[71] Ibid., p. 8.

> **indeed. Mr. Woodhouse told me of it. Mr. Woodhouse saw the letter, and he says he never saw such a handsome letter in his life.**" (*E*, p. 16)

Similar to this is the occasion when the news of Mrs Churchill's death reaches the inhabitants of Highbury:

> Mrs. Churchill, after being disliked at least twenty-five years, was now spoken of with compassionate allowances. In one point she was fully justified. She had never been admitted before to be seriously ill. The event acquitted her of all the fancifulness, and all the selfishness of imaginary complaints.
>
> **"Poor Mrs. Churchill! no doubt she had been suffering a great deal: more than any body had ever supposed—and continual pain would try the temper. It was a sad event—a great shock—with all her faults, what would Mr. Churchill do without her? Mr. Churchill's loss would be dreadful indeed. Mr. Churchill would never get over it."** (*E*, p. 422)

These passages seem indeed near equivalents. The second is written in free indirect speech, marked, as Austen's free indirect speech often is, with speech marks. The first, by contrast, is in the present tense, without attribution: in other words, free *direct* speech.[72] Jane Austen is well known for her subtle use of free *indirect* discourse, unprecedented in both quantity and quality, in the English novel. But her writing exemplifies in many ways, further to this, the fluid and contiguous relationship between free indirect and free direct styles.

## Free Direct/Indirect Discourse

Jane Austen's private writing provides evidence that, in her case, the origins of free indirect discourse lie in speech and in verbal imitation.[73] Jane Austen's letters bear out Roy Pascal's intuition that the propensity for "incidental mimicry" in Austen's fiction lay in everyday speech with a close confidant[74] and, likewise, Daniel P. Gunn's description of free indirect style as "a kind of narratorial *mimicry*, analogous to the flexible imitations of

[72] Moler has suggested that this passage may modulate into the voice of a specific speaker (Mr Woodhouse), ibid., p. 10.

[73] Monika Fludernik outlines the debates about the origins of free indirect discourse and endorses its oral roots in *The Fictions of Language and the Languages of Fiction: the Linguistic Representation of Speech and Consciousness* (London: Routledge, 1993), p. 93.

[74] Roy Pascal, *The Dual Voice: Free Indirect Speech and Its Functioning in the Nineteenth-Century European Novel* (Manchester: Manchester University Press, 1977), p. 57.

others' discourse we all practice in informal speech and expository prose".[75] This is the 'dual voice' theory that one voice takes on the characteristics of another.[76]

Austen would have absorbed much about free indirect discourse from literary pioneers of the technique, Frances Burney, Samuel Richardson and Henry Fielding.[77] But the lively mimicry that Austen engages in throughout her letters points to a conversational instinct informing her practice. In the same letter in which Austen describes the missing instances of "said he" and "said she" in *Pride and Prejudice*, for instance, she uses a free form of reported speech when she writes to Cassandra:

> What a vile Character M^r^ Digweed turns out, quite beyond anything & everything;—instead of going to Steventon they are to have a Dinnerparty next tuesday! (*L*, p. 211; 29 January 1813)

Austen discernibly adopts the locutions of another speaker here, as Deirdre Le Faye tells us, Harry Digweed's wife, Jane.[78] If Austen had used quotation marks (or another graphic indication),[79] the phrase "quite beyond anything & everything" would be more straightforwardly a quotation (though Cassandra would of course recognize the extent of her sister's lifting). This example shows the symbiotic nature of speech forms: how indirect speech can embed direct speech, while, without contextual knowledge, a quotation becomes something recognizable as free direct speech.

We see in Austen's letters, as here, that what she began in narratorial summary developed fluidly into the living voice. As Austen composed her fiction, too, there is manuscript evidence to show that indirect summary is spontaneously inflected with the direct speech of her characters. Or to put it differently, that she found her characters speaking through her. There are two examples in *The Watsons*. In the first, an account of young Charles

[75] Daniel P. Gunn, 'Free Indirect Discourse and Narrative Authority in *Emma*, *Narrative*, 12, 1 (2004), 35–54, pp. 35–6.

[76] See also Joe Bray 'The "Dual Voice" of Free Indirect Discourse: Report on a Reading Experiment', *Language and Literature*, 16, 1 (2007), 37–52, for an empirical endorsement of the identification of 'dual voice' when reading.

[77] For Richardson's possible influence on Austen in this respect, see Joe Bray, *The Epistolary Novel: Representations of Consciousness* (Routledge, 2003). On free indirect speech in Henry Fielding's *Joseph Andrews*, see Pascal, *The Dual Voice*, pp. 35–6.

[78] Deirdre Le Faye comments on how Austen quotes Mrs H. Digweed's "favourite expression": "beyond anything & everything" (*L*, p. 420, note 10).

[79] When Henry Austen was reading *Mansfield Park*, Austen wrote to Cassandra: "Henry has finished Mansfield Park, & his approbation has not lessened. He found the last half of the last volume extremely interesting." (*L*, p. 273; 9 March 1814). Does Austen's underscoring indicate her own emphasis or is she signaling for Cassandra the exact words that Henry used?

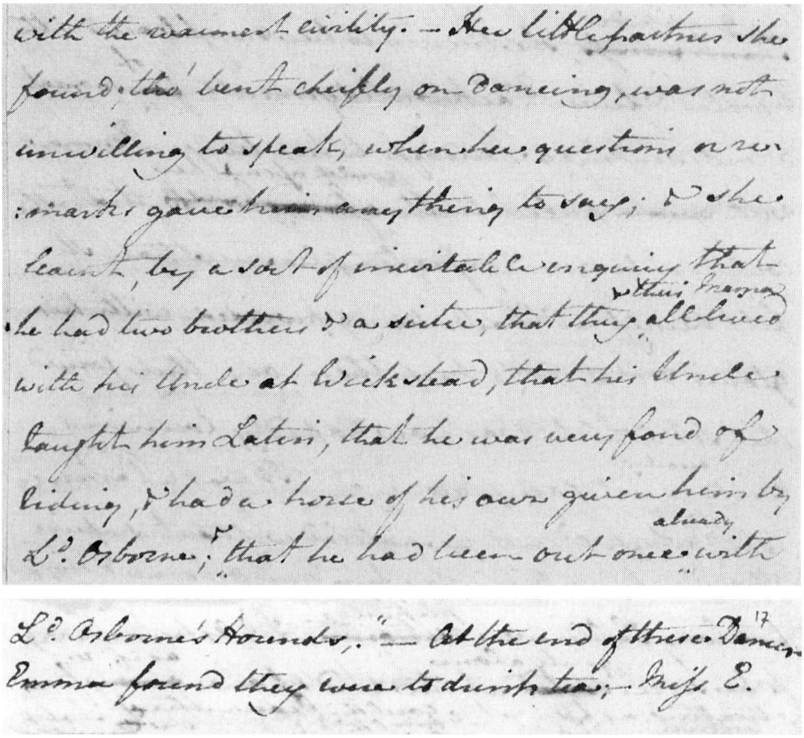
with the warmest civility. — Her little partner she
found, tho' bent cheifly on dancing, was not
unwilling to speak, when her questions or re-
:marks gave him any thing to say; & she
learnt, by a sort of inevitable enquiry that
he had two brothers & a sister, that they & their Mama all lived
with his Uncle at Wickstead, that his Uncle
taught him Latin, that he was very fond of
riding, & had a horse of his own given him by
Ld. Osborne; that he had been out once already with
Ld. Osborne's Hounds." — At the end of these Dances
Emma found they were to drink tea; — Miss E.

Illustration 3.6 Jane Austen, *The Watsons*, b4-4–5. By permission of the Bodleian Libraries, The University of Oxford. MS.Eng.e. 3764

Blake conversing excitedly with Emma begins in summary, but becomes increasingly possessed by the quality of a heard voice. While no quotation marks indicate the opening of the speech, they close it. This points to the development, in the act of writing, of a movement from indirect report to free indirect speech (with the sentence's childish accretive rhythms) and to something close to direct speech, which the closing quotation marks signal (see Illustration 3.6):

> Her little partner she found, tho' bent cheifly on dancing, was not unwilling to speak, when her questions or remarks gave him any thing to say;

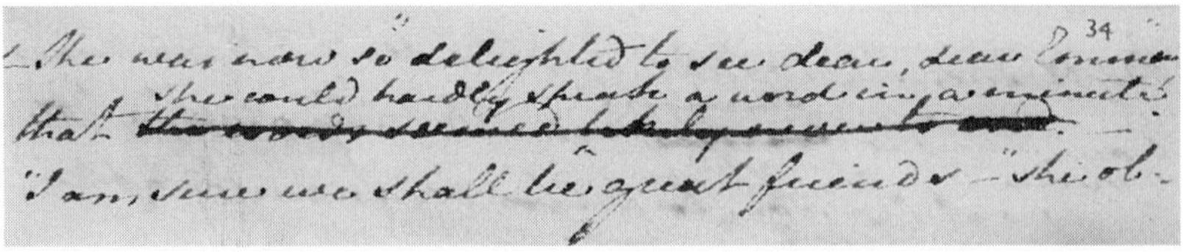
She was now so delighted to see dear, dear Emma
she could hardly speak a word in a minute
that ~~the words seemed likely never to end~~ —
"I am sure we shall be great friends —" she ob-

Illustration 3.7 Jane Austen, *The Watsons*, b8-5. By permission of the Bodleian Libraries, The University of Oxford. MS.Eng.e. 3764

> & she learnt, by a sort of inevitable enquiry that he had two brothers & a sister, that they ^ & their Mama all lived with his Uncle at Wickstead, that his Uncle taught him Latin, that he was very fond of riding, & had a horse of his own given him by L$^{d}$. Osborne; ^ & that he had been out once ^ already with L$^{d}$. Osborne's Hounds." (*W*, b4-4–5)

The half-and-halfness of this narrated speech, with only one half of its pair of quotation marks present, symbolizes appositely the essence of free indirect discourse which is in part indirect and in part direct. It also endorses Kathryn Sutherland's sense of Jane Austen as an immanent writer whose writing, on the evidence of the working drafts, was not significantly pre-planned.[80]

Later in *The Watsons*, Emma meets her sister, Margaret for the first time (see Illustration 3.7):

> She was now **so "delighted to see dear, dear Emma",** that ^ she could hardly speak a word in a minute ~~the words seemed likely never to end.~~ — "I am sure we shall be great friends—" she observed, with much sentiment, as they were sitting together. (*W*, b8-5)

In the first line, the quotation marks do not fall within the line and seem to have been added subsequently, hanging high over already-written letters (the "o" of "so" and between the "m" and "a" of "Emma").[81] The spoken quality of "delighted to see dear, dear Emma" within an indirect account is belatedly acknowledged by punctuation. There is a similar case, thirteen years later, in *Sanditon*, when Diana Parker first turns up in Trafalgar House (see Illustration 3.8):

[80] Sutherland, *Jane Austen's Textual Lives*, pp. 127–8.

[81] The position of the second of these speech marks may have been occasioned by reaching the edge of the page, but the positioning of the first seems disconnected from the flow of the prose.

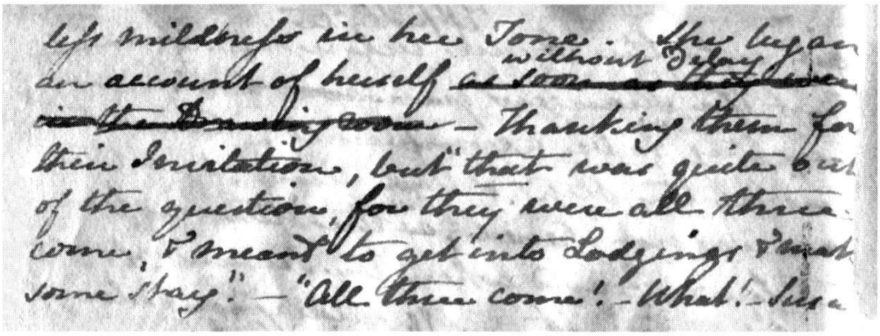
left mildness in her Tone. She began an account of herself ~~as soon as they were in the Drawing room~~ without Delay — Thanking them for their Invitation, but "that was quite out of the question, for they were all three come, & meant to get into Lodgings & make some stay." — "All three come! — What! — Sus...

Illustration 3.8 Jane Austen, *Sanditon*, b2-48. By permission of the Provost and Fellows of King's College, Cambridge (no accession number)

> She began an account of herself without delay. ~~as soon as they were in the Drawing room~~ — Thanking them for their Invitation, but "that was quite out of the question, for they were all three come, & meant to get into Lodgings & make some stay." (*S*, b2-48).

While Austen tends to give a lot of manuscript space to her quotation marks, as in the second of this pair, the first seems to be a retrospective thought, put in once Austen finds Diana's voice emerging. These examples again testify to a fluidity between the indirect and the direct, as Austen's subsequent punctuation transforms indirect narration into something that is notated as spoken.

While today quotation marks tend primarily to indicate direct speech, in the eighteenth and early nineteenth centuries indirect forms of speech could also be distinguished in this way. In Austen's fiction, free indirect discourse is often signalled by quotation marks.[82] While quotation marks – whether by virtue of their presence or their absence – feature rather rarely in expository accounts of free indirect discourse, Roy Pascal describes Austen's use of them as showing her awareness of "the difference between this stylistic form [free indirect speech] and others, for instance, simple indirect speech or narratorial description; and further, it shows that the author was aware of its nearness to direct speech, even though the third person is used".[83] Quotation marks may indeed provide a clue to Austen's sense of distinction between her speech forms, but that she doesn't *always* mark free indirect discourse with quotation marks equally shows their closeness and hybridity.

[82] Page, *Speech in the English Novel*, pp. 30–1, p. 38.
[83] Pascal, *The Dual Voice*, p. 46.

Free direct speech has also been identified as inner, present-tense monologue.[84] Understood in this way, another form of continuity between an indirect and a direct style can be identified in Austen's fiction. As in the following example from *Emma*, free indirect discourse and free direct discourse offer different intensities of the same train of thought:

> Emma sat down to think and be miserable.—It was a wretched business, indeed!—Such an overthrow of every thing she had been wishing for!—Such a development of every thing most unwelcome!—Such a blow for Harriet!—That was the worst of all. Every part of it brought pain and humiliation, of some sort or other [...] and she would gladly have submitted to feel yet more mistaken—more in error—more disgraced by mis-judgment, than she actually was, could the effects of her blunders have been confined to herself.
>
> **"If I had not persuaded Harriet into liking the man, I could have born any thing. He might have doubled his presumption to me—But poor Harriet!"**
>
> How she could have been so deceived! (*E*, p. 145)

There are questions here as to whether Emma thinks first and then speaks aloud the words given in the direct form between quotation marks (marked here in bold). Or do the words in quotation marks represent a different level of consciousness: a thought that is more conclusive and therefore more vividly articulated in Emma's mind? In *Sense and Sensibility*, too, a movement between free indirect and free direct discourse similarly suggests such differing levels of consciousness. The following is an early instance of free indirect discourse in published Austen's fiction, as the narrator's summary becomes infused with the deductive and increasingly excited locutions of Elinor:

> But—it was *not* Colonel Brandon—neither his air—nor his height. Were it possible, she should say it must be Edward. She looked again. He had just dismounted;—she could not be mistaken;—it *was* Edward. She moved away and sat down. "He comes from Mr. Pratt's purposely to see us. I *will* be calm; I *will* be mistress of myself". (*S&S*, pp. 405–6)

The free direct discourse seems to be used here, in part, to resolve the ambiguity of free indirect discourse. That we have been encountering Elinor's inner speech, rather than simply the narrator's summary, is

[84] Monika Fludernik describes Brian McHale's account of 'free direct discourse' in the realm of thought representation as synonymous with inner monologue, not marked by typographical means or third-person narrative framing; *The Fictions of Language and the Languages of Fiction*, p. 290. Fludernik refers to McHale's 'Free Indirect Discourse: a Survey of Recent Accounts', *Politics and Theory of Literature*, 3 (1978), 249–87.

confirmed by the direct speech in which this extract culminates. The direct speech rounds off the sense that this is Elinor's own excitement, and the combined view of narrator and character in the indirect mode is narrowed down to the singular 'I'. We may choose to describe Elinor's words, "He comes from Mr. Pratt's purposely to see us. I *will* be calm; I *will* be mistress of myself", simply as direct speech, with an implied reporting clause (said Elinor, exclaimed Elinor), and this is a valid interpretation of all 'free' forms of discourse. But, given the context, it is just as likely that Elinor thought rather than said these words. Freed from explicit narratorial direction, we do not know definitively whether her instructions to herself were thought or whether they were said aloud.

For all of these links between (free) indirect and direct discourse, commentators tend to agree that two strongly definable grammatical features distinguish them: indirect speech utilizes the third person and past-tense forms and direct speech the first person and present-tense forms. But in *Emma*, among the published novels, there is an episode in which Jane Austen ostentatiously removes these basic distinguishing elements of direct and indirect speech to create an extraordinarily mimetic and experimental depiction of the entangledness of human interaction and exchange.

## *Emma* and the Subjectless Sentence

The "voice of Highbury" is one that can be heard in the free direct and the free indirect mode. In the former,

> "I suppose you have heard of the handsome letter Mr. Frank Churchill had written to Mrs. Weston? I understand it was a very handsome letter, indeed"

the subject 'I' is unspecified and is representative of the collective. Either it is an exchangeable 'I' denoting different speakers with near-identical sentiments. Or the quoted speech typifies a collective view. Even though multiple speakers may be indicated here, quotation marks include them all in one utterance. In the latter, free indirect form,

> "[…] It was a sad event—a great shock—with all her faults, what would Mr. Churchill do without her? Mr. Churchill's loss would be dreadful indeed. Mr. Churchill would never get over it"

the indirect voice is indicated through back shifted tense rather than person "Mr. Churchill would never get over it" rather than conversation in the present ("Mr. Churchill will never get over it"). The closeness of the two forms is apparent in the opening of this second extract where the speech of Highbury could be direct or indirect, and sourced to a singular speaker or to several:

> "Poor Mrs. Churchill! no doubt she had been suffering a great deal: more than any body had ever supposed [...]"

But in one of the most innovative passages in her fiction, Austen makes free indirect and free direct speech indistinguishable over a prolonged period. This is in Mrs Elton's 'monologue'.

The inhabitants of Highbury have been invited to pick strawberries at Donwell Abbey. Mrs Elton leads the party and her chat dominates the group. Mrs Elton's monologue is introduced by Emma's self-satisfied musings about Donwell Abbey and Isabella's marriage to Mr John Knightley, until she like the others has to assemble at the strawberry beds (see Illustration 3.9):

> These were pleasant feelings, and she walked about and indulged them till it was necessary to do as the others did, and collect round the strawberry beds.—The whole party were assembled, excepting Frank Churchill, who was expected every moment from Richmond; and Mrs. Elton, in all her apparatus of happiness, her large bonnet and her basket, was very ready to lead the way in gathering, accepting, or talking—strawberries, and only strawberries, could now be thought or spoken of. —"The best fruit in England—every body's favourite—always wholesome.—These the finest beds and finest sorts.—Delightful to gather for one's self—the only way of really enjoying them.—Morning decidedly the best time—never tired—every sort good—hautboy infinitely superior—no comparison—the others hardly eatable—hautboys very scarce—Chili preferred—white wood finest flavour of all—price of strawberries in London—abundance about Bristol—Maple Grove—cultivation—beds when to be renewed—gardeners thinking exactly different—no general rule—gardeners never to be put out of their way—delicious fruit—only too rich to be eaten much of—inferior to cherries—currants more refreshing—only objection to gathering strawberries the stooping—glaring sun—tired to death—could bear it no longer—must go and sit in the shade."
>
> Such, for half an hour, was the conversation—interrupted only once by Mrs. Weston, who came out, in her solicitude after her son-in-law, to inquire if he were come—(*E*, pp. 389–90)

Mrs Elton's voice is undoubtedly singled out here: Bristol and Maple Grove pin particular utterances to her. But otherwise, the provenance of speech in this passage is profoundly uncertain. As has been noted by Kathryn Sutherland, there is a significant complexity to the passage in that Mrs Elton's eulogy may be filtered through Emma's mind: "What we appear to hear is Mrs Elton's voice unmediated. But her speech is

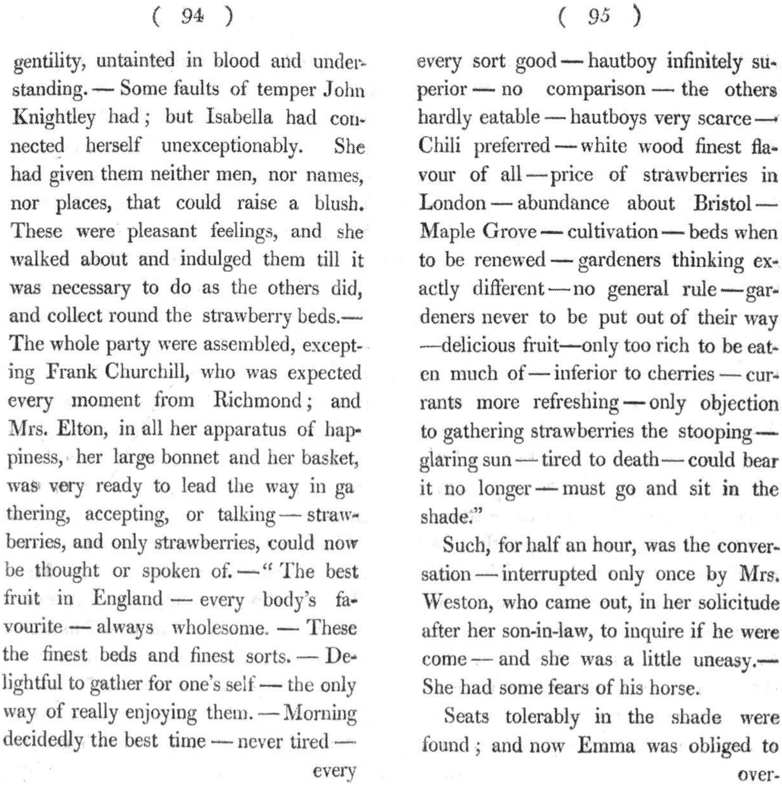

( 94 )

gentility, untainted in blood and understanding.—Some faults of temper John Knightley had; but Isabella had connected herself unexceptionably. She had given them neither men, nor names, nor places, that could raise a blush. These were pleasant feelings, and she walked about and indulged them till it was necessary to do as the others did, and collect round the strawberry beds.—The whole party were assembled, excepting Frank Churchill, who was expected every moment from Richmond; and Mrs. Elton, in all her apparatus of happiness, her large bonnet and her basket, was very ready to lead the way in gathering, accepting, or talking—strawberries, and only strawberries, could now be thought or spoken of.—"The best fruit in England—every body's favourite—always wholesome.—These the finest beds and finest sorts.—Delightful to gather for one's self—the only way of really enjoying them.—Morning decidedly the best time—never tired—every

( 95 )

every sort good—hautboy infinitely superior—no comparison—the others hardly eatable—hautboys very scarce—Chili preferred—white wood finest flavour of all—price of strawberries in London—abundance about Bristol—Maple Grove—cultivation—beds when to be renewed—gardeners thinking exactly different—no general rule—gardeners never to be put out of their way—delicious fruit—only too rich to be eaten much of—inferior to cherries—currants more refreshing—only objection to gathering strawberries the stooping—glaring sun—tired to death—could bear it no longer—must go and sit in the shade."

Such, for half an hour, was the conversation—interrupted only once by Mrs. Weston, who came out, in her solicitude after her son-in-law, to inquire if he were come—and she was a little uneasy.—She had some fears of his horse.

Seats tolerably in the shade were found; and now Emma was obliged to over-

Illustration 3.9 Jane Austen, *Emma: a Novel* (London: John Murray, 1816), vol. 3, pp. 94–5. By permission of the Syndics of Cambridge University Library. Keynes.K.2.4-6

edited in such a way as at least to suggest that it comes to the reader only in snatches. As the surrounding paragraph shows, it also comes to our ears by way of Emma's, and it is by no means certain that what we overhear is not after all Emma's selective mimicry of Mrs Elton".[85] More than this, I would propose that it is by no means certain that what we overhear, through Emma or freestanding, is Mrs Elton alone. Can the long passage between quotation marks be described as a 'monologue' at all?

Remarkably, there is no indication of person in this passage. Austen avoids personal pronouns entirely. She also, again remarkably, avoids any

[85] Sutherland, *Jane Austen's Textual Lives*, p. 307.

main verbs, until the last two clauses. Dashes repeatedly take the place of subject and verb:

> —never tired

In other words, Austen avoids those key grammatical indicators of person – pronoun and verb form – and in the absence of verb *tense* we do not know whether this is direct or indirect speech. For instance:

> —Morning decidedly the best time—never tired—every sort good—hautboy infinitely superior

This can be completed as direct speech (I am never tired); indirect speech (she was never tired):

> —Morning decidedly the best time **[I am/she was]** never tired—

Or to take another example:

> "The best fruit in England—every body's favourite—always wholesome"
> "The best fruit in England **[they are/they were]** every body's favourite—always wholesome"

Do the gaps read, assertively "they are every body's favourite" or indirectly "they were every body's favourite"? This persistent absence of person and tense is striking. A 'sentence', in virtue of its capital letter and full-stop – such as "**These the finest beds** and finest sorts." – is compressed to be verbless.

Whether direct or indirect, without the attribution of person it is conceivable that the passage contains snapshots of communal discussion:

> hautboy infinitely superior—no comparison—the others hardly eatable—hautboys very scarce

These fragments could be the confirming echoes of other members of the party, following Mrs Elton's "lead".[86] The dashes stand in the place of any definitive attribution or a line break. After all, the narrator twice emphasizes the communal nature of this expedition: "[t]he whole party were assembled"; "Such [...] was the conversation", though this could be understood ironically, if Mrs Elton has spoken over them all. We have already encountered in *Emma* how group speech is collectively embraced by quotation marks and how the manuscript of *The Watsons* provides

[86] Casey Finch and Peter Bowen say apropos the workings of gossip that there is "the establishment of a "naturally" enforced hierarchy, *within* its circle of inclusion, by which certain citizens are privileged over others"; '"The Tittle-Tattle of Highbury": Gossip and the Free Indirect Style in *Emma*', *Representations*, 31 (1990), 1–18, pp. 7–8.

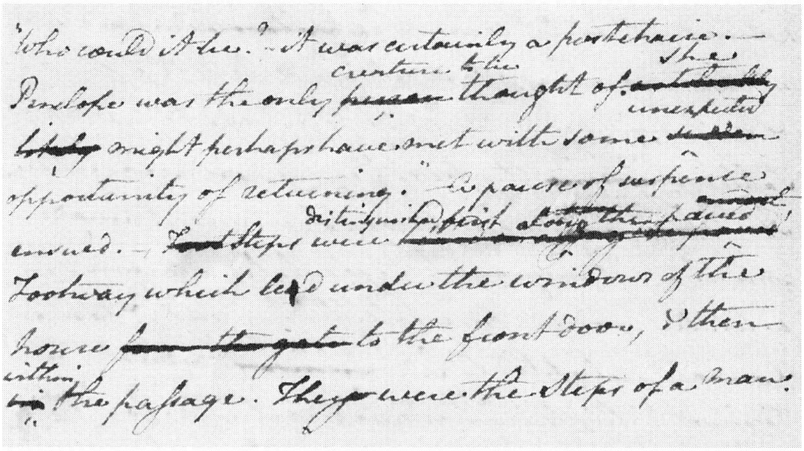

Illustration 3.10 Jane Austen, *The Watsons*, b9-5. By permission of the Bodleian Libraries, The University of Oxford. MS.Eng.e. 3764

evidence that Austen herself punctuated group speech in this way (see Illustration 3.10):

> "Who could it be? —it was certainly a postchaise. —Penelope was the only creature to be thought of. She might perhaps have met with some unexpected opportunity of returning." —A pause of suspense ensued. (*LM*, p. 126)

Alan Palmer asks, "Can two or more minds form a cognitive unit of whatever sort, however casual and ephemeral?"[87] Palmer has advocated the importance in fiction of the depiction of intermental thinking, that is, thinking distributed across a group. In *Persuasion*, the "party" is an ever-shifting category of people in which Anne is involved, that makes decisions and can act together.[88] However, it also seems that Austen's interest in group thought is bound up innovatively with her speech presentation. Casey Finch and Peter Bowen have suggested that, like gossip, free indirect style in Austen's fiction "blurs the narrative distinctions between objective and subjective discourse", and thus Austen "blurs too the proprietary difference between communities and individuals".[89] The strawberry-picking episode exemplifies a blurring of community and individual: the voice of the individual, Mrs Elton, is vividly apprehended,

[87] Palmer, *Fictional Minds*, p. 162.

[88] Alan Palmer, *Social Minds in the Novel* (Columbus: Ohio State University Press, 2010), pp. 147–50.

[89] Finch and Bowen, '"The Tittle-Tattle of Highbury"', p. 10.

yet in places it becomes indistinguishable from a much wider scope of speakers. This passage shows the possibility of displaying collective, messy speaking and also innovatively reveals the character of group thought, the mood of a collective, shaping itself around an individual, and working in consensus, confirming each other, as well as changing their minds, growing tired together with the activity they are undertaking.[90]

It is only at the end of the strawberry-picking passage that finite verbs are used: "could bear it no longer—must go and sit in the shade". While free indirect discourse here seems confirmed by the verb form "could" (rather than "*can* bear it no longer"), person remains in doubt – "[She/they] could bear it no longer". "Must", however, destabilizes things again. "Must" does not inflect for person or tense, and therefore capaciously allows past/present, singular/plural, direct/indirect forms: "[I/she/they] must go and sit in the shade". The last phrase may even demonstrate, in the manner of passages we have already encountered, a concluding shift to the present tense. There seems no grammatical or orthographical reason to read this passage as spoken entirely by Mrs Elton (though that is not to say definitely that it is not). On the contrary, the grammar of this long passage works to *prohibit* any conclusion that there is a single speaker. The concluding verbs do not shut down or negate the possible multiplicity of free forms that precede it. Austen's refusal to situate the sources of speech from the outset of this passage exemplifies the heterogeneity and spontaneity of discourse provenance, in a prose that is alive with unsourced voices.

What we encounter then in the strawberry-picking episode in *Emma* is a virtuosic experiment in non-attribution. Austen explores the porousness between monologue (Mrs Elton), inner monologue (Emma) and a communal conversation involving multiple speakers. She explores the porousness between direct speech and indirect report, as well as between the single speaker and the group. It is significant that the narrator introduces this passage as one potentially of thought as much of speech: "strawberries, and only strawberries, could now be thought or spoken of". "The best fruit in England" could be a phrase uttered by Mrs Elton or ventriloquized by Emma, it could be spoken or thought by any individual in the party, or it could represent a communal echo (spoken individually by

[90] It is even conceivable that in places narratorial summary can merge with the other voices. "Chili preferred" may be a phrase uttered by Mrs Elton or someone else, "Chili [is much to be] preferred", or the narrator summarizing the suddenly prevailing counterview in favour of chili rather than hautboy. Similarly, in the last example from *The Watsons*, "Penelope was the only creature to be thought of" reads as narrative summary within quotation marks. Visually and grammatically the whole passage from *Emma* even seems to resemble summarizing chapter headings. I am grateful to Mark Faulkner for suggesting this last point to me.

more than one speaker) or it could signify the collective mindset. Not only does Austen manage to create in this passage a tour de force of stylistic innovation, it is one of the funniest episodes in her fiction.

## Blunders

The "greatest blunder" in the printing of *Pride and Prejudice* was the compression of two speeches into one. And yet, it is exactly this – the compression of multiple speeches into one – that is an innovative and complex aspect of Austen's style. In *Emma*, Austen also returned to the word "blunder", almost obsessively, at one point using it to dramatize the misattribution of speech.

Frank Churchill attributes a letter containing news of Mr Perry's plans to set up a carriage to Mrs Weston. She denies ever having written such a letter or being in possession of such information. Frank dismisses the matter as a dream, while Mrs Bates acknowledges that she had been privy to such a plan some time ago, and is unable to promise that she hadn't mentioned it to someone or other. Frank goes on to send Jane a message through a box of alphabets:

> The word was *blunder*; and as Harriet exultingly proclaimed it, there was a blush on Jane's cheek which gave it a meaning not otherwise ostensible. Mr. Knightley connected it with the dream; but how it could all be, was beyond his comprehension. (*E*, p. 377)

The last sentence here establishes Mr Knightley as the observing consciousness, carefully examining the participants in this episode of the carriage. Frank, by contrast, comes out poorly in the matter of being mindful about others, failing even to remember what Jane has written to him, in letters one would hope he might cherish. He is unable to distinguish the bearer of the information he possesses.

The majority of the fifteen uses of "blunder" in *Emma* relate to individuals' – especially Emma's – ability or inability to discern another's character correctly. 'Blunder' is used when Mr Knightley and Mrs Weston discuss Emma's attachment to Harriet ("she will make no lasting blunder" says Mrs Weston misguidedly [p. 40]). The word is repeated when John Knightley suggests to Emma that Mr Elton's attentions might be directed towards her rather than Harriet, while Emma ends up berating herself (four times) about her "blunder" in mistaking Mr Elton's affections. Emma also uses "blunder" to describe her mistake in confiding in Frank Churchill her suspicions about Jane Fairfax and Mr Dixon. Finally, Emma's realization that she has been blind to her affections for Mr Knightley is described as a blunder. In each case, Emma, priding herself on her ability to penetrate into the characters and affections of others, acknowledges that her analysis of character is consistently misdirected. Mr Elton admires Emma herself and not Harriet; Frank admires Jane and not Emma; and she does not admire Frank but Mr Knightley. One character is consistently mistaken for another and Emma has to face her inability to assess character successfully.

In another important passage in the novel relating to blunders, Jane deflects the unwelcome attentions of Mrs Elton by introducing the topic of the post-office with Mr John Knightley:

> "The post-office is a wonderful establishment!" said she.—"The regularity and dispatch of it! If one thinks of all that it has to do, and all that it does so well, it is really astonishing!"
>
> "It is certainly very well regulated."
>
> "So seldom that any **negligence or blunder appears**! So seldom that a letter, among the thousands that are constantly passing about the kingdom, **is even carried wrong**—and not one in a million, I suppose, actually lost! And when one considers the variety of hands, and of bad hands too, **that are to be deciphered**, it increases the wonder!"
>
> "The clerks grow expert from habit. —They must begin with some quickness of sight and hand, and exercise improves them. If you want any further explanation," continued he, smiling, "they are paid for it. That is the key to a great deal of capacity. The public pays and must be served well." (p. 320)

This conversation leads to a discussion of the discernment of hand-writing:

> "I have heard it asserted," said John Knightley, "that the same sort of handwriting often prevails in a family; and where the same master teaches, it is natural enough. But for that reason, I should imagine the likeness must be chiefly confined to the females, for boys have very little teaching after an early age, and scramble into any hand they can get. Isabella and Emma, I think, do write very much alike. I have not always known their writing apart."
>
> "Yes," said his brother hesitatingly, "there is a likeness. I know what you mean—but Emma's hand is the strongest."
>
> "Isabella and Emma both write beautifully," said Mr. Woodhouse; "and always did. And so does poor Mrs. Weston"—with half a sigh and half a smile at her. (pp. 320–1)

John Mullan describes Austen "pursuing" the word "blunder" through *Emma*, in the manner of Shakespeare, "testing [a word's] powers".[91] The word also resonates beyond *Emma*, evoking the "greatest blunder" of *Pride and Prejudice* where two speeches are made into one.

[91] John Mullan, *What Matters in Jane Austen? Twenty Crucial Puzzles Solved* (London: Bloomsbury Publishing, 2012), p. 213.

There is an intriguing correspondence between Austen's disparagement of "dull elves" who cannot with a little ingenuity work out who speaks when;[92] her compositors' inability to distinguish Jane's speech from Elizabeth's; and this discussion of family members declaring their inability to tell one Woodhouse sister from another. Mr Knightley is here a superior reader in knowing Emma and Isabella's hands apart, unlike their own father and one of their own husbands. True, it is possible that Mr Knightley only believes he can tell them apart because of his own preference for Emma. His statement is one way in which he is able, perhaps even unconsciously, to declare his attraction. But the novel as a whole dwells on Knightley's sound abilities in reading and distinguishing character, even, as it turns out here, 'character' in a written sense. While Austen deliberately obfuscates the differences between other of her fictional sisters – the Steeles, the Bertrams, the Musgroves – the ability to know the difference between Elizabeth and Jane, Emma and Isabella, Anne and Elizabeth is a significant part of her fiction's purpose, that is, to borrow a phrase from *Persuasion*, the "discernment of character".

This discussion of blunders in *Emma* reflects back then on *Pride and Prejudice*'s printing "blunder". In praising the post-office, Jane acknowledges the efficiency of systematic procedures in the circulation of letters: "So seldom that any negligence or blunder appears! [...] And when one considers the variety of hands, and of bad hands too, that are to be deciphered." These words are entirely relevant to the printing industry too, where manuscript hands have to be deciphered. Likewise Mr John Knightley's practical sense of the professional demands that ensure the accuracy of those working in the distribution of letters is relevant to the work of composition in the printing house: "The clerks [...] must begin with some quickness of sight and hand, and exercise improves them". This latent analogy between the blunders that occur in *Emma* and those that can occur in the process of printing novels, is endorsed by Frank Churchill's blunder over Perry's carriage. That he chooses to spell out his blunder to Jane through the sorting and distribution of letters similarly evokes the printer's hand. The business of postal clerks and printing compositors is to discern character in the sense of hand.

In *Persuasion,* the narrator tells us that "[t]here is a quickness of perception in some, a nicety in the discernment of character, a natural

[92] Mullan alludes to the dull elves when he describes Frank Churchill's covertly acknowledged blunder over Perry's carriage allowing a "really ingenious interpreter to understand just what has been going on"; ibid., p. 213.

penetration, in short, which no experience in others can equal" (*P*, p. 271). Austen seemed to show equanimity in the fact of the great "blunder" of *Pride and Prejudice* "where two speeches are made into one", where the compositor could not follow Austen's hand in terms of her orthographic conventions *nor* her character portrayal. Nonetheless, Austen continued to experiment with the omission of speech attribution, evolving in myriad ways the merging of variant speeches or speakers into one.[93] The 'discernment of character' thus is as much the business of her readers, as her characters and her compositors. In fact, she may even have seen the creative potential of the compositor's blunder in *Pride and Prejudice* for her own experiments in speech and as material for her own plots.

93 Stuart Burrows has described how *Persuasion* "betrays a remarkable lack of interest in specifying who is speaking and when", in 'The Privatization of Public Life' (para. 10), as well as pointing to the novel's blurring of direct and indirect speech (para. 9).

# *Conclusion*
## Sanditon's *Shorthand*

The style of *Sanditon* has long produced critical disquiet. Among the many puzzles of Austen's enigmatic last work is the compressed, fragmentary quality of its language. In its early reception, the work's "coarse strokes"[1] and 'sketches'[2] were signs of an early stage of drafting that Austen would inevitably have wanted to revise, while by the late twentieth century, the stylistic fragmentation signalled a bold new experimental phase of writing. At the other extreme and more recently, *Sanditon* has been described as the breakdown of Austen's style.[3] My suggestion, in these closing pages, is that the elliptical compressions that characterize many parts of *Sanditon* provide a clue to a long-standing style of composition.[4]

Reginald Brimley Johnson's 1934 preface to *Sanditon*, published in the seventh volume of his *Works of Jane Austen*, exemplifies an early critical dismissal of the fragment's style. While R. W. Chapman, *Sanditon*'s first editor in 1925, deemed the fragment a first draft, Johnson moved the compositional identity of the manuscript back in time. *Sanditon* was not even a rough sketch but "the beginning of a rough sketch", a series of "shorthand notes", "a few interesting and suggestive notes for reference" that would eventually form the basis of a draft. The "carelessness" of this manuscript revealed an author "merely jotting down ideas for characters and scenes as they came into her mind without a thought for sequence

[1] R. W. Chapman thought that Austen would have "smoothed these coarse strokes", in *Jane Austen: Facts and Problems* (Oxford: Clarendon Press, 1948), p. 208.

[2] James Edward Austen-Leigh, in the first public acknowledgement of the existence of *Sanditon*, described the characters as "sketched in with a vigorous hand", in *A Memoir of Jane Austen* [...] *Second Edition to Which Is Added Lady Susan and Fragments of Two Other Unfinished Tales by Miss Austen* (London: Richard Bentley and Son, 1871), p. 182.

[3] D. A. Miller, *Jane Austen, or The Secret of Style* (Princeton, NJ, and Oxford: Princeton University Press, 2003), p. 80.

[4] I have written about this subject also in 'Jane Austen Jotting: The Manuscript of *Sanditon* and the Question of Style', *Persuasions On-Line*, 38, 2 (2018).

or arrangement".[5] Johnson pointed to features of the manuscript style that went beyond characterization alone, although the ampersands and dashes (which he may have had in mind when he described *Sanditon*'s "broken sentences") are both now established as routine parts of Austen's compositional practice. In the 1960s, Brian Southam overturned the received sense of the novel's incipient status in his study of Austen's literary manuscripts. Rather, he transformed the aspects of *Sanditon*'s writing that seem so unlike Austen into a new thematics and stylistics of disconnection. Austen's indebtedness to an eighteenth-century prose tradition fully gives way to the fragmentary and elliptical: "a new, experimental style".[6]

It is Mr Parker's language that best emblematizes the elliptical tendencies of *Sanditon* and he is at his most disjointed in the novel's two opening chapters where he conveys to Mr Heywood his passion for the newly established resort. His syntactical unorthodoxy allowed Tony Tanner ingeniously to conflate topographical and grammatical erosion:

> His [Mr Parker's] speech is conspicuously marked by asyndeton (i.e. omitting particles which usually begin sentences). This is exactly right; for in his hurry he does 'omit' (forget) 'beginnings' and connectives. He is no longer concerned with the syntactic rules which govern the correct linkings and relationships and positionings of society. Among other things, Sanditon is built on – and by – careless and eroding grammar. Indeed, one could say that Sanditon is Asyndeton built large.[7]

Mr Parker's language is therefore thematically pertinent to his situation. As the chief speculator promoting the new town, his grammar collapses, like the terrain that Austen is keen to point out is "half rock half sand", such that asyndeton proves a form of moral critique foreboding a damaging speculative collapse. D. A. Miller continues the analysis more pejoratively: this is prose, perhaps like the development itself, of "shoddy construction".[8]

[5] Jane Austen, *Sanditon, The Watsons, Lady Susan; and Other Miscellanea; with an Introduction by R. Brimley Johnson* (London: J. M. Dent & Sons Ltd, 1934), p. x.

[6] Brian Southam, *Jane Austen's Literary Manuscripts: a Study of the Novelist's Development through the Surviving Papers* (London and New York: the Athlone Press, 1964), pp. 108, 125.

[7] Tony Tanner, *Jane Austen* (London: Macmillan, 1986), p. 260.

[8] Miller, *Jane Austen, or The Secret of Style*, p. 78.

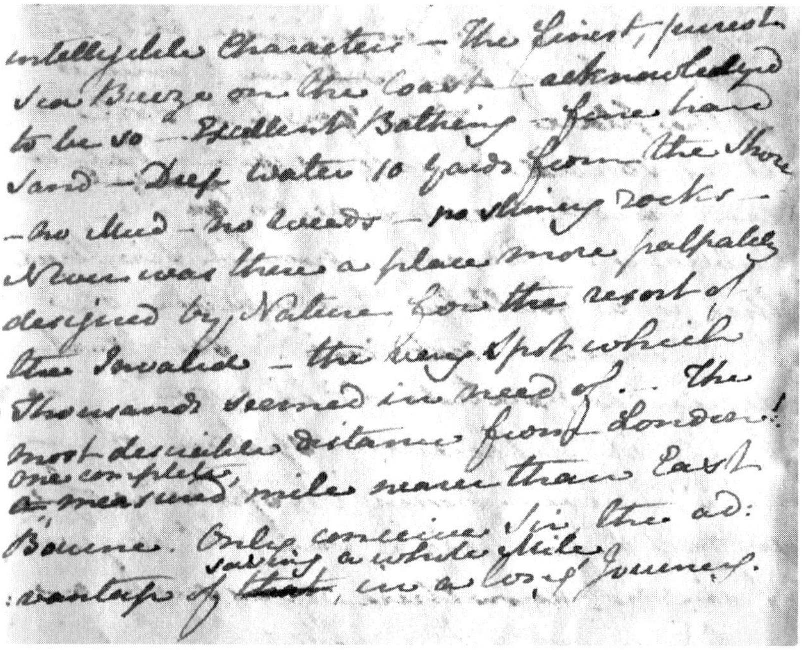
intelligible Characters – The finest, purest
Sea Breeze on the Coast – acknowledged
to be so – Excellent Bathing – fine hard
Sand – Deep Water 10 yards from the Shore
– no Mud – no Weeds – no slimey rocks –
Never was there a place more palpably
designed by Nature for the resort of
the Invalid – the very Spot which
Thousands seemed in need of. – The
most desirable distance from London!
One complete,
a measured mile nearer than East
Bourne. Only conceive Sir, the ad:
saving a whole Mile
:vantage of ~~that~~, in a Journey.

Illustration C.1 Jane Austen, *Sanditon*, b1-13. By permission of the Provost and Fellows of King's College, Cambridge (no accession number)

This is part of Mr Parker's speech which Tanner and Miller describe (see Illustration C.1):

> "Our Coast too full"—repeated M$^{r}$. P.—On that point perhaps we may not ‸ totally disagree; — At least there are enough. […] Such a place as Sanditon Sir, I may say was wanted, was called for.—Nature had marked it out—had spoken in most intelligible Characters—The finest, purest Sea Breeze on the Coast—acknowledged to be so—Excellent Bathing—fine hard Sand—Deep Water 10 yards from the Shore—no Mud—no Weeds—no slimey rocks—Never was there a place more palpably designed by Nature for the resort of the Invalid—the very Spot which Thousands seemed in need of.—The most desirable distance from London! ~~a~~ ‸ One complete, measured mile nearer than East Bourne. (*S*, b1-12–13)

Mr Parker produces a series of promotional highlights that summarize Sanditon's blessings. But while he begins by addressing Mr Heywood directly here – and resumes with the direct address at the end of this extract – the sentence fragments that accrue in between make it uncertain whether Mr Parker continues in direct speech or whether the speech is an indirect summary ('[He believed that] Nature had marked it out'). The possibility of indirect speech becomes more exposed, the more Mr Parker becomes rhetorically fervent:

> Never was there a place more palpably designed by Nature for the resort of the Invalid —the very Spot which Thousands seemed in need of.

Mr Parker speaks in the language of advertising, but what advertiser distances their wares by situating them in the past? Why would Mr Parker promote Sanditon's benefits historically ("the very Spot which Thousands seemed in need of") rather than in the here and now: the very Spot which Thousands seem in need of. The words are conceivable as direct speech, but the shift to the past tense seems as likely to register an indirect voice, with the main verb and subject elided, '[it was] the very spot which Thousands seemed in need of'.

Mr Parker is an extreme example of this elliptical speech characteristic, but it is less commonly noted, and indeed is less obvious, that a fragmented syntax is also associated with the more sensible characters. In these opening chapters, Mr Parker seems to be contrasted with the solid Mr Heywood, who disputes the flighty characteristics of his interlocutor, preferring a stable and traditional home life and economy. But Mr Heywood, in the first chapter, adopts speech patterns that are also grammatically elided and paratactic, as he gives his view on seaside towns (see Illustration C.2):

> How they can half of them be filled, is the wonder! ~~amazing to me~~! Where People can be found with Money or ~~&~~ Time to go to them!—Bad things for a ~~any~~ Country;— ^—sure to raise the price of Provisions & make the Poor good for nothing ^as—I dare say you find, ~~it so~~ Sir." (*S*, b1-11)

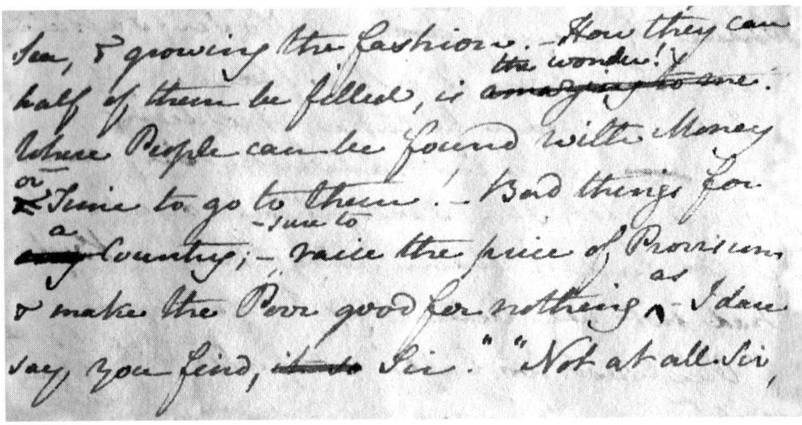

Sea, & growing the fashion. — How they can
half of them be filled, is the wonder! ~~amazing to me~~.
Where People can be found with Money
or ~~&~~ Time to go to them! — Bad things for
a ~~any~~ Country; — sure to raise the price of Provisions,
& make the Poor good for nothing ^ as — I dare
say, you find, ~~it so~~ Sir." "Not at all Sir,

Illustration C.2 Jane Austen, *Sanditon*, b1-11. By permission of the Provost and Fellows of King's College, Cambridge (no accession number)

Mr Heywood's speech is more heavily revised than Mr Parker's. But the result is equally a fragmentary propensity, as he elides subjects and finite verbs: "Bad things for a country—sure to—raise the price of Provisions". If Mr Heywood were speaking in something other than a strange exclamatory muttering, surely he would say '[they are] Bad things for a country' '[they are] sure to raise the price of provisions'. The subject and verb have been elided, and with them the indication as to whether this is direct speech or reported indirectly – '[He thought they were] Bad things for a country'. Austen's addition of "sure to" before "raise the price of provisions" reveals that Mr Heywood's utterance was even more truncated in its first iteration.

The experimental quality that Southam attributed to *Sanditon* must be modified by accounts of Austen's propensity towards elliptical language elsewhere. Most strikingly, the fragmentary and loquacious speeches of *Sanditon* are similar to the experiments with speech in *Emma* and Mr Parker's grammatical elisions, the heavy dashes and the uncertainties about direct or indirect speech recall the elliptical strawberry-picking scene that I detailed in the last chapter. Looking at this extended passage in *Emma*, with its scope for multiple speech forms, Mr Parker's fragments seem rather mild than experimental or new. Kathryn Sutherland has also pointed to something like *Sanditon*'s fragmentary style in *Persuasion*, as Austen uses short clauses to capture the mounting pace and emotional breathlessness of Louisa's fall from the Cobb:

> He advised her against it, thought the jar too great; but no, he reasoned and talked in vain; she smiled and said, "I am determined I will:" he put out his hands; she was too precipitate by half a second, she fell on the pavement on the Lower Cobb, and was taken up lifeless![9]

Indeed, from *Sense and Sensibility*, Austen deployed short, staccato clauses and dashes to convey mounting emotion.[10] Interestingly, Sutherland describes the larger passage in *Persuasion*, from which this extract is taken, in the same words as Brimley Johnson, though without the dismay. Sutherland describes how the passage is "like a sequence of notes for a scene before the imposition of subordination". The writing suggests "the dissolution of style, its decomposition into the jottings and memoranda that precede writing".[11]

[9] Sutherland, *Jane Austen's Textual Lives*, p. 173.

[10] "But—it was *not* Colonel Brandon—neither his air—nor his height. Were it possible, she should say it must be Edward. She looked again. He had just dismounted;—she could not be mistaken;—it *was* Edward. [...] "He comes from Mr. Pratt's purposely to see us. I *will* be calm; I *will* be mistress of myself"" (*S&S*, pp. 405–6).

[11] Sutherland, *Jane Austen's Textual Lives*, p. 173.

Was, then, Reginald Brimley Johnson so wrong? Is it possible to entertain the idea of *Sanditon* as containing, in places at least, Austen's notes and jottings? That Mr Heywood's staccato utterances are here like Mr Parker's suggests a compositional manner rather than an individuated stylistic choice according to character. Furthermore, reading Mr Parker in manuscript leads to questions that would not arise were we to encounter him in a published form. When his direct speech moves into a fragmented indirect style in praising Sanditon, do we encounter free indirect speech or can the indirect speech indicate the summary of Austen as she composed, listing for herself the key elements of Mr Parker's view. The text compresses into shorthand as Austen seeks to capture the energy and spontaneity of his flow. Elsewhere in the fragment, Austen even seems close to providing a memo to herself in describing how Charlotte "allowed her Thoughts to form themselves into **such a Meditation as this**" (*S*, b2-39–40). In other words, in this manuscript, the style of which is inseparable from its draft status, free forms of speech can seem curiously akin to compositional notes to oneself. *Sanditon* reveals how Austen may well have channelled the contingencies of the drafting process so as to generate her most forward-reaching technical and dramatic developments, in the transcription of an apprehended voice.[12]

It has been the purpose of this book to show how compression was an aspiration and source of innovation for Austen. This is the case from the largest to the smallest features of her writing. Austen espoused a reduction of novelistic length, deploying rhetorical techniques of omission to bypass description. She also took away key supports for the delivery of dialogue to generate new speech forms. By the time Austen was composing *Emma*, at least, she was drafting sentences that were innovatively compressed in terms of their grammar. Crucially, the strawberry-picking episode provides us with evidence that she did not always wish to redraft or expand them. We are unlikely to ever know what she intended for *Sanditon*, but its grammatical contractions are another manifestation of a foundational economy and, in this case, the sadly unfulfilled promise of further stylistic growth.

[12] See also my discussion of manuscript quotation marks in Chapter 3, pp. 170–73 above.

# *Bibliography*

## Primary Sources


[Anon.], *The Child of Providence: a Novel* (London: for William Lane, at the Minerva Press, 1792).

[Anon.], *The Complete Letter-Writer; or, Polite English Secretary.* [...] *The Twelfth Edition, Improved* (London: for Stanley Crowder; and Benjamin Collins in Salisbury, 1768).

[Anon.], *A New English Dictionary: Containing a Brief and Clear Explication of Most Words in the English Language* (Glasgow: for Charles Hutcheson, 1759).

Austen, James (ed.), *The Loiterer, A Periodical Work, in Two Volumes: First Published at Oxford in the Years 1789 and 1790* (printed for the author, 1790); *A facsimile reproduction*, ed. with an introduction by Li-Ping Geng (Ann Arbor, MI: Scholars' Facsimiles & Reprints, 2000).

Austen-Leigh, James Edward, *A Memoir of Jane Austen and Other Family Recollections*, ed. with an introduction and notes by Kathryn Sutherland (Oxford: Oxford University Press, 2002).

*A Memoir of Jane Austen* [...] *Second Edition to Which Is Added Lady Susan and Fragments of Two Other Unfinished Tales by Miss Austen* (London: Richard Bentley and Son, 1871).

Austen, Jane, *Emma: a Novel* (London: John Murray, 1816).

*Emma*, eds. Richard Cronin and Dorothy McMillan (Cambridge: Cambridge University Press, 2005).

*Jane Austen's Fiction Manuscripts: a Digital Edition*, ed. Kathryn Sutherland (2010). Available at https://janeausten.ac.uk/index.html. ISBN: 978-0-9565793-1-7.

*Jane Austen's Letters*, collected and ed. by Deirdre Le Faye, 4th ed. (Oxford and New York: Oxford University Press, 2011).

*Juvenilia*, ed. Peter Sabor (Cambridge: Cambridge University Press, 2006).

*Later Manuscripts*, eds. Janet Todd and Linda Bree (Cambridge: Cambridge University Press, 2008).

*Letters of Jane Austen*, ed. with an introduction and critical remarks by Edward, Lord Brabourne (London: Richard Bentley & Son, 1884).

*Mansfield Park: a Novel* (London: T. Egerton, 1814).

*Mansfield Park: a Novel*, 2nd ed. (London: John Murray, 1816).

*Mansfield Park*, ed. John Wiltshire (Cambridge: Cambridge University Press, 2005).

*Northanger Abbey; and Persuasion* (London: John Murray, 1818).

*Northanger Abbey*, eds. Barbara M. Benedict and Deirdre Le Faye (Cambridge: Cambridge University Press, 2006).

*Persuasion*, eds. Janet Todd and Antje Blank (Cambridge: Cambridge University Press, 2006).

*Pride and Prejudice: a Novel* (London: T. Egerton, 1813).

*Pride and Prejudice*, in *The Novels of Jane Austen*, ed. R. W. Chapman, 3rd ed. (Oxford: Oxford University Press, 1932; 1st ed., 1923).

*Pride and Prejudice*, ed. Pat Rogers (Cambridge: Cambridge University Press, 2006).

*Sanditon; The Watsons; Lady Susan, and Other Miscellanea; with an Introduction by R. Brimley Johnson* (London: J. M. Dent & Sons Ltd, 1934).

*Sense and Sensibility: a Novel* (London: T. Egerton, 1811).

*Sense and Sensibility: a Novel*, 2nd ed. (London: T. Egerton, 1813).

*Sense and Sensibility*, ed. Edward Copeland (Cambridge: Cambridge University Press, 2006).

*Teenage Writings*, ed. with an introduction and notes by Kathryn Sutherland and Freya Johnston (Oxford: Oxford University Press, 2017).

Bage, Robert, *Hermsprong; or, Man as He Is Not*, ed. Pamela Perkins (Peterborough, ON: Broadview Literary Texts, 2002; first published 1796).

*Man as He Is: A Novel* (London: for William Lane, at the Minerva Press, 1792).

Bailey, Nathan, *An Universal Etymological English Dictionary* (London: for E. Bell, J. Darby, A. Bettesworth, F. Fayram, J. Pemberton, 1721).

Barbauld, Anna Letitia, *The British Novelists; with an Essay; and Prefaces, Biographical and Critical, by Mrs Barbauld* (London: F. C. and J. Rivington, et al., 1810).

*The Correspondence of Samuel Richardson* [...] *Selected from the Original Manuscripts* [...] *to Which Are Prefixed, a Biographical Account of That Author, and Observations on His Writings* (London: Richard Phillips, 1804).

Barrett, Eaton Stannard, *The Heroine, or Adventures of Cherubina* [...] *Second Edition, with Considerable Additions and Alterations* (London: for Henry Colburn, 1814).

Beckford, William, *Modern Novel Writing, or The Elegant Enthusiast*, ed. with an introduction and notes by Robert J. Gemmett (Stroud: Nonsuch, 2008; first published 1796).

Blair, Hugh, *Lectures on Rhetoric and Belles Lettres* (London: W. Strahan; T. Cadell; and Edinburgh: W. Creech, 1783).

Bland, Charles, *The Art of Rhetorick, as to Elocution; Explain'd: and Familiarly Adapted to the Capacityes of School-Boys, by Way of Question and Answer* (London: for S. Sturton, 1706).

Brydges, Samuel Egerton, *Arthur Fitz-Albini, a Novel* (London: for J. White, 1798).

Burney, Frances, *Camilla, or, a Picture of Youth*, eds. Edward A. Bloom and Lillian D. Bloom (Oxford: Oxford University Press, 2009; first published 1796).

*Evelina, or, the History of a Young Lady's Entrance into the World*, ed. Margaret Anne Doody (London: Penguin, 1994; first published 1778).

*The Wanderer; or, Female Difficulties*, eds. Margaret Anne Doody, Robert L. Mack and Peter Sabor; with an introduction by Margaret Anne Doody (Oxford: Oxford University Press, 1991; first published 1814).

Dickens, Charles, *The Posthumous Papers of the Pickwick Club*, ed. with an introduction by Robert L. Patten (Harmondsworth: Penguin, 1972; first published 1836–7).

Edgeworth, Maria, *Belinda*, ed. Kathryn J. Kirkpatrick (Oxford: Oxford University Press, 1994; first published 1801).

*Patronage*, introduction by John Mullan (London: Sort of Books, 2011; first published 1814).

Fielding, Henry, *The History of the Adventures of Joseph Andrews and of His Friend Mr Abraham Adams; and, an Apology for the Life of Mrs Shamela Andrews*, ed. Douglas Brooks-Davies; revised with a new introduction by Thomas Keymer (Oxford: Oxford University Press, 1999; *Joseph Andrews* first published 1742).

*The History of Tom Jones, a Foundling*, eds. John Bender and Simon Stern, with an introduction by John Bender (Oxford: Oxford University Press, 1996; first published 1749).

Fisher, Anne, *A Practical New Grammar, [...] the Seventh Edition Enlarged, and Much Improved* (Newcastle: for Thomas Slack, 1762).

Ford, Ford Madox, *Joseph Conrad: a Personal Remembrance* (London: Duckworth & Co., 1924).

Gibbons, Thomas, *Rhetoric; or, a View of Its Principal Tropes and Figures, in Their Origin and Powers* (London: by J. and W. Oliver, 1767).

Gilpin, William, *An Essay upon Prints; Containing Remarks upon the Principles of Picturesque Beauty* (London: J. Robson, 1768).

*Observations on the River Wye, and Several Parts of South Wales, &c. Relative Chiefly to Picturesque Beauty* (London: for R. Blamire, 1782).

*Observations, Relative Chiefly to Picturesque Beauty, Made in the Year 1772, on Several Parts of England; Particularly the Mountains, and Lakes of Cumberland, and Westmoreland* (London: R. Blamire, 1786).

*Three Essays: On Picturesque Beauty; on Picturesque Travel; and on Sketching Landscape: to Which Is Added a Poem, on Landscape Painting* (London: R. Blamire, 1792).

Goldsmith, Oliver, *The History of England, from the Earliest Times to the Death of George II*, 4 vols. (London: T. Davies; Becket and De Hondt; and T. Cadell, 1771).

*An History of England, in a Series of Letters from a Nobleman to His Son* (London: for J. Newbery, 1764).

Green, J., *A Short Grammar, or Rudiments of the Latin Tongue* (London, 1759).

Guazzo, Stefano, *The Art of Conversation* (London: for J. Brett, 1738).

Inchbald, Elizabeth, *A Simple Story*, ed. with an introduction by J. M. S. Tompkins (London: Oxford University Press, 1967; first published 1791).

Hawkins, Laetitia Matilda, *Rosanne; or a Father's Labour Lost* (London: F.C. and J. Rivington, 1814).

Henry, Robert, *The History of Great Britain, from the First Invasion of It by the Romans under Julius Caesar. Written on a New Plan* (London: printed for the author, 1771).

Hume, David, *The History of England, under the House of Tudor*, 2 vols. (London: for A. Millar, 1759).

Hunter, Rachel, *Lady Maclairn, the Victim of Villany. A Novel* (London: for W. Earle and J.W. Hucklebridge, 1806).

Johnson, Samuel, *A Dictionary of the English Language* (London: by W. Strahan, for J. and P. Knaptor; T. and T. Longman; C. Hitch and L. Hawes; A. Millar; and R. and J. Dodsley, 1755).

Knight, Richard Payne, *An Analytical Inquiry into the Principles of Taste* (London: for T. Payne and J. White, 1805).

*The Landscape, a Didactic Poem*, 2nd ed. (London: by W. Bulmer and Co., 1795).

Lennox, Charlotte, *The Female Quixote, or The Adventures of Arabella*, ed. Margaret Dalziel; with an introduction by Margaret Anne Doody; chronology and appendix by Duncan Isles (Oxford: Oxford University Press, 1989; first published 1752).

Lewes, George Henry, *The Principles of Success in Literature*, with an introduction by Geoffrey Tillotson (Farnborough, Hants: Gregg International Publishers, 1969; first published in the *Fortnightly Review*, May–November 1865).

Marmontel, Jean-François, 'Direct' (1754), in *Encyclopédie, ou dictionnaire raisonné des sciences, des arts et des métiers, etc.*, eds. Denis Diderot and Jean le Rond d'Alembert, (1751–72). Available at University of Chicago: ARTFL Encyclopédie Project (Autumn 2017 Edition), Robert Morrissey (ed.), http://encyclopedie.uchicago.edu/.

Mudford, William, *The British Novelists; Comprising Every Work of Acknowledged Merit Which is Usually Classed Under the Denomination of Novels* (London: by W. Clarke etc., 1810–16).

Price, Uvedale, *An Essay on the Picturesque, as Compared with the Sublime and the Beautiful; and, on the Use of Studying Pictures, for the Purpose of Improving Real Landscape* [...] *A New Edition, with Considerable Additions* (London: for J. Robson, 1796).

Radcliffe, Ann, *The Mysteries of Udolpho*, ed. Bonamy Dobrée; with an introduction and notes by Terry Castle (Oxford: Oxford University Press, 1998; first published 1794).

Richardson, Samuel, *Clarissa, or the History of a Young Lady*, ed. Angus Ross (Harmondsworth: Penguin, 1985; first published 1747–8).

*The History of Sir Charles Grandison*, ed. with an introduction by Jocelyn Harris (London: Oxford University Press, 1972; first published 1753–4).

Scott, Walter, *Sir Walter Scott on Novelists and Fiction*, ed. Ioan Williams (London: Routledge & Kegan Paul, 1968).

*The Antiquary*, ed. David Hewitt (Edinburgh: Edinburgh University Press, 1995; first published 1816).

*Guy Mannering*, ed. P. D.Garside (Edinburgh: Edinburgh University Press, 1999; first published 1815).

*The Miscellaneous Prose Works of Sir Walter Scott* (Edinburgh: for Cadell and Co.; London: Longman, Rees, Orme, Brown, and Green, 1827).

*Waverley*, ed. P. D. Garside (Edinburgh: Edinburgh University Press, 2007; first published 1814).

Shaw, John, *A Methodical English Grammar* [...] *To Which Is Subjoined, an Epitome of Rhetoric*. The Fourth Edition, Carefully Revised, Corrected, and Improved (London: for W. Richardson; and J. Prescott, Manchester, 1793).

Sheridan, Thomas, *A General Dictionary of the English Language* (London: [by William Strahan] for J. Dodsley; C. Dilly; and J. Wilkie, 1780).

Smith, Charlotte, *Desmond, a Novel* (London: for G.G.J. and J. Robinson, 1792).

*Desmond: A Novel*, ed. Stuart Curran (London: Pickering & Chatto, 2005; first published 1792).

*Emmeline, the Orphan of the Castle*, ed. Judith Stanton (London: Pickering & Chatto, 2005; first published 1788).

*Ethelinde, or the Recluse of the Lake*, ed. Stuart Curran (London: Pickering & Chatto, 2005; first published 1789).

Smith, John, *The Mystery of Rhetorick Unveiled* (London: for R. Wilkin, B. Tooke, D. Midwinter, B. Cowse and G. Mortlock, 1721).

Spencer, Herbert, 'The Philosophy of Style', in *Essays: Scientific, Political, & Speculative* (London: Routledge/Thoemmes Press, 1996; first published in the *Westminster Review*, October 1852), vol. 2, pp. 333–69.

Sterne, Laurence, *The Life and Opinions of Tristram Shandy, Gentleman*, eds. Melvyn New and Joan New; with an introductory essay by Christopher Ricks; and an introduction and notes by Melvyn New (London: Penguin Books, 1997; first published 1759–67).

Ward, John, *A System of Oratory, Delivered in a Course of Lectures Publicly Read at Gresham College, London: to Which Is Prefixed an Inaugural Oration* (London: for John Ward, 1759).

## Reviews (Supplementary to Editions of Collected Reviews, Listed Below)

Austen, Jane

[Mary Augusta Ward], 'Style and Miss Austen', *Macmillan's Magazine*, 51 (December 1884), 84–91.

Scott, Walter, *The Antiquary* (1816).

*Antijacobin Review; and True Churchman's Magazine*, 50 (July 1816), 625–32.

*British Critic*, 5 (June 1816), 633–57.

*European Magazine, and London Review*, 70 (September 1816), 248–50.

*Gentleman's Magazine: and Historical Chronicle* (June 1816), 521–3.

*Monthly Review, or, Literary Journal*, 82 (January 1817), 38–52.

*Scots Magazine, and Edinburgh Literary Miscellany* (May 1816), 365–73.

Scott, Walter, *Waverley* (1814).

*Monthly Review, or Literary Journal*, 75 (November 1814), 275–89.

*Quarterly Review*, 11 (July 1814), 354–77.

## Secondary Sources

Allentuck, Marcia, 'Scott and the Picturesque: Afforestation and History', in *Scott Bicentenary Essays: Selected Papers read at the Sir Walter Scott Bicentenary Conference,* ed. Alan Bell (Edinburgh; London: Scottish Academic Press, 1973), pp. 188–98.

Alston, R.C., *A Bibliography of the English Language from the Invention of Printing to the Year 1800* (Ilkley: Janus Press, 1974).

Austin, J.L., *How to Do Things with Words: The William James Lectures Delivered at Harvard University in 1955,* 2nd edition, eds. J. O. Urmson and Marina Sbisà (Oxford and New York: Oxford University Press, 1975; first published 1962).

Babb, Howard S., *Jane Austen's Novels: The Fabric of Dialogue* (Columbus: Ohio State University Press, 1962).

Bachelard, Gaston, *The Poetics of Space*, trans. Maria Jolas; with a new foreword by John R. Stilgoe (Boston: Beacon Press, 1994; first published as *La Poétique de l'espace*, 1958).

Banfield, Ann, *Unspeakable Sentences: Narration and Representation in the Language of Fiction* (London: Routledge & Kegan Paul, 1982).

Barchas, Janine, *Matters of Fact in Jane Austen: History, Location, and Celebrity* (Baltimore: Johns Hopkins University Press, 2012).

'Very Austen: Accounting for the Language of *Emma*', *Nineteenth-Century Literature*, 62, 3 (2007), 303–38.

Bautz, Annika, *The Reception of Jane Austen and Walter Scott: a Comparative Longitudinal Study* (London: Continuum, 2007).

Benedict, Barbara M., 'Jane Austen's *Sense and Sensibility*: the Politics of Point of View', *Philological Quarterly*, 69, 4 (1990), 453–70.

Bermingham, Ann, *Landscape and Ideology: the English Rustic Tradition, 1740–1860* (London: Thames and Hudson, 1987).

Braudy, Leo, *Narrative Form in History and Fiction: Hume, Fielding & Gibbon* (Princeton, NJ: Princeton University Press, 1970).

Bray, Joe, 'The "Dual Voice" of Free Indirect Discourse: a Reading Experiment', *Language and Literature*, 16, 1 (2007), 37–52.

*The Epistolary Novel: Representations of Consciousness* (London: Routledge, 2003).

'The Figurative Language of *Sanditon*', *Persuasions On-Line*, 38, 2 (2018).

Bree, Linda, 'Style, Structure, Language', in *The Cambridge Companion to Emma*, ed. Peter Sabor (Cambridge: Cambridge University Press, 2015), pp. 88–104.

Brophy, Brigid, 'Jane Austen and the Stuarts', in *Critical Essays on Jane Austen*, ed. B. C. Southam (London: Routledge & Kegan Paul, 1968), pp. 21–38.

Brower, Reuben A., 'Light and Bright and Sparkling: Irony and Fiction in *Pride and Prejudice*', in *Jane Austen: a Collection of Critical Essays*, ed. Ian Watt (Englewood Cliffs, NJ: Prentice-Hall, 1963), pp. 62–75.

Burrows, John F. *Computation into Criticism: a Study of Jane Austen's Novels and an Experiment in Method* (Oxford: Clarendon Press, 1987).

'Style', in *The Cambridge Companion to Jane Austen*, eds. Edward Copeland and Juliet McMaster (Cambridge: Cambridge University Press, 1997), pp. 170–88.

Burrows, Stuart, 'The Privatization of Public Life: Free Direct Discourse in *Persuasion*', in *The Prose of Romanticism*, ed. Yoon Sun Lee (February, 2017), *A Romantic Circles Praxis Volume*, www.rc.umd.edu/praxis/prose/praxis.2016.prose.burrows.html.

Burton, Antoinette, '"Invention Is What Delights Me": Jane Austen's Remaking of "English" History', in *Jane Austen and Discourses of Feminism*, ed. Devoney Looser (Basingstoke, Hampshire: Macmillan Press, 1995), pp. 35–50.

Butler, Marilyn, 'Disregarded Designs: Jane Austen's Sense of the Volume', in *Jane Austen in a Social Context*, ed. David Monaghan (London: Macmillan, 1981; first published in 'The Jane Austen Society Report for the Year 1978', pp. 49–65).

*Jane Austen and the War of Ideas* (Oxford: Clarendon Press, 1975).

Byrne, Paula, *Jane Austen and the Theatre* (London: Hambledon and London, 2002).

*The Real Jane Austen: A Life in Small Things* (London: HarperPress, 2013).

Chapman, R. W., *Jane Austen: Facts and Problems* (Oxford: Clarendon Press, 1948).

Clery, E. J., *Jane Austen: the Banker's Sister* (London: Biteback Publishing, 2017).

Copley, Stephen and Peter Garside, eds., *The Politics of the Picturesque: Literature, Landscape and Aesthetics since 1770* (Cambridge: Cambridge University Press, 1994).

Crosby, Richard Benjamin, 'Mitt Romney's Paralipsis: (Un)Veiling Jesus in "Faith in America"', *Rhetoric Review*, 32, 2 (2013), 119–36.

Dabundo, Laura, 'Jane Austen's Opacities', in *Jane Austen and Mary Shelley and Their Sisters*, ed. Laura Dabundo (Lanham, MD: University Press of America, 2000), pp. 53–60.

Davis, Lennard J., *Resisting Novels: Ideology and Fiction* (New York and London: Methuen, 1987).

Delaney, Janice Fogarty, *Chapter Design in Jane Austen's Novels* (PhD, Temple University, 1970).

Deresiewicz, William, 'Community and Cognition in *Pride and Prejudice*', *ELH*, 64, 2 (1997), 503–35.

*Jane Austen and the Romantic Poets* (New York: Columbia University Press, 2004).

Doody, Margaret Anne, *Jane Austen's Names: Riddles, Persons, Places* (Chicago: University of Chicago Press, 2015).

'Turns of Speech and Figures of Mind', in *A Companion to Jane Austen*, eds. Claudia L. Johnson and Clara Tuite (Oxford: Wiley-Blackwell, 2009), pp. 165–84.

Duckworth, Alistair M., *The Improvement of the Estate: a Study of Jane Austen's Novels* (Baltimore and London: The Johns Hopkins University Press, 1971).

'Landscape', in *Jane Austen in Context*, ed. Janet Todd (Cambridge: Cambridge University Press, 2005), pp. 278–88.

'"Spillikins, Paper Ships, Riddles, Conundrums, and Cards": Games in Jane Austen's Life and Fiction', in *Jane Austen: Bicentenary Essays*, ed. John Halperin (Cambridge: Cambridge University Press, 1975), pp. 279–97.

Ehrenpreis, Anne Henry, '*Northanger Abbey*: Jane Austen and Charlotte Smith', *Nineteenth-Century Fiction*, 25, 3 (1970), 343–48.

Elfenbein, Andrew, 'Austen's Minimalism', in *The Cambridge Companion to Pride and Prejudice*, ed. Janet Todd (Cambridge: Cambridge University Press, 2013), pp. 109–21.

Empson, William, 'Argufying in Poetry', in *Argufying: Essays on Literature and Culture*, ed. John Haffenden (London: Chatto & Windus, 1987; first published in *Listener*, 22 August 1963), pp. 167–73.

Everett, Nigel, *The Tory View of Landscape* (New Haven, CT, and London: Paul Mellon Centre for Studies in British Art by Yale University Press, 1994).

Ferguson, Frances, 'Jane Austen, *Emma*, and the Impact of Form', in *Reading for Form*, eds. Susan J. Wolfson and Marshall Brown (Seattle and London: University of Washington Press, 2006; first published in 2000 as a special issue of the *Modern Language Quarterly*), pp. 231–55.

Finch, Casey and Peter Bowen, '"The Tittle-Tattle of Highbury": Gossip and the Free Indirect Style in *Emma*', *Representations*, 31 (1990), 1–18.

Fludernik, Monika, 'Collective Minds in Fact and Fiction: Intermental Thought and Group Consciousness in Early Modern Narrative', *Poetics Today*, 35, 4 (2014), 689–730.

*The Fictions of Language and the Languages of Fiction: the Linguistic Representation of Speech and Consciousness* (London: Routledge, 1993).

Galperin, William H., 'Afterword: the Picturesque and the Work of Regulation', *European Romantic Review*, 13 (2002), 95–104.

'Austen's Earliest Readers and the Rise of the Janeites', in *Janeites: Austen's Disciples and Devotees*, ed. Deidre Lynch (Princeton, NJ: Princeton University Press, 2000), pp. 87–114.

*The Historical Austen* (Philadelphia: University of Pennsylvania Press, 2003).

Gamer, Michael, 'A Select Collection: Barbauld, Scott, and the Rise of the (Reprinted) Novel', in *Recognizing the Romantic Novel: New Histories of British Fiction, 1780–1830*, eds. Jillian Heydt-Stevenson and Charlotte Sussman (Liverpool: Liverpool University Press, 2008), pp. 155–91.

Gard, Roger, *Jane Austen's Novels: the Art of Clarity* (New Haven, CT, and London: Yale University Press, 1992).

Garside, Peter, James Raven, and Rainer Schöwerling (general eds.), *The English Novel 1770–1829: a Bibliographical Survey of Prose Fiction Published in the British Isles; vol. I: 1770–1799*, eds. James Raven and Antonia Forster, with the assistance of Stephen Bending; *vol. II: 1800–1829*, eds. Peter Garside and Rainer Schöwerling, with the assistance of Christopher Skelton-Foord and Karin Wünsche (Oxford: Oxford University Press, 2000).

Geng, Li-Ping, '*The Loiterer* and Jane Austen's Literary Identity', *Eighteenth-Century Fiction*, 13, 4 (2001), 579–92.

Gilson, David, *A Bibliography of Jane Austen: New Introduction and Corrections by the Author* (Winchester: St Paul's Bibliographies, 1997).

González-Díaz, Victorina, 'Round Brackets in Jane Austen', *English Text Construction*, 5, 2 (2012), 174–207.

Grundy, Isobel, 'Jane Austen and Literary Traditions', in *The Cambridge Companion to Jane Austen*, eds. Edward Copeland and Juliet McMaster (Cambridge: Cambridge University Press, 1997), pp. 187–210.

'Rachel Hunter and the Victims of Slavery', *Women's Writing*, 1, 1 (1994), pp. 25–34.

'Why Do They Talk So Much? How Can We Stand It? John Thorpe and Miss Bates,' in *The Talk in Jane Austen*, eds. Bruce Stovel and Lynn Weinlos Gregg (Edmonton: University of Alberta Press, 2002), pp. 41–56.

Gunn, Daniel P., 'Free Indirect Discourse and Narrative Authority in *Emma*,' *Narrative*, 12, 1 (2004), 35–54.

Halsey, Katie, *Jane Austen and her Readers, 1786–1945* (London: Anthem Press, 2012).

Harris, Jocelyn, 'Anna Letitia Barbauld, Jane Austen's Unseen Interlocutor', in *Anna Letitia Barbauld: New Perspectives*, eds. William McCarthy and Olivia Murphy (Lewisburg, PA: Bucknell University Press, 2014), pp. 237–57.

'Jane Austen, Samuel Johnson, and the Academy', *Persuasions*, 30 (2008), 27–37.

*Jane Austen's Art of Memory* (Cambridge: Cambridge University Press, 1989).

*A Revolution Almost beyond Expression: Jane Austen's Persuasion* (Newark: University of Delaware Press, 2007).

Hartman, Geoffrey H., 'Wordsworth, Inscriptions, and Romantic Nature Poetry', in *Beyond Formalism: Literary Essays 1958–1970* (New Haven, CT, and London: Yale University Press, 1970), pp. 206–30.

Hayden, John O. (ed.), *Scott: the Critical Heritage* (London: Routledge & Kegan Paul, 1970).

Heydt-Stevenson, Jill, 'Liberty, Connection, and Tyranny: the Novels of Jane Austen and the Aesthetic Movement of the Picturesque', in *Lessons of Romanticism: a Critical Companion*, eds. Thomas Pfau and Robert F. Gleckner (Durham, NC: Duke University Press, 1998), pp. 261–79.

Holly, Grant I., 'Emmagrammatology', *Studies in Eighteenth-Century Culture*, 19 (1989), 39–51.

Honan, Park, *Jane Austen: Her Life*, revised and updated (London: Phoenix Giant, 1997; first published 1987).

Jarrells, Anthony, 'Short Fictional Forms and the Rise of the Tale', in *English and British Fiction, 1750–1820*, eds. Peter Garside and Karen O'Brien (Oxford: Oxford University Press, 2015), pp. 478–94.

Johnson, Claudia L., *Jane Austen: Women, Politics, and the Novel* (Chicago and London: University of Chicago Press, 1988).

*Jane Austen's Cults and Cultures* (Chicago and London: University of Chicago Press, 2012).

'"Let Me Make the Novels of a Country": Barbauld's *The British Novelists* (1810/1820)', *NOVEL: a Forum on Fiction*, 34, 2 (2001), 163–79.

'The "Operations of Time, and the Changes of the Human Mind": Jane Austen and Dr. Johnson Again', *Modern Language Quarterly*, 44, 1 (1983), 23–38.

'The "Twilight of Probability": Uncertainty and Hope in *Sense and Sensibility*', *Philological Quarterly*, 62 (1983), 171–86.

Johnston, Freya, 'Johnson and Austen', in *Samuel Johnson after 300 Years*, eds. Greg Clingham and Philip Smallwood (Cambridge: Cambridge University Press, 2009), pp. 225–45.

*Samuel Johnson and the Art of Sinking 1709–1791* (Oxford: Oxford University Press, 2005).

Johnston, Kenneth R., *Unusual Suspects: Pitt's Reign of Alarm and the Lost Generation of the 1790s* (Oxford: Oxford University Press, 2013).

Jones, Vivien, '"The Coquetry of Nature": Politics and the Picturesque in Women's Fiction', in *The Politics of the Picturesque: Literature, Landscape and Aesthetics since 1770*, eds. Stephen Copley and Peter Garside (Cambridge: Cambridge University Press, 1994), pp. 120–44.

Jung, Sandro, 'Sensibility, the Servant and Comedy in Radcliffe's *The Mysteries of Udolpho*', *Gothic Studies*, 12, 1 (2010), 1–12.

Kelly, Helena, *Jane Austen: the Secret Radical* (London: Icon Books, 2016).

Kent, Christopher, 'Learning History with, and from, Jane Austen', in *Jane Austen's Beginnings: the Juvenilia and Lady Susan*, ed. J. David Grey; foreword, Margaret Drabble (Ann Arbor: UMI Research Press, 1989), pp. 59–72.

'"Real Solemn History" and Social History', in *Jane Austen in a Social Context*, ed. David Monaghan (London: Palgrave Macmillan, 1981), pp. 86–104.

Knoblauch, Cyril H., 'Samuel Johnson and the Composing Process', *Eighteenth-Century Studies*, 13 (1980), 243–62.

Knowlson, James, *Damned to Fame: the Life of Samuel Beckett* (London: Bloomsbury, 1996).

Knox-Shaw, Peter, *Jane Austen and the Enlightenment* (Cambridge: Cambridge University Press, 2004).

Kornbluh, Anna, 'The Economic Problem of Sympathy: Parabasis, Interest, and Realist Form in *Middlemarch*', *ELH*, 77 (2010), 941–67.

Lambert, Mark, *Dickens and the Suspended Quotation* (New Haven, CT: Yale University Press, 1981).

Lane, Maggie, 'Brothers of the More Famous Jane: the Literary Aspirations, Achievements, and Influence of James and Henry Austen', *Persuasions*, 31 (2009), 13–32.

Lascelles, Mary, *Jane Austen and Her Art* (Oxford: Oxford University Press, 1939).

Leech, Geoffrey and Mick Short, *Style in Fiction: a Linguistic Introduction to English Fictional Prose*, 2nd ed. (Harlow: Pearson Education Limited, 2007; first published 1981).

Le Faye, Deirdre, *Jane Austen: a Family Record* (Cambridge: Cambridge University Press, 2nd ed., 2004; first published 1989).

'Jane Austen and Mrs Hunter's Novel', *Notes and Queries*, 32, 3, (1985), 335–6.

Le Hir, Yves, 'Dialogue et Typographie', *L'Information Littéraire*, 13 (1961), 215–16.

Leighton, Angela, 'Sense and Silences: Reading Jane Austen Again', in *Jane Austen: New Perspectives. Women & Literature. New Series. Vol. 3*, ed. Janet M. Todd (New York: Holmes & Meier, 1983), pp. 128–41.

Lennard, John, *But I Digress: the Exploitation of Parentheses in English Printed Verse* (Oxford: Clarendon Press, 1991).

Lindstrom, Eric, 'Austen and Austin', *European Romantic Review*, 22, 4 (2011), 501–20.

'*Sense and Sensibility* and Suffering; or, Wittgenstein's Marianne?', *ELH*, 80, 4 (2013), 1067–91.

Litz, A. Walton, 'The Picturesque in *Pride and Prejudice*', *Persuasions*, 1 (1979), 13–15, 20–24.

Liu, Alan, *Wordsworth: the Sense of History* (Stanford, CA: Stanford University Press, 1989).

Lock, Charles, 'Double Voicing, Sharing Words: Bakhtin's Dialogism and the History of the Theory of Free Indirect Discourse', in *The Novelness of Bakhtin: Perspectives and Possibilities*, eds. Jørgen Bruhn and Jan Lundquist (Copenhagen: Museum Tusculanum Press, 2001), pp. 71–87.

Looser, Devoney, *British Women Writers and the Writing of History, 1670–1820* (Baltimore and London: The Johns Hopkins University Press, 2000).

Lupton, Christina, 'Contingency, Codex, the Eighteenth-Century Novel', *ELH*, 81, 4 (2014), 1173–92.

Lynch, Deidre, 'Clueless: About History', in *Jane Austen and Co.: Remaking the Past in Contemporary Culture*, eds. Suzanne R. Pucci and James Thompson (Albany: State University of New York Press, 2003), pp. 71–92.

*The Economy of Character: Novels, Market Culture, and the Business of Inner Meaning* (Chicago and London: University of Chicago Press, 1998).

*Loving Literature: a Cultural History* (Chicago: University of Chicago Press, 2014).

Mandal, Anthony, *Jane Austen and the Popular Novel: the Determined Author* (Basingstoke: Palgrave Macmillan, 2007).

Mayhead, Robin, 'The Problem of Coherence in *The Antiquary*', in *Scott Bicentenary Essays: Selected Papers Read at the Sir Walter Scott Bicentenary Conference*, ed. Alan Bell (Edinburgh and London: Scottish Academic Press, 1973), pp. 134–46.

McCarthy, William, *Anna Letitia Barbauld: Voice of the Enlightenment* (Baltimore: The Johns Hopkins University Press, 2008).

McKeon, Michael, 'Prose Fiction: Great Britain', in *The Cambridge History of Literary Criticism*, vol. 4, *The Eighteenth Century*, eds. H. B Nisbet and Claude Rawson (Cambridge: Cambridge University Press, 1997), pp. 238–63.

Mee, Jon, *Conversable Worlds: Literature, Contention, and Community 1762 to 1830* (Oxford: Oxford University Press, 2011), chapter 5, 'Jane Austen and the Hazard of Conversation'.

'Austen's Treacherous Ivory: Female Patriotism, Domestic Ideology, and Empire', in *The Postcolonial Jane Austen*, eds. You-me Park and Rajeswari Sunder Rajan (London: Routledge, 2000), pp. 74–92.

Mellor, Anne K., *Mothers of the Nation: Women's Political Writing in England, 1780–1830* (Bloomington: Indiana University Press, 2000).

Miller, D. A., 'Austen's Attitude', *The Yale Journal of Criticism: Interpretation in the Humanities*, 8, 1 (1995), 1–5.

*Jane Austen, or The Secret of Style* (Princeton, NJ, and Oxford: Princeton University Press, 2003).

*Narrative and Its Discontents: Problems of Closure in the Traditional Novel* (Princeton, NJ: Princeton University Press, 1981).

Millgate, Jane, '*Persuasion* and the Presence of Scott', *Persuasions*, 15 (1993), 184–95.

*Walter Scott: the Making of the Novelist* (Edinburgh: Edinburgh University Press, 1984).

Moler, Kenneth L., '"Group Voices" in Jane Austen's Narration', *Persuasions*, 13 (1991), 7–12.

*Jane Austen's Art of Allusion* (Lincoln: University of Nebraska Press, 1968).

"Truth Universally Acknowledged", *Persuasions*, 8 (1986), 25.

Mooneyham, Laura G., *Romance, Language and Education in Jane Austen's Novels* (Basingstoke: Macmillan, 1988).

Moore, Catherine E., '"Ladies ... Taking the Pen in Hand": Mrs. Barbauld's Criticism of Eighteenth-Century Women Novelists', in *Fetter'd or Free? British Women Novelists 1670–1815*, eds. Mary Anne Schofield and Cecilia Macheski (Athens: Ohio University Press, 1986), pp. 383–7.

Moran, Michael G. (ed.), *Eighteenth-Century British and American Rhetorics and Rhetoricians: Critical Studies and Sources* (Westport, CT, and London: Greenwood Press, 1994).

Mudrick, Marvin, *Jane Austen: Irony as Defense and Discovery* (Princeton, NJ: Princeton University Press, 1952).

Mullan, John, *What Matters in Jane Austen? Twenty Crucial Puzzles Solved* (London: Bloomsbury Publishing, 2012).

Murphy, Olivia, *Jane Austen the Reader: the Artist as Critic* (Basingstoke: Palgrave Macmillan, 2013).

Mylne, Vivienne, 'The Punctuation of Dialogue in Eighteenth-Century French and English Fiction', *The Library*, 1 (1979), 43–61.

Nell, Edward, '"Found Wanting?": Second Impressions of a Famous First Sentence', *Persuasions*, 25 (2003), 76–84.

Neumann, Anne Waldron, 'Characterization and Comment in *Pride and Prejudice*: Free Indirect Discourse and "Double-Voiced" Verbs of Speaking, Thinking, and Feeling', *Style*, 20, 3 (1986), 364–94.

Page, Norman, *The Language of Jane Austen* (Oxford: Basil Blackwell, 1972).

*Speech in the English Novel*, 2nd ed. (Atlantic Highlands, NJ: Humanities Press International, 1988; first published 1973).

Palmer, Alan, *Fictional Minds* (Lincoln and London: University of Nebraska Press, 2004).

*Social Minds in the Novel* (Columbus: Ohio State University Press, 2010).

Parks, Edd Winfield, 'Jane Austen's Lure of the Next Chapter', *Nineteenth-Century Fiction*, 7, 1 (1952), 56–60.

Pascal, Roy, *The Dual Voice: Free Indirect Speech and Its Functioning in the Nineteenth-Century European Novel* (Manchester: Manchester University Press, 1977).

Phillips, Mark Salber, *Society and Sentiment: Genres of Historical Writing in Britain, 1740–1820* (Princeton, NJ: Princeton University Press, 2000).

Pinch, Adela, *Strange Fits of Passion: Epistemologies of Emotion, Hume to Austen* (Stanford, CA: Stanford University Press, 1996).

Poovey, Mary, 'From Politics to Silence: Jane Austen's Nonreferential Aesthetic', in *A Companion to Jane Austen*, eds. Claudia L. Johnson and Clara Tuite (Oxford: Wiley-Blackwell, 2009), pp. 251–60.

*The Proper Lady and the Woman Writer: Ideology as Style in the Works of Mary Wollstonecraft, Mary Shelley, and Jane Austen* (Chicago and London: University of Chicago Press, 1984).

Rawson, C. J., '"Nice" and "Sentimental": a Parallel between *Northanger Abbey* and Richardson's *Correspondence*', *Notes & Queries*, 11, 5 (1964), 180.

Ricks, Christopher, 'Clichés', in *The Force of Poetry* (Oxford: Clarendon Press, 1984), pp. 356–68.

Robbins, Bruce, *The Servant's Hand: English Fiction from Below* (Durham and London: Duke University Press, 1993; first published 1986).

Robinson, Sidney K., *Inquiry into the Picturesque* (Chicago and London: University of Chicago Press, 1991).

Sabor, Peter, '"Finished up to Nature": Walter Scott's Review of *Emma*', *Persuasions*, 13 (1991), 88–99.

'Jane Austen: Satirical Historian', in *Swift's Travels: Eighteenth-Century British Satire and Its Legacy*, eds. Nicholas Hudson and Aaron Santesso (Cambridge: Cambridge University Press, 2008), pp. 217–32.

'Preface', in *The Cambridge Companion to Emma*, ed. Peter Sabor (Cambridge: Cambridge University Press, 2015), pp. xi–xiv.

Said, Edward W., *Culture and Imperialism* (London: Chatto & Windus, 1993).

Schor, Naomi, *Reading in Detail: Aesthetics and the Feminine* (London: Methuen, 1987).

Seeber, Barbara K., *Jane Austen and Animals* (Farnham, Surrey: Ashgate, 2013).

Shaw, Narelle, 'Free Indirect Speech and Jane Austen's 1816 Revision of *Northanger Abbey*', *SEL* 30, 4 (1990), 591–601.

Snoeck Henkemans, A. Francisca, 'Manoeuvring Strategically with *Praeteritio*', *Argumentation*, 23, 3 (2009), 339–50.

Sorensen, Janet, *The Grammar of Empire in Eighteenth-Century British Writing* (Cambridge: Cambridge University Press, 2000), Epilogue. 'Jane Austen's Language and the Strangeness at Home in the Center'.

Sorensen, Knud, 'Johnsonese in *Northanger Abbey*: a Note on Jane Austen's Style', *English Studies*, 50 (1969), 390–97.

Southam, B. C. 'General Tilney's Hot-Houses: Some Recent Jane Austen Studies and Texts', *Ariel*, 2 (1971), 52–62.

(ed.), *Jane Austen: the Critical Heritage* (London: Routledge & Kegan Paul, 1968).

(ed.), *Jane Austen: the Critical Heritage 1870–1940*, vol. 2 (London and New York: Routledge & Kegan Paul, 1987).

*Jane Austen's Literary Manuscripts: a Study of the Novelist's Development through the Surviving Papers* (London and New York: The Athlone Press, 1964).

*Jane Austen's 'Sir Charles Grandison'*, transcribed and ed. by Brian Southam; foreword by Lord David Cecil (Oxford: Clarendon Press, 1980).

Spacks, Patricia Meyer, *Boredom: the Literary History of a State of Mind* (Chicago and London: University of Chicago Press, 1995).

*Gossip* (Chicago: University of Chicago Press, 1986).

Spencer, Jane, 'Not Being a Historian: Women Telling Tales in Restoration and Eighteenth-Century England', in *Contexts of Pre-Novel Narrative: the European Tradition*, ed. Roy Eriksen (Berlin and New York: Mouton de Gruyter, 1994), pp. 319–40.

Sternberg, Meir, 'Point of View and the Indirections of Direct Speech', *Language and Style*, 15 (1982), 67–117.

'Proteus in Quotation-Land: Mimesis and the Forms of Reported Discourse', *Poetics Today*, 3 (1982), 107–56.

Stevick, Philip, *The Chapter in Fiction: Theories of Narrative Division* (Syracuse, NY: Syracuse University Press, 1970).

Stokes, Myra, *The Language of Jane Austen: a Study of Some Aspects of Her Vocabulary* (Basingstoke: Macmillan, 1991).

Stone, Donald D., 'Sense and Semantics in Jane Austen', *Nineteenth-Century Fiction*, 25, 1 (1970), 31–50.

Stovel, Bruce and Lynn Weinlos Gregg, eds., *The Talk in Jane Austen* (Edmonton: University of Alberta Press, 2002).

Sunder Rajan, Rajeswari, 'Critical Responses, Recent', in *Jane Austen in Context*, ed. Janet Todd (Cambridge: Cambridge University Press, 2005), pp. 101–10.

Sutherland, Kathryn, 'Chronology of Composition and Publication', in *Jane Austen in Context*, ed. Janet Todd (Cambridge: Cambridge University Press, 2005), pp. 12–22.

'From Kitty to Catharine: James Edward Austen's Hand in *Volume the Third*', *The Review of English Studies*, 66 (2014), 124–43.

'Jane Austen's Dealings with John Murray and His Firm', *The Review of English Studies*, 64 (2012), 105–26.

*Jane Austen's Textual Lives: from Aeschylus to Bollywood* (Oxford: Oxford University Press, 2005).

Tandon, Bharat, *Jane Austen and the Morality of Conversation* (London: Anthem Press, 2003).

Tanner, Tony, *Jane Austen* (London: Macmillan, 1986).

Tave, Stuart, 'Introduction' to the facsimile reprint of Robert Bage, *Hermsprong; or, Man as He Is Not*, edited, annotated, and with an introduction by Stuart Tave (University Park and London: Pennsylvania State University Press, 1982).

*Some Words of Jane Austen* (Chicago and London: University of Chicago Press, 1973).

Taylor, Megan, 'Jane Austen and "Banal Shakespeare"', *Eighteenth-Century Fiction*, 27, 1 (2014), 105–25.

Thomas, Bronwen E., 'Multiparty Talk in the Novel: the Distribution of Tea and Talk in a Scene from Evelyn Waugh's *Black Mischief*', *Poetics Today*, 23, 4 (2002), 657–84.

Thompson, James, *Between Self and World: the Novels of Jane Austen* (University Park: Pennsylvania State University Press, 1988).

Thomsen, Inger Sigrun, 'Words 'Half-Dethroned': Jane Austen's Art of the Unspoken', in *Jane Austen's Business: Her World and Her Profession*, eds. Juliet McMaster and Bruce Stovel (Basingstoke: Macmillan, 1996), pp. 95–106.

Tieken-Boon van Ostade, Ingrid, *In Search of Jane Austen: the Language of the Letters* (Oxford: Oxford University Press, 2014).

Todd, Janet, *The Cambridge Introduction to Jane Austen* (Cambridge: Cambridge University Press, 2006).

Toner, Anne, 'Anna Barbauld on Fictional Form in *The British Novelists* (1810)', *Eighteenth-Century Fiction*, 24, 2 (2011–12), 171–93.

'Apophatic Austen: Speaking about Silence', *RSEAA XVII–XVIII* (2017), 179–97.

*Ellipsis in English Literature: Signs of Omission* (Cambridge: Cambridge University Press, 2015).

'Free Speech: Jane Austen, Robert Bage, and the Subversive Shapes of Dialogue', *Textus. English Studies in Italy*, 30, 3 (2017), 167–87.

'Jane Austen Jotting: The Manuscript of *Sanditon* and the Question of Style', *Persuasions On-Line*, 38, 2 (2018).

'Landscape as Literary Criticism: Jane Austen, Anna Barbauld and the Narratological Application of the Picturesque', in *Critical Survey*, 26, 1 (2014), 3–19.

'A 'Said He' or a 'Said She': Speech Attribution in Austen's Fiction', *Persuasions*, 34 (2012), 140–9.

Tuite, Clara, *Romantic Austen: Sexual Politics and the Literary Canon* (Cambridge: Cambridge University Press, 2002).

Vilihora, Karen, *Austen's Oughts: Judgment after Locke and Shaftesbury* (Newark: University of Delaware Press, 2010).

Wall, Cynthia, *Grammars of Approach: Landscape, Narrative, and the Linguistic Picturesque* (Chicago and London: University of Chicago Press, 2019).

Wheeler, David, 'The British Postal Service, Privacy, and Jane Austen's *Emma*', *South Atlantic Review*, 63, 4 (1998), 34–47.

Williams, Ioan (ed.), *George Meredith: the Critical Heritage* (London: Routledge & Kegan Paul, 1971).

Wiltshire, John, 'Comfort, Health and Creativity: a Reading of *Emma*', in *Jane Austen's Emma*, ed. with an introduction by Harold Bloom (New York: Bloom's Literary Criticism/Infobase Publishing, 2010; previously published in *Jane Austen: Introductions and Interventions* (Basingstoke and New York: Palgrave Macmillan, 2003)), pp. 65–74.

*The Hidden Jane Austen* (Cambridge: Cambridge University Press, 2014).

*Jane Austen and the Body: 'The Picture of health'* (Cambridge: Cambridge University Press, 1992).

Wimsatt, W. K., *The Prose Style of Samuel Johnson* (New Haven, CT: Yale University Press, 1941).

Woloch, Alex, *The One vs. the Many: Minor Characters and the Space of the Protagonist in the Novel* (Princeton, NJ and Oxford: Princeton University Press, 2003).

# Index

# HOW TO SEND A MESSAGE

## A Short Story Collection

CAIMH MCDONNELL

McFori Ink

Caimh McDonnell

Visit my website at www.WhiteHairedirishman.com

ISBN: 978-1-912897-03-2

Created with Vellum

# FOREWORD

Hello and welcome to *How To Send a Message* – a collection which gathers together in paperback form all of the short fiction I have published between the years 1975 and 2018. (Note: I wrote most of it from 2015 to 2018, but if I use my whole lifespan it means my ma will feel slightly happier when she remembers all that time I spent as a teenager staring out windows and studiously not studying.)

I bloody love short stories. If I'm honest, I've read a lot of novels that would've made great short stories. That's the beauty of 'em you see, they last the exact perfect length to capture an idea. There's no unnecessary flim-flam or navel-gazing. It's not you and the author trading blows until somebody gives up, it's the author aiming one bodacious boot to the bollocks and they either hit you in the proverbials or they turn tail and run for it. That's the other wonderful thing about short stories, if you're not feeling it, you dear reader can make a run for it too. There's another one right around the corner - there is no need for long term commitment here, short stories are the literary world's Tinder. (As a happily married man I don't understand Tinder – but in the case of at least one fella I know, it did involve a boot to the knackers. Hello Rob!)

For your delight and delectation, this collection has been divided

into two sections. Section one is the Bunnyverse, and it features characters you can find in my novels. So yes, there's Bunny McGarry, the irrepressible Sisters of the Saint, Smithy, Diller and Cheryl, and even Maggie the dog. The second section is the Looniverse and there, you can expect pretty much anything to happen. There's time travel, a bit of romance, even a bit of horror, which is weird because I scare way too easily to read horror.

I hope you enjoy it and that at least one or two of these well-intentioned boots connect with you somewhere deep and meaningful.

Cheers,

Caimh McDonnell

# PART 1 – THE BUNNYVERSE

# DOG DAY AFTERNOON

WARNING: THE FOLLOWING STORY CONTAINS A KICK-ASS DOGGIE AND MAY BE UPSETTING TO THE OWNERS OF TESTICLES.

---

**12:12pm June 18**

"I need a dead dog."

People, thought Noreen. People really were the problem. If people were a bit easier to deal with, she'd probably have become a doctor like her father and his father before him, instead of being the unspoken family disappointment of a veterinarian. She really had tried to like people, but it was very hard to based on the available evidence – war, famine and the films of Adam Sandler. Animals, on the other hand, were infinitely more lovable. In fact, their only downside was that they were invariably owned by people. It was the Peter principle on a massive evolutionary scale. Humanity had been promoted to the position of dominant species, a role they managed with utter incompetency.

Take this specimen, for example; standing on the opposite side of the counter in a black sheepskin coat, which smelled like it hadn't

been cleaned since the sheep had worn it. His large bulbous face was a shade of red only meant for beetroot and heart attacks, and a lazy left eye only added to the impression of him being unhinged. To be fair, in other circumstances he'd probably have just looked intense as opposed to deranged, but those circumstances would've involved him not bursting into her surgery demanding a dead dog.

"We don't have any dead dogs."

"Have you any that are looking a bit peaky?"

He looked about fifty and was blessed with the kind of Cork accent that managed to lilt and grate at the same time, like somebody was trying to get a tune out of an industrial sander.

"May I ask the nature of your enquiry?"

"I need a dead dog and you're a vet. Now can you help me or not?"

"Absolutely not. I'd like you to leave or I'm going to call the Gardaí."

The man pulled an overstuffed wallet from his inside coat pocket and flipped it open to his official Garda ID. "DS Bunny McGarry at your service. Now about that dead dog; ideally an Alsatian but I'll work with what you've got."

"Sure. Let me just rummage through my extensive collection of corpses out back and I'll see what I can rustle up."

"Really?"

"No."

Bunny sighed heavily and leaned on the counter. "This is no time for sarcasm, Doc. A Garda officer's life is in danger."

Noreen's mouth opened and closed without producing any words. DS Bunny McGarry glowered at her and then looked over her shoulder, presumably for somebody else to glower at. He'd be lucky. Darren had called in sick yet again. People.

"Look," said Bunny, looking at his watch, the anger in him seemingly subsiding, to be replaced by weariness. "I have forty-seven minutes to find a dead dog to take the place of a decorated police officer in front of a firing squad."

"But—"

"I should mention, the police officer is also a dog."

"Ah," said Noreen, getting at least within waving distance of understanding. "You need to – wait – what kind of monster is putting a dog in front of a firing squad?"

"Well, I dunno – they're putting her down."

"That's normally done by a painless injection."

"Well this one will definitely be painless because it's going to be given to a dead dog. At least it will be if you start helping. I tried driving up the M50, but you can never find roadkill when you need it. All I got was half a rabbit and that's gonna be a tough sell."

"Why's this dog being put down?" asked Noreen.

"It's not important."

"It is if you want my help."

"It'll sound bad when you hear it."

"Try me."

"She sort of attacked a few children."

"Oh."

"See, I told ye it'd sound bad. There were mitigating circumstances."

"Which were?"

"Well, she was high on drugs at the time."

"Is that normally a compelling legal defence?"

"She's a good dog. The best on the force until some drug peddling scumbag with a grudge found where she was kennelled and spiked her food with LSD."

"That's awful. Is she OK?"

"Ah she's A1 tip-top, other than the whole being on death row thing. I mean, I've been told she spends quite a lot of time staring at lights but ... look, are you going to help me or not?"

"Isn't there an appeal process?"

He shook his head. "She went mad at the Garda summer barbecue, snarled at a few kids and then shat in a bouncy castle that the Commissioner herself had paid for." He looked at his watch again. "We've got forty-six minutes or else the poor doggie is deader than disco."

"What're you going to do with this dog once she is free?"

"I'd not thought that far ahead."

"I'll only help if you can guarantee her a long and happy life."

"Love, look at me," he said, spreading his arms wide. "If I could provide that to any female, do you think I'd be standing here with a half-eaten kebab in my pocket, begging you for a dead dog? Now are we dancing or not?"

Noreen looked around and then leaned in. "We normally have one or two in the freezer but the crematorium van came around yesterday."

Bunny ran his hands through his hair and puffed his cheeks out.

"Where's the crematorium?"

"Nearest one is out on the Naas Road."

"Feck it, too far. Any other vets nearby?"

"They'd all have—"

"Been collected at the same time by the crematorium van," finished Bunny. "Bollocks!" He pushed himself off the counter with his hands and stared down at the floor. "C'mon Doc, work with me here. Where can we find a German shepherd-sized dead animal in central Dublin in the next forty-something minutes?"

"Well ..." said Noreen.

"What?"

"Never mind. It's a ridiculous idea."

"I'll take it."

"But ..."

**12:54pm June 18 – Kilmainham Garda Station**

Garda Patrick Lennox was making Noreen extremely uncomfortable. He didn't mean to, quite the opposite in fact. His teary brown eyes were filled with gratitude and he'd already attempted to hug her a couple of times. Noreen did not like being touched, by anyone in general and tearful men in particular.

"I really appreciate what you're doing and I know how big a deal it is. I mean, you could get in all kinds of trouble for this."

"Paddy," interjected Bunny, "stop saying that, there's a good lad."

Noreen finished filling out the clipboard full of paperwork and handed it back to Lennox. She gave it one last lingering look as she did so. He wasn't wrong. She could be struck off for this. She looked down again at the white sheet under which the body lay. She'd met Bunny McGarry about forty-two minutes ago, instantly disliked him, and was now committing a crime at his behest. She had never had the greatest taste in men.

"And you're sure that the vet you normally use—"

"Relax," interrupted Bunny. "He's been called home by a family emergency."

"Do I want to ask?"

"Best not."

The door opened and a fresh-faced female guard stuck her head in. "Paddy, Mara has just pulled up."

"Oh Christ."

"Is that the vet?" asked Noreen, her career flashing before her eyes.

"No," responded Bunny. "Worse. Feck's sake, you'd think the Assistant Commissioner would have better things to be doing with his time."

"But, you said someone was coming to verify ..."

"Yes," said Lennox, "Someone being Sergeant McCullough, who'd just nod at the sheet and sign the form. Not Mara."

Noreen looked at Bunny.

"He's right, that snivelling little prick would happily take a selfie with a corpse."

"Jesus," said Noreen, "He lifts that sheet and we're all done for."

Bunny started pacing back and forth. "Alright, we're OK. Doc, you just follow my lead."

Noreen nodded; what choice did she have?

Bunny stopped and looked at Lennox. "Paddy, you look terrified, we need grief."

Paddy attempted to make his face a mask of appropriate misery. He looked like Robert DeNiro trying to pass a whole watermelon.

"Christ," said Bunny. "You're not exactly a great loss to the acting profession."

"Sorry Bunny, I'm trying. I just ..."

"It's OK, relax. Take a deep breath ..."

Lennox nodded and obediently complied. The breath exploded out of him a second later when Bunny punched him in the stomach. Bunny gently held him for a moment and then pushed him back into the chair in the corner, where Lennox sat doubled over, unable to speak. Bunny patted him sympathetically on the shoulder.

"Greater good Paddy, greater good."

Bunny looked at Noreen. "Just follow my ..."

And the door opened.

Bunny clasped his hands together as a short, balding man in a dress uniform entered. "As we forgive those who trespass against us; and lead us not into temptation, but deliver us from evil. Amen."

"Amen," responded Noreen. The man, who she assumed was this Mara fella, awkwardly took his peaked hat off and reflexively joined in with them blessing themselves.

"DS McGarry, what are you doing here?"

"I came to console Sergeant Lennox, Sir, he's not taking this well."

Bunny nodded over at Paddy, who did indeed look like a man drowning in a sea of very personal grief. Mara looked down at the sheet.

"This was supposed to happen at precisely 1pm."

"The usual vet, Damian Hickey was called away on a family matter, Sir. Doctor Richards here kindly agreed to step in."

Noreen added nervously, "Yes, I felt it best if we get things moving."

"Well that's as maybe, but I promised the Commissioner I would verify proceedings properly. How do I know that animal is dead?"

Noreen's heart jumped into her mouth as Mara bent down towards the sheet.

"Oh for feck's sake, Mara," said Bunny, nodding at Lennox, "have a heart, would you?" Bunny roughly nudged the body with his foot. "See ... dead."

"Nobody asked for your input DS McGarry," snarled Mara. "Now, get the hell out of my way." Noreen didn't have to be an expert in reading people to see the obvious animosity that existed between the two men.

Bunny placed himself between Mara and the sheet and then leaned over and poked the body with his finger."'E's not pinin'! 'E's passed on! He has ceased to be! 'E's expired and gone to meet 'is maker! 'E's shuffled off 'is mortal coil, run down the curtain and joined the bleedin' choir invisible! This – is an ex-parrot!"

Mara attempted to shove Bunny out of his way.

"Are you drunk Bunny? Consider yourself on report. Now get out of my way. I ..." Bunny kept shifting himself to stay between Mara and the body, like a basketball player determinedly holding onto possession.

Noreen took a deep breath and stepped forward. If she was getting struck off, she might as well go down swinging.

"What the hell is going on here?" Her harsh tone caused Bunny and Mara to stop scuffling and look up at her. She pointed down at the body beneath the sheet. "This poor animal has had to be put to sleep due to injuries it suffered in the line of duty. Is this how the Garda Síochána treats a fallen hero? No respect. No basic common decency. Instead you ..." pointing at Bunny, "are using it for some tawdry comedy routine and you ..." pointing at Mara, "wish to parade the poor animal's body through the streets like some deposed third-world dictator. Shame on you. Shame on both of you. I think the press will be very interested to hear about this."

Mara backed away, as if punched in the chest. "I'm sorry ... I just ... I have to verify ..."

Noreen moved forward. "I assure you, this animal is very dead." Technically not a lie. "Or are you now questioning my professional competence as well?"

"No, no ... "

"Good, then if that is all. Excuse me, as I remove this animal and bring it to the crematorium to be disposed of in the appropriate dignified manner."

"Right, I ... of course. Sorry about ... There's no need to bring the press into—"

"Good day, sir!"

"Right I—"

"I said good day!"

**5:24pm June 18 – Garda HQ, Phoenix Park**

Mara placed his Cajun chicken wrap and his copy of the *Evening Herald* on his desk. It'd been a long day. He'd not eaten since the few biscuits at this morning's policy meeting and he had a Chamber of Commerce reception tonight, standing in for herself. The mess with the dog had been embarrassing. McGarry had been his usual buffoonish self. Ah well, not long now and his retirement would finally come through and the stain of having such a walking anachronism on the Garda payroll would be removed.

He cracked open the seal on his wrap and flicked through the first couple of pages of the paper.

**5:27pm June 18 – Garda HQ, Phoenix Park**

Health and Safety Incident Report: Garda Maureen O'Sullivan is to be commended for her quick thinking in administering the Heimlich manoeuvre to Assistant Commissioner Justin Mara, who was choking on a Cajun chicken wrap.

***Evening Herald* June 18 – page 4**

***Cat-napped!***

*The Irish National History Museum on Merrion Square was the site of one of the most bizarre crimes in Irish history today as a stuffed model of a sabre-toothed tiger was stolen from its display case. The theft occurred at 12:30pm when a man, wearing what visitors described as an improvised balaclava made out of a Tesco bag for life, walked in and used a hurley to*

*smash open the display case. The animal was then removed and the catnapper made his getaway.*

*In an odd twist in the tale, the cat was returned unharmed just two hours later.*

*The Gardaí are mystified although one unnamed source did point out that it was a reading week at nearby Trinity College.*

**3:27pm June 18 – O'Hagan's pub, Baggot Street**

Tara Flynn surveyed her domain. The lunchtime rush had been dealt with and now there was the mid-afternoon lull, before the post-work crowd barrelled in and messed the place up again. She knew that busy was better but there was still a part of her that enjoyed the quieter moments. It gave you a chance to catch your breath and have a bit of a chat with the customers. She noticed the familiar figure of Bunny McGarry shambling through the doorway and started pouring his usual stout. He was a creature of habit and he'd no doubt been called an awful lot worse than that. He was not a bad sort truth be told, once you got by the bluster. Besides, every good publican knew you could never have too many friends in law enforcement.

Bunny unbuttoned his ever-present sheepskin coat and deposited himself on one of the high stools beside the bar. "Usual please, Tara."

"On its way."

And then Bunny's arse barked.

Tara leaned over the bar to see a German shepherd sitting beside him on the floor. "Have you made a friend Bunny?"

"Something like that. Long story."

"Technically, we don't allow dogs in here."

"I'm legally blind."

"Oh are you now?"

"I must be, otherwise I'd have noticed that those packets of cigarettes behind the bar don't have a custom duty stamp on them."

Tara could feel herself blush, not something she was known for.

"I've got a few sausages left over from lunch if he's hungry?"

"He's a she and you're an angel."

Tara laughed as she topped the pint up and placed it in front of him. "Finally found yourself a woman. What's her name?"

"Maggie. Possibly named after the mad bitch of the same name."

In the corner of her eye, Tara noticed the bloke in the beanie hat and the Captain Birdseye beard, who'd been camped out in the cubby hole with his two friends all afternoon. He was waving a twenty euro note at her from the far end of the bar. Tara rolled out her best fuck-you glare. "The lap dancers start at six love."

"I'm just looking for three Heinys when you're done flirting with your da."

He then turned and leaned back against the bar, basking in his dazzling wit. Tara noticed that little twitch in Bunny's face. This was bad. The last time she'd seen that, some bloke on his Chrimbo party who'd got handsy with one of the waiting staff had found himself with an ornamental Christmas tree shoved somewhere memorable.

"What did you say there, fella?" Bunny actually smiled when he said it. This was very bad.

"Calm down, Grandad, I just ..."

And then he stopped. Tara stopped. Bunny stopped. There'd been no music playing, but if there had been, it surely would have stopped. That's the kind of thing that happens when a German shepherd places its jaws around a man's crotch and growls. It wasn't loud. It didn't need to be.

He spoke in a whisper. "Fuck's sake Grandad, get your dog off me."

Bunny took a slow sip of his pint before responding. It wasn't like the younger man was going anywhere. "Couple of things, firstly ..." Bunny whipped his wallet out, "that's Detective Sergeant Grandad to you. And secondly, that's not my dog. She's just been let go from the force in less than ideal circumstances. I don't think you want me to give her an order right now. She has a bit of a problem with

authority." Maggie growled softly as if to emphasise the point. "By any chance, you're not carrying any illegal narcotics are you?"

Captain Birdseye exchanged a worried look with his mates.

"No. You can't search me, I know my rights."

"Fair play. Good luck explaining them to the dog."

"I've nothing on me."

"Right so, must be something else. Have your genitalia recently been in contact with a dead body?"

"No."

"Well then, unless your bollocks are made of Semtex, I'm out of ideas."

"Look, just ..."

The words caught in his throat as the dog tightened her grip on proceedings.

His voice went up an octave. "I might have a small bit of ..."

"I'd get rid of it if I was you."

Slowly, very slowly, Birdseye reached into his pocket, took something out and dropped it on the counter. Tara placed it in front of Bunny. About three joints' worth, by her reckoning.

"Tut tut, young people these days, and he seemed like such a nice boy. Seeing as I'm in a good mood, we'll let you off with a warning."

Nobody seemed more surprised than Bunny when the dog released her grip and calmly padded back to sit beside him. Birdseye nearly collapsed as he staggered for the door, followed by his two friends.

Tara noticed his twenty euro note on the counter and placed it in the charity box. "And a big thank you from the orphans." She turned to Bunny. "Jesus, Bunny!"

"Don't look at me."

As if on cue, Maggie hopped up onto the high stool adjacent to him.

Tara looked at the dog's happy face. She didn't look like she'd hurt a fly. "I'll get them sausages."

Maggie leaned forward and gulped down the lump of hash in one fluid motion, cling-film and all.

"Holy fuck! Ease up there, Janis Joplin," exclaimed Bunny. He turned to face Maggie, who was panting happily away on the stool beside him. She looked calmly back at him. It was accepted Dublin criminal lore that, due to his unnervingly wonky eye, nobody, not even the hardest nutbags on God's green earth, could stay locked in a stare with Bunny McGarry. Until now.

After what seemed like an eternity, Bunny turned back to his pint and took a long pull on it. He then smacked his lips and regarding the half empty glass as if seeing it for the first time.

"Y'know, one of us is going to have to be good cop."

Maggie licked her chops and belched.

"We'll work on that."

# HOW TO SEND A MESSAGE

WARNING: THE FOLLOWING STORY CONTAINS SCENES OF A GRAPHIC NATURE AND MAY LEAVE THE READER UNABLE TO LOOK AT ICING GUNS THE SAME WAY EVER AGAIN.

---

"I'm just saying—"

"Well don't," said Keith. "Alright? Just don't."

Scanner had been 'just saying' things since they were eight. Twenty years later, and he was still full of opinions. He always seemed honestly mystified when his thoughts went unappreciated, often to the point of physical violence. These days he spent a lot of time in the gym. He was now a fully-grown five feet six of bristling muscles and unrestrainable opinions. Keith reckoned Scanner was under the false impression that people picked on him because of his size. They didn't. They picked on him because he was Scanner and Scanner was fucking annoying.

"All I'm saying," continued Scanner as he turned the wheel and took them onto the Cabra Road, "is that us driving over there and posting a bullet through the guy's letterbox, is a bit of a cliché."

"It's a message," said Keith.

"It's a clichéd message."

"And what would you do?"

"Shit in his letterbox."

Keith turned in his seat, truly appalled. "And what message exactly does that send?"

"It says, don't mess with us, we're the kind of people who are capable of anything."

"Does it?" said Keith, "Or does it send the message that we're full of shit?"

"You lack imagination, that's your problem."

"Imagination? Alright, say we do this, Mister Picasso. How would you even go about it?"

"What do you mean?"

"I mean, do we sit there and wait until you feel ready to pop one out or do we do it beforehand and bring it with us?"

"I'm pretty confident I could knock one out as required."

"Impressive," said Keith.

"You could too if you started having proper fibre in your diet."

"Ah, don't start that again," said Keith. "Alright then smartarse, pun intended, what happens if it's one of those up-high letterboxes? Do I pick you up and use you like an icing gun?"

"Nobody has those letterboxes anymore."

"My Auntie Margo does."

"Well, your Auntie Margo is weird."

"Says the man who wants to shit through her letterbox."

"Didn't her husband leave her to go off and live as a woman?"

"Yes he did. He's been going through a difficult life change. We're all trying to be supportive."

"He's a freak."

"And you're a small-minded prick."

Keith turned to stare out the window. He'd had more than enough of Scanner to last him a lifetime. The only reason they were still friends was habit. It was a hell of a lot easier to break up with a bird than it was to break up with a mate. The arsehole had been nice

to him twenty years ago when Keith had moved to a new school, and he's been living off it ever since.

They merged onto the Navan Road and Keith looked longingly at the Merc dealership. Even at this time of night, they always had the windows lit up, showing off the goods. He'd gone in there once but the saleswoman had been a bit dismissive when she'd smelled he'd not got the wedge. He dreamed about going back and slamming it down in cash, given her a wink and driving out. That'd show the judgy bitch.

"DNA," said Keith, cutting Scanner off. "They could get your DNA off the turd."

"Bollocks they can."

Keith took out his iPhone and typed it in as he spoke. "DNA in faeces."

"Faces?"

"Faeces, you idiot. It's the medical word for shite."

"Well la-dee-dah. What's wrong with just saying shite?"

Keith scrolled down through the search results. "Cop yourself on. You can't have doctors saying things like 'I'm sorry Mr Williams, you've got bowel cancer, we can tell from your shite'."

"I don't think people would care. If Mr Williams was that concerned, he would have had more fibre in his diet in the first place."

"You're like a broken bleedin' record with the ... Yes! Jog on ye shit cannon, you can even buy a DNA testing kit specifically for faeces."

"Feck off."

"Yep. Your first day in prison would be fucking hil-ar-i-ous. What are you in for? Me? Shitting through a letterbox."

A car in the oncoming lane honked as Scanner tried to look at Keith's phone. "Eyes front. You need to take a right onto Nephin Road up here."

"I know," said Scanner, huffily.

"Yeah, you know everything."

They turned, Keith flicking the required Vs at Cabra Garda station on the corner as they did so.

"Alright," said Scanner, a man utterly incapable of accepting defeat. "You pay a homeless bloke to do it."

"Right, and do we bring him with us or go for the 'here's one we prepared earlier' approach?"

Scanner considered this. "Earlier. You could have him do it into one of them Tupperware containers, so it doesn't stink the car out." Scanner was very particular about his car.

"So, let me get this straight. We're now paying homeless guys to shit in a lunchbox? This is sounding less like a message and more like a cry for help. Take a right up here."

Scanner grumbled under his breath as he turned into the road.

"Alright, stop here," said Keith, pulling on his gloves as he did so. "It's number 26, that'd be that one four from the end I reckon. You come with me. Keep an eye on the surrounding windows and make sure nobody clocks us. When it's all clear, give me the nod and I'll nip in and deliver the bullet. Clear?"

"Could we not..."

Keith opened his door and was out in a flash. He was not in the mood for another one of Scanner's suggestions.

Four minutes later, both car doors reopened and they sat in.

"Job done," said Keith.

"I'm just saying ..." said Scanner.

"D'ye know ..." said a voice that was neither Keith or Scanner, hence the reason that Keith screamed and Scanner punched a crack into his own windscreen.

"Jesus!" said Keith.

"Fuck's sake!" said Scanner.

"You alright there lads?" said the man sitting in the back seat eating a kebab. "You seem a tad jumpy?"

Keith and Scanner exchanged a look. The man, who definitely hadn't been there before, seemed unnervingly calm. He was large bloke in a black sheepskin coat, blessed with the kind of Cork accent that sounded like a cat in a slow moving blender.

"As I was saying," he continued, "d'ye know what really bothers me? In loads of films, people pop up in the back seat of cars and ye think, how in the hell did you not notice somebody crouching down back there? It's how Grace Jones knocks off Patrick Macnee in that Bond film where Duran Duran did the tune. Happens in the *Godfather* too. One of them *Back to the Future* films. I think it even happens in one of the Bourne things ..."

"Who the fuck are you?" said Scanner.

"It's him," said Keith.

"Him who?"

"Who do you think?" said Keith, nodding back in the direction they'd just come from.

"DS Bunny McGarry," said Bunny, in between messy mouthfuls of kebab. "Delighted to be making your acquaintance. The point I was making is, I didn't think anyone was stupid enough to miss somebody sitting in the back seat of a car and yet here's you two gobshites, proving me wrong." Bunny casually tossed the remains of his kebab onto the floor.

"Ah, for Jaysus's sake," said Scanner, "you're getting it all over me car."

Bunny looked at Keith, who, even panicked as he was, couldn't help but feel a little bit embarrassed.

"I don't think the muscle hamster here has fully grasped the gravity of the situation, has he?" asked Bunny. "Let's recap for the hard of thinking, shall we? You two just made a delivery to my abode. I'm going to guess ... a bullet?" Bunny looked between the two men. "Bit of a cliché, isn't it?"

"I told ye," said Scanner.

Keith felt like slamming his head through the window. "You just confessed, you know-it-all prick."

"Oh dear," said Bunny. "Bit of tension in paradise, is there lads?"

Scanner made as if to speak.

"Don't say a word," said Keith.

"The bullet means they'll have you on at least threat to kill under the Non-Fatal Offences Against the Person Act, 1997. That's a

maximum twelve months and seeing as yours truly is a card-carrying member of the Garda Síochána, you'll get the full whack. That's small time to hard men like you though, isn't it?" He looked at them both in turn. Even in the dim glow from the streetlights, the guy had a very off-putting wonky left eye that made it hard for Keith to look directly back at him. "That's not your big problem though."

"Isn't it?" said Keith.

"No," said Bunny. "That'd be the gun."

"What gun?" said Scanner, "We've not got a g..."

There was a loud thunk. Keith didn't need to look to know that the object that'd landed in the rear footwell was a handgun.

"Oh dear, oh dear, oh dear," said Bunny. "You boys are really in over your heads, aren't you?"

"Are we?" said Scanner. "There's another way of looking at it."

"Is there?" said Bunny, a disconcerting hint of glee to his voice.

"Yeah. You're the one in a car with two proper Gs that have now got a gun, ye fat old prick."

"Very true," said Bunny, pointing at Keith. "Your friend here looks like he can handle himself and I bet you'll be invaluable if the situation requires anything heavy being picked up and put down again in the same place. I'm no athlete and as you pointed out, I've got twenty-five hard years on either of you. Plus, as you said, I've now given you a gun. Thing is... wait!" Bunny McGarry held his hand up and then walloped Keith's headrest with it. "Tom Cruise in *A Few Good Men*, that's another one."

"What?" said Scanner.

"Where someone pops up from the back seat. Anyway what was I talking about? Oh yeah. See, you're dead right, you have 'a gun' but I have what could be termed in this situation as 'the gun'."

In the darkness of the car, the click-click of an unseen safety being slipped off and a hammer being pulled back echoed, if only in Keith's mind. It sounded like a coffin lid slamming shut. Bunny grinned widely at him.

"I'll do you a deal, boys. Whichever one of you bleeds first, I'll say he was the one holding the gun."

"What?" said Scanner.

"I do so hate repeating myself," said Bunny. He spoke slowly, pointing to add a visual aid. "I said – whichever one of the two of you, who gets the other to bleed first, doesn't cop for carrying the gun."

"And you think..." said Scanner, who didn't get any further because Keith had just punched him full in the face.

Dessie Kearns was rudely awoken by the doorbell. Actually, he was rudely awoken by his wife's elbow in his ribs, but that had been prompted by the doorbell.

"Fuck's sake!"

"Doorbell," she responded.

"You like it so much, why don't you go and answer it?"

One of the many current sources of friction in their marriage was the cost of that bloody doorbell. Like the house wasn't expensive enough, she'd made him spend four grand on the damn thing. She had seen it on some programme. It felt like every time she turned on the TV or opened a magazine, it cost him money. The stupid thing contained actual bells. Now every time they got a pizza delivered it sounded like Christ Church bleedin' Cathedral.

He could feel her sitting up in the bed beside him, pulling her eye-mask off.

"Let me get this straight..."

He hated when she started a sentence that way, it never ended well.

"... It is three o'clock in the pissing morning, and you want to send your wife, the mother of your children, down to answer the door to God-knows-what?"

"Rapists don't generally ring, love."

She clapped twice to turn the lights on and then slapped him right on the earhole.

"Jesus!" he said, now fully awake and loving life. "Ye mental bitch."

"Tell whichever of your drunken buddies wants you to go out whoring with him that you are unavailable."

He rolled out of bed and grabbed his robe off the floor. As he left the room, he heard her clap again to turn the light off. Like she wasn't going to be sitting there listening, loading up on ammunition for when he got back. Whoever this was, somebody had better be dead or somebody was going to be.

Through the ornate swirling glass beside the door, he could see the outline of two figures in the porch-light. Something wasn't right.

"Who is it?"

"Sorry Dessie," came back a shaky voice. "It's Keith and Scanner."

"What the..."

As he opened the door, the words died in his throat. Keith and Scanner were standing there bollock naked. Scanner was holding a tissue to his bleeding nose with one hand and cupping his nether region with the other. Keith had a swollen eye and both hands covering his modesty. They both sported various other cuts and bruises, and stood awkwardly hunched over like nature wasn't calling so much as hollering.

Dessie looked down the drive and around at the neighbouring houses. Thankfully he couldn't see anyone taking notice. They'd objected to their gnomes at the last resident's association meeting. He glanced back up the stairs; please God don't let her see. He couldn't afford to move again.

He stepped out and pulled the door nearly shut behind him.

"What the fuck?" whispered Dessie.

"We were doing..." started Scanner.

"You – shut up. Keith?"

"We were doing that thing," said Keith.

Dessie nodded.

"And it didn't go well."

"I can see that!" he hissed. "Where the hell are your clothes?"

"He took them."

"And he beat you up?"

Keith averted his eyes and looked down at the rosebushes. "Not exactly."

Scanner removed the hand from his modesty and pointed accusingly at Keith. "This fucker went and..."

Dessie pointed at Scanner without even looking at him. "Keith, what have I said about this dickhead talking?"

"Please, Dessie," said Keith, "can we just come in?"

Dessie glanced back over his shoulder, truly horrified. "No you can not."

"Please. He said as soon as he dropped us off, he was calling a patrol and reporting two naked perverts roaming the area."

"Oh for..."

Dessie looked around again, trying to decide between what would be the lesser of two evils. Out of the corner of his eye, he couldn't help but notice that Scanner's hand had now moved around to his posterior area.

"What on earth do you think you're doing?"

Scanner and Keith exchanged an awkward look. Keith looked between them both.

"Well?"

"He..." said Keith, and then stopped, his voice choking.

"What?"

"He..."

"Fuck's sake," said Scanner. "He made us shove bullets up our arses."

"Jesus."

"Yes," said Keith, again unable to make eye contact with anything but the ground. "And he gave us something to tell you."

"Which was?"

"This is how you send a message."

# SISTERS GONNA WORK IT OUT

Warning: The following novella features the Sisters of the Saint – a badass bunch of nuns who were first introduced in the novel Angels in the Moonlight, which is a prequel to The Dublin Trilogy.

If you think you don't like nuns, then you've not met these sisters. They're like the A-Team without the bizarre habit of firing off thousands of rounds of ammunition and never ever hitting anything.

# HANGING WITH THE SISTERS

## CAUCA PROVINCE, COLOMBIA – 1985

"This noose is very uncomfortable."

Sister Dionne very carefully turned her head to look at Sister Bernadette to see if she was joking. She already knew the answer but some statements still deserve to be double-checked. Sure enough, there was Bernadette, all five foot nothing of her, standing ramrod straight, the noose around her neck, glowering pointedly at the guards standing over by the stable door.

There were only two guards. One was a man in his forties who had the mistaken belief that his moustache gave his face character, and the other was an acne-pocked kid who couldn't have been more than nineteen and who looked incapable of growing any form of facial hair. The younger was brimming with nervous energy; the older was full of concern regarding a lot of things, not least his young compatriot. Dionne recognised the signs, she had been taught how to do so at a very young age. If you can recognise the signs, you can find an angle. Admittedly, she was not in a great position to work the room – her hands were tied and, not for the first time in her life, she

was standing on a tall bar stool. This, however, was the first time she had done so with a noose tied tightly around her neck.

Bernadette, to Dionne's left, was standing on a similar stool to the one Dionne found herself on. To Dionne's right, Sister Assumpta stood on a stepladder in deference to her significantly greater weight. They couldn't have her dying ahead of schedule.

The bar stools had come from the fully stocked bar in the corner. As stables went, this one had a surprisingly lounge lizard vibe to it. There was also a jukebox and a pool table.

"I said," repeated Bernadette, "this noose is very uncomfortable."

Dionne sighed. "I don't think he can understand you."

"Oh yes he can, and besides I'm not talking to you."

"Really? That is so you. Spending your last few minutes on earth holding a grudge."

Bernadette temporarily diverted her withering gaze from the guard to aim it in Dionne's direction. "Holding a grudge against the eejit who got me killed? I can think of nothing better to be doing."

"Well, that and lodging your complaint with the customer services department over there about the quality of their nooses."

Bernadette turned back to focusing all of her energies on giving the guard the evil eye. "I said, don't talk to me."

"Actually," said Dionne, "you said you weren't talking to me, you said nothing about me not talking to you. And besides, Sister, didn't I hear somewhere that to forgive is divine?"

"Don't you quote the Bible at me. You're not even a real nun."

Dionne shook her head and smiled at the younger guard, who was busy staring at a piece of ground as if he was expecting it to move. If anything, he looked like the most nervous person in the room which, given he was one of the only two people present who could take a step forward without dying, was really saying something.

One of the horses behind Dionne neighed. She had taken note of them as she'd been dragged into the barn. Knowing everything possible about your surroundings was another skill she had picked up from her father before she could walk. There were six horses in total; three black, two brown, one grey. Each one had their own stall

complete with water, oats, hay and so on. Dionne knew little about horses but they appeared to have a pretty sweet deal going here, even if the pool table and bar were presumably not for their benefit. General Rivera took considerably better care of his horses than he did of the people who worked for him. She wondered if that had occurred to the guards.

Dionne felt her nose itch and braced herself. An additional wrinkle to their current predicament was that she was a hay fever sufferer trapped in a room featuring an abundance of hay. She was one violent sneeze away from dancing the dead man's jig. Her dying in the hangman's noose had always seemed like a reasonably strong possibility, although the exact circumstances would at least come as a shock to the people she'd grown up with.

She turned to her right to look at Sister Assumpta. While she was the youngest of them, she was also the least capable of standing upright for an extended period of time. At a guess, Dionne reckoned she must be a good 300 pounds now and she knew from her old Aunt Bessie that her feet must have been killing her from standing still for so long. She stood on the second to top rung on the ladder, sweat gathering under her armpits as she stared intently up at the beam above their heads to which the ropes around their necks were tied.

Dionne lowered her voice. "Are you OK, Sister?"

Assumpta looked down at her with a start, as if surprised by the presence of anyone else in the room, and gave her a nod. To say Assumpta wasn't the talkative sort was an understatement of epic proportions. She could speak, she just mostly chose not to. It'd been weird at first but you soon got used to it. With Bernadette there, it wasn't like there was an abundance of silence to be filled.

Assumpta went back to intently staring at the beam.

The barn door flew open and a sheet of blinding sunlight washed through the dimness, causing Dionne to flinch. The distinctive figure of General Rivera in his immaculately pressed uniform, riding crop held under his arm, leather boots on his feet, strode in. He looked like a budget version of General Patton.

"Ah Sisters, sorry to have kept you 'hanging around'."

The general looked back at the guards for an appreciative audience for his joke, but they were too busy closing the doors behind him to have caught it.

For a man in his fifties Rivera looked fit. His slim build showed no signs of middle-aged spread, the sprinkle of salt and pepper in his otherwise robust head of hair being one of the few signs of his advancing years. His beard still held its original dark brown colouring. He favoured them with a smile that might have appeared to hold warmth if it wasn't for the circumstances.

He stopped a few feet in front of them. "I'm afraid your little plan is all for naught. The two trucks that you loaded my people onto have been spotted trying to make their way to the Panamanian border and I have sent my men to intercept. They have no chance of escape. They will soon be back here minus a couple of the ringleaders who will, of course, have to be executed."

"Monster." Bernadette spat out the word.

Rivera looked up at her and then stepped towards her. "Monster? Me? How am I the monster? I'm not the one who came in here, disturbing the happy balance of the community, trying to stir up revolt amongst my people."

"If they're 'your people'," said Dionne, "how come they are so keen to leave this hell-hole behind?"

"Hell-hole?" said Rivera, stretching his arms wide, "how is this a hell hole? I am but a simple farmer."

"My father back in Tipperary is a simple farmer," interjected Bernadette. "He has fifty head of cattle on a few acres. What he doesn't have is a hundred acres of coca plants and his own cocaine processing plant."

Rivera shrugged. "Potato, potatoe."

"We'd none of them either."

"And to think, when you turned up a couple of months ago, asking to create your school in the village, I was so accommodating. I allowed you to use one of my properties, I changed the work schedules to allow the children to work later in the day. And this is how you repay me?"

"Yes," said Dionne, "by trying to free the people who you keep as slaves."

"Slaves?" Rivera said with a grin. "How dramatic you are. You are the American one, no? Where do you think all of my product will end up? You people are so quick to condemn and yet there never appears to be any shortage of buyers."

"Very true," said Dionne. "For every person you're killing here, you're probably killing a hundred back home."

Rivera shrugged. "People decide for themselves what they want to do. Neither I nor any of my business associates force our wares on anybody."

"Yes," said Dionne, "you're all for freedom of choice, except when it comes to the people on those trucks."

The smile dropped from Rivera's face. "Those are my people, I am their papa. I protect them, I provide for them. A father must make hard choices for the good of his family."

"Yes," said Bernadette, "like deciding which ones to kill for being, what was it you called them? Oh yeah, ringleaders."

"I grow tired of this tedious conversation. Which of you is in charge?"

"Me," said both Bernadette and Dionne at the same time, before turning to look at each other.

"Hold on a second," said Dionne, "a minute ago it was all my fault that we were in this mess."

"That's right, and that is why you're no longer in charge."

"Oh, because your ideas are always so great. Remember what happened in Bolivia?"

"That wasn't my fault. That donkey almost certainly had an existing heart problem. What about that time in Somalia?"

"That was the interpreter's fault. How was I to know the word for—"

"Ladies!"

They both stopped and looked back down at Rivera, who seemed irritated at no longer being the focus of attention. "I really thought nuns were supposed to be more... how do you say, serene?"

"Ah,"said Bernadette, "blow it out your arse."

"Tut tut, Sister," said Rivera, leaning the heel of his boot on the stool that Bernadette was precariously perched on. "Such language is very un-nun-like."

"Nonsense. Nowhere in the Bible does it say you can't swear."

"Really? How interesting. Still, it seems to lessen you. Perhaps you should consider a different line of work?"

# A JOB FOR LIFE

## BALLYPOREEN, TIPPERARY – EIGHT YEARS EARLIER

'Perhaps you should consider a different line of work?' – that's what he'd said – bloody cheek. Tommy Riordan was her second cousin, once removed. Bernadette's father had helped out his father many a time. Tommy had also asked Bernadette if he could see her boobs and she'd done him the courtesy of not telling anyone. In his defence, they had both been seven at the time but still, Bernadette was fairly confident that Tommy would've got the belt if his father had found out. She had of course turned down his request, as indeed she had to any of a similar nature from any source ever since.

She sat at the bus stop and looked hard at the tarmac road, as if seeing if her glare combined with the summer sun could melt it. She was focusing her energies on being angry as the very last thing she wanted to be seen doing was crying. She had gone to the bus stop outside of town so people wouldn't see her sitting at the one outside Riordan's pub in the middle of the day, waiting to go back home already. Not that the news of her continuing fall from grace wouldn't be around the place within the hour. Trying to keep something

private in a small country town was like trying to hold boiling water in your hands.

Three cars had already slowed to offer her a lift. She'd waved them all on. She wanted to get the bus. Actually, she didn't want to do that either. What she really wanted was for the ground to open up and swallow her but so far it seemed unwilling to do so.

She glanced to her left and right. The road was barely wide enough for two cars to pass each other without one going into the ditch, and the bushes on either side clambered to touch passing traffic. It was currently deserted in both directions. Bernadette turned her eyes to the heavens.

"Well, this week hasn't exactly been going gangbusters, has it?" She had spoken directly to God since she had been a child. In the convent, she had asked one of the sisters if it was all right to do so and been advised that it was probably best to keep it to herself, but it was fine as long as God didn't start talking back. "Y'know, I get that you move in mysterious ways and all but, I've got to be honest, I'm not seeing it. Am I being punished? If so, for what? Have I not always tried to please you?" Bernadette looked down briefly and shook her head before returning her glare to the clear blue sky. "First, I'm thrown out of the Order and, as previously discussed, I was right. They can if and but it all day long, but I was right – and we both know it. Then, I've to come home and explain it to Da, which was... I mean, the look on his face. He didn't even know you could stop being a nun. Neither did the Job Centre for that matter, and what an ignominious trip that was. Siobhan Cunningham behind the counter too, absolutely loving it. Y'know, all she was thinking about was how I'd told on her and Deirdre Doyle for smoking behind the prefabs that time. It was a wooden structure for God's sake!" Bernadette kicked her foot at a stone in the ground that was too embedded to move. "So, I've to go cap in hand to Tommy Riordan for a job and then two days later he fires me! I mean, enough is enough, surely? What's the point of any of this? I mean seriously, if you've got some big ta-dah moment planned can I get a sign just to, y'know, let me

know that life isn't going to just be an endless stream of humiliations from here on out?"

Bernadette looked down again then glanced to her left and right. To the right, heading out of town, she could see someone striding purposefully around the bend in the road. It was a black woman in a nun's habit.

Bernadette glanced towards the heavens again and with a significantly lowered voice said, "OK then. I mean, it's not exactly subtle, but I'll take it."

Bernadette's eyes stayed fixed on the nun as she walked the hundred or so yards to the bus stop. The nun's eyes remained locked on hers the whole time too, putting them in a peculiar form of staring contest. Bernadette was aware that staring at someone like that was considered rude but she didn't care. As had been pointed out numerous times throughout her life, she seemed almost wilfully unconcerned with the proper etiquette for normal social situations. To be fair to her, this didn't feel like a normal social situation.

The nun sat down beside her, smoothed out her habit and only then did she speak.

"You are a hard woman to find."

"I wasn't aware anybody was looking."

The nun extended her hand to shake. "I am Sister Dorothy."

Two firm handshakes met and battled to a stalemate.

"I'm Sis... I'm Bernadette. Just Bernadette."

"Yes. You have been thrown out of your order."

Bernadette turned to look at the nun who looked back at her with an unreadable expression. She was mid-forties at a guess, a few years older than Bernadette. Her accent sounded West African but she couldn't place it any more accurately than that.

"You're very direct," said Bernadette.

"An attribute I am told we share."

Bernadette nodded at the ground. "True enough."

"I was told you worked at the off-licence in the town there..." She said the words 'off-licence' as if she was unsure that it really was a

thing. "But the man told me that you had recently left his employment."

"He fired me."

"Ah. I see."

"Apparently I was scaring off the customers. He showed me the figures. While I was behind the register the sales of alcohol were down 215% and the sale of peanuts were up 180%. He said seeing me made people feel guilty. Apparently, I have a very judgey face."

"That is unfortunate."

"I told him he should just whack up the price of peanuts but he wasn't having it. Turns out I'm not nun-like enough for the Order's liking, but I'm far too much of a nun for anything else."

"We shall see about that."

Bernadette turned to regard Dorothy again. What was this? They didn't want her back, that had been made extremely clear. Further punishment? They had already expelled her. They weren't going to involve the Gardaí for very obvious reasons.

"Who sent you?"

"I sent me. I wish to speak about what you did."

"I don't."

"You put a priest's head through a wall."

"Did you not hear what I just said?"

"I did but I am choosing to ignore it. I want to talk about you putting the priest's head through a wall."

"It sounds bad when you say it like that."

"How would you say it?"

"For a start, it wasn't a solid wall. I put his head through the plaster bit. It wasn't like a load-bearing wall or anything."

"Did you know that beforehand?"

Bernadette shrugged in lieu of an answer. Father Phelan was six foot two and had been a boxer in his days at the seminary. Bernadette was small enough to wear some children's sizes in clothing. Still, she had been the biggest opponent Father Phelan had seen in quite some time.

"Do you have any regrets?"

"Yes," said Bernadette, "I'm sorry the wall got damaged."

"Nothing else?"

Bernadette turned in the seat to look at Dorothy again. "Do you know why I did it? I mean, the actual reason?"

Dorothy looked her directly in the eye. "I do. I was just wondering if, given all that has happened to you since, you would choose the same course of action again?"

"In a heartbeat."

Dorothy gave a slight smile. "Good. That is why I am here."

"OK, but last I heard, Phelan was in a neck brace and had a cast on his hand, so there's a fair chance we might actually kill him this time."

"I have an offer for you. I am from The Sisters of The Saint."

"The who?"

"We are not well known."

"No kidding. I've never heard of you and I am, well was, a nun. And what kind of a name is that? The Sisters of Saint who?"

"Just the saint." Dorothy brushed dust that wasn't there off the knee of her dress. "We once had a full name but it was taken away from us. We... upset some of those in authority. Something I would imagine you could relate to."

"When did this happen?"

"1654."

"The Catholic Church does know how to hold a grudge."

Bernadette glanced up at Dorothy. There was a far-off look in her eyes as she spoke. "We are not without friends there too; how do you think I heard about you?"

"So, you've come to recruit me – is that it?"

"There are charitable organisations throughout the world, of all religions or of no religion, doing good work. Still, for all that... there are places where they cannot go. Where it is too dangerous to send people or where it is not politic to interfere. There are problems that nobody wishes to touch or solutions that are outside the realm of what is considered acceptable. We do not play by those rules. Wherever the innocent are in danger we are willing to go." Dorothy

spread her hands to indicate her habit. "This offers a small amount of protection, as does the element of surprise. Still, the work we do carries great risks. All I can promise you is a chance to make a difference."

Over Dorothy's shoulder Bernadette noticed her bus chug around the corner, barely twenty minutes late. She glanced up at the heavens as she spoke. "So, it has finally arrived."

# BLOWING IN THE WIND

## CAUCA PROVINCE, COLOMBIA – 1985

General Rivera pushed his foot against the base of the stool that Bernadette stood on. Dionne could see the delight on his face as he enjoyed the feeling of power as it wobbled under her. She could also see he was dangerously close to getting Bernadette's boot right in the kisser. They were painted black to look inconspicuous but Dionne knew she wore steel caps on her footwear for just this purpose. The action would almost certainly cost Bernadette her balance and hence her life, but Dionne could see that calculation in her eyes and she didn't like where the results were heading. They were seconds away from Rivera having a lifetime free of posing for family photographs and Dionne's team going from a trio to a duo.

"What exactly is it you need?" said Dionne.

General Rivera stood back and smiled up at her. "The names of the ringleaders."

"OK, and what do we get in return?"

Rivera laughed. "You are not in the strongest of negotiating positions."

Dionne gave him her best winning smile. "That don't mean we can't be friends, does it?"

"Oh for God's sake."

Dionne didn't take her eyes off Rivera as she spoke out of the side of her mouth. "Shut up Bernadette, I am talking to the general."

"You're an embarrassment to the habit. Batting your eyelashes at a tyrant. It's not nun-like."

"Well, you've already established that I'm not a nun, so—"

"You're damn right you're not. Look at her: tall, blonde, perfect teeth – she looks like a nun dreamed up by Hollywood."

"I apologise for flossing regularly, maybe if you—"

"Enough!" interjected Rivera. "I am tired of your little Marx Brothers routine. My men will have seized the trucks any moment now and then your usefulness will be entirely at an end. Now give me the names of the organisers." He stopped and looked up at Dionne. "Your friend is right, you are an attractive woman. I have a lot of men working for me, perhaps we could introduce a bonus programme?" He then looked up at Assumpta. "Some men do also like the larger lady."

Assumpta remained staring fixedly at the beam above their heads.

Rivera looked back at the other two. "Is there something wrong with her?"

"That's an interesting question to ask," said Dionne, "giving what you were threatening seconds ago."

Rivera's response stalled in his mouth as the walkie-talkie of the older guard at the door beeped loudly. He snatched it off his belt and spoke quietly into it.

"Ah," said Rivera, "I'd imagine this call is to tell me that your pointless little revolution is at an end." He raised his voice and spoke to the guard while smiling up at Dionne. "Ramón, what is the good news?"

The guard stepped forward nervously. "They have stopped the trucks, General."

"Excellent news. Good, good, good."

"They, ehm... they are empty."

Rivera whirled around on his heels. "What do you mean empty? How can they be empty? This is not possible. They were seen getting on those two trucks, they..."

Ramón's mouth flapped open and shut a couple of times but no words came out. Rivera turned to look at the nuns before pulling out his gun and pointing it at Dionne. "Where are my people?"

Dionne smiled down at him. "Are you familiar with the game Three-card Monte?"

# THREE-CARD MONTE

## WOMEN'S CORRECTIONAL FACILITY, FORT WORTH, TEXAS – FOUR YEARS EARLIER

"Are you familiar with the game Three-card Monte?"

Dionne Featherstone was sitting at one of the metal all-in-one tables specially designed to give you nothing to throw in a riot. She shuffled a pack of cards expertly, flipping the cards back and forth from hand to hand. She was sitting with Patricia, her cellmate of three years, but that wasn't who her question had been aimed at. It had been meant for Tina DeLuca, who was currently leaning over the table in a threatening matter. Tina tried to do everything in a threatening manner – Dionne imagined as a child she had lined her dollies up and then tried to squeeze them for chocolate cigarettes.

Tina's default expression of intimidation was currently muddied with confusion. "What the shit do I care about that, Featherstone? I asked you if you're all excited about getting out on parole next week? Y'know, free as a bird. Won't have to put up with this shit no more."

While she could have meant the incarceration experience in general, Dionne knew that wasn't it. At least not just it. What she meant was the current random cell inspection that was happening on

the four floors above them which meant that all the inmates of Block C were currently gathered in the downstairs communal area.

"I know what you were asking me," said Dionne, smiling up sweetly at Tina, "and by way of an answer, I was asking if you were familiar with the game Three-card Monte?"

She said it slow, in a voice that implied she thought Tina was a bit hard of thinking for not understanding. It was fair to say there was no love lost between them. When she had first arrived Tina had tried to 'tax' Dionne and Patricia, an offer which Dionne had declined. There had then been three attempts to 'deal' with Dionne, all of which had gone very badly. So much so that Tina's position as alpha bitch of the wing was now being openly questioned. Tina needed to deal with that. People, thought Dionne, were so tediously easy to predict at times.

"Why I give a shit about some faggoty card game?"

"Well, Tina, I'm glad you asked as it explains our current predicament beautifully." Dionne's fingers flew across the deck and without looking she withdrew three cards from it. She placed them on the table in front of her. The queens of hearts, diamonds and clubs. "Now, in the traditional 'find the lady' version of this game there's a queen and two other cards, and your job is to find the queen. I like to play it differently. See these three queens..." Dionne indicated the cards with an open-handed gesture, "... I'm going to turn them over and move them around, and if you can find the lady, I'll give you ten bucks. OK? Good."

Dionne flipped all three of the cards over and started moving them around on the table with lightning speed. "Just keep your eyes on the lady."

"But," said Tina, "they're all ladies."

"Just like in this prison, so that should make it pretty easy for you." Dionne's hands left the cards and then she held them out palm up again. "So, find me a lady."

Tina looked around nervously, aware that all the nearby inmates were taking an interest now. She tried to smile, aware that, in a way

she didn't understand yet, the situation was going sideways. "That one."

She slammed her index finger down onto the back of the card on the far left.

"Oh, are you sure?"

"Yeah, no... alright, that one."

She moved her finger over to the middle card and held it there.

"Well," said Dionne, "let's see. If you'd have stayed here..." She flipped over the left-hand card to reveal the Queen of Diamonds. "You would have been a winner, or if you'd have gone here..." Dionne flipped over the right-hand card to reveal the Queen of Hearts, "again, winner! But you went—"

Dionne tried to lift up the middle card but Tina held her finger firmly on it. "No way bitch, you ain't touching the card. Back off."

Dionne held her hands up in surrender. "Alright boss, just take it easy. I—"

Tina flipped the card over – Jack of Spades. Laughter and a smattering of applause broke out behind Tina as her face grew red.

"Oh dear," said Dionne, "you got jack. You're a loser."

"You cheated."

"Nah honey, I misdirected."

"What's the difference?"

"I'll explain; look up there." Dionne pointed to the entrance to her and Patricia's cell, 117, that two of the guards were just about to enter. "My cell is about to be searched. You sticking that little bundle of contraband drugs in there to be found so as to mess up my parole, that was cheating."

Tina at least had the wherewithal to look embarrassed. "I don't know what you're talking about."

"Sure you do," said Dionne with a wide warm smile, "but that's OK because they aren't going to find anything in that crevice under the toilet because there's nothing there to find. Misdirection. However, when they get to cell 208..."

Tina lunged across the table at her. It had been expected and was hence easy to avoid. Being physically intimidating meant that Tina

had never learned the art of being unpredictable and that made her easy for Dionne to play. "Whoa, easy there Tina. Your mood swings are so erratic. Is this because of the drug problem?"

A shout came from behind her – Hardy, one of the male guards. "Featherstone."

"No problem here, chief. Me and Tina from cell 208 were just reminiscing about old times."

"Whatever. You've got a visitor."

Dionne wasn't sure what to expect. She had been inside for three years and received the grand total of zero visitors in that time. Her father was dead, mother long gone, and the crew she worked with, they would have been crazy to put their heads above the parapet by coming to see her. On the walk down the corridor she had been trying to guess who her unexpected visitor might be and what trouble it might mean. Trying to find the angles, just like her dad had taught her. The black nun with the piercing stare sitting on the other side of the Perspex glass hadn't made her list of guesses, but Dionne still smiled at her with a genuine sense of relief. As she picked up the receiver from the side of the booth, she was confident she knew both why the nun was here and how this conversation was going to go. Reading people was her thing. She was wrong on all counts.

"Hello Miss Featherstone. My name is Sister Dorothy."

"Hi. So, which one are you from?"

"I'm sorry?"

"Which order?"

"Of the ones you have contacted?" The nun shook her head so vigorously that there was a crackle of interference on the line. "I am from none of them."

"Oh, OK… so who are you, then?"

Sister Dorothy withdrew a folder that was several inches thick and placed it on the desk in front of her. "Who I am is not important right now. I am here to discuss who you are."

Dionne sighed. "OK. I'm in prison. I am paying for my crimes. Like I told the parole board, I have seen the error of my ways."

"Oh, Miss Featherstone—"

"Please, call me Dionne."

"Very well, Dionne... you are certainly not paying for your crimes."

Dionne raised her eyebrows. "Excuse me?"

"You are paying for one of your crimes. You are now thirty-one years of age. You have been working as a 'confidence trickster' since you were at least fifteen. I would imagine you have been involved in hundreds, if not thousands, of frauds in that time. You are only in prison, Dionne, for the one for which you were caught."

"I've changed my mind. Call me Miss Featherstone, and what exactly is this? Am I on *This Is Your Life* or something?"

Dionne's mind was racing, trying to figure the angles. Was she trying to mess up her parole? It didn't help that this woman appeared to have one of the finest poker faces Dionne had ever come across. She'd spent a summer shacked up with a professor from Berkeley who specialised in body language. They'd taught each other a hell of a lot about many things and one of them was reading people. He had the science, she had the natural ability. She'd instinctively known what a micro-expression was long before he had explained the concept. Most people's faces were a sea of emotions and tells; this woman's was a desert. It was throwing Dionne as much as anything she said.

Sister Dorothy patted the large folder. "In a manner of speaking, this is your life. Certainly, it is probably the most comprehensive picture of it that anyone has ever assembled. I have spent several weeks on it. I have spoken to law enforcement in four states and at a federal level. I have also spoken to criminals, those you worked with and those, I suppose, who you would consider your contemporaries. I know more about you than I am guessing anyone does."

"Well, your interest is really sweet but I'm kinda already seeing someone."

"I know you use humour as a defence mechanism."

"Look, I'm not that person any more."

"I know you lie expertly too."

"Ah, to hell with this."

Dionne stood, an angry snarl forming on her lips, ready to slap the receiver back into its cradle. Dorothy looked up at her with the same placid expression, again showing no emotion that could be read. "And I know you will not put that phone down because this," Dorothy tapped her fingers on the folder, "is about your life up until now. I am here about your life after this point."

A long moment of silence stretched out between them. In her peripheral vision Dionne noticed the guard, Hardy, take a step towards her. She sat back down and waved him away. Then she turned back to look at Dorothy on the other side of the glass.

"OK, but let's not dwell on ancient history, shall we?"

Dorothy nodded. "Very well, how about more recent history? In the last three months you have written to every order of nuns in North America explaining to them that you have felt a calling to Christ. That you wanted to explore your vocation with a view to joining the Sisterhood."

"And every last one turned me down flat."

Dorothy gave a shrug. "In their defence, some of them at least looked into you before doing so. Your history scared them off. They thought that you were using them in some form of confidence trick."

"Con, it's just called a con in this country. And I wasn't."

"I actually believe you."

Dionne gave Sister Dorothy a sceptical look. "Really?"

"Well, I am at least open to the possibility that you are not lying. That it is not a 'con', as you call it. In fact, I have a theory."

"Is that so?"

"Yes. If you will permit me..."

Dionne nodded. It didn't seem she had much to lose, and she was curious.

Dorothy cleared her throat. "You were born in Las Vegas to a showgirl mother and a magician father. She, your mother, didn't really take to the role and abandoned you both when you were just a year old."

"Oh God, if this is some psychobabble bull—"

Dorothy calmly held her hand up to stop Dionne.

"To get to the future we need to travel the road of the past."

Dionne puffed out her cheeks then nodded begrudgingly.

"Your father, as far as I can tell, did his best to raise you. When the work dried up he dealt blackjack. He also drank too much, got in a little trouble which seems to have led him into a lot more trouble. From what I can gather, your first 'con' was in order to get him out of a particularly bad fix."

He'd been in fifty large to Gerry Rancone and Rancone had been looking for someone to make an example of. While pleading his case, Pops had spilled coffee on Gerry's Persian rug. He'd really loved that rug. Pops's luck had always stunk. Dionne had gone to work with some friends of her Aunt Bessie that Aunt Bessie wasn't too proud about having.

"Your path into crime being for good reasons stands somewhat in your favour."

"Gee, thanks."

"Not much that follows does, however. I only have pieces of course. There are many reports of 'cons', as you call them, involving a tall, attractive, blonde lady in Nevada and further afield. There are no shortage of ladies who match that description around here though."

"Oh yeah honey, shake a tree and get half a dozen."

Dorothy kept talking as if Dionne wasn't even there. "Of course, as it was explained to me, in many of your cons the victims would not come forward or perhaps did not even know they had been conned. Still, when you were arrested the authorities went looking. They seem a mixture of frustrated and impressed that despite what they suspect, they were not able to prove any other charges."

Dionne smiled. "Not that I know anything about what you're talking about as I was convicted in a case of mistaken identity, but I do remember my daddy once said to me 'you can't cheat an honest man'."

"Ah," said Dorothy, wagging a finger in the air, "but here is where we come to my theory. Firstly, your arrest. I spoke to Detective Winershaw from the Fort Worth Police Department. You and your associates had

successfully defrauded the Lone Star Bank of one hundred and twenty-seven thousand dollars. You were free and clear. Then you just walked into the bank. You were seen by the branch manager you had dealt with calmly standing in line. To quote Detective Winershaw: 'it was like watching an Olympic gymnast complete a perfect routine then trip over her own feet leaving the mat'. It made no sense."

Dionne said nothing, focusing on maintaining a blank expression as Sister Dorothy looked searchingly into her eyes.

"I think you wanted to get caught. You did it in such a way that your associates were free and clear but, even if you didn't know you were doing it, that is what it was. On some level, you wanted to be stopped. You wanted to be punished."

"Well," said Dionne, "you're quite the spooky mindreader. Spank me, I've been a bad girl. Are we done here?"

Dionne wanted to move, to stand up and leave, but something wouldn't let her. The nun merely paused briefly and then continued as if Dionne had not spoken.

"Do you know what I think?" She patted the file again. "Somewhere in here, amidst this pile of unprovable theories of your involvement in all of these schemes or perhaps in one of the schemes that nobody in law enforcement has any idea about, you finally found a victim to your victimless crime."

Dionne ran her tongue across her dry lips.

"You had been blanking it out all these years. Companies are insured, you can't cheat an honest man... I am certain you had many excuses in your head. Then something happened. Something you couldn't brush off. Your conscience, so long dormant, woke up and you couldn't make it stop. Tell me, do you see their faces when you try and sleep?"

"What would you know about it?"

"Considerably more than you would think. I wouldn't be sitting where I am right now if I hadn't been where you are."

"Done a lot of hard time have you, Sister?"

The only answer Dorothy gave was another dose of that

implacable stare. Dionne looked down at the scarred Formica table top, a collage of cigarette burns, coffee stains and scuff marks.

When Dorothy spoke again it was in a quieter, more conciliatory voice. "The orders were right when they rejected you... up to a point. They thought you were engaged in some kind of trick and you are. Trying to join an order, that wasn't it though, was it? No. You being in here, that is the trick and it is one you played on yourself. You weren't caught in any real sense. No, you tried to put yourself somewhere were you couldn't do any more harm. You thought that would make it stop but it didn't. Now you're facing getting out next week and you're terrified. Terrified of the person you were and that you fear you'll become again. You wrote to all those orders because you wanted to put yourself somewhere else where you could do no harm because you hate what you have done and who you have become."

Dionne wiped a single hot tear from her right cheek. "Alright, it was a stupid idea, I get it. No order of nuns is going to want me. I'm a liar, a cheat, a con artist. I get it."

"One order might."

Dionne looked up, despite herself, a little hope lighting her heart.

"But we are not your ordinary order. We take on work others won't do and we have, at times, had to step outside the conventional methods to achieve results."

"What does that mean?"

"What that means, Dionne Featherstone, is that I am offering you a unique opportunity. I want you to be a liar, a cheat, a con artist. I want you to use all you have learned on a grander scale than you have ever dreamed of."

"But—"

"I want you to be who you are, while at the same time being a much better person than you've ever been, because this time you will be on the side of the angels."

# GENERALLY UNHAPPY

## A BARN IN CAUCA IN 1985 WITH A VERY ANGRY GENERAL

General Rivera was at the far end of the barn screaming invectives into a radio and threatening to shoot everybody. So far, this vigorous piece of man management had not resulted in the trucks that he thought contained his workforce being any less empty.

"What was all that nonsense about card tricks?" whispered Bernadette.

"It was a little piece of showmanship," said Dionne. "You've got to sell the sizzle as well as the steak."

"It just seemed like you were antagonising him unnecessarily."

"Me? I was antagonising him? Really? Need I remind you Sister that you were the one that told him to... what was it? Oh yeah, blow it out his ass."

"That's entirely different. And besides, it was arse not ass."

"What difference does that make?"

"A very big one."

Bernadette had that haughty expression on her face that Dionne had known would be there. If she was ever proven wrong in an argument Bernadette's go-to play was acting like the whole argument

was beneath her. It was one of the many, many ways that she was a massive pain in the ass/arse.

A thought struck Dionne. "By the way, is that thing you said about it not saying anywhere in the Bible that swearing isn't allowed true?"

"It is, at least as far as anyone in this room knows. You should read it sometime, Sister."

"Oh for God's sake..."

"Taking the Lord's name in vain, on the other hand—"

Dionne blew out an exasperated huff of air. "Really? You're going to keep banging that 'you're not a real nun' drum, even when we're minutes from death?"

"Ah ha," said Bernadette, turning triumphantly, "so you admit it! We're going to die and it is all your fault!"

"I will admit things have not exactly gone to plan."

Dionne looked down. Truth be told, she was not a big fan of heights. Her feet were only about four feet off the floor on the tall bar stool, but it was a very significant height when a rope was around your neck with maybe six inches of slack. "Do you know what I don't understand? If you hate working with me so much, how come you've never asked Dorothy to transfer you somewhere else?"

"What? And leave you alone to go off and get poor Sister Assumpta killed?"

"Assumpta can look after herself just fine."

They both turned to look at Assumpta. The sweat patches under her arms had now extended down her black dress to near waist level, and she was leaning on the step ladder at a precarious angle, still staring up at the beam the three ropes were tied around. Her face was red from the strain of standing in the one spot for too long in the heat.

"You OK, Sister?"

"Don't keep looking up," said Bernadette, "you'll make yourself dizzy."

Dionne and Bernadette shared a look. They may well have been the two people in the world that were most familiar with Sister

Assumpta's eccentricities, but that didn't mean they didn't find them unsettling on occasion.

They were interrupted by a radio being hurled across the room and destroying several hundred dollars' worth of rather good brandy.

"OK," said Rivera, striding towards them, a slightly unhinged laugh in his voice. "Most amusing, Sisters. Well done. This, what did you call it, Three-card Monte. Most amusing. We think they are somewhere but they are somewhere else. My people are not on the trucks. What a clever trick. So, where are they?"

"Well..." said Dionne.

"No. No," said Rivera, pulling his hand gun from his holster. "No more silly games, no more Three-card Monte. A straight answer or..." he turned to point the gun at Assumpta, "...or the fat one dies. Clearly, you two do not like each other but I bet everyone likes the fat one."

Dionne glanced at Assumpta, whose gaze remained fixed on the beam.

"She's not fat," said Bernadette.

"It's a glandular problem," said Dionne.

Rivera took a step towards her. "She is about to have a lead problem, closely followed by a gravity problem."

"OK, OK," said Dionne, glancing at her watch, "relax. The villagers never left the mountain. They're over in the caves."

"The caves? The caves that are a few hundred yards away from where we now stand? I don't believe you."

"You haven't looked there, have you?" said Dionne. "Of course you haven't. Your little spy saw them getting on the trucks, didn't he?"

"Paulo."

The younger of the guards saluted and then hurried out the door.

"If you are lying," said Rivera, "then you are all dead."

"And if we aren't?" said Dionne.

He shrugged. "There are easy and hard ways to die. What I don't understand is, if they are just hiding in the cave, then what was the point of all this?"

"Well," said Dionne, "do you like puzzles?"

# DO YOU LIKE PUZZLES?

## THE SISTERS OF SAINT KATHERINE, BARCELONA – THREE YEARS EARLIER

*Do You Like Puzzles?* Assumpta regarded the cover of the magazine sceptically. In her opinion, titles should not be questions. The picture below the title was of a puppy. She was unsure whether the question was being asked to or by the dog. Assumpta liked puppies. Assumpta liked puzzles. Assumpta did not like the two of them being thrown together in such an illogical way.

As a child, when she had told her parents back in Florence that she liked puzzles, they had insisted on buying her books in which the objective was to find a man who went by the name Waldo or Wally. She assumed that the multiple names were to protect his identity; a concept she understood only too well. These books made her cry. Assumpta did not like large crowds of people and she assumed Wally/Waldo to be a kindred spirit. She imagined how terribly stressful being lost in these vast throngs was for him. Her brother Leo had been the only one who had understood her point of view. Ten years older than her, he had got her to sleep by telling her a story about Waldo moving to the country and living alone save for three chickens. Assumpta liked chickens.

When it came to people, it wasn't so much that Assumpta disliked them, so much as she knew that they found her confusing and that seemed to upset them. They would then try and make sense of her, and she found that unpleasant not least because, although she was too polite to mention it, they were far more confusing than she was. She liked numbers. She liked patterns. She liked measurable and definable things. People, on the other hand, hurt those they said they loved, found offence in the innocuous and when they got what they wanted, never seemed that happy. Actually, they seemed very happy initially and then inevitably that happiness degraded. If happiness was H and the object of their desires – be it a person, an achievement or an actual object – was D, then:

$$H = D/T$$

with T of course being time. Everything degraded.

Then they would need another thing, call it D2 and it would be:

$$H = D1/T + D2/T$$

and so on, with T eventually reducing all to zero. The more they got, the more they wanted in order to maintain the value of H.

As far as Assumpta was concerned, happiness equals P – that being peace. That being zero, the absence of all else, should be easily achieved – at least in theory. If her life proved anything, it was that finding a way to just be left alone with numbers and perhaps a couple of chickens, was an almost impossible objective.

*"How could this happen?"* That was the voice of Reverend Mother Margareta coming from behind the large oak door to Assumpta's right. It was the door to Principal Cisneor's office.

*"What do you mean how could this happen?"* And that was the voice of Principal Cisneor. Both he and the Mother Superior had spent quite a lot of time trying to make sense of Assumpta. They were talking in Spanish but Assumpta understood them. Spanish was one of fourteen languages Assumpta could speak, not that she ever really

spoke them. Almost nobody knew about this skill. In fact, most people spoke to Assumpta like she could barely comprehend one language.

*"You told me to find a use for her in the school. What was I supposed to do? Make her a teacher? She doesn't speak!"*

Assumpta looked up to see Principal Cisneor's secretary, Mrs Bagello, trying not to look at her while making a poor attempt at looking busy. She was exhibiting the signs of giddy excitement. Assumpta did not know why. Perhaps she was ill.

*"But the school accounts? That's a lot of responsibility."*

*"You said she liked numbers!"*

The principal was speaking faster than usual and at a higher pitch. The Mother Superior, on the other hand, was lowering her voice at the end of sentences. Assumpta noted this as she flipped through the pages of the puzzle book, spending about fifteen seconds looking at each page. That was how long it took to solve the puzzles in her mind.

*"I didn't say give her access to bank accounts! How much did she take out?"*

*"All of it."*

Assumpta heard a soft swish of material. She had been surrounded by nuns long enough to know that was the sound of someone blessing themselves with a vengeance. Assumpta had become a nun because her family had initially not known what to do with her and then were forced into making a swift decision by circumstance. She had gone willingly, although she had been disappointed to find out she had not joined one of those silent orders.

*"How much,"* said the Mother Superior, a peculiar tremble in her voice, *"is all of it?"*

*"Sixteen thousand pesos."*

*"Sweet mother Mary!"*

A change in the light caused Assumpta to look up. There was a nun standing over her but not one she had ever met. She was black for a start. Assumpta had never met a black person before.

"Hello Assumpta, my name is Sister Dorothy. Do you mind if I sit down?" she asked in English.

Assumpta shrugged and the nun grabbed the chair beside her and moved it so they were sitting opposite each other.

The secretary coughed one of those coughs that people do when they don't really need to cough and then followed it up with, "Excuse me, I am Principal Cisneor's secretary, can I help you with something?"

Sister Dorothy said, "I am sorry, I cannot understand your question as I do not speak Spanish. No assistance is required, thank you." She said this in perfect Spanish before lowering her voice and switching back to English. "Sometimes it is just easier to pretend. I know I don't have to explain that to you."

*"How did she even know how to go into a bookmaker's?"*

*"One of the porters showed her apparently, I don't know. All I know is she put all of it on what they call an accumulator bet on three different horses in three different races."*

Sister Dorothy looked at the door. "They think they are in there deciding on your future, don't they?"

Assumpta shrugged.

"I think we can decide your future out here. Do you remember the tests you did a couple of years ago?"

Assumpta knew which ones she meant. She hadn't been supposed to do them as they were only meant for the older male students. Her taking them had caused all kinds of trouble. There had been a lot of people trying to make sense of her after that.

"Well, I saw the results. I think you have special skills..."

*"She lost it all?"*

*"Worse than that..."*

"Skills that are wasted here."

*"... She won."*

*"She won?!"*

"And it seems I have got here just in time."

*"Two hundred and seventy thousand pesos. The bookmaker is livid, he is accusing the church of cursing him."*

Dorothy looked at the door again before continuing. "How would you like to join my order?"

*"Oh my God. If the press were to find out."*

*"He is refusing to pay. I think maybe, maybe we make a deal..."*

"The work will be dangerous, but I promise you will be allowed to be your true self..."

*"We could agree to take only some of the money."*

*"Yes. I mean, we did win."*

*"But not all of it, in exchange for him keeping quiet."*

"You just need to do the things you are good at, and I promise we will not try and change you..."

*"The, ahem, the Order will of course be entitled to a..."*

*"A small part, yes."*

Assumpta looked at the ceiling for a moment and then nodded.

*"I mean, she is <u>our</u> sister after all."*

*"She could have ruined <u>this</u> school."*

Assumpta reached across and took Sister Dorothy's hand. Without another word both women stood up.

"Excuse me, where are you going?" asked the secretary, sounding flustered.

"I can still not understand your question, may God bless you."

They walked out of the waiting room and down the hallway, Sister Assumpta clutching Sister Dorothy's hand all the way.

*"How did she do it?"*

*"I asked her. Was it a message from God? A miracle?"*

*"And what did she say?"*

*"She said it was just numbers."*

*"Numbers?"*

*"Numbers."*

# HANG TIME

## A BARN IN CAUCA IN 1985 WITH A LESS ANGRY GENERAL

General Rivera was beginning to calm down. The younger guard had called in on the radio to say that he had found the people, all eighty-nine of them, huddled together in the caves exactly where Dionne had told him they would be.

Rivera tapped the radio handset's aerial to his chin contemplatively as he looked up at the three nuns.

"Do I like puzzles?" he repeated. "I guess I must do because you are still alive. I am fascinated to find out what you thought any of this could achieve."

Dionne smiled at him. "Well, to explain that, I have to give you the puzzle: so, you have four plastic containers; one six gallons in size; one three gallons; and the final two are both two gallons. The six gallon one is full of water, the others are empty. You also have four half inch pipes. How would you connect them all together so that in," she looked over at Assumpta, "sixty-three?" Assumpta didn't look at her. "Assumpta?" she repeated.

Assumpta lowered her head from her vigil of staring at the beam.

"Sixty-three minutes?"

Assumpta nodded once and returned to what she was doing.

Dionne turned back to the general. "Sorry, yes, you have to connect the containers and the pipes in such a way that the water comes out of the last pipe and falls into a waiting cup in sixty-three minutes' time."

The general shook his head, "I have no idea, nor do I care... and that is what proves I am intelligent. For this task I would hire a plumber."

Rivera laughed and turned to the moustachioed guard, who smiled the smile of underlings everywhere when a superior has made a bad joke.

"The puzzle I want an answer to is why my guards caught three nuns trying to break into my facility this afternoon? And why they convinced my people to go and cower in a cave? Were you expecting to be able to overpower my men?" Rivera turned to the guard behind him again. "Hey Ramón, do you think these three unarmed women could take you?"

Ramón smiled nervously under his thick moustache and shook his head.

Rivera turned back to Dionne. "He thinks he could handle you. Even if he couldn't, Paulo would have. Even if you'd managed to take out both of them, the rest of my men would be back from chasing the trucks pretty soon. So, I'm afraid, I still don't get it."

Dionne turned to Bernadette. "Would you like to field this bit, Sister?"

"Thank you, Sister." Bernadette cleared her throat. "For the record, we were not breaking into your facility."

"No?" said Rivera.

"No," confirmed Bernadette. "Although, let's call it what it is... your cocaine processing plant where you make children and women work sixteen-hour days, processing and packaging your filth."

"They could work out in the fields with the men under the blazing sun, but my mother raised a gentleman."

Bernadette rolled out one of her best facial expressions of

absolute disgust; Dionne considered herself to be a connoisseur of her extensive collection.

"Anyway," continued Bernadette, "we weren't breaking in because we already had. We had broken in, and then broken out again."

"Is that right?" said Rivera, with a smirk.

"Yes. Then we realised that your two men, Ramón here and..."

"Paulo," interjected Dionne.

"Paulo," continued Bernadette, "were not out on patrol as we expected but inside the facility."

"Yes," said Rivera. "I am a general. I did not leave the source of my power unguarded."

"Well," said Bernadette, "we consider all life to be sacred. Even men who worked for an evil tyrant such as yourself."

Rivera pulled a wounded facial expression and clenched his hands to his chest mockingly.

"And," said Bernadette, "our 'plan' had not accounted for their presence." She looked pointedly at Dionne.

"No," agreed Dionne, "my bad. We had to improvise a way of getting them out of there and, as you already said, us overpowering them was risky. So I came up with the idea of us getting captured. We thought—"

"You thought."

"I thought," said Dionne with a roll of her eyes, "that they'd bring us to that cell you have over behind your house on the far side of the compound, but instead they brought us here. To your stables, which is right beside your facility."

"Yes," said Rivera, "my orders. I do all my 'interviews' here." He walked over and patted the mane of the large grey horse. "I find being surrounded by my beauties most relaxing." He rubbed his cheek against the horse's neck. "Isn't that right, Pegasus?"

He turned back to Dionne. "You thought with my facility unguarded that my people would rise up and destroy it, instead of cowering in the cave like frightened children?"

"Many of them are frightened children," snapped Dionne, for the first time letting emotion slip through her calm demeanour.

"We got caught," said Bernadette, "deliberately... to save the lives of your men, because on the day of judgement, I don't want to stand before God and say that I didn't do everything I could to prevent the needless loss of life. In the same way, I wouldn't want to be you if I was standing there saying I had allowed innocent people to be slaughtered by a man who cares for nothing save money, power and his damn horses."

"If you are trying to plead for your life," said Rivera, "you are doing a particularly bad job of it."

Dionne noticed how pale Ramón had now turned. It was him and not the general that Bernadette's fearsome gaze had been fixed on as she spoke. If there was one thing Bernadette knew how to do, it was to put the fear of God into someone. Nobody did fire and brimstone quite like her.

The digital watch on Sister Assumpta's wrist beeped loudly. She wriggled her bound hands around until she was able to turn it off.

Dionne looked across at her. "Have you figured the problem out?"

Assumpta spoke for the first time. "Maybe."

"Ahhhhh!" said Rivera excitedly, "it speaks at last! And tell me tubby girl, what is the answer to your little problem with vessels and pipes and water?"

Assumpta shook her head. "That isn't the problem."

"No?" said Rivera.

"No," confirmed Dionne. "I mean that was a problem, but she figured that out about sixty-four minutes ago. I explained it wrong the first time. You see, the containers... there isn't water in them. No, they're full of the ethanol that you use to process the coca into cocaine."

The smile dropped from Rivera's face.

"And the cup? Not a cup. It is a welding torch with its flame ignited."

And now it was Rivera's turn for his face to go a deathly shade of white. "Ramón, go and check."

"I really wouldn't do that," Bernadette said in what passed for her

softer voice, “not unless you want to be having that chat with Saint Peter a lot sooner than you’d expect.”

“Ramón! Do as I say this instant.”

Ramón nodded, as if agreeing, and then drew his pistol and pointed it at the general.

“Ramón!”

Ramón looked at his own shaking hand, as if he were as surprised by its actions as anyone, although no-one could have been as outraged as Rivera.

“This is mutiny! You will swing for this.”

His eyes blinking through the sweat teaming down his face, Ramón looked back at his now ex-employer. “I don’t want to burn in hell, I don’t want to burn in hell, I don’t want to burn in hell.”

Just then there was a massive explosion outside and all hell broke loose.

The sheer force of the first explosion blasted the barn’s loft doors open. The ground shook and debris slammed against the walls, splintering the wood in places. It felt like a giant was trying to rip the building from the earth.

Dionne managed to maintain her balance on the wobbling stool beneath her while shoving her fingers in between the noose and her neck to provide some semblance of protection if she slipped.

Once she had steadied herself she looked to her right. The stool lay on the ground and above it Sister Bernadette’s feet dangled helplessly. As her body turned in the air Bernadette’s hands scrabbled desperately at the rope gradually cutting off her air supply. Their eyes locked briefly and Dionne saw something there she had never seen before – fear.

Assumpta had to act fast. She had calculated out fourteen different scenarios over the last forty minutes but the current predicament didn’t exactly match any of them. She stood on the topmost step of the ladder as it wobbled under her. She tried to shut out the world.

Tried to shut out Sister Bernadette struggling like a hooked fish.

Assumpta calculated her to have three minutes at most, assuming she fought. That was a safe bet. Bernadette would always fight.

She tried to shut out the general and Ramón rolling around on the floor. Typical men – the building was on fire and they were engaging in physical combat.

And finally, Assumpta tried to shut out the flames that had already started amidst the dry straw of the loft. They would spread fast. Eventually, they would eat through the beams and collapse the building in on itself. Even if they did, there was at best a three per cent chance of that happening in time to save Bernadette's life. That assumed the smoke and flames hadn't got them first.

Another secondary explosion followed the initial blast as the greedy fire in the processing plant found something else to consume. It hadn't reached its main course yet – the vats of ethanol at the back of the building. That would be quite the feast for the flames.

Assumpta used the two feet of slack in her rope to tug her knot along the beam as close to Dionne as possible. Dionne watched her intently.

"Catch me!"

Assumpta grasped the rope above her head with both hands and swung. She was relieved the assumption that her arms were strong enough to support her weight while gripping the rope was correct. If it hadn't been, the fall would have snapped her neck and at least granted her the grace of being the first to go.

The horses behind her neighed and kicked at their stalls as the smoke reached them and primal instincts screamed for survival.

Dionne, always stronger than she looked, managed to grab Assumpta without falling off her stool. The ladder crashed to the ground behind her. Dionne held her for a moment, like two old friends awkwardly embracing. Without meaning to, Assumpta caught sight of Bernadette twisting back and forth on the end of her rope, her eyes starting to bulge now. Her face was bright red from the exertion.

"Up!" shouted Assumpta amongst the cacophony of flame and frightened animal. Dionne looked confused as Assumpta swapped

her grip from her rope to Dionne's. It would have been far easier for Assumpta to boost Dionne up rather than vice versa but that wouldn't work for what she had planned.

Assumpta started messily climbing up Dionne's body. Her hands heaving on the rope for dear life as her legs gracelessly clambered around her friend. Dionne grabbed a foot and tried to boost her up as much as she could. Assumpta felt a sickening crunch as her knee accidentally made contact with Dionne's nose. No time. Dionne managed to maintain balance. Assumpta kept heaving at the rope, straining to pull herself up. Her arms were screaming now. Dionne's hands were on her ass, shoving as hard as she could. Assumpta pulled herself further upwards. Her hands were a couple of feet from the beam now. Her feet found Dionne's shoulders. Nearly there – with one last push off Assumpta managed to get her right arm around the beam.

She felt the rope beneath her going taut, the last push having cost Dionne her balance. She blocked it all out. Her whole world was the beam now. She tried to throw her right leg over it – but failed. Her grip starting to slip, the sweat making it hard to hold on. The pain in her arms begging her to let go.

Assumpta clenched her eyes shut and with a roar managed to swing her leg up enough for her foot to hook itself above the beam. She heaved herself up.

The smoke was getting thicker now, burning her eyes. The panicked neighing of the horses growing louder and more frenzied beneath her. She pushed herself along on her ass until she reached the wooden column, then she used it for support as she hauled herself to a standing position.

She took a deep breath and shifted the rope that still clung to her neck so that it wouldn't get in her way.

A memory came back to her, unbidden, of one of her rare happy days in school. She had slipped out of class and found the school gymnasium unlocked. Alone, with no-one to laugh, she had mounted the gymnastics beam. Walking back and forth, growing in confidence with every step, she had discovered her grace. She had finished by

executing a cartwheel. It didn't matter that they would never know; she would know.

This was the same, only different.

She held her hands above her head and sprinted four steps down the four-inch-wide beam and jumped, executing a half turn in the air as she did so. She landed hard on her backside, just to the right of the end of the rope now taut around Dionne's neck.

Numbers.

A jolt of pain shot up her spine.

A cracking noise issued from the beam beneath her. She balanced there for a precarious moment and then started falling backwards, just as the beam broke in half.

Assumpta thumped hard into the ground, the sound of her collarbone breaking echoing around her head as a screaming pain shot through her.

Mercifully, she had landed to the right of Dionne who coughed and spluttered, hunched over on the ground. In her peripheral vision, Assumpta was aware of Bernadette lying motionless on the ground beside them.

Dionne scrabbled across the dirt floor to where Bernadette lay. She seemed so small now; unmoving, limbs akimbo – like a doll that a child had cast aside. Not knowing what else to do, Dionne started slapping her repeatedly across the face.

"Bernadette, wake up! Wake up!"

Nothing.

A shadow passed over her. Dionne looked up to see Assumpta clutching her arm to her side, looking down in concern. Dionne didn't know what to do. The only one of them who had proper first aid training was Bernadette.

"Should I give her mouth-to-mouth?"

Assumpta gave a pained half-shrug in response.

Dionne parted Bernadette's tightly clasped lips and bent towards her.

Bernadette's eyes flickered opened and her voice came out as a whispered croak. "Get off me, Tommy Riordan, or I'll tell your da."

"What?"

Bernadette blinked a couple of times. "Help me up. I don't know if you two have noticed but the building is on fire."

Dionne dragged Bernadette back to her feet. The flames had now found the straw on the lower floor, the horses kicked furiously against their stalls and screamed. Dionne hadn't known that horses could scream, it was a sound she didn't ever wish to hear again.

They turned towards the stable's door. Ramón, the guard, lay groaning in a heap on the floor to one side of it. In front of it stood General Rivera, a demented look in his eyes and Ramón's gun in his hand. His wide smile showed blood-stained teeth.

"Ah Sisters, you saved yourselves only to die anyway. This is really not your day."

Much has been made of the futility of closing a stable's doors after the horses have bolted. However, not nearly enough has been made of the dangers of opening said doors before the horses have bolted, particularly if the stable is on fire at the time.

General Rivera was framed in the shaft of light that spilled in behind him as Paulo returned, concerned primarily for his Uncle Ramón, whom he had pressurised into getting him this job that he now thoroughly hated.

Horses are not the brightest of creatures but even they can recognise the chance for life when they see it. The three sisters clung to each other as the six demented creatures rushed by them.

Paulo dived out of the way just in time, being blessed with the fast reactions of youth. Then he picked himself up and rushed in to try and find his uncle. He hadn't immediately realised that the trampled object lying in front of the door was the general. Six horses is a small stampede as stampedes go, but they can still do an awful lot of damage to anything foolish enough to stand in their way. Paulo threw up on what little remained of his former employer's head, then three remarkably forgiving nuns led him and his uncle outside where the air was filled with the sweet stench of burning coca.

# THE SECOND MOST STUBBORN CREATURE

## SIX DAYS LATER

Dionne looked into the eyes of pure hatred. "I don't think this ox likes me very much."

Bernadette was walking behind her, placing her bag up on the cart. "Very intelligent animals, oxen."

Maria, the young woman in her twenties who it seemed was now the leader of the village, smiled and patted the ox. "Tito doesn't like anybody, but he is very dependable for pulling the cart. He'll get you where you want to go."

"Not with her driving," came a croaky whisper from the back of the cart.

Dionne rolled her eyes. Bernadette was almost back to her old self, in all its glory. "Aren't you supposed to be resting your throat?"

Bernadette did so by muttering something under her breath. The doctor that had arrived yesterday had fixed Dionne's nose, bandaged Assumpta's broken collarbone and placed her arm in a sling, then, after a thorough inspection of a thoroughly uncooperative patient, had determined that given plenty of rest, Bernadette's voice would soon be making scathing remarks at its normal volume. He had

trekked up the mountain on a donkey for two days once word had got through that the village was no longer under the general's control and in need of help. Dionne suspected that the nice young man had probably hoped for a warmer welcome for his troubles than an Irish nun informing him that he required a haircut. She had also caught the nervous glances between the doctor and Maria, and was fairly sure that it'd take a lot more than a heavy dose of Bernadette to dissuade him from becoming a regular visitor to the village. Nobody had put Maria in charge in any official capacity, she had just been the person people had looked at when decisions had needed to be made. Dionne knew how that was all too well.

The ox was one of the village's prized possessions but they had insisted on lending it to the sisters to get them down the mountainside. The fuel for the trucks had gone up in the fire, so what little they had was being used for a supply run. The cart was small but it was just big enough to fit the three of them. Maria had insisted, assuring the sisters that when they reached the train station at Malapache, all they had to do was ask for Pablo's cousin and he would return the cart to the village. Apparently, it didn't matter which of Pablo's cousins it was, he came from a long line of famously honest men. Dionne hadn't argued. Assumpta was in no fit state to walk and Bernadette was still recovering from her ordeal. Her recovery had not been aided when on the first night of the village's freedom, she had stood in the wrong spot and been downwind as the coca crops had burned. Despite her condition, it had taken her a day to fall asleep and the local women had giggled as the alarmingly energised nun had suddenly decided to bath all of the children in the village.

When the general's men had returned, the scuffles had been brief and thankfully bloodless. The guard Ramón and his nephew had changed sides seamlessly, helped by them coming bearing the gifts of the remaining weapons from the general's armoury. Maria had greeted the trucks containing the returning guards with a simple proposition – join us or leave. Some stayed, some ran, lighter of load for having been relieved of their weapons. The general's right-hand man was a short fat man that Dionne had known only by his

reputation for brutality. He had been stripped naked and chased out of the village by an elderly woman with a stick and a vicious aim.

The ox would be needed back in the village soon to plough the fields. Coffee and bananas. That was what all of this area had been before and that was what it would be again. The villagers had sworn to the sisters that it would never go back to coca and given that they now believed the three women to be angels of the Lord sent down to administer his righteous vengeance, Dionne didn't doubt their sincerity. She believed they would make it too. They had the confidence brought from liberation, and they had Maria. One determined woman could be worth ten men with guns if the world would just let her get on with it.

Dionne climbed up into the front seat of the creaking cart.

"Oh for God's sake."

She turned to look behind at her three passengers. Assumpta took up most of the back of the cart, with Bernadette having to squeeze herself in between the bags.

Dionne sighed. "What's wrong now?"

"We're not seriously taking that with us?"

She was pointing at the third passenger who Assumpta held gingerly in her hands. The villagers had little in terms of material wealth, but all of it had been offered to the sisters in thanks, and all of it had been rejected. All of it but one thing. Assumpta looked down at the chicken in her arms, pointedly ignoring Bernadette's complaint. One of the children had asked and been told that she had named it 'Chicken'.

"We've been over this Bernadette, the chicken is a gift and if Assumpta wants it, she can keep it. Don't forget, she saved your life six days ago."

Bernadette folded her arms grumpily. "I'd have been fine. Big fuss over nothing."

Dionne shook her head and picked up the reins attached to the ox. "OK, time to go." She looked around. The whole village had lined the square to form an impromptu guard of honour for their departure. She realised that every pair of eyes was looking at her

expectantly. Dionne cleared her throat and raised her voice. "Thank you for your hospitality, The Sisters of The Saint wish you well. May God bless you and keep you safe for the future."

They all cheered. Dionne nodded and smiled awkwardly, then she jerked the reins. "Yah!"

Tito the ox, having no sense of how to make a dramatic exit, did not move.

Dionne jerked the reins again. "Yah! Ándale arriba!" She was painfully aware that she was now quoting a cartoon mouse. Tito had either never seen Speedy Gonzales or else he was not a fan, as he remained steadfastly still.

"In the name of Jesus Christ our saviour, I command you to move!"

Dionne was shocked and not a little appalled at the words that had just come out of her own mouth. She'd just gone full evangelist at the ass of an ox. That ass made its feeling known on this state of affairs by passing wind loudly.

Nobody in the town square laughed, which showed the immense respect they had for the sisters. Instead they continued to wave, warm smiles affixed to their faces. Their arms must be getting tired by this point.

"This is going well."

Dionne spoke through gritted teeth. "Shut up, Bernadette."

She looked across at Maria, who smiled an embarrassed smile, before stepping quickly forward and slapping Tito on his immense behind.

He lurched into a march of such speed, Dionne barely maintained her balance. The crowd cheered again, as much in relief as anything.

Dionne waved and smiled as she went, glowing faces beaming back from every direction. The children ran behind them, waving all the while – passing around two bends in the road before some of the older children called them back. Dionne made no effort to direct the ox, guessing that their best chance was the hope that Tito felt like going in the approximate direction they were heading.

Soon, they found themselves alone on the road, with nothing to hear but the low-level buzz of nature carrying on regardless and Tito, clomping steadily onwards.

"Well that was embarrassing."

"I can't hear you, Sister Bernadette, did you say something?"

"I particularly liked the bit where you commanded a cow to move by the power of the Holy Spirit."

"No, I can't make anything out. Assumpta, is that your chicken clucking away that I hear?"

"Although arguably the part where you butchered some Spanish was the real low point."

"Never mind, Assumpta. I think what I'm hearing is Tito's stomach working its way through his dinner. There's clearly a lot of hot air in there."

Sister Assumpta cradled the chicken gently in her arms and closed her eyes, lulled into sleep by the sway of the cart's steady progress, and the sound of two people not having a conversation.

# SMITHY'S REVENGE

Warning: The following novella features Smithy and Diller, a dangerous duo who we meet in the novel Disaster Inc. This is the story of how Smithy tries to get revenge on the man who put him in the most humiliating situation he has ever experienced. It also contains scenes of muppet decapitation which some readers may find upsetting. To be honest, if you don't – have a word with yourself, you're a stone-cold psycho!

# ADDITIONAL WARNING

This Novella was originally written as a fun freebie to be included with Disaster Inc. However, the author enjoyed writing it too much, to the point that he might well make it the first act of a full novel somewhere down the line. If he ever does that, you are contractually obliged to buy that book and not point out:

A) That you've already read the first bit

or

B) That some bits of the first bit have changed

Essentially, the author reserves the right to Bobby Ewing this whole thing and pretend you only dreamed reading it previously.

# A TERRIBLE PLAN

Diller took a long, thoughtful suck on the straw of his drink as Smithy watched him expectantly.

"Well?"

They were sitting in the back booth of the Porter House Lodge. Over the last few months it had become their unofficial clubhouse. They liked its casual ambiance. They liked Jackie and Phil the regular barmen who were the primary sources of the casual ambiance. Most of all, Smithy liked the fact that it was one of those rarest of establishments; one that would allow him to have a tab. A resting actor greatly appreciates such things.

Along with all that, Smithy liked it for the privacy the back booth offered. He had spent the day looking after the dog that was sort of his, sort of Cheryl his girlfriend's and sort of stolen. It was a Siberian husky that Smithy had 'acquired' from his ex-employer's dog grooming shop to prevent its previous a-hole owner having it spray-painted to look like Gene Simmons from Kiss. Cheryl had started taking care of it as Smithy had guessed, correctly as it turned out, that someone would come looking for it at his place. Then, they'd bonded and the dog had stayed there, without it being discussed much. A lot of Smithy's and Cheryl's relationship worked on a 'don't ask, don't

tell' basis. The dog's original name had been abandoned and he'd been referred to as 'Not Gene Simmons' for a couple of weeks – which had led to N.G.S before eventually arriving at Nogs.

Smithy had spent the day minding Nogs because Cheryl's landlord was dropping around and there was a strict no pets policy. Smithy didn't mind at all, he had kind of dumped the dog on her after all. The only downside was that being a dwarf walking a large Siberian Husky around Manhattan had gotten him a lot of unwanted attention. He was used to people staring but it didn't mean he liked it. A four-foot-five guy walking a dog that wasn't far off being nearly as tall as him, Smithy had a sneaking suspicion that people kept expecting him to hop on and try and ride off into the sunset. So, it'd been a long day and he'd been glad of the comfort of the back booth at the Porter House Lodge, where Nogs was happily snoring away under the table.

Having finally finished taking his deliberately long drink, Diller placed his fist to his mouth and belched softly. "'Scuse me. That's a kick-ass lemonade. That's why this place is the bomb. Most bars have really crappy ones. I guess they figure they're just gonna mix it with—"

"Diller?"

Diller shifted nervously on the padded seat in the booth. "My mom always says, if you can't say anything nice, don't say anything at all."

"She's such a font of wisdom."

Diller squinted his eyes. He was very sensitive about his mother.

Smithy raised an apologetic hand. "I meant no disrespect. What d'ya think is wrong with the plan?"

"First off, the fact you have a plan," said Diller. "Nothing good can come from this."

"Oh, for Christ's sake," said Smithy, picking up his whiskey and then putting it back down again. "Need I remind you what this bastard did to me?"

"No."

"He gets me, and a dozen other people..."

"I don't need to be reminded."

" ...And makes us dress up as leprechauns! Leprechauns."

"But you're going to remind me anyway."

"On Saint Patrick's Day! And the guy is on a quadbike. He's like four hundred pounds. Massive. As if the prick couldn't do with the exercise of chasing us on foot!"

"I know all this, but I'm gonna let you get it out."

"Then him and his rich asshole buddies hunt us, like... like..."

"Leprechauns?"

"Animals! Like we're less than human. And let me tell you, those paintballs hurt. They leave bruises – physical and emotional."

Smithy was absentmindedly shredding a bar mat into strips with his fingers as he spoke. Diller watched him with concern. He was mostly a calm and thoughtful guy, right until the point he wasn't. His temper had got him into trouble before – and that was just the trouble Diller knew about.

"I know," said Diller. "It was horrible. No question. You only did it because you needed the money."

"He took advantage of me needing the money."

"Five grand."

"Five grand," repeated Smithy, "that I was in to Benny Wong for. Benny doesn't mess around. His guns don't shoot paintballs."

"I said you should never have taken a loan from him."

"Whose side are you on?"

"I'm just saying, you needed the five grand."

"I could've done with the fifty grand first prize, but that other little bastard cheated me out of it. Still thought, if this fat... I mean, I don't mean to be harsh but the dude is a whale. Screw it, I'm gonna call him the whale."

Diller pulled a face. "Let's not make it a weight thing."

"I'm not... You know me, I don't judge. Me and Big Dom are tight."

"Dom is looking good these days."

"I think that gastric band thing he got is really working for him."

Diller nodded enthusiastically. "I'm so pleased for the guy. He's

been trying real hard. Did you know seventy percent of weight gain is genetic?"

"Really?"

"Yeah. I'm reading this book called *The Obesity Code*. Calorie counting doesn't work."

"Why are you reading that book? You're as skinny as a rake."

Diller shrugged. "The library had it and I've read most of the stuff there."

"Well, he... Wait." Smithy looked up from his rant, distracted. "Did you say you've read most of the stuff in the library? Seriously?"

"They don't get a lot of new stock coming in, so..."

"That's insane! Marello's over by the Brooklyn Bridge has a quiz night. We should hit that."

"Isn't that the one you got barred from?"

"People cannot use their phones to google stuff." Smithy prodded the table to emphasise his point. "There's no point having rules if nobody is enforcing them. What were we saying?"

"You were explaining how you don't overreact to stuff."

Smithy shot Diller a look that was notable for its lack of appreciation for the last remark. "My point is, this rich fucking... Well, now I don't know how to describe him without referring to his weight."

"Just use his name."

"I can't. His name is Lou Reed."

"And?"

"That's the same name as, well, Lou Reed. I love Lou Reed."

"Who is Lou Reed?"

"What? You've never heard of Lou Reed? The Velvet Underground?"

Diller gave Smithy a blank expression.

"C'mon. They're one of the definitive rock bands of the twentieth century."

"The twentieth century?!" exclaimed Diller. "I'm twenty-two. I was barely here for any of it. You're really surprised that a twenty-two-year-old black dude from Hunts Point doesn't know who this guy is?"

"The point is that Lou Reed, Bowie and Iggy Pop are my holy trinity."

"I heard of Bowie."

"I'm going to do you a mix tape."

"A what?"

Smithy squinted at Diller. "Are you trying to distract me from talking about the plan?"

"Hey, I'm not the one getting irate about dead guys."

"They're not all dead. Iggy is still alive," said Smithy, then paused. "I'm ninety per cent certain he's still alive. I gave up reading the news for the last couple of months to focus on the play."

"Time you spent on this plan, apparently."

Smithy glowered. "Man, for such a sweet guy, you've got a real eye for the low blow."

"I'm just saying, maybe you're..."

"What?"

"Is it possible..." Diller ran his hands over the tabletop, like he'd left the right choice of words on it and couldn't quite believe they'd disappeared.

"What?" repeated Smithy.

"Is it possible that your writer's block has maybe made you focus on this a teeny tiny bit more than perhaps you should be?"

"No."

"Just—"

"No," repeated Smithy emphatically. "In fact, now you mention it, I think it's this wrong – this big, massive, throbbing, monumental wrong – sitting there, festering away on my subconscious, that is draining the creative spirit out of me. I think if I resolve this situation then the play will just flow."

"Making it one of the many fine ones written in prison."

"Oh for... Now you're just being dramatic."

"At least one of us is."

Alright," said Smithy. "Anyway, point is, this rich... Damn it, what do we call him? I refuse to refer to him as Lou Reed."

"OK," said Diller, pausing to push around the ice cubes at the

bottom of his glass with his straw. "How about we call him Fat Lou? No, that's not good. Big Lou?"

Smithy shook his head. "I knew a guy called Big Lou. One time, he helped me get back into my trailer when I was locked out."

Diller's eyebrows shot up. "You lived in a trailer? When did you live in a trailer? You've got a whole backstory we have never discussed."

Smithy shrugged. "It's not uncommon."

"I've never known anyone who has lived in a trailer."

"That's because you've never left New York. I mean, have you ever even seen a real-life cow?"

"Yeah," said Diller, before running his hand over his tightly cropped hair. "I've seen one at a petting zoo the school took us to this one time. I remember it because it didn't seem that happy."

"How so?"

"Y'know, just its general vibe."

"Vibe?" repeated Smithy. "Have you ever met a happy cow?"

"I dunno. Like I said, I only ever met one."

"Precisely. You've got no frame of reference. Cows are not creatures predisposed to joy. The only one you've ever seen smiling is the cartoon one on those ads. Come to that, how messed up is that? This cow is supposed to be delighted because you're eating yogurts made out of the milk that it produces to feed its babies? That ain't natural."

"Doesn't the cow also talk?"

"Whatever. You're dragging us off the point here, Dill."

"Me? You're the one asking about cows. I just wanted to know about you living in the trailer, but you never talk about your mysterious past."

"No big mystery, just picture me in a trailer with a bunch of Lou Reed LPs. Speaking of which, back to the topic in hand..."

"What's an LP?"

"Don't even... Wait. How about Louis? The rich a-hole – we can call him Louis."

Diller nodded. "I don't know anybody called Louis."

"Perfect."

"Lousy Louis?" offered Diller.

"Done. Point is, this Lousy Louis fucking fucker" – Smithy was enjoying the name now it was freed from unkind stereotypes and musical legends – "what he did, it cannot be allowed to stand."

"Can't it though?" said Diller. "I mean, it has for a couple of months already."

"Only while I was forming my plan."

"Or," said Diller, "you could just move on. Living is the best revenge."

"Only for those people who don't have a plan. And besides," said Smithy, picking up his glass again, wafting it around in order to make his point rather than drinking its contents, "if we let the rich assholes run riot – do what they like – what happens to the world? This is America, godammit."

"Umm," said Diller, "the rich do pretty much—"

"Not on my watch!" interrupted Smithy. "If the system doesn't stop these monsters, then the individual must. I'm going to do it for me and for the other persons of reduced height that were involved."

Diller eyes widened with concern. "Oh Lord!"

"What?"

"Do you not say dwarf any more?"

"What does that matter?"

"You promised me that if the right word ever changed, you'd tell me. I don't want to end up like that old guy in that diner that time. Remember? He looked horrified when the waitress said you can't say 'coloured' any more. You could see he didn't mean to be, y'know... Poor guy looked so upset. I think most people don't mean to offend, but you've got to try and help the good ones because language can get confusing. I met a British guy at that audition last week – told me that Asian means a whole different bunch of people over there than it does over here. Isn't that crazy?"

"Diller," said Smithy, "stop trying to distract me."

"I'm not."

"You were."

"Alright, I was, but only for your own good."

"You can't distract me," said Smithy. "I'm on a mission."

Diller's eyes opened even wider and his mouth gaped. "Oh my God, why didn't you say? Is this from...?" Diller pointed at his head and then looked around, before nervously turning his finger towards the ceiling.

Smithy sighed. "No, it's not from the voice."

Diller slumped in his seat, clearly disappointed. "Oh."

"We've discussed this: it ain't God."

"I disagree."

"You disagree? It's in my head."

"Exactly. You're the worst person to judge. It's like cutting your own hair."

"It's nothing like that. The damn thing is just an auditory hallucination caused by post-traumatic stress following a car accident."

"Or," said Diller, "the voice of God is speaking to you following a near-death experience."

"That's a matter of interpretation."

"Everything is."

"Well," said Smithy, glancing around and lowering his voice, "as it happens, it's much of a muchness, seeing as I've not heard 'it' in weeks. I think 'it' might be, y'know..."

"Gone?"

"Shush. Don't say it. You'll jinx it."

"I hope I do. I liked the voice. I think it helped you to make very good life decisions."

"You're welcome to it in your head then, my friend, because I was getting sick of it."

"Speaking of voices of reason, what does Cheryl think of this plan of yours?"

Smithy shifted awkwardly. "She doesn't need to know."

"Meaning that you're too chicken to tell her because you know exactly what she'll say."

"If we know what she'll say, why do we need to tell her?"

"That's..." Diller scrunched his eyes up. "It feels like all the words in that sentence make sense on their own, but they're somehow collectively stupid."

Smithy sat back in his chair and tossed his hands up. "OK. Fine. Don't help."

"What?!"

Smithy was taken aback by the edge of outrage in Diller's voice.

"If you don't want to—"

Diller cut him off. "I said it was a terrible plan. I never said I wouldn't help. I'm your friend. You ask me to help, I'm gonna help."

"Oh. OK. Well, thank you."

"Yeah, well," said Diller, still looking put out, "you're welcome."

Smithy held his drink up in a toast. "You're a good friend, Dill."

"Yeah, and it's still a terrible plan."

# OVER THE TOP

They sat on the large wooden crate in silence, save for the quiet rocking of the van as it moved down the street. The only illumination was a sliver of sunlight that could be seen at the bottom of the roll-top rear door. It was uncomfortably warm – an unseasonably hot May in New York that felt more like July. The back of the truck had an uncomfortable lack of air conditioning – unsurprising, given that it was not designed for human transportation.

Diller pulled at his shirt, which was already starting to cling to him. "Do you think this feels like the D-Day landings?"

Smithy looked up in the direction of Diller's voice. "Nope."

"Y'know, the tension. Waiting to go over the top?"

"That's the wrong war you're thinking of. They didn't go over the top in World War II."

"Actually, they did. There were still trenches. I accept your point though. On D-Day it was landing crafts. 'Storming the beaches' is what I should have said. Do you think this is a bit like storming the beaches on D-Day?"

Smithy shook his head. "No, Dill. I don't think we can compare our current endeavour – namely, you delivering me in a dishwasher crate to a penthouse apartment on West 57th Street –

to the sacrifices made by so many members of our greatest generation on the beaches of Normandy. The comparison falls down on several levels, not least of which is that, as far as I'm aware, nobody on either side on that fateful day came in a silly costume."

"I'm not in a silly costume," said Diller, sounding defensive. "I'm in the correct costume for my part."

"I know."

"A costume you provided, I might add. I ain't been to many costume parties, but I don't think many people turn up dressed as a UPS guy."

"True."

"You, on the other hand..."

"My being dressed as a leprechaun is the whole point. You know I hate it."

Diller nodded. "I do. In fact, you hating it is what got us into this mess. Actually, come to think of it..."

"What?"

"Nothing."

"What's nothing?" insisted Smithy.

"You won't like it."

"Try me."

"OK, well, I mean – you know how you brought your normal clothes in your gym bag to change into when you're making your escape?"

"Yes. So?"

"Could you not have just brought the leprechaun suit in the bag and changed into it later on?"

"No, because..." Smithy stopped to consider this. "I..."

There was an awkward moment of silence, save for the van's creaking suspension as they took a right turn.

"Damn it!" said Smithy.

Diller sucked his teeth. "That's the thing with a plan. You think you've got it all laid out, but..."

"It's nothing," said Smithy. "It doesn't affect anything."

"Yeah, but if you missed that teeny tiny detail, what else did you miss?"

The van took a left turn.

"Seriously?" said Smithy. "You're trying to mess with my head this close to go time?"

"I'm just pointing it out. It's not too late to—"

"I'm doing this."

"Sure. OK," said Diller. "I just think maybe you should take one last long, hard look at the plan."

There was a little more of that awkward silence.

"Don't look at me like that," said Diller.

"It's dark. How the hell can you know I'm looking at you?"

"I just know."

"Hey," said Smithy, "hang on a minute – you hate the dark. How come you didn't just ride up front with Big Dom?"

"It's like, y'know – your last few minutes before the thing. I figured you probably could do with some company."

"Oh. Thanks."

"And besides, I don't think we can call him Big Dom any more."

"I know," said Smithy. "He told me he's lost 126 pounds now. That's basically what I weigh."

"That's incredible," agreed Diller. "And I'll tell you what else. He looks great. I mean, it's not just the weight, it's how he's lost it. He's not got that flappy, jowly skin stuff that some people get."

"He's a new man," said Smithy, then he raised his voice. "Hey, Dom, should we still call you Big Dom?"

"Yeah," came the shout back. "But more importantly, shut up. It's against company policy for people to be riding in the back."

"Right. Sorry."

"S'alright. We're five minutes out. You sure about this?"

"Damn it, Dom – not you too?"

"I'm just saying… Whatever, man. We're three blocks away, time to batten down the hatches."

The two men hopped down and Smithy turned on the torch on his phone. He pushed off the wooden lid and looked into the crate.

"Helium – check. Balloons – check. Bag full of clothes – check. Paintball gun – check. Crowbar – check. Douchebag Bluetooth headset – check. Phone..." Smithy waggled the phone in his hand. "Check." He pulled on the pair of leather gloves he had brought with him. "Gloves – check. Right that's—"

Diller pointed into the crate. "Leprechaun hat. You didn't say leprechaun hat."

Smithy sighed. "Yes, alright. Leprechaun hat – check. I was trying to maintain a bit of my dignity."

"Oh right," said Diller. "Sorry."

"OK then."

Smithy flashed his torch all around the back of the truck.

"Something wrong?" asked Diller.

"Not as such, but..." Smithy sighed again. "I can't see anything to stand on. Could you lift me into the crate please?"

"Oh. Right. Yeah."

# DELIVERANCE

Sitting in the dark, Smithy listened to the *thunk-thunk, thunk-thunk* rhythm of the hand truck as it trundled over the sidewalk. It provided a slightly out-of-sync backbeat to the sound of Diller whistling *Born to Run*. Diller wasn't a fan of Springsteen any more than he was a fan of Lou Reed, but Dale Grayson – the character he'd come up with for the delivery guy he was playing – was. He had gone into far too much detail, but Smithy had let him run with it. Diller tried to turn everything into some form of acting training, and today he was a twenty-three-year-old UPS delivery guy from Jersey, adopted at age six by white parents, who had found acceptance in his new world through sport and been offered a shot at playing baseball in the minors – but declined, because his mother was sick, and stayed home and took night classes at the local community college in aquatic engineering instead. And if that's what it took for him to help out with the plan, then fine – he could be all that. As long as he also delivered the crate.

Big Dom actually worked for a rival courier firm to UPS, but while he was happy to give them a lift with the crate, he had said he would not take part in a fraudulent delivery, as it was against the code of the courier. Smithy was pretty sure the code of the courier didn't

exist, at least to anyone but Dom, but he hadn't queried it. Dom was a very serious guy and Smithy could respect that. They had met when Dom was the prop manager with a theatre company he'd briefly worked with before it had imploded, as so many of these things do. Big Dom was a great guy, and when he occasionally needed someone to listen while he talked, Smithy was happy to be that ear. It was just over a year since the big guy had been jilted while literally standing at the altar and it had left him with some understandable trust issues. The best man and his intended had taken the honeymoon to Cancun. Despite it all, Dom was a kind soul with a good heart. Even now, he was sitting around the corner in his van, waiting to give Diller his bike on his return.

Smithy had more confidence in the plan than Diller, but that was because he hadn't wanted to tell his friend exactly how much time he had dedicated to its formulation. For the last two weeks, Smithy had taken a job in the florist across the street, just so he could watch the comings and goings at Lousy Louis's apartment building. The two daytime door persons split shifts – four days one week, three the other. The woman was in her late forties and conscientious. She liked things to be just so. She paid a great deal of attention to deliveries, kept the reception area studiously neat and was polite to the other staff. The man, on the other hand, was in his late twenties, and while he was gushingly effusive to the residents, laying the charm on thick, he was lazy and rude to the other staff, particularly the Guatemalan cleaner who had rebuffed his sexual advances. He was, in short, a lazy douchebag – which was perfect. You could rely on a lazy person to be lazy, and him being a douchebag meant that if it cost him his job, well – instant karma. If they'd any sense, they would give the job to the nice Guatemalan cleaning lady, who would be an awful lot better at it.

Smithy had learned all of this by carefully watching the building's toings and froings through the roses, tulips and peonies in the window of Petal to the Metal florist. It was amazing how much you could learn if you paid enough attention. He'd also discovered that he both enjoyed and had a flair for arranging flowers. That's not to say

he'd been sad to give the gig up two days ago. Being hit on by Phillip, the bitchy old queen who owned the place, hadn't bothered Smithy in the least, but his statement that "I find myself weirdly attracted to you" meant he could go take a long walk off a short pier. Weirdly? Seriously, did he think that was some kind of compliment? It always amazed Smithy how some people seemed to have no grasp of even basic manners. There were a lot of weirdos out there – and coming from a dude dressed as a leprechaun and hiding in a crate so he could gain vengeance on someone who'd paid him five grand for an afternoon's work, that was really saying something.

The crate took a right turn and Smithy steadied his breathing. He heard the whoosh as the automatic doors opened and the change in the sound as the wheels transferred from the sidewalk to cold, smooth marble.

"Hey, how ya doing?" said Diller – or rather Dale, in his admittedly well-judged New Jersey accent.

"I am fine, thank you. How are you today, my friend?" said a bright and chipper voice that was not supposed to be there. Smithy had planned it so that the lazy douchebag doorman would be on. He'd never heard him speak, but he was willing to lay good money that he didn't have a West African accent.

"Yeah, y'know, I'm getting by. Like The Boss sang, it's just the working life."

That seemed a little much.

"What boss?" said the unknown doorman. "Whose boss? I don't understand."

"The Boss. Bruce Springsteen."

"Ah right, the singer. Is that crate a delivery from him?"

"No," said Diller. "I was just... hey, never mind. I got a delivery here for apartment 2601. The penthouse."

"I see," said the doorman. "Well, I have nothing on the list here. I will take it and put it into the back room."

"What? No. I was told it's gotta be delivered up into the apartment. Got to be left in there."

"Hmmm... I have not been told anything about this."

"Yeah," said Diller. "The guy left really clear instructions. If you don't mind me asking – are you the regular doorman?"

"No, I have been sent here by an agency."

I should have come by and checked this morning, thought Smithy. Why did I not come by and check?

"Right," said Diller. "Maybe he left instructions with the regular guy?"

"Well, we cannot ask him. He has been fired."

"Oh."

"Yes. He was found attempting to have sex with a domestic appliance."

"Excuse me?"

"Yes. A vacuum cleaner. He has been removed from his position with immediate effect. I do not know what they have done with the vacuum cleaner."

"Right," said Diller.

"No, it is very wrong."

"Yeah, I mean, obviously."

"There are some very sick people in this world, let me tell you."

"You ain't kidding, buddy. All kinds of weirdos."

Smithy, while focusing on staying calm, couldn't help thinking that this new information put the doorman's interest in the Guatemalan cleaning lady into a new and even more disturbing light.

"Yes," said the doorman. "Follow me and we can leave this delivery in the storage area."

"I wish I could, fella, but my instructions were really clear. This has got to be delivered right into apartment 2601."

"Hmmm. What is it?"

"It's a dishwasher."

"I see. Perhaps the tenant was concerned that the doorman might attempt to have sex with it? Such a disgusting man."

"Too right," said Diller. "This is what happens when people do not let the light of Jesus into their lives."

"Praise the Lord."

"Praise the Lord."

This was why Smithy had wanted Diller to be the one to deliver the crate. It should have been straightforward. The former doorman, being lazy, used to accompany delivery men up to the apartments to drop big deliveries off directly. He didn't want to do what the doorwoman did and bring them up personally when the tenant came home. You could rely on lazy – except if lazy got caught being a sicko with a vacuum cleaner and then, well, you couldn't rely on it. Smithy could rely on Diller though. He was a people person. It was a remarkable instinct. He knew how to get on with anybody. Praise the Lord.

"So," said Diller, "can we just drop this crate upstairs, please? I would hate to have to come back. My church has a social tonight and I promised my auntie I'd help with putting the chairs out."

"Hmmm," said the doorman. "I will tell you what I will do – I shall ring the tenant and confirm the instructions. We have a sheet of work hour contact numbers for residents for just this eventuality."

"Umm. Oh, there's no need to trouble the guy."

"It is no trouble – Apartment 2601 you say?"

"Yes," said Diller, because what else could he say.

"I have a number here that says it is for his office. Let us call and see."

Smithy sat in the dark, listening as a firm hand punched buttons on a phone.

"It is ringing," said the doorman.

"Honestly, you don't need to—"

"Hello, may I speak to a Mr Lou Reed please?" Pause. "Thank you." There was another short pause. "They are putting me through. Isn't that the name of a famous singer? Maybe that is why Bruce Springsteen is sending him a— Yes, hello. My name is Jacob Anan and I am the temporary doorman at Mr Reed's building. I am contacting you regarding a delivery."

Pause.

"I see, will he be in the meeting long?"

Pause.

"Oh, I see. I believe it is a delivery from Bruce Springsteen."

"No," said Diller, "it's..."

"Yes. I just wanted to know if he wants it delivered directly to his apartment?"

"Sorry," said Diller, "I think there's—"

"OK," said Jacob. "Thank you for your time."

The phone was put firmly back in its cradle.

Diller sounded increasingly exasperated. "It's not a delivery from Bruce Springsteen."

"Oh," said Jacob. "She said you could take it straight up if it was."

"It's less of a delivery. More of a gift."

"Ah, OK. Well, follow me. This Bruce Springsteen, he seems like a very generous man."

"Yes," said Diller. "Yes, he is."

# LIFESTYLES OF THE RICH AND THE SHAMELESS

"Aw, hell no!"

Smithy had already put his Bluetooth headset on, so he took his phone out of his pocket and speed-dialled Diller.

Diller spoke in a whisper. "Is everything OK?"

"No."

"Oh God. Have you been arrested?"

"What? No. And why are you whispering?"

There was a moment's pause as Diller realised he didn't have a good reason for doing so. He coughed. "I'm... My throat is sore."

"Yeah. Hey, great improv with the doorman, by the way, I thought we were royally screwed there."

"I know," said Diller. "I'm just glad that Lousy Louis was in a meeting, otherwise we would have been done for."

"Yeah."

"Did everything go OK with getting out of the crate? Oh my God, are you stuck in the crate? You're stuck in the crate, aren't you? I knew it!"

"Dill, relax. I'm not stuck in the crate."

In fact, Smithy had discovered that crates were harder to open from the inside than the outside, but it had been nothing the crowbar

couldn't sort out. He'd then blown up a dozen helium balloons and filled the crate with them. When Lousy Louis came home, he'd discover someone had inexplicably sent him a crate full of balloons, but hey, who didn't love balloons? Last year, Smithy had gotten a short-lived delivery gig for a gift company. In the two weeks he'd worked there, he'd delivered a colonic irrigation gift set, a basket of muffins, upon each of which was an iced picture of a supreme court justice, and a "Congratulations on Your Divorce" basket that contained everything a person might want for spending some quality alone time – unless you were this building's ex-doorman. In short, a crate full of balloons wasn't that weird. More importantly, you wouldn't open it and think someone had used it as a method of sneaking into your apartment. Smithy was particularly pleased with this part of the plan. It was essentially a modern-day take on the classic Trojan Horse. If it ain't broke...

"OK," said Diller. "If you're not stuck in the crate, what's the problem?"

"Guess what this a-hole has on his bedroom wall?"

"You know I love a guessing game, Smithy, but this feels like it could take a while."

"I'll give you a clue – it's a sort of trophy."

"Oh God, the guy who won the leprechaun thing. He had him stuffed and mounted?"

"What?" said Smithy. "No, of course not. Why on Earth would you guess that?"

"Well, I dunno. You seem pretty angry."

Smithy looked up at the wall again. "He has – I shit you not – Han Solo encased in carbonite. I mean, like, the real one."

"Yeah, that would've taken a while to guess. Define 'real' here?"

"I mean the actual prop from the film. There's a framed certificate beside it and everything. Signed by George Lucas."

"Cool!"

"It is not cool, Diller. It is annoying. Something like this should be in a museum somewhere, not hanging in this douchebag's bedroom. I mean, of all places! Who has that in a bedroom? I bet that sets the

mood with the ladies." Having been understandably distracted by the sight of Harrison Ford trapped in carbonite, Smithy hadn't paid much attention to what else was on the wall. "Holy crap."

"Now what?"

"He's got one of Han Solo's blasters from the movie too."

"Sweet!"

"How are you not outraged by this?"

"Because I'm a dude from Hunts Point who has only ever seen one cow and this guy's place sounds awesome."

"Your priorities are messed up, Dill."

"Says the guy in dressed in costume in the middle of a B & E. Speaking of which, aren't you supposed to be hiding somewhere? What happens if he comes home?"

"Relax. It's Tuesday. He goes to see some lady every Tuesday. I'd like to think therapist but best not to ask."

"How long have you been following this guy?" asked Diller, incredulous.

"Not that long." This was technically true-ish. Most of Smithy's time had been spent just trying to find the guy – it turned out the filthy rich weren't in the phonebook. "The point is, he's not going to be home for ages. What I'm doing right now is figuring out a hiding spot. I got plenty of time – I've not even been in the front room yet. I'm going to have to stay hidden for hours, so I want to be comfortable and— Holy shit!"

"Now what?"

"He's got a floating bed!"

Smithy hadn't noticed it when he walked in because, well, Han Solo was on the wall, but now he saw that the large bed, up on a platform in the centre of the room, was actually floating in mid-air.

"Cool. Do you mean it's hanging from wires or something?"

"No, I mean it's actually floating in mid-air. Seriously, is this some kind of voodoo? How evil is this dude?"

"I bet it's magnets," said Diller.

"Magnets? How can it be magnets?"

"I've seen it in a magazine. In fact, I'm pretty sure it was *TIME*

magazine's innovation of the year a while ago. Damn, I wish I was with you. This place sounds tight!"

"It's not tight," said Smithy. "What it is - is grossly, offensively decadent. And what stops the bed floating off?"

"Science."

"Science," mumbled Smithy disapprovingly. "Science wasting its time on crap like this is why we don't have a cure for cancer."

"Take a picture of the bed."

"Really? I've broken into somebody's apartment and you want me to take pictures so I can have incriminating evidence on me?"

"Take a picture, send it to me and then delete it."

"So, to be clear, Dill, you want me to send you incriminating pictures linking you to this crime?"

"Oh, never mind. You've taken all the fun out of it. So what other cool stuff has he got?"

"What is this? Lifestyles of the rich and the shameless? It's a big, gaudy, expensive-looking penthouse with a floating bed, an actual original Han Solo in carbonite on the wall and a bona fide laser pistol. I'm getting out of the bedroom before I throw up."

"How big is his TV?"

Smithy looked around. "D'you know, I've not actually seen one."

"Oh. I don't trust peeps who don't have a TV."

"You don't have a TV, Dill."

"Yeah, but I can't afford one. That's different. I'm guessing this dude can."

"True enough." Smithy looked at the various doors in the room. There were two, in addition to the one he had entered through. He walked towards the nearest and stopped.

"These doors don't have handles."

"What?"

"They don't have... Wait a sec." He waved his hand in front of a dimly glowing panel on the wall and the door whooshed left, *Star Trek*-style, to reveal a large walk-in closet.

"What was that?" Diller asked.

"Nothing."

"I bet it was something cool and now you won't tell me."

"It was nothing exciting. I'm in the dude's walk-in closet."

"What's that like?"

Smithy looked around. Rows of expensive-looking suits hung beside about three dozen shop-fresh shirts, with sweaters neatly folded on shelves, followed by slacks, T-shirts, chinos and several drawers that were no doubt full of freshly laundered underwear. There were about fifty pairs of shoes, most of which were buffed to such a high shine that you could get a migraine from looking at them for too long. "Just lots of expensive clothes. He's probably got a suit made out of Dalmatians somewhere in here."

"So is this where you're going to hide?"

Smithy spun around slowly, giving it an appraising eye. There wasn't anywhere he could actually hide himself – at least not where he wouldn't be spotted as soon as someone walked in. "Nah."

"You need to find somewhere."

"No kidding. I'm guessing under the bed is out – I ain't lying in magnetic fields all night, that don't sound healthy. I'll find somewhere. This place is massive, and it's just me and the bag."

Smithy shifted the gym bag on his shoulder, which contained his street clothes, leprechaun hat, paintball gun and a small canister of helium.

"Is the plan still...?"

"To wait until he's asleep? Yes."

For reasons Diller didn't fully understand and wasn't entirely comfortable with, a lot of Smithy's recent ideas seemed to draw inspiration from the films of Mel Gibson. He'd used *Lethal Weapon 2* to help a friend with an issue a couple of months back. He'd watched *What Women Want* with Big Dom in an effort to get him primed for his return to the rigours of the dating game. Then there was this idea, which drew its inspiration from *Braveheart*.

After William Wallace, played by Mel Gibson, is betrayed by the Scottish lords, he escapes and hunts them down one by one. In one particular scene, a lord is asleep in his bed, having a nightmare in which Mel is coming after him on horseback, wild-eyed, in full face

paint. The full Gibson. The lord wakes up, terrified, and is relieved to realise it was all just a dream. Then his bedroom door flies open and in rides Mel on horseback, a vision of terrible vengeance made real, and proceeds to slam a kind of cannon ball on a chain into the lord's head, smashing it like a pumpkin. Admittedly, in the Smithy version, a lot of that had changed. For a start, he wasn't actually going to kill Lousy Louis, and despite what his acting CV said, Smithy couldn't ride a horse. Even if he could, he would have needed a much bigger crate. No, in his version, Lousy Lou is asleep in his douchey floating bed and wakes to find a leprechaun standing over him, holding a paintball gun. Smithy had a shortlist of four versions of the speech he was going to do, but he hadn't settled on one yet. He thought he would just see what felt right at the time. Then, when Louis was lying there thinking he was about to die, he'd be hit with the mother of all paintball barrages. Smithy had spent quite a lot of money he didn't have on a gun that the guy in the shop said had something called a motorised gravity-fed hopper. Smithy hadn't understood most of the technical lingo, but he'd got the important bit – it could shoot twenty paintballs a second. The dude had waxed lyrical and called it a triumph of engineering elegance and excellence. Smithy considered that a phrase really more appropriate for something like the Brooklyn Bridge, but he had let it slide. Besides, he was fully intending to take the gun back in the morning and say it was a present that hadn't been appreciated. Failing that, he'd have to stick it on eBay and hope for the best. This project had gone way over budget, not least because it wasn't supposed to have one.

The other change in Smithy's version of events was that, unlike with the deceitful lord, this would be the beginning of Lousy Louis's nightmares. If Smithy's plan went as he hoped, Lousy was going to learn a valuable lesson about how to treat human beings – one that would stay with him for the rest of his life.

Smithy walked up to the other *Star Trek* door and waved his hand in front of the sensor.

"Aw, hell no times a hundred!"

"Now what?"

"He's got a whole wall of Lou Reed's album covers – like the actual, proper musical genius Lou Reed. Full vinyl LP covers – all thirty-five – that's twenty-two studio and thirteen live albums."

"Oh," said Diller. "OK."

"OK? OK? It is not OK!"

"What, so this guy can't like the same music as you?"

"He can, but he doesn't. Because if you properly like Lou Reed, you would not have his album covers on the wall of your bathroom."

"Oh."

"Yes. One of the greatest artists to ever grace the planet deserves more respect than having his life's work gazed upon by some fat asshole while he takes a dump."

"We said we weren't going to mention his weight again."

"All bets are off! This is an affront that will not stand."

"Oh boy. And so it begins."

"What are you talking about?"

"Well," said Diller, "I can always tell when you're properly losing your temper because your speech gets more and more Shakespearian."

"That is ridiculous."

"Is it though? That fight in the karaoke bar, the last thing you said was, 'If this brute dares to place his hands on me once more, I shall smite him.'"

"I never—"

"You did. You said you were actually going to smite that Australian dude, which turned out to mean putting his head through a framed picture of Gloria Estefan."

"How do you know who Gloria Estefan is but you don't know Lou Reed?"

"Now who's changing the subject?"

"Alright, I'm just... I once had every Lou Reed album on vinyl, y'know. They got lost in a fire."

"Oh."

"I know these aren't the exact same ones, but it's just..." Smithy

ran his gloved hand over them, as if trying to comfort a wounded animal. "This is just... aw, hell no! Hell no! Hell no!"

"Now what?" asked Diller. "Has he stuffed and mounted Lou Reed?"

Smithy looked up at the wall. "I think he..." Smithy had to work to hold back the emotion in his voice. "I think these album sleeves still have all the original records still inside them."

"So?"

"So?!" Smithy could feel his blood starting to boil. "So? So? Dill, do you have any idea what being in a steamy bathroom will do to rare vinyl recordings?"

"No."

"Well, neither do I, but I bet it isn't good. I'm going to rip every single one of these down and take them with me. This is an affront in the eyes of God!"

"Hello again, Mr Angry Shakespeare," said Diller. "Seeing as you're stealing stuff, can you get me the Han Solo laser pistol?"

"I am not stealing stuff. I'm here to make an important point."

"Couldn't that point be that bad people don't deserve nice things?"

"Dill, don't—"

Smithy froze. It was only 4:30pm – Lousy Louis wasn't supposed to be home for at least three hours. So why had he just heard the front door open?

# HI HONEY - I'M HOME!

Lou Reed – the one that wasn't dead – came barrelling through the front door, his phone pressed to his ear. "I don't give a fuck, Morris. Just get it done, or else go fill out a job application for Dunkin' Donuts, because that is where you'll be working next week." He snapped his phone shut with a pleasing thunk. Flip phones were hard to get these days, but he'd found a place in South Korea that could build one for you custom. He enjoyed being able to snap it shut to terminate a call. It felt boss. Speaking of bosses...

He looked at the big crate sitting in his kitchen amidst the polished marble surfaces and glittering chrome. His fridge had more processing power than all of NASA had when they'd put a man on the moon. It currently contained some pickles and an expired jar of mayonnaise.

"Alright, alright, alright." He walked around the crate as if admiring a fine work of art. He'd hurried home right after he'd gotten the message from his assistant. Last year, Lou had spent a lot of time chasing Springsteen's people to try and book him for the company's Fourth of July party. He'd been told that Bruce did not do private bookings, no matter what. He'd doubled the offer – hard no. Then he had doubled it again, and he had gone to great lengths to find out

where Springsteen lived. He had sent an intern over to personally deliver the offer with a bottle of champagne. The intern had been told to not take no for an answer. He had returned covered in champagne and defeat. Last Lou had heard of him, that intern was now working in Starbucks. That was too good for him – coffee is for closers.

Lou ran an affectionate hand over the crate. He'd known that Springsteen would have a price – all that "man of the people" stuff was just marketing.

"Samantha, call Pamela."

"Calling Pamela, sir." Samantha was the state-of-the-art home management system that he'd had installed earlier this year. It controlled everything. He'd also paid a small fortune to get that hot chick from that show he liked that'd got cancelled to record the voice for it. It was a totally customised one of a kind. Lou was all about rarity.

"Hello, Mr Reed." Pamela's voice came from the speakers in the ceiling. Louis could take calls anywhere in the penthouse.

"How the hell am I supposed to open this thing?"

"Umm, what exactly?" said Pamela.

"What? The crate! The crate from Springsteen!"

"Right. Of course. Sorry. Do you want me to send somebody over?"

"No. I want... Wait a second." Lou had spotted something on the floor. "It looks like they left a crowbar. I guess I'll have to do it myself, seeing as nobody has thought of this."

"Sorry, sir."

Lou took off his suit jacket and tossed it on the marble counter. Then he took a long, hard look at the crate.

"Do you have any idea why he would send you a dishwasher?"

"Well, it's a gift. Obviously."

"It's kind of odd though."

Lou looked around the crate again. "Musicians are all odd. We booked Bowling for Soup a few years ago and they sent us a crate of Fresca. Did Hiroshi's people call back?"

"Not yet, but—"

"Call them again."

"It's 5:30am there now, boss."

Lou stopped and glared up at the ceiling. "Did I ask you what time it was in Tokyo or did I ask you to make a call?"

"Yes, Lou. Sorry, Lou."

He placed the tip of the crowbar under the lid and rested his weight on it. It unexpectedly offered little resistance, as if it had been only loosely held in place. Lou stumbled messily against it as the lid flew off. And then he looked up.

His scream, carried by the speakers, echoed around the entire apartment.

"What is it?" asked Pamela. "Are you OK, sir? Lou? I'm calling 911."

Lou fell to the ground and stared up at the kitchen ceiling in horror. "B... b... balloons!"

Pamela's voice was now a mixture of confusion and terror. "I'm... Lou? Do you need...?"

"He..." Lou was breathing hard. "He sent me fucking balloons! What kind of monster sends somebody balloons?!"

There was a pause at the other end of the line. "Right. That's... weird. Are these... are these ordinary balloons?"

Lou looked up at the ceiling as the balloons bobbed there creepily. "They're balloons, Pamela. Big, fucking creepy balloons. What about that can you possibly not understand?"

"Right. Maybe he thought they'd be" – her voice lowered, as if she was already regretting starting the sentence, but she couldn't avoid finishing it – "nice?"

"Nice?" said Lou, as crawled on his hands and knees out of the kitchen. "Nice? Are you out of your fucking mind? Everyone knows I hate balloons. Springsteen is a sick bastard. Jesus Christ, Pamela. Get over here now. I need you to get rid of them."

"Right. I'll send somebody."

Lou, having reached the hall, placed his hand on the wall and dragged himself back to his feet. "No. You. I want you."

"I can't, Lou. Remember, we discussed this. I've got to take Michaela to that doctor's appointment about her throat."

"Cancel it."

"I... I can't do that. It took six months to get the appointment."

"Fine."

"I'm sorry. I could come after? Or..."

"No, no – it's fine. If you're not dedicated to your job, then that's not a problem."

"Look, I'll send someone else."

"No," said Lou, firmly. "Nobody else. I don't want strangers. Not now."

"The building's concierge then?"

"No. He's new. He tried to talk to me on the way in. I don't want him. It's fine."

"If you're sure."

"Yes. I'll just have a room in my home I can't use because you can't fix a simple problem."

"I can come over after the—"

"No," said Lou as he walked through to his bedroom, pulling his tie off and tossing it on the floor. "I need a shit."

"OK, I'll leave you to—"

"Take me through my schedule for tomorrow."

"I... Right."

Lou went into his bathroom and proceeded to drop the kids off at the pool while Pamela took him through his schedule of meetings for the next day. He was just straining to push out a particularly big one when he heard a whooshing noise from the other room. "Goddammit, Pamela, you said the guy had been around to fix that problem with the doors."

"He did. He came Monday morning. He assured me it was fixed."

"Well, it isn't. Get him back first thing tomorrow. Christ. Can't anyone do their job around here? I've got a stressful week ahead. The last thing I need is doors opening at random in the middle of the night. It freaks me the fuck out! I'm a sensitive sleeper."

"Right, sorry, I'll—"

"Samantha, end call."

"Sorry, Lou, can I just..."

"Call terminated," came the automated voice from the ceiling.

"Wah, wah, wah," Lou whined in a mocking tone. "Like it's my fault your kid is sick. Samantha, place a call to Steffon Birch."

Then, while he wiped his ass, he informed the company's head of human resources that his secretary wasn't working out and he'd need yet another new one.

Having unburdened himself of both lunch and his useless secretary, Lou walked back into the bedroom. "Samantha, how come nobody can do even simple things right?"

"Sorry," said the automated voice. "I do not have that function."

"No," he said to himself, "you don't." He walked into his closet and changed into slacks and a sweater, leaving his suit on the floor for the maid to deal with in the morning.

When he left the bedroom, he passed the glass enclosure of the kitchen. Since he'd bought the place, he'd had the kitchen redesigned three times, which was also the same number of times he'd used it to cook an actual meal.

"Samantha, darken kitchen glass to max."

He watched with satisfaction as the glass tinted until it was impossible to see into the room. It was a useful feature, allowing the maid to cook his breakfast in the morning while he moved around his apartment in privacy. Lou liked to go clothes-free for the start of his day.

He needed to take his mind off the balloons. Fucking Bruce Springsteen, trying to play some kind of sick and twisted joke on him. People were weird.

"Samantha, TV."

Lou sat down on the couch and placed his feet up on the coffee table as the floor-to-ceiling windows darkened and the twelve-foot screen descended from the ceiling.

# THE MAN COMES AROUND

Smithy felt his phone silently vibrate in his pocket. That was about the tenth or eleventh time now. He slowly reached his hand down, careful not to disturb any of his cuddly friends, and took it out of his pocket, cupping the screen with his hand so that the light wouldn't reflect off any of the windows. He looked at the screen.

Diller: 'What happened?'

Diller: 'You OK?'

Diller: 'Smithy?'

Diller: 'Answer me!'

Diller: 'Oh God, this is bad.'

Diller: 'Why aren't you answering?'

Diller: 'Not that I know where you are.'

Diller: 'Or had anything to do with whatever you are doing.'

Diller: 'I've been busy all day.'

Diller: 'I'm going to call Cheryl.'

Smithy cursed silently to himself and then quickly thumbed a response.

Smithy: 'All fine. DO NOT CALL CHERYL!!!'

After twenty seconds, the phone vibrated again.

Diller: 'What happened?'

Smithy: 'He came back early. I think he was excited to see what Springsteen had sent him.'

Diller: 'Oh.'

Diller: 'Oops! (Smiley face)'

Diller: 'How did he not see you?'

Smithy: 'I was always good at hide-and-seek.'

Actually, it had been a combination of luck and quick thinking. Mostly luck. Smithy had been in the closet when he'd heard the front door open. Luckily, it was a big apartment and Lousy Louis was loud, so he'd been able to close the closet's *Star Trek* door without drawing any attention. Smithy had nearly screamed when the automated voice of Samantha had come blaring over the speaker in the otherwise silent walk-in closet. Between Lousy Louis's booming voice and the phone call being carried right around the house, he had been able to ascertain where Lousy was. He had also heard more than enough to reaffirm his opinion that the man was indeed an unspeakable asshole – one that was inexplicably afraid of balloons. If Smithy had known that sooner... Still, too late now. As it was, he'd barely managed to avoid being seen. Then Lousy had loudly proclaimed he was going for a dump, so Smithy had been able to get himself out of the closet. He'd also been lucky that when Lousy had heard the door open, he'd assumed it was a recurrence of some fault in the system. What on earth was wrong with an ordinary door handle? It had worked fine for centuries. Lousy Louis deserved all the problems he'd got – and a whole lot more.

As soon as he'd escaped from the bedroom, Smithy had looked around, desperate to find somewhere to hide. There had been that moment – the point of no return. He'd stood with the glass-enclosed kitchen in front of him, considering whether to make for the front door and freedom to his left, or sticking with his faltering plan to his right. Then he had heard Louis make that crack about the secretary's kid and Smithy had turned right. Then he'd turned back. Not to leave – he'd realised that he'd messed up and left the crowbar behind. He

padded into the kitchen, snatched it up and then headed back into the apartment.

He'd only been in the kitchen, bedroom and bathroom so far. The main room had a massive sunken lounge with a sofa stretching the length of it that could comfortably seat about ten people. The enormous wooden coffee table in front of it was about the size of Smithy's entire apartment. Even as he'd looked around in panic, he couldn't help but wonder how they'd managed to get it in. Had they taken out some of the windows that led out to the enormous balcony? The view of the sun crawling across the Manhattan sky was a billion-dollar one, literally. They didn't call this billionaire's row for nothing. Smithy had considered the balcony as a possible hiding place, but rejected it. There was some furniture out there, but not a great deal, and the shrubbery wasn't the kind that'd offer much cover. Besides, all he'd need was for Lousy to lock it and he'd be stuck out there all night.

The open-plan sunken lounge offered no concealment. There was a bar in the far-left corner of the room, but that didn't seem strategic either. Lousy Louis struck Smithy as being highly likely to be a solo drinker. On his right was a wall hung with massive movie posters. Smithy had scanned the room, pointedly ignoring them. He couldn't afford to get distracted. He'd walked further into the apartment, between the sunken lounge and the wall of posters. There must be somewhere in this... Smithy had turned the corner and stopped dead. Leonard Nimoy was staring right at him.

Smithy's phone vibrated again.

Diller: 'Where are you hiding?'

Smithy: 'I'm in the muppets.'

Diller: 'What?'

Around the corner from the lounge lay an area about twice the size of the massive bedroom, and it was filled with... everything. Lousy had the most ridiculous collection of memorabilia known to man. He had a life-sized waxwork of Leonard Nimoy as Spock, his hand held aloft in the tradition Vulcan salute. He had the pinball

machine from the film *Tron* – the original film, not the awful remake. He had a Batman suit, a Captain America suit, a suit of samurai armour – all displayed on man-sized mannequins. Alongside them was a velociraptor from *Jurassic Park* and life-sized models of both the Alien and the Predator. In the centre of the room, dominating proceedings, was what appeared to be a full-sized Batmobile from the original TV series. That made getting the immense coffee table in look like a walk in the park. And there, against the far wall, was a massive collection of what appeared to be full-sized versions of every single member of *The Muppets*.

There was a closed door at the back of the "museum area" which Smithy had been considering going for when he heard "Samantha, darken kitchen glass to max." He'd panicked and dived in amongst the Muppets, burying himself in their furry safety. It was instinctive. He came from a generation that didn't trust politicians, the press or damn near anyone else on TV, but everyone trusted the Muppets. He rearranged them hastily, placing five-foot tall Fozzie to the left of him, with Gonzo and a few of the chickens to his right side, and the bass player from the band Dr Teeth and the Electric Mayhem standing behind him. Elmo sat on Smithy's lap. It left Smithy with just enough room to look out, but invisible to all but the most interested of observers.

Diller: 'You're hiding with the Muppets?'

Smithy: 'Long story.'

Diller: 'Has he got loads of other cool stuff then?'

Smithy: 'I'll tell you later.'

Diller: 'Does he really not have a TV?'

Smithy: 'Bit busy right now Dill.'

Diller: 'Oh right, sorry. Good luck.'

Diller: 'And if you happen to get your hands on that pistol...'

Smithy: 'No.'

Smithy was starting to worry he was bad influence on Diller. After all, the kid had enough on his plate – maybe he should stop involving him in his dumb ideas?

Over the next few hours, he had made good use of Lousy's – well, not TV. You couldn't call a twelve-foot HD screen that appeared out of the ceiling a mere TV. It was no doubt a "home entertainment system" or something. They watched a hockey game, which the Islanders had lost 4–3 to Arizona, bringing an unexpected trip to the play-offs to its expected end. There had been a point when Lousy had frozen the picture on one of the Islanders' scantily clad "ice girls". These women were like NFL cheerleaders, only they had to clean the ice between periods while waving at drunken fans. As Lousy had sat and stared at her frozen image, Smithy had feared the worst. He had looked away and covered Elmo's eyes. Then, thankfully, Lousy had gone back to live TV in time to see the Islanders massacre another breakaway.

Then Lousy had put on the *Watchmen* movie, which Smithy had always quite liked, and then an episode of *Elementary*. That was annoying, as it was the season finale and Smithy and Cheryl had been saving them up to watch together. He hated watching stuff out of order. There was nothing this guy couldn't ruin. Halfway through the episode, the two large pizzas Lousy had ordered from some place called Ragadoni's turned up. Lousy had offered the delivery girl a hundred bucks if she came in and burst some balloons for him – no questions asked. The kid had called him a pervert and hightailed it out of there.

Once the initial terror of being discovered had receded, Smithy had found himself becoming quite relaxed. His presence had clearly gone undetected, and Lousy, while not exactly a gracious host, seemed uninterested in admiring his ludicrous horde of collectibles. By about 11pm, Lousy had nodded off while a bunch of talking heads argued over who should play quarterback for the Jets. Smithy could feel his own eyelids growing heavy too. He needed to stay awake – bar anything else, he had been informed by Cheryl that he talked in his sleep. That would be a really dumb way to get found.

Then suddenly he was wide awake. Something had caught his attention. His instincts had caught it and they were just waiting for

the rest of him to catch up. What was it? Lousy hadn't moved; he was still snoring away happily. The TV continued to talk to itself. What was wrong? Was it just a jolt of paranoia at falling asleep that had sent a shock of adrenaline through him? Then, without a whisper of noise, one of the doors to the balcony opened and a figure clad in black stepped in from the night.

# GOD'S SAVING GRACE

*Not my problem.*

Those were the first words that popped into Smithy's head. Whatever the hell this was, it was not his problem. Lousy Louis was an appalling human being and it stood to reason that he had pissed off a great deal more people than just Smithy. Or maybe he just had a lot of highly steal-able stuff.

Smithy sat amongst the plush toy Muppets and watched as the black-clad figure looked down at the slumbering form of Lousy Louis Reed – who seemed to be in a pizza-induced coma, drooling contentedly onto himself. The figure was framed by the light of twelve-foot-wide sports centre in the background, so details were hard to make out – not that there was a great deal of detail to see. The intruder – well, technically the second intruder – was entirely clad in the head-to-toe black apparel of a... well, Smithy felt embarrassed even thinking it, but a ninja. One person breaking into an apartment in costume was admittedly odd, but two doing it separately? Mind you, while the ninja outfit was a bit much, the person wearing it had just magically appeared on the balcony of a twenty-six-storey building, so maybe it was unfair to lump them into the same category as a dude who'd run the New York Marathon dressed as a chicken.

The ninja stepped neatly onto and over the immense coffee table and leaned in close to look at the slumbering Louis. Smithy couldn't say exactly what it was, but something about this person's gait made him feel sure it was a man. He clicked his fingers – no response. It appeared Louis was an incredibly heavy sleeper. But as soon as that thought occurred to Smithy, another one bounced up from somewhere to contradict it. According to Lousy's own whiny complaint delivered to his soon-to-be-ex-secretary, he was a light sleeper who got woken up by phantom doors whooshing open in the night.

Smithy didn't have much time to think about that, as the ninja had just done something unexpected. Although, could a ninja who'd just walked in from the sky ever truly be said to do anything unexpected? Still, pulling the sleek black rucksack from his back and taking out a camcorder was surprising. He looked around the room and seemed to make a decision, placing the camcorder at the end of the coffee table on its small inbuilt tripod. Smithy still had no idea what was happening, but he now had a very bad feeling about it. It only got worse when the figure then took out what appeared to be a phone and held it in front of the screen for five seconds. Smithy caught a glimpse as he turned it back around – it appeared to show a clock. Then – oh no... With a sense of dread, Smithy recognised the tingling sensation at the back of his mind. He'd thought it was gone. He'd thought wrong.

*HELP HIM.*

He felt queasy suddenly.

*HELP HIM.*

Smithy closed his eyes and tried having a strong word with himself/the voice of God. *Look, this isn't my problem. I don't know what any of this is about.*

*HELP HIM.*

*It's really none of my business. How do I know that he doesn't deserve whatever this is?*

*HELP HIM.*

Smithy opened his eyes and shook his head. He was done being dictated to by his own psychological illness.

*HELP HIM.*

The black-clad figure stood in front of the comatose Lousy Louis, looking back in the direction of the camcorder. Its small screen was turned forwards, so the person in front of it could see themselves being filmed and frame the shot. Seemingly satisfied, the ninja nodded at the camera and then reached over his shoulder and pulled out a sword. It was one of those fancy curved blades that Smithy had seen used in martial arts films – he had no idea what they were called though. As the blade caught the light, he was also certain that it was very real and very deadly.

Oh crap.

*HELP HIM.*

*HELP HIM.*

*HELP HIM.*

Could he really watch an innocent man die? No, wait – that sentence didn't fit. Could he really watch a man who was guilty of an awful lot of things die? No, that wasn't it either. Could he really watch an asshole who was guilty of being an asshole be executed in cold blood?

*HELP HIM.*

*HELP HIM.*

*HELP HIM.*

Crap.

*If I die doing this bloody stupid thing, there'd better be a heaven, and this better get me some serious brownie points.*

*HELP HIM.*

*HELP HIM.*

*HELP HIM.*

*If you really are God, then no offence, but you're not much of a conversationalist.*

As quietly as he could, Smithy stood up and – for no reason he could readily understand – he put on the hat.

. . .

Chikao placed the edge of the sword's blade to Lou Reed's throat and prepared to pull it back to deliver the death blow. After a moment's consideration he bent down and carefully moved Reed's head to lean on the other shoulder. The man mumbled in his sleep but otherwise did not stir. From his research, Chikao knew it was almost impossible to detach a head cleanly with one stroke but, as requested, he would try. The client had been insistent on this point.

He glanced once more at the camera to confirm that he had framed the shot correctly, and then he pulled the sword back.

As the sword made its final descent, a flash of movement in Chikao's peripheral vision caused him to alter its course. A figure was hurtling towards him. The blade sung as it ripped through the air and then tore through his attacker in one fluid motion. Chikao watched in confusion as the severed head of Fozzie Bear spun off into the distance. He turned to see the only slightly less incongruous figure of a leprechaun charging down the coffee table towards him. He swung the blade again, missing the Celtic mythical creature as it fell flat on its back and slid along the table's polished surface. As he pulled the sword back to strike a downward blow, the last thing he saw clearly was the gun. Then, in a triumph of engineering elegance and excellence, twenty paintballs hit him square in the face.

As the man howled in pain, Smithy rolled right and dropped off the table. The ninja staggered back and brought his hands to his paint-soaked face, dropping the sword in the process. As he rubbed furiously at his eyes, the sword impaled itself into the table at the exact spot where Smithy's chances of reproduction had been just a moment before. A paintball travels at approximately 280 feet per second, which isn't fast enough to break the skin in most circumstances. However, receiving a barrage of them into a virtually unprotected face is considered a very bad idea – even by people on YouTube. As ridiculous risks go, Smithy felt that the one he had just taken had worked out remarkably well. His opponent's howls were enough to cause Lousy Louis to finally come around. He looked up to see a ninja with a face splattered in pink paint and screamed. Smithy didn't have the luxury of time to scream, because his opponent was

coming to terms with his surprising change in circumstances and had started reaching his right hand around to the back of his outfit.

Smithy started running.

He dived over the end of the couch just as the TV exploded in a shower of sparks behind him. Not unlike a stopped clock's ability to be right twice a day, a temporarily blind man can still kill you by shooting in the right general direction. A rapid series of shots from the gun that Smithy had correctly anticipated rattled off in quick succession.

Smithy felt the whoosh of air over his head as a bullet passed through the hat that thankfully started a foot before the top of his head did. Amidst the exploding TV and the sound of bottles of – no doubt shamefully expensive – booze in the bar shattering, Smithy counted possibly twelve shots. That would have been a really useful piece of information if he had the first clue what gun his opponent was holding and how many bullets it held. He didn't. Smithy didn't like guns in general – and this one in particular.

He tossed the leprechaun hat in the air, hoping to draw a couple more shots. Nothing. When he risked a glance over the top of the sofa, he found himself looking down the barrel of a gun, behind which lay the half-covered and entirely pink face of his opponent, who was all kinds of pissed off.

"Who the fuck are you?" His accent was clipped, hard to place.

Smithy sighed and sat back on the floor. "I'll be honest, it's a really long story, and I'm guessing we don't have that kind of time."

Smithy closed his eyes.

*WELL, YOU TRIED.*

Smithy's last thought was about to be something very unkind about God, but then he heard the noise. He opened his eyes just in time to see the immense form of Lousy Louis Reed, who had managed to get to his feet and was hurtling towards his would-be assassin with all the energy he could muster. He caught the black-clad figure just as he tried to turn, wrapping his massive arms around him.

It was the nature of Smithy's existence that he was used to most of

life towering over him. The everyday world was designed by men, about six feet in height, who assumed that the rest of the planet was on their eyeline. Still, nothing had loomed over Smithy with such ominous presence as Lousy Louis Reed grappling inexpertly with a pink-faced ninja. Smithy was trying to scamper away when, like an avalanche of asshole, the duo came crashing down on top of him, expelling all the air from his lungs and possibly shattering a few things. It was impossible to tell where the most damage lay – everything hurt too much to individualise the agonies. Hell was other people, or at least other people lying on top of you.

Lou was pinning both Smithy and his assailant to the ground. The good news was that Smithy knew where the gun was; the bad news was where the gun was. The ninja's weapon-holding hand was pinned beneath Lousy Louis's girth, leaving the gun pointing directly at Smithy's face. Smithy needed to move his head quickly if he wanted to maintain its structural integrity in the long term. Above them, Louis was panting and groaning almost rhythmically. Smithy guessed this meant that the assassin's other hand was free and throwing punches into Lousy's body in an effort to move him.

Straining, Louis raised his voice. "Samantha... call... nine... one... one."

Smithy was trying to pull his head further away from the gun, but he was pinned down and there was no give in that direction. He also couldn't breathe, which was becoming an issue. Smithy had learned not to expect a great deal from life, but dying while Lousy Louis grunted and groaned above him felt like a particularly ignominious way to die.

The automated voice of Samantha boomed over the speakers. "Calling... Olivia Munn."

It wasn't like the evening had gone to plan or indeed made a great deal of sense up until this point, but still – this was a bit much. As Smithy began wiggling in the other direction while attempting to pull some air into his lungs, the thought did occur to him that surely this couldn't be *the* Olivia Munn.

The sound of a phone ringing filled the apartment.

The only Olivia Munn that Smithy had ever heard of was the Hollywood actress. She'd been brilliant in Aaron Sorkin's *The Newsroom*, and criminally underused in the X-Men film she was in. He couldn't imagine that Lousy Louis actually knew her, but then he hadn't expected him to be the target of an honest-to-God ninja assassin either. The asshole was defying expectations left, right and centre.

After two rings, the phone was picked up and a female voice boomed over the apartment's speakers.

"Hello."

It was hard to tell if it was her or not. Smithy was now inches from his goal. Louis continued to grunt and groan, his weight shifting slightly, putting yet more pressure on Smithy and shoving his nose into the carpet.

"Hello. Who is this?" asked the woman. It did sound quite like her.

Louis shifted again, giving a pained gasp as his weight shifted back the other way. Smithy drew in a desperate breath and sweet, sweet air re-entered his lungs.

"Is this you again, you fucking pervert?"

Smithy was beginning to think it really was Olivia Munn.

Lights were flashing before his eyes now. Smithy summoned every last desperate ounce of strength he had left in his body and prepared to do the world's hardest push-up.

"I don't know how you keep getting my number, but I'm going to hunt you down and kill you, you useless, pathetic ball sack of depravity."

Damn. Munn Burn.

The phone hung up.

Smithy kept his eyes locked on the barrel of the gun and heaved with all his might. Louis moved a few inches above him...

Smithy pushed his head to the side and sunk his teeth into the black-gloved hand holding the gun. Somewhere in the distance there was a scream – and then the gun fired three times.

Smithy's ears rang, and as the sound of the explosion faded, he

realised he was temporarily deaf. The pain in his ears was mitigated by the fact that Lousy Louis, keen to avoid getting shot, had rolled his body completely off him.

Smithy reared up, gasping greedily at the air, born again. After a few moments, he placed a hand on the side of the couch and laboriously pulled himself to his feet. Amoebas of light were floating across his field of vision and he reached up a hand to feel wetness running out of his right ear.

Having detected the smoke from the exploded TV, the sprinklers in the ceiling started showering the apartment in water. Smithy felt like Andy Dufresne after he made his escape from Shawshank. An alarm was sounding, but with his ears still ringing, it felt as if it was happening miles away, in a whole other life.

Regaining his sense of his surroundings amidst the man-made rainstorm, Smithy looked around him. Lousy Louis was on the floor, propped between the couch and the coffee table. His assailant was now limping towards the balcony door. He opened it and stepped back into the night, heading straight for the edge of the balcony. Smithy watched in incomprehension as the black-clad figure clambered up onto the stone facade and, in one fluid movement, rolled himself off.

Smithy got to his feet and rushed out as fast as the stabbing pain in his right leg would allow. The cool night air felt glorious. He'd developed a new-found appreciation for the joys of breathing. He staggered across and clambered onto the stone facade just enough to allow him a view of the street. Down below, he could see a small parachute landing on the ground. A vehicle sped up the street and scooped up the ninja, leaving only the parachute behind as the evidence that the whole thing hadn't been a weird if remarkably physical dream.

"You have got to be kidding me!"

Smithy turned back. The ringing in his ears was starting to die away and he could hear the alarm more clearly – clearly enough that he was relieved when it stopped. When he limped back inside, the

sprinklers had ceased too. The room was drenched. He glanced across at the soggy mass of muppetry and gave a sigh.

He looked back to see Lousy Louis gawping at him, his eyelids flying at half-mast, like a drunk trying to find sense in the world.

"Are you... an angel?"

"No," said Smithy. "No, I'm not."

"But... you saved me."

"Not my idea."

"What're you... what're you doing here?"

Smithy ignored the question as he limped over and picked up his hat. He looked at the bullet hole in it, about two inches above where his head would have been. "Well, that's a deposit I'm not getting back." That thought led to another. He turned and saw the paintball gun lying on the ground. The barrel was now pointing at an angle and the hopper was cracked. "Goddammit! Do you have any idea how much these things cost?"

Smithy picked it up, pointed it at Louis and pulled the trigger. Nothing happened. "Great. That's just great."

"I'll pay."

Smithy glowered at the man who did not deserve the name Lou Reed. "That's your answer to everything, isn't it? You narcissistic, megalomaniacal piece of shit."

Louis attempted to drag himself up onto the couch but found it too much and slumped back to the floor. He waved a hand at Smithy. "You're one... one of the leprechauns."

"I'm not a fucking..."

Smithy looked at the sword still sticking out of the centre of the coffee table and took a few deep breaths. The tempting idea of making Lousy Louis into a kebab had just popped into his brain, and while he wasn't going to do it, he still enjoyed the thought for a few seconds.

"You saved me!" Reed now wore a weirdly blissful smile.

Smithy looked down at the sodden carpet below his feet, took a very long and slow deep breath and then let it all out. "Shut up. You are a

terrible person. Do you understand that? Awful. I don't know why that guy was trying to kill you, but I bet you deserve it. You treat people like objects. You think money gives you the right to do what you like? Well, it doesn't. Alright? It doesn't. And show the actual Lou Reed some respect. Take those records off your bathroom wall. You are the most pathetic human being I've ever come across – and believe me, that is really saying something. Re-hire your assistant and, and, and… don't ever ring Olivia Munn again. Just… just try and be… a person. Just a decent person."

Smithy raised his head and looked over at Louis to see what effect his words had had.

The man was fast asleep again, snoring away happily.

"Great. Just great." Then he looked up at ceiling. "Well, I hope you're happy?"

Smithy limped over to the far side of the room, picked up his rucksack from where he had discarded it, placed the sodden hat and broken paintball gun inside it and headed for the apartment's front door.

He'd just reached it when a thought struck him and he turned and headed back into the front room. He walked over, picked something up and did a hasty about-turn.

As he walked by, he held it up in front of the unconscious form of Lousy Louis Reed. "I'm taking Elmo. You don't deserve Elmo."

A minute later, he stood on the landing outside the door of Louis Reed's penthouse. He opened the door to the stairs and heard the sound of boots quickstepping. Two of the lifts were on their way up too. It made sense. Shots are fired somewhere on the darker edges of the city, they'll send a patrol car. Shots are heard on billionaire's row, they'll send a SWAT team. Someone might miss their target and accidentally hit some of the money.

With a heavy sigh, Smithy opened the nearby garbage disposal chute and climbed in, clutching a sodden Elmo to him.

As the door closed behind him, he placed his legs against the wall and gradually started shuffling his way down, ignoring the pain

coming from his damaged leg. For a plan that had been so meticulously prepared, none of it had gone as it should have. Such was Smithy's painstaking level of planning that he had even managed to get hold of the building's architectural plans. He knew this chute led to a trash collecting area three floors down that would in turn feed into the compactor in the basement. It wasn't on at this time of night. He just had to make it there and then he could find a way to slip out of the building.

He felt that sickly tingle again.

*YOU DID WELL.*

"Shut up, God."

# GOOD DEEDS BAD INTENTIONS

Warning: The following novella is frankly a little bit Christmassy. If it is June when you're reading this, feel free to throw this book at a wall in disgust, but do come back and pick it up in December. Also, while it is festive, it does feature Bunny, Smithy, Diller and Cheryl and they are messing with some very bad hombres in their own inimitable style.

# TWAS THE NIGHT BEFORE CHRISTMAS

"You ain't nothing but bull."

Bunny looked down to see a face, scrunched up with anger, glowering up at him from between pigtails. He wasn't exactly a leading expert on children, but he reckoned the girl was eight or nine at most.

"Excuse me?" said Bunny, trying to give what he hoped was a winning smile.

The girl pointed up at him. "You heard me. Ain't no such thing as Santa, and this whole thing is a scam! A straight-up scam!"

Bunny glanced around and noticed that they were getting noticed by passers-by. Seventh Avenue had no shortage of foot traffic, and while he had come to appreciate just how good most people were at ignoring anything going on around them, a little girl standing on the sidewalk hollering at Santa Claus on Christmas Eve was the kind of thing that'd pique the interest of all but the most insular of New Yorkers.

"Are you OK, little girl?"

"Don't you 'little girl' me. I'm sick of all this nonsense. You're fake. I bet even that belly is fake."

She poked Bunny in what was very definitely his real belly.

"Ouch! Go easy, would ye? That's all me."

"Oh. Well then you should lose some weight."

"Thanks for the advice. And before you rip it off my face, this beard is mine too." He gave it a tug to emphasise his point. None of these facts seemed to do anything to take the angry wind out of the little girl's sails.

"None of that makes you Santa Claus. You're just some fat old guy with a beard!"

Bunny looked around, hoping to see a parent, but while several people were now paying attention, none of them had that parental air about them. "Jesus, love, is your charm school on a day off or something?"

She wrinkled her nose and wafted her hand in front of it. "And you smell of booze. I know that smell."

Bunny tried to smile. "Santa has been out here all day in the freezing cold, ringing this bell, raising money for the homeless..." He pointed at the bucket next to him, which contained mostly coins. "And he may have taken a little nip of something to take the edge off."

"Stop calling yourself Santa. You ain't Santa."

Bunny scratched his beard. She had him there. He wasn't the real Santa. In fact, he wasn't even the real fake Santa – that guy was in a bar down the block getting wasted. Bunny had needed an excuse to stand around on this street corner and not look suspicious. This had seemed like a good idea at the time. It turned out the other guy was doing this as part of his community service for a public urination citation, and he'd been more than happy to be liberated from his bell-ringing responsibilities.

"OK," said Bunny, lowering his voice and leaning down to look at the little girl. "You're absolutely right, sweetheart – I'm not 'the' Santa. I'm a friend of his, and he let me borrow his suit so I could raise money for charity to help homeless people have a nice Christmas."

"So you're a friend of Santa?"

"Yes."

"OK, then explain this: there are, like, two billion children in the world – how is he delivering presents to all of them?"

"Well," said Bunny, "his reindeer can fly, and—"

"Yeah," she interrupted, "but to visit every house, they'd have to be clocking at least 650 miles per second. At that speed, reindeers are gonna spontaneously combust. BOOM!" She threw her arms out in an extravagant gesture to emphasis the violence of this untimely end. "I googled it in the library at school. The top speed of a reindeer is fifteen miles per hour. Per hour! They reach 650 miles per second and Santa's hurtling towards the earth with a face full of fried reindeer, and that's gonna leave a big old fat-white-guy-sized crater. That's science! You can't argue with science."

"Right," said Bunny. "Well, that's very impressive. You know a lot about science, don't you?"

"Yeah. I like science. Science don't lie to you, unlike everybody else." She pointed around them. "Look at all this. Spirit of goodwill? It's all rich people buying other rich people fancy things."

Despite the cold weather, Bunny was sweating. Down the block, amidst the throng of tourists, last-minute shoppers and pickpockets, he could see two members of the NYPD looking in his direction.

"So, are you going to be a scientist when you grow up?"

The little girl folded her arms and narrowed her eyes. "I'd like to be, but I ain't gonna be. I looked that up too. To do science, you gotta go to college. That costs a lot of money, and I'm an orphan. Where am I gonna get that kind of money? Ain't gonna happen."

"Oh," said Bunny.

"Yeah," said the girl. "I'm gonna end up in some crappy job where I don't get to use my brain. I'll probably end up standing on a street corner ringing a bell."

"Ouch."

"No offence," she said, with the air of someone who was aware she had an inadvertent tendency to cause an awful lot of it. "I saw some comedian guy on TV talking about how angry the staff are at the DMV. I bet that's because they couldn't afford to be scientists either. Life ain't fair." She nodded – agreeing with herself emphatically.

Bunny was floundering. The little girl had a relentless line of

argument, which he was having a hard time countering. "Santa's reindeer are magic?" He could hear the disbelief in his own voice as he said it. He knew it was futile, but he felt the need to at least attempt it anyway.

"Oh, please," said the little girl, throwing her arms up in disgust. "If Santa has all this magic at his fingertips, what's he doing with it? Take a look around – world needs a hero, not some fat dude who works one day a year."

"Annabelle Watson!" The shout came from a large, sweaty white woman who was rushing down the sidewalk towards them, her face a mix of panic, relief and outrage. "There you are!"

The little girl looked back at the woman. "What? I wasn't doing nothing."

"You weren't doing *anything*," said the woman, almost on automatic.

"See, you agree with me."

"No, I..."

The lady reached them, her breathing now heavy and laboured. "You most certainly were doing something, and you know it was something you weren't supposed to."

"Make up your mind," said the little girl, just quietly enough to not be heard.

"What was the one thing I said before we left Saint Augustine's this morning?"

"Pee now as we can't—"

"Not that! I said don't wander off. And what did you do, missy? You wandered off. We will be having some serious words about this when we get back."

The woman leaned down and took Annabelle's hand, and then she looked up at Bunny, her face full of apology. "I am sorry, sir. I hope she wasn't a bother?"

"Oh no, not at all. We were just having a nice chat."

She gave a tight smile. "Thank you. She's a smart child, but she is a handful."

"But Mrs Tandy—"

"Not another word, missy. Not one word. Well, at least you got to meet Santa."

Annabelle pointed at Bunny with her free hand. "He ain't Santa; he's just some fat dude in a suit."

"Annabelle!" Mrs Tandy exclaimed, her voice full of genuine outrage. She looked at Bunny. "I do apologise, sir."

Bunny waved it away. "Ah, don't worry about it. She speaks her mind – not enough of it about."

Mrs Tandy leaned in. "I'm sorry – she's acting out. We brought all the children into Manhattan on a day trip. Danelli's department store gives us a free visit with Father Christmas on Christmas Eve – you know, as a PR thing. The kids really look forward to it."

"Ah, right," said Bunny. "That's nice of them."

"Yes, it would have been, only we turned up to find out they'd bumped us. Some NBA team is in town to play a game tomorrow and they brought their kids to see Santa instead."

"Oh," said Bunny.

"Yes. The PR woman said orphans at Christmas were a bit depressing. They'd rather have Santa taking free throws with millionaires." Despite giving it some effort, Mrs Tandy failed to keep the anger from her voice. "We load twenty-seven kids onto the subway from Queens because the home's bus has broken down – again – only to get here and find that. Not exactly the most Christian thing, is it?"

"No," agreed Bunny, "'tis an absolute disgrace."

"Yes. As if that wasn't bad enough, the woman gave us discount vouchers for toys, like that's some kind of a thing. Giving orphans money off on toys – might as well be giving me free parking for my Ferrari. I don't know how some people—"

Mrs Tandy's cell phone interrupted her. She fished it out of her pocket with her free hand. "Hey, Samantha... Yes, I found her. We'll meet you over by the station... What? Anthony needs to go again? You'd think with all that crying, he'd be tapped out. OK, I'll be back over in a second."

She hung up the phone.

"Come on, Annabelle, we have to be getting back. Say goodbye to the nice man."

Annabelle shot a begrudging nod in Bunny's direction.

Mrs Tandy shook her head again. "A merry Christmas to you, sir."

Bunny nodded. "And to you too," he said, raising his voice, as the duo were already hurrying back down the sidewalk.

Bunny watched them go, Mrs Tandy weaving in and out of the torrent of pedestrian traffic, a truculent Annabelle dragged in her wake. He stood transfixed for a full minute, until, from the corner of his eye, he saw an object arc its way into the bucket that dangled from the stand beside him.

His hand shot out on instinct, and grabbed the source of the object around the throat: a blond guy in his mid twenties, wearing a suede jacket and a smug grin – although the grin didn't survive a coarse hand wrapping itself around his body's primary avenue for oxygen consumption.

"What the—"

The rest of the sentence was lost as Bunny tightened his grip. The tosser found himself eye to eye with Father Christmas, whose right eye glowered at him while the left seemed to be gazing off in an entirely different direction. "'Tis the most magical time of the year, fella. And to prove that, a couple of miracles are about to happen. In particular, the soda can you just tossed into the bucket – which you know is there to collect money for the homeless – is going to magically transform itself into all the cash in your wallet."

The guy went to push Bunny away, but this resulted in a firm grip being applied to his right wrist, sending pain shooting up his arm. He gave a strangled yelp.

"And if that miracle does happen," continued Bunny, "then the other miracle will be you walking away from here with the same number of bollocks as you came with. Are we clear?"

Five minutes and an ostentatious donation of two hundred bucks later, Bunny was back to ringing his bell and trying not to attract attention. Then he saw Helena Martinez step out of the side door of the theatre where she worked, just as she had done for the last three

days. Everything around her wasn't the same though. You'd have had to know what to look for to see it, especially in the Christmas rush of people moving in all directions. Still, Bunny knew what to look for. He hadn't been watching Helena Martinez so much as he'd been waiting to see who else was watching Helena Martinez. A large man with a shaven head, who, despite the just above freezing weather, was only wearing a black hoodie, walked quickly out of a nearby coffee shop and, with his eyes fixed on her, followed her down the street.

Bunny took the burner phone out of the pocket and hit speed dial.

"We got a bite."

# A WALK IN THE PARK

Helena checked the bench was clean and then sat down. In reality, it really was far too cold to be sitting in Central Park eating her lunch, but she didn't care. Even as a kid, she had weirdly loved the cold weather. Everyone else longed for summer, but not her. There was something about that bite in the air that made her feel alive. And so it was that, at the same time every day, rain allowing, she would nip out of the theatre and hurry the three blocks up to Central Park, so she could sit there in the closest thing you could find to peace and quiet on the Island of Manhattan. When Helena was a child, her momma had often joked that, seeing as she loved the cold and the quiet so much, she should go live in Alaska with the penguins. Helena had known there weren't any penguins in Alaska outside of a zoo, but she hadn't corrected her momma, as then she would have had to admit that she had not only looked it up but studied it in embarrassing detail. Everyone else dreamed of Hollywood; she was the little girl who had gone to bed every night dreaming of Alaska. She'd grown into a woman who had never even left New York. With a sigh, she pulled the package of sandwiches she had brought from home out of her bag and unwrapped it. A few pigeons swooped down as she did so. She recognised the one with the unusual white

and brown markings – he was a regular who knew she was an easy mark.

She was halfway through her second sandwich when a red-headed woman sat down at the other end of the bench. Helena let out an involuntary yelp of surprise. The woman held out a hand.

"Pardon me, honey – didn't mean to frighten you."

Helena blushed. "Oh no, not at all. Sorry. I was engrossed in feeding the birds."

The woman nodded. "I can see that. They sure do love you."

Helena gave a polite laugh. "They love anybody with bread. Not many people sit around feeding them this time of year."

The redhead gave a warm laugh and hugged her arms around herself. "Ain't that the truth. Too damn cold. I'm from Texas – we don't keep our iceboxes this frosty."

Helena smiled in response.

"Still," continued the woman, "sitting here, we got more space around us than you get anywhere else in Manhattan, huh?"

Helena nodded. "That's why I come here."

"Yeah," said the woman with a nod. "It's broad daylight and we've got plenty of wide-open ground around us. I want you to remember that."

Helena's head whipped around to look at the woman.

"Oh gee, I'm sorry. That came out wrong. Didn't mean to sound quite so stalkery. Apologies." The redhead held her hands up. "I'm kinda new to this."

"New to what exactly?"

The woman gave her a smile. "I promise you, I'm here as a friend. Relax, Helena."

Helena sat up ramrod straight. "How do you know my name?"

"That's what I'm here to explain. My name is Cheryl, and I want to help you."

"I don't need help."

Cheryl nodded. "I'm afraid you do. Try not to look, but there's a big, muscly dude with a shaven head over on the far side there, on the left, at the treeline. He followed you here."

Helena tried to look casual as she looked around. She could see the man now, staring over at them.

"Oh God." She said it to herself as much as anything.

"It's OK," said Cheryl.

"It's not. You don't understand."

"I do. I really do. You think that man has something to do with your ex-husband, and you're right – he does."

Helena grabbed her bag, ready to stand and run.

"Wait, wait – please. Just give me sixty seconds. I swear to you, honey, I'm here to help."

Helena eyed the woman suspiciously, but she didn't move.

"Thank you," continued Cheryl. "I'm helping out a friend of mine. He got hold of a list of women like yourself who are trying to get away from abusive partners."

"How would you get that? They don't just hand that kind of information out."

"No. I know somebody who works in an emergency room. Let's just say he got tired of seeing a certain kind of injury."

Helena said nothing, instead looking down at her hands clasped in her lap.

"We," continued Cheryl, "well, mainly my friend – he keeps an eye on these ladies, just in case the abusers show up again. We know the law doesn't offer enough protection, and we're just trying to fill in the gaps."

"And what's in it for you?" The fear in Helena's voice was turning to anger now.

"First and foremost, we want to stop bad things happening. I get you being suspicious, I really do. That's why I'm approaching you like this. We want to help you. Also..." The woman shifted in her seat. "Also," she repeated, "to be completely honest with you, honey, my friend... he's trying to find a bunch of nuns that operate in New York, helping women in situations like yourself. We figure we help out enough people, somebody might know them, put us in contact."

Helena shook her head. "I don't know any nuns."

"OK, not a problem. Like I said, we want to help regardless, and

we can. Believe me. We've done this a few times now."

Helena gave her a suspicious look. "Why can't you just go talk to these nuns?"

Cheryl shrugged. "He can't find them. He's been here looking for them for like..." She took a moment to think. "Damn, nine months now. They don't officially exist. It's complicated, but if they're here at all, they don't want to be found. So this is what we came up with."

"It doesn't make any sense."

Cheryl pursed her lips. "You might be right, honey, but – to be straight with you – this is his last hope. He's kinda desperate. And besides, he likes helping people – people who need help. And no offence, but that is you."

Helena ran her hand over her brow. "Jonny said he'd kill me if he found me. I've got to run."

"You do that, he'll find you again."

She shook her head. "You don't understand. He's a dangerous man."

"Jonny Risbury, suspected lieutenant for the Los Zetas Cartel, on the run after skipping bail in Miami on two serious assault charges. He was previously charged but not convicted in three first-degree murder cases and was a person of interest in several more investigations."

Helena gulped and put her head in her hands. "Oh God."

"He's a dangerous man alright. The good news is so is my friend."

Helena looked into the distance and didn't speak for about thirty seconds. Finally, she pushed her hair back behind her ear and spoke in a soft voice. "You're probably wondering how I could ever go with a guy like that?"

Cheryl shook her head. "No, I'm not. I know as well as anyone, sweetheart, the evil bastards can be just as charming as the good guys – sometimes even more so, precisely because they are the evil bastards."

Helena nodded, tears in her eyes now. "He wasn't always... When we met, he was just a nice guy working in a bar. Mostly."

"His actions are his actions. None of this is your fault. If you'll let

us, we'd like to make it so he'll never bother you again."

"I've got a son."

"We know. If it makes you feel better, right now my beau is outside his school, making sure he's safe."

"This guy you work with," said Helena. "The one looking for the nuns, he is your...?"

Cheryl laughed. "Oh no. Lord, no. He's a friend. Me and my man just help him out."

"How do you know him?"

Cheryl smiled. "That's a long story. Let's just say the crazy Irishman dropped into our—"

"He's Irish?" asked Helena with such abruptness that Cheryl sat back.

"Ehm, yes."

"Big guy? Beard?"

It was Cheryl's turn to look surprised. "You know him?"

"He has a..." She waved a hand at her face. "Y'know, a sort of 'off' eye?"

Cheryl nodded. "You really have met him."

Helena shook her head. "No, but I got a friend. Well, I mean, I know her. We're in this support group together. Her name's Marcia. She lives out in Brooklyn somewhere, I think."

"Ah. Right."

"Her old boyfriend came looking for her. Came after her with a baseball bat."

Cheryl nodded. "Like I said, we've done this before."

"Your friend? That was the guy who bust in and...?"

Cheryl nodded again.

"Is it true they found her ex hanging upside down from a street light?"

"My friend has a... Let's call it a certain sense of flair."

"Carol told us it took them hours to remove the bat."

Cheryl tried to suppress a smile. "He ain't a big fan of baseball."

Helena bit her knuckle and then turned back to Cheryl with a very different look in her eyes. "What would I have to do?"

# SMILE – IT CONFUSES PEOPLE

Jackson Diller leaned against the lamp post and smiled. He was a young black guy standing on a street corner in one of New York's nicer suburbs, and that made people nervous. People being nervous because a black dude was just standing doing absolutely nothing really shouldn't be his problem, but it was. Rather than taking steps to bring about meaningful social change at 8pm on Christmas Eve, he was smiling just to stop the white people from calling the cops. Smiling had been Diller's preferred mode of defence since birth, and that had seen him through more challenging situations than this. He had been stationed here for over two hours now and it was getting cold. He'd found a thick duffle coat in a thrift store a few weeks ago and it was proving to be a superb purchase. It was two sizes too big for his skinny frame, but Diller loved it. He clapped his hands together to keep the blood flowing. An old lady looked at him nervously and Diller upped the wattage on the smile.

"Happy Christmas to you, ma'am."

The woman nodded, smiled and noticeably increased her pace. Diller was between meaningful positions of employment. He wondered if he could get a gig as a personal trainer for the elderly? He'd had two weeks of acting work booked in, but that had gone

south after the one-act play's opening night turned out to be its closing night too. Not only had there been only one performance – well, there hadn't even been that, really. Their leading lady/director/writer/backer had shimmied down a drainpipe mid-performance and disappeared. It turned out she had stolen a painting from her psychiatrist's office and had been shocked to see him sitting in the audience – although not as shocked as he was to see his painting hanging on the back wall of the set. Diller had finished the play by performing both parts. The consensus was that it had improved it greatly.

Diller returned to watching the six-storey brownstone about a hundred yards away on the opposite side of the street. It was the building where Helena Martinez and her son lived, up on the fourth floor. He had followed them home earlier that day. Actually, he had followed the guy who was following them home, and then watched as he'd checked their precise address before leaving. The theory was that he and his boss, Helena Martinez's ex, would be back later tonight, which was why Diller was standing on a street corner smiling at nervous strangers. His job for this part of proceedings was to be lookout. They had a plan. He personally felt that at least one part of it was terrible and another part was verging on the suicidal, but nobody seemed keen to hear his thoughts, and besides, his mom had always told him that if you can't say anything nice...

Diller's upbringing had been, to say the least, unconventional, but his mom had always made a big effort for the holidays. They'd never had much, but she had done everything in her power to make something out of it. Looking at all of these apartments, their windows aglow with warm lights, snapshots of lives festooned with decorations and presents under the Christmas tree, felt like looking into a different world, one he'd only ever seen on TV.

He heard a noise and glanced behind him, then he turned again, executing a textbook double take.

"Is that a pig?"

The slight woman in a bobble hat and thick-rimmed glasses did nothing to hide her eye-roll. "Yes, it's a pig," she said, before adding

with a sigh, "just once it would be nice to bring him for a walk without people asking us questions."

Diller pulled back. "Sorry, but you're walking a pot-bellied pig in New York. I think you're going to have to get used to the fact that people will have questions." Diller gave his best winning smile which still lost.

"Honestly, you'd think people haven't seen a pig before."

The woman would have undoubtedly liked to storm off, but the pig had taken this moment to engage in a large dump.

There was an awkward silence – or at least there would have been, but for the sounds of the pig popping out a prodigious poop. Diller wasn't a big fan of silences.

"So what's his name?"

"Mr Oinks."

"Right. Hey, Mr Oinks!" Diller gave a wave in the pig's direction, but the pig seemed preoccupied.

His owner shuffled her feet. "Sorry about snapping before. It's just... It's my last day with him."

"Oh," said Diller, before lowering his voice. "Is he...?"

"What?"

"Going to be Christmas dinner?"

The woman reared back in outrage. "No! I am a strict vegan, as is Mr Oinks."

"Right. Sorry," said Diller, who happened to know pigs were omnivores by nature and Mr Oinks was very unlikely to be vegan by choice, but elected, rightly, not to mention it.

"It turns out that *technically*" – she said "technically" like it was a very bad word – "it is illegal to keep a pig as a pet in New York City. It's fine to slaughter them en masse, of course."

"Right," said Diller. He glanced over at the building he was supposed to be watching, aware that he was getting dragged into a distraction he could not afford.

"One of my neighbours complained. Bitch! So now Mr Oinks has to go live with my Uncle Jeffrey in Jersey. I'm taking him over there tomorrow."

"I see. Is it legal to keep him in Jersey?"

"Have you been to Jersey? It's barely fit for human habitation."

The woman bent down before storming off, or at least as much as it was possible to storm off with a pig's lead in one hand and a freezer bag full of pig poop in the other.

In the opposite direction, Diller noticed a yellow Mustang pulling up to park. The man Diller recognised from earlier got out of the driver's side, and another man got out on the passenger side. They had a brief discussion over the hood and then the driver stayed with the car while the other one headed towards the building's front door.

Diller casually took his mobile out of his pocket and sent a group text.

THEY ARE HERE.

# THE MAN COMES AROUND

Jonny Risbury stepped back as a hassled-looking guy, laden with too much luggage and with his phone clamped to his ear, emerged from the building's front door.

"No, Mom, Janice said she was getting the cranberry sauce. I don't even eat it. Why would I... No, I'm not... I have... Alright, fine, I'll get it. I'll ask the Uber driver to stop on the way. OK."

He dropped his bags and looked at Jonny, who gave him a polite smile in return.

"So, where are you parked?" He looked at Jonny expectantly and then, after a few moments of blankness, looked mortified. "Oh my God, I'm so sorry. You're not my Uber driver, are you?"

Jonny shook his head. "No."

Designer leather jacket, Rolex on his wrist – this guy obviously thought the people-ferrying business paid really well.

"Sorry, dude. Sorry. I'm a little stressed out, y'know – family!"

Jonny gave him a big grin and caught the door before it closed behind him. "Yeah. Tell me about it." Then he moved inside and headed for the stairs.

# NO GOOD DEED

Rolo sat in the Mustang and fiddled irritably with the heater. It somehow managed to blow a lot of hot air around without making the car warm. He'd already spent most of the day trudging around New York following the boss's ex, and he was getting royally sick of this. Not that he'd say anything. Jonny was real friendly and amicable, right up until the point he wasn't. Rolo had been there the night Jonny had messed up Xavier Fuentes bad, when they had been playing cards. Jonny was alright with losing, but Xavier had had to go twisting the knife, making it all personal. Xavier wouldn't be running his mouth off like that again – the dude spoke with a permanent slur now, like his tongue was too big for his mouth. Last Rolo heard, Xavier had got himself deliberately arrested robbing a five-and-dime, because he couldn't cope with being outside since he was all messed up. These days he pushed a broom up in Rikers and didn't say nothing to nobody.

Rolo didn't like this. If it was up to him, Jonny would just forget about his ex-wife and kid, but it very definitely wasn't up to him. They were supposed to be making money for the bosses. Jonny got a lot of rope because he was an earner, but that only went so far. They had something they were meant to be doing, and this wasn't it. Rolo

knew better than to bring it up though. Jonny was full-on crazy on this particular subject – like he took the whole thing as a personal insult. Rolo didn't get it. it wasn't like Jonny didn't have plenty of women, and it wasn't like he was a contender for dad of the year either. He had another kid he never saw. This was all because she had walked away from him and the man couldn't take losing. It was messed up. Rolo wasn't sure what the endgame was supposed to be. Did Jonny think they were going to see each other again and it'd be happy families? Did he just want to scare her? Or worse? Rolo had plans for the night; the last thing he wanted was to have to go dump a body in the river on Christmas Eve. He had surf and turf at Marco's booked in.

A van pulled up in front of him and a blonde got out. She was cute, and not exactly dressed for the weather. Leather miniskirt and a mirrorball top that clung in all the right places. She had legs to die for. She looked around, searching for something that wasn't there. Rolo watched as she twirled around and then pulled out her phone. She rang a number and swore into somebody's voicemail. Rolo looked up from checking out her body to find her eyes on him. He felt himself redden, but she gave him a big smile and headed straight for him. As she reached the window, he pressed the button to bring it down. She leaned in with a big smile and Rolo tried to look without looking at what was on display below the smile.

"Hey, baby, I'm real sorry to bother you. I'm supposed to be meeting my friend but he ain't here. I've got to drop a sound desk just over there to my girl Janice's apartment. Is there any chance you could help me lift it?"

Rolo looked up. "Sorry, I'm just waiting for somebody."

"Please?" She gave him a little pout. "I'd be real grateful. It's just over there. We're in a band. I'll give you tickets to a show we got coming up at the Roxy."

Rolo thought about it. Jonny was likely to be a while yet.

"Please, baby. I'll make sure you get the VIP treatment too."

She said it with a sly smile that won him over.

"Alright then."

"Oh, thank you. You're such a sweetheart."

Rolo got out of the car and moved around.

"It'll just take a second."

"Sure, no problem. So what's the name of the band?"

"Shocker. We're funk metal."

"Right," said Rolo. "Sounds cool." It didn't, but Rolo was warming to the idea of the VIP treatment and what exactly that might entail.

"Can you get the doors there, baby?"

Rolo opened the van doors. "I ain't been to the Roxy for—"

He stopped talking because, upon opening the van doors, he'd seen it was empty. A flicker of suspicion flashed through him a millisecond before the 1200 volts of electricity. He fell to the ground. As Rolo's scrambled brain tried to process this unexpected turn of events, he was dimly aware of the woman's knee digging into his back and then a hand pressing a material with a sweet chemical smell to his face.

Diller moved over to stand beside Cheryl as she kneeled on top of the big guy's back. He looked around.

"Are we cool?" asked Cheryl.

"Yeah. I don't think anybody saw."

"Excellent. I told you this would work."

Diller nodded. "You did. Don't take this the wrong way, but you would make an excellent serial killer."

Cheryl looked up at him and smiled. "And what exactly is the right way to take that?"

Diller shrugged.

"How long do I have to hold this chloroform over his mouth?"

"I'd give it another minute. People think it acts instantly because they've seen it go down like that in movies, but it doesn't."

"OK," said Cheryl, pulling her blonde wig off with her free hand and tossing it into the back of the van. "Damn, I'm freezing my ass off."

Diller nodded. "You should've worn a thick coat."

Cheryl laughed and shook her head. "Dill, honey, for such a smart dude, there are some big things you don't understand – like if I was wearing a big warm coat, this guy would still be sitting in his car. Anyway, do you think that's enough?"

Diller looked at the big dude's face. "Yeah, he looks out of it. Besides, too much chloroform could kill him."

Cheryl pulled the rag away. "Jesus, Dill, couldn't you have mentioned that before?"

"Sorry. I thought I had?"

"Nope, you definitely didn't." Cheryl stood up and glanced around. "C'mon, let's get him into the back before somebody sees."

They bent down to the unconscious man and each grabbed an arm. "This dude is heavy," said Cheryl.

"Yep," said Diller through gritted teeth.

The man's face hit the tow bar on the van.

"Oops," said Cheryl. "Where did you get the chloroform from anyway?"

"I made it."

"You're kidding?"

With a heave they got his upper body in the back of the van.

"You just need some acetone and a gallon of six per cent sodium hypochlorite bleach. I'll get the rope and tie him up. I'm good with knots."

"Right," said Cheryl. "And remind me again why *I'm* the one who'd make a good serial killer?"

# LIKE THE FELLA ONCE SAID...

Jonny stood to the side, out of view of the peephole, and then knocked politely on the door.

"Amazon delivery."

He waited. He'd been careful to disguise his voice, going for an inoffensive Midwestern accent like all those companies used in their adverts. Apparently it was the most trusted – they'd done a study or something. He'd read a thing in a magazine once while waiting in a doctor's office.

Nothing happened. There was no sound from within the apartment. He had checked the windows from the street; there had definitely been lights on.

He knocked again, more loudly this time.

"Amazon delivery for a Helena Martinez." He knew she had changed her name. It should be Risbury, but even if you accepted this bullshit divorce the judge had granted, her maiden name was Ortega. She had changed it again when she'd run and taken his son away from him. It had made finding them harder, but not impossible. Not when you knew the right people.

There was still no noise from inside. Jonny reached inside his jacket and checked the Glock holstered under his left armpit. Then

he stood and listened for a full minute to make sure nobody was coming. He glanced up and down the hallway. He could hear a TV from across the hall, and a selection of festive tunes sung by a choir could be made out playing elsewhere in the building, but there didn't seem to be many people moving about. He put his hand in his inside pocket and pulled out the picks. This had never been his greatest skill, even in his early days, but the lock didn't look like much. As long as nobody disturbed him, he'd be fine.

He placed his hand against the door and was surprised to feel it give. The crazy bitch had left it open. She'd never been the smartest. Jonny slipped his picks back into his pocket and then discreetly withdrew the gun. He took a deep breath and moved inside, closing the door behind him. The apartment was now in darkness save for the wan light spilling in from the street outside. He listened but he still couldn't hear anything.

"Hey, baby. Daddy's home."

He was about to reach around for a switch when the lights came on.

"Howerya, Daddy."

Now illuminated, Jonny could see it was a studio apartment. There was an open-plan kitchen to his left and a bunk bed pushed against the far wall, with a small dining table and chairs beside it. A raggedy couch faced an old-looking TV to his right, behind which sat a small Christmas tree. At the far side of the room, about twenty feet from where Jonny stood, a large man in a Santa Claus outfit was sitting in an armchair giving him an amused look. Jonny pointed the gun at him.

"Who the fuck are you?"

The man raised his eyebrows. "Really? Jolly fat lad, red suit, beard? You're not exactly the world's greatest detective, are you?"

"Hilarious. Where's my wife?"

"You don't have a wife."

Jonny stepped forward. "You've got a hell of a mouth on you for the man who ain't holding the gun."

The man shrugged. "Well, I've been standing on a street corner

for a lot of the day and I may've had a couple of nips against the cold. Sure, 'tis Christmas."

"She's picking up drunk Scottish bums now?"

"Scottish? Scottish?! I'm Irish, ye cloth-eared gobshite."

"I don't give a fuck. Where is my wife?"

"If you mean your ex-wife, then she and her son are miles away."

"Our son. I'm his father."

"Only in the sperm-donor sense."

Jonny looked around. There was a door that presumably led to a bathroom. Maybe they could be in there?

"And what are you doing in my wife's apartment?"

The man stretched his arms out and yawned expansively. "Well, appropriately enough, you're on my naughty list."

"Who do you work for?"

The man gave Jonny what he may have thought was a smile. One of his eyes was messed up, making him look more than a little crazy, even before you factored in the suit. The beard was real, although it looked like he'd made a half-assed attempt to make it whiter. "I don't work for anybody. Think of me as a freelancer."

"Well, I ain't and believe me, you don't want to mess with who I represent."

"What? Amazon? Just leave the card saying you tried to make the delivery and feck off, there's a good lad."

"You got jokes. Ain't that sweet. You really need to shut up now, old man."

"Ohhh, there's no need to be hurtful, ye drug-peddling, wife-beating shiteburger."

"Your mouth is gonna get you into a world of pain."

The man shrugged. "To be honest with you, it wouldn't be the first time."

"I don't know what she told you, but my wife..."

"Ex-wife."

"Has put you in the middle of somewhere you shouldn't be. You're in my way. Bad things happen to people that get in my way."

"Yeah, I read the hospital report. You left her with a broken collarbone and a cracked—"

Jonny raised his voice. "You better mind your goddamn manners."

The man scratched at his beard. "Fecking weird moment to break into a lesson on etiquette there, fella."

"I'm done with your bullshit. You either tell me where my wife and son are or the first bullet goes through your leg. And that's just the first one."

"They want nothing to do with you. This is your last chance to walk away."

Jonny looked around. This fat a-hole seemed inexplicably confident, given the circumstances. Either Jonny was missing something or the guy was straight-up insane.

"My last chance? My last chance?" repeated Jonny. "There's a word for someone who comes between a man and his wife."

All pretence of jollity left the Irishman's voice, which dropped to a low, growling register. "And there are lots of words for someone who raises his hand to a woman, and none of them are 'man'."

"Alright, that's it. Which leg do you want first, motherfucker?"

"Yeah, you're a big man with a gun, aren't you, Jonny? You only go toe to toe with women, is that right? Macho. Why don't you dance with someone your own size for a change?"

"You are one dumb son of a bitch."

"Tell you what there, John-boy. You beat me one-on-one and I'll tell you the exact address of where they are."

"Like I can't get it out of you anyway?"

"Yeah, but where'd be the fun in that?"

Jonny was twenty years younger, sixty pounds lighter and in considerably better shape. He'd gone to the state championships as a boxer in his teen years, and since then his fast hands had ended a lot of fights quickly.

"Stand up."

Santa Claus did as he was told, rising slowly from the chair.

"Show me you haven't got any weapons."

"Only my dazzling wits." The Irishman opened the stupid red suit

and lifted it up as he turned slowly around. As he did so, he hummed 'It's Beginning to Look a Lot like Christmas' happily to himself. Jonny wanted to wipe the smile off this idiot's face. Rotation completed, Jonny pointed at the legs of the Irishman's Santa Claus outfit. He raised each of them in turn to show there was nothing strapped down there either. Then he rolled up his sleeves.

"I've also got nothing up me arse, but you're welcome to check?"

"No, thank you."

"Suit yourself. People have made that mistake before."

Jonny stood and looked at him for a long moment before placing the Glock down on the kitchen island. He could take this asshole easy, and if something went wrong, he still had the 22 strapped to his ankle. It'd feel real good to smash his face into the floor. He deserved a little Christmas treat.

The Irishman gave a sarcastic clap. "Fair play, Jonny. I would say I misjudged you but I haven't."

Jonny took his jacket off and tossed it on the floor. "Let's do this," he said, moving forward.

"Hang on a sec," said the Irishman, raising his hands. "Before we do – no knocking over the Christmas tree, it's bad luck."

Jonny cracked his knuckles. "Whatever."

"And, as it's Christmas, what do you say to no bollock shots?"

"Stop talking."

"Also" – the Irishman pointed back over towards the counter – "any disputes will be decided by the referee."

"What the...?"

Jonny glanced behind him. Standing beside the counter was a dwarf, holding Jonny's gun and pointing it at him.

"Fuck!"

"Yep," said the Irishman, before addressing the dwarf. "You owe me ten bucks, by the way." He turned back to Jonny. "I bet him I could make you give up the gun, and bless your fucking stupidity, you did. It was either that or he'd have used that stun gun thing he has. Thing is, that'd make you have a muscle spasm – never the cleverest thing to do to somebody holding a gun."

Jonny prepared to dive for his ankle holster.

"Don't," said the dwarf. "Just don't. I will if I have to."

Jonny looked at him and then relaxed his body. Nothing about the little guy indicated he was bluffing. "You better let me walk out of here. You think I came alone?"

"No," said the dwarf. "But the big dude outside in the car has already been dealt with. I got a text. Looks like you're having a bad day."

Jonny looked between the two men. "What's the plan here? You want me to leave Helena alone? Fine. You have my word."

"Well," said the Irishman, "if you can't trust a wife beater."

Jonny was just about done with this nonsense. "Who the fuck do you people think you are?"

The fat man held his hands out. "Sure, didn't I tell you. I'm Santa and he's my..."

"Don't say it," said the dwarf.

"I'm not. I didn't say it."

"You said you wouldn't say it."

"I haven't said it," pleaded the Irishman.

"You both need to listen to me," said Jonny, "and listen good. Anything happens to me, the people I work for will come for you. You'll meet your end begging for death. I've seen it. They get real creative." He pointed at the Irishman. "Believe me, they'll come for you, Santa Claus." He said it with a sneer. "And your little helper."

"That's it," barked the dwarf.

"I didn't say it. He—"

Jonny didn't hear the rest of the conversation. He watched as the dwarf pulled a yellow device from his pocket and fired it at him. Time slowed as Jonny watched the two metal probes arc through the air. He tried to run, but that just meant he got hit in the back. He went down hard. The last thing he remembered was seeing Santa's boot heading straight for his head.

# CHRISTMAS AT BERNIE'S

They'd be fine.

Cheryl sat behind the wheel of the van and looked up at the apartment window. The light had come on a few minutes ago. She looked at her phone again: no message from Smithy. She'd give it another five minutes and then she would go and check. If it had gone south, she'd ring the cops and they would just have to deal with the consequences. She'd felt OK about her part of the plan, but now it was over, she was starting to realise just how many flaws were in the other half of it. If she had to explain to a cop why some hired muscle was hog-tied and unconscious in the back of the van, then so be it. OK, it wasn't her van, which was awkward, but her friend Carol could just say she hadn't known what Cheryl was using it for. She drummed on the steering wheel and looked at the clock on the dash, trying not to think of Smithy and Bunny bleeding out on the floor of an apartment. Smithy hadn't wanted her involved in this, but Bunny's little side project being what it was, he needed a woman more than he needed Smithy or Diller, not least because Diller was a non-combatant. Although the guy certainly had his uses.

Cheryl jumped as Diller's face appeared at the window right beside her. "Jesus, Dill!"

He waved apologetically as she wound the window down. “Sorry, didn’t mean to startle you.”

“Any sign of…?” started Cheryl.

“What? Oh, no.”

Diller didn’t seem worried. He appeared to have complete faith that Smithy and Bunny would be fine.

“Y’know how you said to take the keys and check their car?”

“Yeah.”

“Well, I found something in the trunk.”

“What did you…?”

Cheryl never finished the thought, as the door to the apartment building opened and three drunks exited. At least that was what it would look like to any passers-by. Santa Claus and a dwarf messily carried an unconscious man between them. They passed a female jogger making her way back into the building.

“Sorry, m’darling, sorry there. Jonny here is a bit worse for the drink.”

“I told him,” added Smithy in a slur, “you can’t go drink for drink with an Irishman.”

The jogger gave them a tight smile as she moved past them.

As she watched them make their way down the steps, Cheryl laughed, as much from relief as anything. Diller, for his part, applauded appreciatively. “They’re *Weekend at Bernie’s*-ing it. Gotta respect that. Quality touch.”

# GIFTS OF ALL KINDS

Sergeant Marlon Watts punched his fist on his chest and issued a resounding belch. He didn't know when this obsession with baking had hit the precinct, but it was reaching epidemic levels. Since two weeks before Thanksgiving, people had been bringing in all manner of homemade cookies and confections and it was becoming a nightmare, albeit a delicious one. Everybody knew he had a sweet tooth and that he was in charge of setting rotas, and this had led him to eating his own weight in baked goods over the last month. It was getting to the point that he had found himself craving a salad earlier. Well, craving may have been too strong a word; he hadn't been moved enough to actually go and get one. Still, as the doctor had said at his last physical, his feet problem was really a weight problem, and every other problem he would have in later life would end up being a weight problem too. Looking at life from the wrong side of fifty, Marlon couldn't take such things lightly anymore – not when his stomach was so large that he could lean it on his desk to get a little relief. His belt was also digging into him more and more. Damn it – come January first, he would go back to that gym he had been paying for every month for two years now. Marcia joked that he went

religiously, in the sense that like church, he went a couple of times every year, usually around Christmas.

The doors flew open and Marsden and Gianelli came charging in. "Sarge, Sarge, Sarge – you gotta come outside!" insisted Gianelli.

Marlon didn't look up from the arrest reports he was scanning through on his desk. "I don't know if you're familiar with the chain of command in the sainted New York Police Department, Officer Gianelli, but I, like everyone else on the force, do not have to do anything you say."

Marlon didn't like Gianelli. Not even an Italian family could have as many uncles as he'd had 'die' over the last two years. If even half of them were real, he should have set up his own undertaking firm.

"C'mon, Sarge," chimed in Marsden. "I'm telling you, you do not want to miss this. It's a little Christmas treat."

On the other hand, Marlon actually did like Marsden; she was a good kid. She once judo-threw a tweaker across the receiving area after he'd lost it and tried to fight his way out. The woman was a pocket rocket.

"If it's carollers, then I'll give it a hard pass."

"It's better than that," said Gianelli. "I swear, Sarge."

Marlon stopped and looked at both of their faces. He'd not seen such eagerness since his own kids were youngsters on Christmas morning.

"Alright then, what is it?"

Marlon Watts stepped out of the back doors of the Precinct and into the car park. He didn't need to be directed as to where his attention was required. Two men sat tied up and gagged in the back seat of a yellow Mustang. The Mustang was wrapped in a massive bow. "Well, I'll be. There's something you don't see every day."

Unsurprisingly, the two men looked less than happy with their lot in life.

"There's a note, Sarge, there's a note!"

Marlon turned to Gianelli. “Yes, thank you, Officer Gianelli – having not lost the use of my eyes, I can see there is a note.”

Marlon took two steps down to look at the note displayed on the Mustang’s front windscreen, because, while he hated to admit it, his eyes weren’t as good as they once had been.

He read the note aloud.

“Hello, I am Jonny Risbury, a lieutenant in the Los Zetas Cartel. I am a wanted man after skipping bail in Miami on two assault charges. Odds-on my colleague here is also of interest to the authorities. A merry Christmas and God bless us each and every one. Yours sincerely, Santa Claus and his merry men and/or women. PS There are about ten kilos of cocaine in the trunk of this car.”

Marlon Watts looked around the car park. “Is this some kind of Christmas prank?”

“No, Sarge.”

“Because if it is, Gianelli, then you should know the rumours of me having a sense of humour have been greatly exaggerated.”

“I swear it isn’t, Sarge.”

Marsden interrupted. “Well, if it is, it has nothing to do with us, I swear.”

“Alright then,” said Marlon.

“How come you believed her and not me, Sarge?”

“Because, Gianelli, her relatives don’t all die on Fridays. So where’s the coke?” Marlon looked at the two rookies. “Oh, for... Open the damn trunk then!”

# IN THE ABSENCE OF CHIMNEYS

Smithy tapped the screwdriver against his chin, stared hard at the circuit board in front of him and took a deep breath. "Can both of you please stop watching me?"

"What?" said Cheryl.

"We're not watching you," said Bunny.

"I can feel your eyes on me and I'm trying to concentrate."

"You're sounding a bit paranoid there, sweetheart," said Cheryl.

"We're on the roof of a building we're trying to break into, and I'm trying to disable an alarm system. This is exactly the place where being paranoid is a good idea. Can't the two of you just talk amongst yourselves?"

They were indeed on top of a building, and while nobody was drawing attention to it out of politeness, it was bitterly cold. There was the threat of snow in the air and Cheryl was regretting not wearing her woollen gloves over the plastic gloves she was already wearing in order to not leave fingerprints. As Christmas Eves went...

"Alright, Smithy boy," said Bunny. "You relax and take your time. Cheryl and I will talk to each other, alright?"

"Excellent."

"So, Cheryl, do you think your fella can disable this alarm?"

Cheryl pursed her lips. “Don’t ask me. I didn’t know he had any skills in this area until an hour ago. This is yet another part of his mysterious past that he doesn’t talk about.”

“When I said talk amongst yourselves, I thought not talking about what I’m doing kinda went without saying?”

“Sorry,” said Bunny. “You should have said.”

“If I wanted to answer a lot of questions, I’d have brought Diller up here with me.”

“Alright, alright,” said Bunny. “Relax. Jesus, breaking and entering makes him fierce grumpy.”

A low growl issued from Smithy, causing Cheryl and Bunny to exchange a look that said ‘maybe we shouldn’t push this anymore’.

Cheryl turned to Bunny. “Besides, is this even a crime?”

“It is,” said Smithy.

“Well,” admitted Bunny, “technically, yes. Although, as a big believer in law and order, I’m fine with it, which is an indication of the level of seriousness.”

“Hmm,” said Cheryl. “On a related note, is taking the twenty grand from the trunk of Jonny’s car a crime?”

“It is,” said Smithy.

“Again, technically, yes,” said Bunny. “Although, once again, I’m absolutely fine with it. Plus, we did make a citizen’s arrest there of sorts.”

“You’re not a citizen,” said Smithy.

“Can I ask,” said Cheryl, pointing at Bunny’s clothes, “why’ve you not changed your outfit? I mean, I did.” She had, otherwise she probably would’ve been dead from hypothermia by now.

“What?” said Bunny. “It’s Christmas Eve – this suit is the perfect disguise. Who’s going to shoot Santa on a rooftop on Christmas Eve?”

Smithy sighed. “You still haven’t got your head around America, have you? You’re going end up mounted above someone’s fireplace.”

“I thought you were supposed to be concentrating?” asked Cheryl. “Why do you keep talking to us?”

Smithy said nothing, instead putting the screwdriver back into his

small toolkit with more force than was necessary and taking out a slightly smaller screwdriver and tapping that against his chin instead.

"Actually," said Cheryl, turning to Bunny, "I did want to talk to you. How come you've turned down our gracious invite to come over for Christmas dinner tomorrow?"

"Ah, thanks but no thanks," said Bunny. "I don't want to intrude."

"Really?" Sarcasm dripped from Cheryl's voice as she held her arms out. "You're literally about to be an actual intruder, but we invite you into our apartment, through the front door, and you'd rather not?"

Bunny said nothing, which was the wrong answer.

"What have you got planned?"

"I was going to take it easy."

"By which you mean you'll stay in that awful hotel and get drunk."

Bunny said nothing, which was all the answer she needed.

"Nope. Sorry, honey, ain't going to happen. You are coming. Diller is coming too, y'know?"

"Yeah," said Smithy, without turning around, "I'm going to drop him out to Cedarview to see his mom in the morning, and then he's coming back to our place."

Cheryl nodded. "So that settles it."

Bunny went to say something, which was also the wrong answer.

"No argument, you're coming. We're having our traditional Christmas. Smithy cooks a turkey; the turkey is undercooked. Smithy swears at the turkey and then cooks it until it is horribly overcooked. Smithy swears at it a whole lot more. We all eat three bites and then we order Chinese. Also, there's Trivial Pursuit. It's fun, you'll love it. You're family, whether you like it or not. And besides, the dog likes you."

Bunny nodded. "I appreciate what you're saying, but..."

They were interrupted by a cell phone ringing.

Smithy sighed. "Really? We're taking calls in the middle of the robbery now?"

"Shut up," said Cheryl, putting her hand into her jeans pocket and fishing it out. "It's the number."

"What num—? Oh right," said Smithy. The number was something Cheryl had come up with when she started helping Bunny with the list. They had needed a way for the women they were trying to help to get in touch with them, but they couldn't use their personal numbers, for obvious reasons. The number belonged to an unregistered disposable phone.

"It's Helena," said Cheryl.

"Shite," said Bunny. "Answer it."

Cheryl did.

"Helena, are you OK?"

Cheryl listened for a few seconds. "One second, honey," she said, before taking the phone from her ear. "She's fine. The police rang to let her know they have arrested Jonny for violating his parole, skipping bail and more – they didn't specify." She put the phone back to her ear. "That's great news, Helena, we're really pleased."

Much to Bunny's annoyance, Cheryl then held up a finger and walked a few feet away, turning her back on them. "What in the feck is she doing now?"

"I've no idea," said Smithy. "I'm kind of busy breaking into this building for you."

"Right. Yeah." Bunny lowered his voice to a whisper. "Now that she isn't here, can I ask, what does the, y'know…?"

"What?"

"The voice. What does it think of all this?"

Bunny was one of two people in the whole world who knew that, since Smithy had been the victim in a serious hit and run a few years ago, he occasionally suffered what Smithy himself considered auditory hallucinations. In simpler terms, he occasionally heard the voice of God in his head. For an atheist, this was particularly annoying. The other person who knew this secret was Diller, who was entirely convinced it was the voice of God. Bunny was still on the fence. The reason Cheryl didn't know was that Smithy didn't want the woman he enjoyed sexy time with getting distracted by wondering if

God was talking to him at that moment. She was from a family of Texan baptists and that was the kind of thing that could really blow a romantic evening horribly off course.

"I told you I wasn't going to talk about that," said Smithy.

"Right."

"But if you must know, there's been nothing."

Bunny nodded. "Is that good or bad, do you think?"

"Well, speaking as the man whose head it is, I think not hearing voices is a good thing."

"Fair point."

"Although you two have been yacking so much, I probably wouldn't have heard it anyway."

"You'd like me to shut up, wouldn't you?"

"Bunny, you can read me like a book."

Bunny shut up and Smithy went back to staring at the circuit board.

After a minute, Cheryl came back. "OK, I want you to remain calm."

"Do you mean me or him?" asked Smithy. "Because I'm trying and failing to remain focused here."

"I love you, honey, but shut up."

Smithy said nothing. Cheryl looked at Bunny. "OK, so, Helena. She didn't want to mention it before, but she once met a woman in that support group."

"Right," said Bunny.

"And she said this woman told her that a friend of hers got out of New York along with her two kids, thanks to some help from" – Cheryl looked at the name she had hastily scrawled on the back of her hand – "Father Gabriel de Marcos. Apparently he runs some kind of gang intervention thing somewhere."

"The Bronx," said Smithy, without looking up. "There was a big write-up about it in the paper recently."

"OK," said Cheryl. "Well, him."

"Right, but—" started Bunny, but he stopped when Cheryl held her finger up.

"She thinks it might be nothing, but... the woman said this priest knew a bunch of nuns who had helped get them out."

"Jesus!" said Bunny.

"Don't get your hopes up. It might not be the – what do you call 'em?"

"The Sisters of the Saint," said Bunny.

"Right."

"It's a lead though," said Bunny. "I've been here nine months – nine fecking months looking for them, and this is the first thing that's gone right!"

"Thanks," said Smithy.

"Ara shut up, y'know what I mean."

"It's good news," said Cheryl, "but don't get carried a—"

Cheryl was interrupted as Bunny swept her up into a massive bearhug. "I've got a lead!"

"OK, just..."

Bunny spun her around and was two bars into a rousing rendition of "It's Beginning to Look a lot Like Christmas" when Smithy turned around and glowered at them.

"Seriously?"

Bunny plonked Cheryl down rather unceremoniously.

"We are actually committing a crime here. Could you two stop treating it like a fun night out?"

"Sorry," said Cheryl.

"Sorry, but—" started Bunny, but Smithy silenced him with a look.

"I know. A lead. Great. Can we celebrate that after we don't get arrested?"

Bunny nodded. "Right. You're right." He turned to Cheryl. "He is. He is absolutely right."

"Shut up," said Smithy.

"Right."

Smithy nodded. "Now, Cheryl, have you got one of those silver wrappers from your gum?"

"I think so..." She found one in her back pocket. "Yes, here."

"Thank you." She handed it to him and Smithy turned back around to the circuit box. He then did something with the wrapper, after which he jammed the screwdriver into something with a considerable amount of force. There was a popping noise followed by the smell of burning.

"OK," said Smithy, "alarm is dead. We're in."

Smithy picked up his tools and walked off down the roof towards the skylight.

Cheryl looked at Bunny. "Is it weird that I'm a little turned on right now?"

# I LOVE THE SMELL OF EGGNOG IN THE MORNING

Mrs Tandy took a deep breath and tried to remain calm. It had, all told, been a rather stressful week. There had been an even higher than normal level of colds and sniffles, not to mention yesterday's disastrous trip with the children into Manhattan to not see Santa. And then there were the smaller things you had to keep an eye out for, especially at this time of year. Any child living in Saint Augustine's would be painfully aware that they were different to other kids. Acting out was inevitable. Tina Lacroix had got into a fight last night with one of the older girls. Tina's auntie had said she would come from Philadelphia to take her for Christmas, but they'd returned yesterday to find a message on the home's machine saying she wasn't coming. Mrs Tandy sincerely loved her job, but there were days when it felt like having gone twelve rounds with an angry gorilla.

And then she had woken up to this – whatever this was – this morning. It had been one of her nights to sleep over and so she'd been the first one into the cafeteria at 7am, to open up for the cooks. That's when she'd seen it, although it had taken her more than a few moments to believe it. Then she had found the note and the envelope. After giving it some thought, she had phoned the police.

She knew that upstairs there were some annoyed and interested kids, and she knew Sarah was having a hard time keeping them up there.

Mrs Tandy stood with Officer Gianelli as he slurped the coffee she had made him. They had run out of small talk five minutes ago. Mrs Tandy was too nervous to chat – somehow, she knew this would go badly. It had been that kind of a week. Officer Marsden had been on the phone with the station for fifteen minutes. When she finally hung up and turned towards them, there was a palpable sense of relief shared between Mrs Tandy and Officer Gianelli, two people unburdened from the weight of failed conversation.

"OK, Mrs Tandy, here's what we know. All of these" – said Officer Marsden, waving towards the massive pile of wrapped presents that was dominating the room – "were stolen last night."

"Oh Lord," said Mrs Tandy, blessing herself furiously.

"Well, kind of," finished Officer Marsden.

"Kind of? How can something be kind of stolen?"

Officer Marsden rubbed the back of her neck. "The assistant manager from Toytopolis Toys up on Bleecker came in this morning. They had some kind of alarm fault last night. Somebody broke in and took a load of toys."

"Oh heavens..."

"But," continued Marsden, "they left a list of what they'd taken and enough money to cover it, plus repairs to the skylight they'd broken to get in."

"Is that normal?"

Marsden shook her head. "No. Burglars don't normally leave notes and they definitely don't ever leave money."

"In fact," interjected Officer Gianelli, "there was a burglary over on Hillcrest last week and that guy left..." Gianelli stopped talking when Marsden's stare penetrated his bubble of stupidity. "Never mind," he said, looking sheepish.

"So," continued Officer Marsden, turning to look at Mrs Tandy, "my boss talked to his boss, who talked to the owner of Toytopolis, and long story short – no harm, no foul. These gifts are for your kids." Marsden gave a big smile.

"And the" – Mrs Tandy lowered her voice – "money?" There had been just over seventeen thousand dollars in cash in an envelope addressed to her, and a note that said, "Dear Mrs Tandy, you seem like an honest woman. Here is a donation to Saint Augustine's so you can get that bus fixed and maybe bring all the kids to the circus or something. Merry Christmas, Santa Claus."

Office Marsden nodded. "The money is a donation, as far as we can see. All above board, bar the breaking in to leave it – which, again, is a bit unusual."

Mrs Tandy felt faint. Officer Gianelli reached out a hand to steady her. "Are you OK?"

"Sorry. Yes," she said, patting his hand. "It's just – well, this is quite a thing, isn't it?"

Marsden nodded. "A regular Christmas miracle."

"Well," said Mrs Tandy, straightening herself up, "thank you both so much for your time."

"No problem," said Marsden, who shared a look with Gianelli.

"Is that everything?" enquired Mrs Tandy.

"Well," said Marsden, "to be honest, we got Christmas Eve and Christmas Day shifts at the station because we're rookies, and it has been kind of bleak."

"I see."

"If you wouldn't mind," continued Gianelli, "it'd be cool to see the kids open their presents."

Mrs Tandy smiled. Yes, yes it would.

---

What followed was chaos. Joyful chaos, but chaos nonetheless. The presents had come numbered with a helpful list that explained what the content of each parcel was, so Sarah and Mrs Tandy had made sure every child got something appropriate. At the very end of the line, her face a more pronounced version of its usual mix of hope and distrust, stood Annabelle Watson.

"Annabelle," said Mrs Tandy, beckoning her over. "May I speak to you for a moment?"

Annabelle followed Mrs Tandy to the corner of the room, beside the games storage cupboard.

"Now, young lady, do you know anything about this?"

Mrs Tandy knew what the response would be by the way her face scrunched up before answering. "No. Why am I always blamed for stuff? I didn't do nothing."

"You didn't do anything."

"That's what I said."

"I'm not accusing you of... Oh, never mind. You don't have a present in the pile over there."

"Oh."

"Because you didn't get *a* present."

Annabelle just nodded.

"Because young lady, you were the only person here to get multiple presents with your name written on them."

With a smile, Mrs Tandy opened the cupboard to reveal a series of boxes. Ten minutes later, Annabelle Watson was the proud owner of a biology lab, a chemistry lab, an electronics lab and her very own laptop computer.

There had been a note.

*Dear Annabelle,*

*You can be anything you want to be.*

*Merry Christmas,*

*SC*

# PART 2 - THE LOONIVERSE

WARNING: THIS IS THE POINT OF NO RETURN, WHERE THERE ARE NO DRUNKEN GOBSHITES OR ARSE-KICKING NUNS TO SAVE YOU.

YOU HAVE BEEN WARNED.

# THE ONE

WARNING: THE FOLLOWING IS A STORY ABOUT LOVE — WHICH IS NOT THE SAME AS A LOVE STORY.

---

"You're the one."

"Excuse me?" said Ros.

"Sorry. I'm Chris," he said, pointing at the name badge that backed up his story.

"Hi Chris," said Ros.

"Hi Ros," said Chris, because she also had a name badge. "You're the one."

"Yes, you mentioned that. The one what exactly?"

"The one, as in 'The One'." He said it with the capitals letters.

"Ohhh," said Ros, turning her eyes to heaven. "So this is your 'line' then is it?"

Chris looked slightly hurt. "No."

"Really?" said Ros. "So you've not tried this on every other wo..."

Ros stopped talking. The reason she did so was that, to illustrate her

point, she had gestured towards the row of a dozen women sitting at identical tables to her right. She was unlucky thirteen in a row of fourteen speed daters, although, the fact they were here in the first place, probably indicated none of them were overly lucky. Ideally, they should've been sitting in a circle but the room was long and thin. Incidentally, so was Chris. The reason Ros had stopped talking was because daters one to twelve appeared to be staring at her. She looked back at them, perplexed.

"Why are they watching us?"

"I told them."

She looked back at him. "That I was 'The One'?"

"Yes."

At least that explained Ros's paranoia that people had been looking at her all night. They had been.

She took a moment and really looked at Chris. He looked both very nervous and disconcertingly sincere. "So, of the fourteen women in this room," she said, "plus Vanessa, the romance Nazi..."

Ros glanced up to see Vanessa, the speed dating coordinator, looking at her too. She wore a hurt expression on her overly-made-up face. Vanessa's attention had been drawn by the fact that the entire room had stopped talking to each other to watch one couple, in an entirely unprecedented break with speed dating etiquette.

"Sorry Vanessa, but seriously, dial it down a notch. You say 'it's just a bit of fun' that often, it feels like the beatings will continue until morale improves."

Ros returned her gaze to Chris. "As I was saying; of the fourteen women, plus Vanessa, in this room, I'm the lucky gal you've decided is 'The One'. I'm supposed to be blown away by that, am I?"

"No, sorry, I'm not making myself clear," said Chris, taking a deep breath and trying to compose himself. "When I said you were 'The One', I meant, out of all the women on the planet, I've decided you are my best and last chance at happiness."

"Wow."

"I know! It is a dramatic statement. You've got to at least give me that."

"You've certainly got my attention. Couple of follow-up questions for you, Chris—"

"Fire away."

"Are you insane?"

"Not especially."

"Define 'not especially'?"

"What is sane in a world that contains genocide, starvation and—"

"Whoaaa whoaaa," she interrupted. "Ease up there, Bono. I just meant, you've not been recently released from anywhere, have you?"

"No."

"Are you wearing your dead mother's underwear beneath that rather fetching checked shirt and jeans combo?"

"No."

"Ever killed anybody?"

"Not in this country." Chris shot her a nervous smile. "That was a joke."

"A high risk one given the circumstances."

*What's happening?*

*He made a joke?*

*Did she laugh?*

*I'm not sure she's the laughing sort.*

Ros glared at the women to her right. They all looked away, for just long enough to say that they had. The men were now watching Ros and Chris too, mainly because nobody sitting opposite them seemed inclined to chat.

"Alright then," said Ros, "How did I earn my status as 'The One'?"

"You look nice."

Ros's eyes widened with more outrage than is normally engendered by that answer to a question. "I look nice? We all look nice! Vanessa looks nice!" Ros looked up again. "Seriously, you do

Vanessa, that's a killer skirt. I'm sorry about what I said before, that was unfair of me. You're just doing your job."

Vanessa smiled nervously and shrugged.

"See?" said Chris. "You are nice."

"I am not nice!" said Ros. "A nice person wouldn't have said it in the first place."

"We all make mistakes."

"You certainly have, because I am definitely not 'The One'."

She did the bunny ears quotation marks with the fingers of both hands – then looked down at them, horrified by their betrayal. "Shit, when did I start doing that?"

"How do you know you're not?" asked Chris, diplomatically ignoring the bunny ears.

"What? 'The One'?" said Ros. "How do you know I am? And be warned, if you say I look nice, I'm going to open a whole can of 'not nice' on your arse."

"OK. First off, you are physically attractive. That's not the most important thing but let's not deny, it is a thing."

"OK."

"You look good, but you also look like you've not tried too hard, because you don't think people should be judged first and foremost on physical appearance."

Ros grudgingly nodded.

"In fact, you look like you've gone to a lot of effort to look like you've not gone to a lot of effort because, in the end of the day, we're all insecure about stuff like that."

"Thank you, Dr Freud."

"Secondly, you're wearing glasses. I like that. They look good and they also say something. You're a fan of reading, you think such things are important and you don't mind people knowing it."

"Or," Ros interrupted, "I ran out of contact lenses."

"Or," Chris shrugged, "there is that."

"So—" said Ros.

"Not finished," interrupted Chris. "Thirdly, your bag has a picture

of Bat Girl on it, using the original comic book logo, which is unspeakably cool."

"Well—"

"Still not finished. Fourthly, you look nice. Punch away. Sometimes you've just got a feeling."

Ros formed her fingers into a fist, and then rested her chin on it. She looked at him. He looked back at her.

"OK," said Ros, "Well, thanks, I guess, but isn't that all a bit flimsy to base your, what did you call it, 'best and last chance at happiness', on? It sounds like an awful lot of guesswork."

"Isn't it always? I mean, how long does it take you to really know a person?"

"Years," Ros admitted.

"Exactly! By which point, they've got keys to your flat and they're all over your life like the smell of bad meat."

"Evocative imagery."

"Thanks," he said. "My freezer packed in while I was away for a few days last month. Nightmare."

"Sounds it," she said. "Alright, hang on a sec here. You've given me your reasons for me being 'The One', flimsy as they are, but what about me? Just because you think I'm your 'The One', doesn't mean you're my 'The One' does it?"

"You're absolutely right."

"So?"

"So?"

"Convince me."

"I can't do that."

"What?"

"All I'm doing is making a decision for myself, and then telling you about it. What you do with the information is your business. I'm a firm believer in a woman's right to choose."

"Right," said Ros, "well on behalf of women everywhere, thank you for that. However, a note for future speed dating events; I'd maybe steer clear of discussing a woman's right to choose during the three minute introductory chat portion of the evening."

"Good tip. Sadly, I won't ever get a chance to use it. I'm never going speed dating again because..."

"I'm 'The One'," finished Ros. "Sorry, I temporarily forgot my status as 'The Anointed' for a bit there."

Chris leaned forward in his chair. "I've got a theory," he said.

"I thought you might."

"You know how stuff in life seems to come in threes? Wishes, wise men, primary colours."

"Blind mice."

"Stooges."

"Musketeers."

"Little Pigs."

"Celebrity deaths."

"Exactly. Well, I reckon you get three 'The Ones' in life."

"Hold your horses there cowboy, I'm not unique?"

"You," said Chris, "are the final One."

"Wow. Could you make that sound any more serial-killery?"

"Sorry, I'm explaining this badly again, aren't I?" He started checking his pockets for something. "Hang on a sec."

Ros glanced back to her right, to see their audience still entirely engrossed.

"Feel free to take pictures."

Someone did. Ros aimed a silent curse at whoever had removed sarcasm from the national curriculum.

Chris pulled his hand out from his inside jacket pocket. In it he held a small ceramic heart. It was about three inches in height and pale blue in colour, although there was something in the pattern, a subtle fluctuation, which gave it a hint of sparkle.

"This is my heart. I made it. Here."

Chris handed it to Ros.

"You made this?"

"Yes."

"OK, I'm not going to lie, that is impressive." She turned it over in her hands.

"I am a little crafty."

"And I like that about you. However, you do lose points because it's damaged."

"Ah, not so fast," he said. "You see that little hole there?"

Chris indicated a small hole in the top right corner, about the size of an apple pip.

"Uh huh."

"That was Claire – the first of 'The Ones'. I was nineteen. It was like most relationships at that age, all passion and sex and big fights and sex and then, after a few months, the realisation that not all of the sex she'd been having had been with me."

"Ouch."

"Yes. It was over. Nineteen. You get tremendously drunk, write some awful poetry and a lot of unsent letters to Thom Yorke as he is the only person that understands you. The world is ending and then, well, it doesn't. Eventually, you get so thoroughly bored of your own misery that you move on."

"Onto the next 'The One'?"

"Oh no, not immediately. Sure, there are others but not 'The One's. I got to the second half of my twenties before the next 'The One' turned up. Jessica."

Chris used his little finger to point out a tiny hairline crack that ran down the left side of the heart in Ros's hand. It was so thin that she'd not noticed it at first.

"We met through friends and it was nice. It was better. It was good – for quite a while at least. We moved in together. You're in your late twenties though, that's when you start figuring out what you want from life and it might end up you find out that you both want very different things. Plus, and people don't ever admit this, but you are always haunted by that suspicion that the 'The One' you've got, might not be the right one, the best one, the one for you."

"And so?"

"And so, two year relationships can turn into five year ones because two nice people are trying to be polite. Eventually, you break your own heart because someone has to. You split up the possessions, time share the friends and move out and on."

"Well this conversation has taken a depressing turn."

"Sorry."

"So where now?"

"So you find yourself in your thirties and you're just tired. Tired of getting hurt, tired of hurting others and most of all, tired of thinking about it. You spend all your time trying to decide if you like this person, if this person really likes you. It's exhausting. No matter what any of us pretend, it isn't 'just a bit of fun'."

He glanced up quickly. "No offence, Vanessa."

Vanessa was in the middle of a teary-eyed glug of wine and didn't respond.

"And you live your life like that. So scared of making a wrong move that you wake up one morning and discover, you've been standing still for five years."

"And so," said Ros, "you decide to throw yourself at the first woman who looks 'nice'?"

"No," said Chris. "You realise something. Maybe 'The One' we're all waiting for isn't coming. Maybe 'The One' isn't some perfect fit. Maybe it's all about taking a chance, about finding perfection in the imperfect. There are seven billion people in the world. If you lived another fifty years, that'd give you .22 of a second to meet each of them."

"So," said Ros, "three minutes is quite a long time when you think about it."

"Exactly. Maybe the thing required to kick-start your happy ever after is a big ludicrous romantic gesture. A moment of inspired madness."

"And you're not, I don't know, doing this as part of some kind of bet?"

He looked at her with wet brown eyes and a lop-sided sad little grin.

"Only with myself. I don't blame you for doubting it though. We live in cynical times. It's the default position. Believing in anything, anyone, is hard. So, maybe, I woke up this morning and thought, fuck it, why not believe in magic? As corny as it sounds, maybe that is

what it takes. At least this way, I'll know I tried. So, yes – you are 'The One'."

"What if this doesn't work out?"

"Then I'll know I gave it one last big shot. Plus, I've got a plan B for the rest of my life."

"Which is?"

"Night classes. You'd be amazed how many there are. I can sign up for circus skills next Wednesday."

"I'm terrified of clowns."

"Well, you know how to prevent there being one more in the world."

There was a pause, during which Ros resisted the urge to glance at their intrusive audience.

"So what happens now?" she said.

"Now? Nothing. You don't have to sit there and tick or don't tick a box. I'm going to make a dramatic exit."

"Ohhhh!"

"I know! I've always wanted to but the chances in life to make one are few and far between."

"You lucky bugger."

"You bet your sweet arse. I'm looking forward to it. Also, this way, you aren't put under any unfair pressure."

"Good because I think our three minutes must nearly be up."

"By my watch, it was up about two minutes ago."

Chris stood up, took his jacket off the back of his chair and put it on.

"If you're interested, I'll be in the Winchester pub just down the road there, at seven o'clock tomorrow evening. There is a Thai place just opposite that isn't awful if you know about the one dish you definitely shouldn't order."

"Which is?" Ros asked.

"There's only one way to find that out." Chris smiled down at her. "Thanks for being nice."

He turned and walked towards the door.

"Wait!" said Ros.

The room held its breath.
Ros held up the heart.
"You forgot your heart."
"No I didn't."
And he left.

# BREATH

WARNING: THE FOLLOWING STORY CONTAINS LIFE, DEATH AND NERVOUS ELEPHANTS.

## 8,409,600

That's how many breaths the average person can expect to take in a lifetime. Give-or-take, best guess.

As it happens, this man has just taken breath number 8,409,600, but he's unlikely to go much above the average.

The machine keeping him alive is about to be turned off. He knows this and he has come to terms with it. His time is almost done.

It should be known; he is a good man who has lived a truly good life. If you need an explanation for what happens next, that is it.

As his body is left to fend for itself, strange visions appear before his eyes. There's still magic in the world, not as much as there once was and nowhere near as much as is needed but still – it is there. On the ceiling of his sterile hospital room, the world spread out before him, full of lost souls, unseen miracles and wasted lives.

He may only have a few breaths left but he hopes to make each one count.

He breathes out...

## 8,409,601

Meanwhile, 1,429 miles away...

She stands above his slumbering body, tears in her eyes, the knife in her left hand. The fingers of her right are teasing at the rip in her jeans absentmindedly. She'd had to climb the back fence to retrieve the key that he'd forgotten was there, under a plant pot. As she looks down at his face – memories, conflicting emotions tear at her soul. She'd loved him once, although that is not what has brought her here.

It is the rage, the gut-churning anger that fills her every waking moment at the thought she once loved this pitiful excuse of a man. Someone who would take the most private thing, a silly game, an intimate moment between two people and share it with a voyeuristic world. Demeaning the act and disgracing the emotion with an act of grubby vengeance – making her loathe herself to the point that the only thing keeping her alive is a hatred so visceral, so real – it makes it hard to breathe.

She wipes her eyes and raises the knife above her head...

And then, the slightest breath of wind from an open window moves the curtain. The blade catches the headlights of a passing cattle truck and a pattern of light plays across the bedroom wall. It's enough to stop her for a moment and there on the wall, she sees two lives play out like spluttering old home movies.

In one, the knife descends and she becomes a cautionary tale – vilified and glorified in turn – by a world that doesn't see people, only stories. He is ended but she is forced to live on, defined forever by his action and her reaction. She becomes the illustration for the ugly phenomenon.

In the other, the knife doesn't fall. She takes a breath and decides that the harder road is worth taking. She moves on and away. In time

she becomes herself again. She learns to trust and happiness finds her when she least expects it – in aisle four, the international foods section.

She drops the knife and leaves without looking back.

On her way out, she stops and empties the water from the goldfish bowl over his brand new 3D TV. Then she departs a despicable man's life for good.

## 8,409,602

Across a long mahogany dining table that sits in front of a roaring log fire, two people glance nervously at each other. It has the awkward air of an Internet date, which in a way it is. On this date, however, one of them has a lethal cocktail of drugs in front of them and the other has promised to eat their guest once they've died.

As they struggle to make conversation, a gust of wind comes down the chimney and lifts an ember from the fire. As they watch, it sails slowly across the table between them and lands on the host's DVD collection. He quickly jumps up to pat it out.

The guest notices some of the film titles and a lively discussion ensues. They discover a shared love of Clint Eastwood films, Thai food and dachshund dogs. After a while, they conspire to forget why they're there. They talk all night and part in the morning, having agreed to catch an Eastwood double-bill on Tuesday at the Roxy.

In years to come, they'll tell people they met online but will be understandably vague on the details.

## 8,409,603

As the midday sun beats down upon the parched earth, a cow stares at a broken bottle with more intensity than its species is normally credited with. The cow, who is destined to be processed into burgers, is trying to decide whether or not it can eat glass. Before a conclusion is reached, the sunlight hits the bottle just right and a tiny root begins to smoulder. The breeze shifts subtly and guides the spark towards a

patch of tinder-dry vegetation. The cow does not enjoy this unexpected turn of events.

On a long straight road with nothing to draw the eye but pylons and dust, a driver is not paying attention. His mind is fixated on other things and he has the stereo up loud – real loud, which is why the 300 stampeding cattle come as such a surprise. He veers left sharply and looks back to confirm the wild-eyed mass of bovine terror wasn't a figment of his imagination – hence the electricity pylon coming as a second, equally unpleasant, surprise. He's not wearing a seatbelt, so the next-to-last thing he sees as he flies through the air is his car as he sails away from it. The last thing he sees is hooves, lots and lots of hooves.

The car is eventually found by workmen from the power company. At first, they don't notice the body as it has been trampled so badly that it looks like burger meat.

The police are called and it is they who eventually pop the trunk and discover the six human heads in pickle jars.

---

And in the sterile hospital room, the man fights to keep breathing.

He may have accepted his fate but now he is fighting to stay alive.

At the end, at the very end – we all fight.

---

## 8,409,604

Outside a downtown Cowboy Burger outlet, a man sits in the front seat of his SUV and reads his own death warrant. It's written on the greaseproof wrapper of the half-eaten Rio Grande with cheese that dangles from his hand. It's one of six burgers he has just purchased, while pretending to the disinterested girl at the drive-thru window that he was making a run for the whole office. He has always eaten his emotions. His life can be measured in binges followed by shame

spirals followed by binges. It was an ongoing battle but it has just been lost.

There it is, in big bold red letters on the inside of the wrapper. 'Congratulations Partner!! You are the lucky winner of Cowboy Burger's Free For Life Giveaway. You'll never have to pay for another burger again!!'

He sits, staring at it – a sense of desperation running through him that very few will understand.

A gust of wind passes through his open window and lifts the wrapper from his lap. On reflex – he grabs for it but it is already out the driver's side and away. He wordlessly watches as it dances away on the breeze.

## 8,409,605

With trembling hands she pulls the noose over her head, tears streaming freely down her face. She takes one last look at her three grown children beaming at her from the picture on the windowsill. Ungrateful shits, they'll definitely remember her birthday next year.

A clatter from the far side of the kitchen distracts her – the wind having rattled the cat flap. She looks down to see the inquisitive face of Mister Wuffles staring up at her and realises she too is being selfish.

Who will feed him when she is dead?

She thankfully doesn't realise this but the answer either way is 'her'.

---

His breaths are shallow now, his pulse grows fainter. The sadness and joy of the world wash over him and it is overwhelming.

He fights to hold onto it for just a few breaths more.

---

## 8,409,606

On a rooftop, a six-year-old boy is distracted just long enough for his older sister to break his heart.

He is temporarily mesmerised by a burger wrapper dancing giddily upon the breeze as it rises between the buildings.

He watches for just long enough for a realisation to hit his sister, who races up four flights of stairs to inform her brother that, despite the assurances she has given him all morning, he cannot in fact fly.

## 8,409,607

A fully-grown female Indian elephant weighs just over four tons. The Lady is all too aware of this fact as one currently has its foot on her head. Normally, despite the audience's gasps, she would not be concerned as the female in question is under the control of her husband, the world's premier elephant trainer. Unfortunately, fifteen minutes before this evening's performance, he caught her in a very unladylike position with an acrobat. She wasn't sure how angry he was until she just looked into his eyes – it appears the answer is 'very'.

He tries to hold back the tears of rage. How could she do this to him? His chest feels like it might explode. If something should happen, it would look like a terrible accident. Yes, his career would be over but he doesn't care right now. The elephant would do it too; she at least has always been loyal to him.

The elephant can feel the tension. Master is angry – she hopes it is not with her. He is a kind master and she loves him with all her heart. The Lady is not nice, she uses the stick and she had been forced to watch her and the circus's clown doing that thing behind her pen. Now her stomach turns every time she hears the honk of the clown's horn. She would do whatever master wants, she only wants him to be happy.

Just then the wind changes; the noses of audience members wrinkle in disgust as the pungent aroma from the elephant pens slaps them in the face. For him the smell brings an odd sense of

comfort. It reminds him how working with these magnificent beasts has been his sanctuary since he was a boy.

The Lady closes her eyes tightly...

He barks a command...

She raises her foot...

And... puts it down safely on the ground. As the crowd applaud, the elephant turns around obediently.

The Lady is relieved. Her husband has seen sense.

He is relieved. He will eventually be happier without her.

She is relieved. So very relieved...

The crowd gasps.

Because sometimes living is the best revenge...

And sometimes it's your cheating wife being defecated on by a nervous elephant.

---

They're less breaths now – more short desperate gasps.

When all that is left is the fight, then the fight is all. There is so much left to do.

---

## 8,409,608

From a rooftop twelve stories up, she watches the fat man pick his teeth through the telescopic sights of her rifle. For three days she has watched him eat and she is thankful there won't have to be a fourth. His table manners are appalling. She'd do this for free but luckily she doesn't have to. He is a businessman and someone is employing her to facilitate a correction in the market. Judging by his gluttonous habits, she'd guess she was only narrowly beating heart disease to the punch.

He is truly loathsome. Yes, he deals in death but her despising him for that would be the height of hypocrisy. His sins are much more personal in nature. Far worse than his revolting table manners is that he eats in nothing but the finest restaurants and then blasphemes the food by drenching it in butter and salt. Philistine!

Seventeen bullets ago, she had been a chef – a damn good one too; methodical and unflappable, able to hold down her station while those around her were losing their shit. She should've gone places but men make the best chefs, everybody knows that. You can't beat accepted wisdom, at least not when you look like your daddy is more likely to be one of the dishwashers than the owner.

She lays no claims to extraordinary marksmanship. She is an above average shot at best but she's found that to be more than good enough for her needs. Of all the misconceptions about this job, the biggest are about what it really takes to succeed at it. How she'd ended up here was ample proof of that.

Her bad taste in men had run to a big talking ex-military type, who'd done all kinds of things, if his stories were to be believed. He must've told his tall tales to the wrong person because he ended up signing on to fulfil a contract for a certain group of highly motivated people. When he was found lacking in both the intelligence and stomach to do so, they were unhappy. They attempted to re-motivate him by acquiring his seven-year-old nephew for leverage. He ran.

Three days later, a high-velocity rifle bullet passed through the target's chest. At the time, he'd been receiving commercially acquired

oral comfort in the front seat of his BMW from a lady of negotiable virtue. That shot had been only the third she had ever fired. She got many things wrong that day, some embarrassingly so – but the actual shooting part was relatively straightforward. She'd also learned an invaluable lesson. When someone has just been assassinated – people tend to look for the steely-eyed stone-cold killer type and they'll run right by the five-foot-nothing Latina who knows how to cry on demand. She'd found the one profession in the world where not looking the part had been a positive boon.

The boy had been duly released and eight weeks later, the leader of a group of highly motivated people had smirked as he read a hand-delivered note about the ethics of using children as negotiating tools. He'd laughed, crumpled it up and tossed it towards the wastepaper bin. The bullet had hit him before the paper made the trash can.

The following month, an e-mail address that had only been set up for a one-time purpose received another message. As it happened, it was preceded two hours earlier by a sous chef's wandering hand having an unfortunate meeting with a paring knife, which meant she found herself in need of employment.

That's how she has ended up here and why, against all common sense, she is waiting for the fat man to pay his bill. She doesn't want to leave the waitress with nothing but a dead guy at her table. Today's tips are going to be downright diabolical – a fat man's brains landing in your soup being one of the universally accepted reasons to skip out on the cheque.

She watches him pay the bill and throw a cash tip into the middle of the table. She can't be certain but she'd guess it was only about 7% – low-end motherfucker.

She relaxes her breathing, corrects for the cross-wind and pulls back the bolt to chamber bullet number eighteen…

She swears as the wind pastes a burger wrapper to her face. She tosses it away angrily and quickly tries to re-acquire the target in her scope.

She pauses – the scope has picked out an empty unit further down the street with a For Rent sign in the window. It's a good

location, footfall would be excellent. New office buildings were springing up all the time and the area already had a decent nightlife. The right establishment, serving wholesome high quality food with the minimum of pretence could do very well, very well indeed... and she has already built up quite the nest-egg.

In this moment, she can't think of a single reason why not. She calmly slides back from the edge, tosses her rifle into the garbage disposal chute and walks away – already planning menus in her head.

In three hours' time, an arms dealer will die of a massive and well-deserved coronary while on the toilet.

Two days later, a waitress will get an inexplicable large tip.

## 8,409,609

A man, who two independent experts have testified has the mental capabilities of an eight-year-old, is strapped into a chair.

Three people – two men and a woman – have their hands on levers, humanely designed so that they will never know which one of them killed him. They are in a state of panic, working the levers up and down furiously but nothing is happening. The man smiles at them nervously; he doesn't like it when people are upset.

It will later emerge that someone has driven into an electricity pylon forty miles away, interrupting the prison's power supply.

After another two minutes, amidst much recrimination and finger pointing, the execution will be cancelled with the authorities citing cruel and unusual punishment.

This ruling will be overturned on appeal.

God bless Texas.

## 8,409,610

Twenty seconds after she left a despicable man's life for good, she re-enters it with a sense of urgency.

Quickly she refills the bowl and places the gasping goldfish carefully back inside. He has done nothing wrong.

She decides to take it with her as she absolutely definitely leaves a despicable man's life for good.

Although lacking in facilities to express it, the goldfish is truly delighted by this unexpected turn of events. He never liked that prick.

---

And it stops.

Because some fights you cannot win but then winning was never the point.

As the last breath passes from his lips, he takes one final look at the world before slipping away, softly on the breeze.

---

# THE PROCESS

WARNING: NOVELS ARE A LOT LIKE KIDNEYS; EVERYONE HAS AT LEAST ONE IN THEM BUT UNLESS YOU HAVE ABSOLUTELY NO CHOICE, YOU SHOULD JUST LEAVE IT WHERE IT IS.

---

It didn't matter how often he had to go through this, he was a bundle of nerves every time. It's what comes from being beholden to an unfathomable malicious force. Gareth sat on the park bench and tried hard to resist the urge to worry away further at his already badly chewed fingernails. He couldn't remember the last time he'd slept for more than a few hours. He scratched at his raggedy beard with both hands as he let out a growling sigh of frustration. A mother pushing a pram glanced at him with alarm before subtly picking up her pace.

Twelve days was all it had taken, which anyone will tell you is a ridiculously short amount of time in which to complete a full length novel, even a bad one. Gareth hadn't written a bad one though, no – he'd written a masterpiece. It'd come so easy it felt like he was cheating somehow. As if the book had already been written and he was merely transcribing the words whispered in his ear by a sweet-

tempered angel. He'd taken a couple of weeks' holiday from the bank and sat in his study for fourteen hours a day, typing away. Then like clockwork every evening, he'd go to the gym and have dinner with his family, before drifting into a peaceful sleep, having made tender yet vigorous love to his wife Samantha.

On the day after he'd finished the novel, he'd re-read it and wept. He'd known straight away what he had done. Humility be damned, this book was going to change lives – his most of all. He rang the bank and said he wouldn't be coming back. He told his boss some home truths about his management style and personal hygiene, and then he'd taken Samantha out for a meal at a Michelin starred restaurant. They should start getting used to the good life.

The next day, hung-over but happy, he'd walked into his study. It was time to e-mail the finished manuscript to publishers and kick off the inevitable bidding war. He sensed it straight away – something was wrong, very wrong. When you know a room well, you can feel when it has been disturbed – the study felt like it had been violated. It looked just how he had left it the evening before, save for one significant difference. There, propped up on his keyboard was a small rectangle of card with four words printed on it. As Gareth read it, it chilled him to his very core – 'We have your book'.

Frantic, he'd checked his desktop PC, the laptop, his two e-mail accounts, the three data sticks and the wastepaper bin. Everywhere, every last word of the book had disappeared. Gareth forced himself to take a few deep breaths, it didn't matter – it was all still there, inside his head, he'd just write it out again from memory. He sat there for hours staring at the flashing cursor on the screen but nothing would come. The characters that had danced so vividly together across his mind, now tripped and trampled on each other's toes. The previously sweet-tempered angel screeched manic words of unintelligible fury in his ear.

There was a number on the back of the card but first he'd contacted the police and Samantha's cousin, the lawyer. They both said the same thing; seeing as there was no evidence of a break-in and nobody but Gareth had actually read this book, it was his word

against whoever's number it was that it had ever even existed. The cops didn't come right out and say it but the message was clear, if you want it back you've got to play ball.

He rang the number. A calm female voice answered, "Hello Gareth."

The first time he tried anger, the voice hadn't engaged, just hung up on him. The second time, he tried pleading and was met with an identical click followed by the dial tone. The third time, he'd said what he knew whoever 'they' were had wanted to hear. "What do I have to do?"

The instructions hadn't made sense but he'd nevertheless followed them to the letter. He'd completed 46 levels on Angry Birds, twirled around in his office chair 3046 times and spent six hours trying to sketch a portrait of the lesbian songstress k.d. lang from memory, despite having never enjoyed her work. At the end of that week, he'd then been given this location and he'd waited patiently at the allotted time. A man in a long brown Philip Marlowesque mac had sat down beside him and wordlessly handed him an envelope containing the first four pages of his novel. All attempts to engage the man in conversation had been met with a blank stare.

When he got home he'd rung the number again and received his next set of instructions and on it went. Under orders, he now spent his days getting into arguments on one Internet forum advocating passionately for the use of goal-line technology in football, while on another forum, taking the exact opposite stance. He watched every episode of an almost entirely incomprehensible Japanese game show, learned to play the bagpipes – badly, got into a protracted turf war with Mr Patel at number 45 about a perfectly harmless hedgerow. The requests went on and on, each more pointless and futile than the last. Every week he'd do as he was told in exchange for a few paltry pages more.

It was almost two years since it had started and he'd now earned back just over half of his novel while losing almost everything else. Samantha had taken Max and Libby to 'visit her mother', that'd been three months ago now. He'd gone around to visit on Sunday, Max

barely said two words to him. As Samantha had closed the front door behind him, he'd stood on the porch with tears in his eyes. In the hallway he heard his sweet Libby talking to her mother.

"Mummy, daddy smells sad."

"I know sweetheart, I know."

Gareth jumped as the man in the mac sat down beside him. It always unnerved him that he seemingly appeared out of nowhere. As usual, the man wordlessly slid an A4 envelope across the bench. He opened it eagerly. "No – there must be some mistake; there's only one page in here. Look!" Gareth held out the solitary page, making no effort to keep the pleading tone from his voice. "It's not even a full one. It's just a couple of paragraphs!"

He was taken aback when for the first time in two years, the man in the mac spoke.

"You were told to spend five hours a day practising your farmyard animal noises."

"But I did, I did!"

"Do a duck."

Gareth quacked pitifully before the man shook his head in disgust. He was tempted to debate whether a duck really qualified as 'farmyard' but thought better of it, reason had never worked before with these people.

"Also, we told you six months ago to gain forty pounds."

"I tried but—"

"From now on, every meal will have an ice-cream course."

Gareth nodded wordlessly.

"And stop sneaking out to the gym."

How did they know, how did they always know?

The man stood as if to leave. Gareth could feel tears welling in his eyes "I'm sorry I, I ... I'll cancel my membership!"

The man looked up briefly, as if he was receiving instructions from on high.

"No – leave the direct debit, just stop going."

The man pulled his collar up and began walking away into the soft mid-morning drizzle.

"Wait!"

He stopped and slowly turned his head to look at Gareth.

"Please I ... I have to know. Why are you doing this?"

The man's harsh gaze softened at least momentarily, to a look of near pity.

"Because it has to be the same for you as it is for everybody else."

And then he walked away.

# THE TROUBLE WITH ME LAST WEEK

WARNING: THE FOLLOW SHORT STORY CONTAINS TIME TRAVEL, SOME VERY BAD DECISIONS AND FRANKLY, SOME REGRETTABLE BODILY FUNCTIONS. LIKE SWIMMING, READING THIS STORY SHOULD NOT BE ATTEMPT UNTIL AT LEAST ONE HOUR AFTER EATING.

---

Paul took a breath, looked around and drank in the view. He couldn't remember when he'd last felt this relaxed. It'd been an odd few days. He had to admit, every time he killed himself, it seemed to be getting easier.

---

Last Thursday night he'd been sitting alone in his lab in a bad mood, inputting data into the computer simulation of a VanBruder wormhole that formed the core of his PhD. Before she'd left to visit her sister in Belfast, Jessica and he had had an argument. It was about nothing, which was bad. If it was about something it was fixable but if it was just a result of their general frustration, a symptom of a

relationship in its death throes – then nothing could be done, at least not by a clueless idiot like him.

Paul knew Jessica was way out of his league and deep down he knew she knew it too, everyone else sure did. People even pointed it out to him, like they were congratulating him – not realising they were just adding to his terrible sense of unease. He'd caught her on the rebound and against all odds, had clung on for over two years – but lately it felt like his luck was finally running out. He spent his days waiting for the other shoe to drop. This paranoia manifested itself paradoxically with him being a passive-aggressive arse to Jessica. It was like his subconscious was trying to get its retaliation in first.

With all this on his mind, it was no surprise he'd messed up. He'd input entirely the wrong equation into the simulation and hence was asking it entirely the wrong question. This question was so monumentally ludicrous that nobody had ever thought of asking it before. It came back with an answer that re-wrote some of the bigger laws of physics, not to mention making Einstein look like a bit of a dick. The first time he'd read through the results Paul hadn't understood them, the second time he hadn't believed them. The third time – he suspected foul play but who would mess with his simulation?

He shared the lab with Toshiko and Daniel. Toshiko was a foreign exchange student that rarely spoke to either of them but she was hardly likely to go messing with his stuff. She didn't do 'fun'. Daniel, on the other hand, did nothing but. He was Paul's mate and with the best will in the world, a moron. All right, he obviously had a brain but it seemed to rest mainly in screensaver mode. It's amazing what cramming for the odd exam and being captain of the University's first ever championship winning side can do for you. Paul knew he should resent Daniel; he had after all been gifted a scholarship that Paul had sweated buckets for, but it'd be like kicking a puppy. Besides, Daniel did liven the place up – spending his days engaged in an elaborate prank war with the microbiologists upstairs. Only this morning, they'd come in to find one of their rabbits hopping about the lab.

Daniel had christened it Spartacus and spent the day feeding it Toshiko's lunch.

Shit, that was it! The bloody microbiologists had messed up his model, those petty little... Even as he thought it, he realised it couldn't be true. Daniel was at least technically doing a physics PhD and he didn't understand Paul's simulation enough to screw it up, there's no way the bunny boilers would.

Paul's mind was racing now. If he was right, using materials that were in the room with him at that very moment – it would be possible to build a device to send someone or something back in time. Time travel. The first time he allowed those words to form in his head, it felt ridiculous but then he'd gone over the figures again and again. He needed to test it. He could build a simple prototype and then send something back – not a person, that'd be crazy but... The rabbit! Of course, the perfect subject!

The thought walloped into him like an articulated lorry.

"Shit the bed!"

What'd Daniel said? The bunny boilers had refused to take Spartacus back, insisted they weren't missing a rabbit.

In a daze, Paul walked over to the storage container that Daniel was using as an improvised hutch. He lifted the rabbit up and felt around his collar. There it was – a white cylindrical object, about the size of an AA battery with a button on the top. Written on it, in a familiar hand was PMC 121118. He felt suddenly dizzy – Paul McCormac 12 November 2018. Not only could he build a time machine, he already had done – four days from now. Then, he'd stolen a rabbit from the bunny boilers and sent it back in time – to arrive some time between about 10pm last night and 8:15am this morning when Toshiko found it.

Reactions to moments of absolute genius have varied throughout history. Running naked down the street was a popular one if a little showy. Paul went the more traditionally Irish route and decided to get skuttering drunk. It was 9:37pm and he knew Daniel would be in the uni bar, having his weekly argument at the pub quiz. He joined him and without any explanation, started buying drinks, lots and lots of

drinks. Big drinks, little drinks, drinks inside other drinks, drinks that were on fire. He was celebrating – today was the last day of his old life.

The first day of his new life got off to a very bad start. He woke up in his bed beside a girl called Orla, a third year in Applied Physics whose labs he and Daniel were forced to supervise as part of their PhDs. Her distinctive pink hair looked incongruous on Jessica's pillow. Paul's whole existence froze in a moment of gut-wrenching terror – only slightly relieved when he remembered that Jessica was away in Belfast. Nevertheless, he had made a truly terrible mistake. It was clear that last night they'd at least tried to have sex, badly no doubt – but Paul didn't think you regained lost points in this situation for having performed inadequately in your act of abject betrayal. It said something for the level of shame and skull-splitting hangover he was experiencing that it took him a good minute to notice the smell. As well as making a terrible mistake last night, it seemed he'd also had a terrible accident in the bed he was currently occupying. He couldn't bring himself to lift the duvet and look down. Today could not get any worse.

It quickly did. He turned as he felt Orla stirring into blurry-eyed life beside him. For lack of any better ideas, he smiled at her – she didn't smile back. She took a couple of moments to look around the room, to drink in the reality of where they were and what it meant. Paul watched her thought process play out across her face; he saw the exact moment the smell from below the duvet hit. She promptly threw up all over him.

Paul lay there, covered in his own filth, her vomit and their collective shame as, sobbing, Orla gathered up all of her clothing that she could find and quickly fled. Neither of them said anything, some situations there really are no words for.

Once it'd become painfully clear that he wasn't going to die as he so fervently wished, he got out of bed. He clambered into the shower for an hour, where he cried and threw up a couple of times. He spent

the rest of Friday lying naked on his sofa, their sofa – feeling like the lowest of the low. Yes, he'd also made one of the greatest discoveries in the history of science but he was in no fit state to think about that now.

Saturday morning he awoke to a truly pungent smell and the horrific idea that he'd somehow re-enacted the most shameful night of his life. He hadn't. What he'd done is refused to face up to the consequences of that night, which is why the stench from the bedroom was now pervading the whole flat. He got dressed, and retching, threw all of the unspeakable mess into two bin bags. He passed Mrs Goring on his way to the big bins behind the building, her wrinkled old face formed into such a disgusted scowl it looked like it was trying to eat itself.

The whole flat stunk; he opened every window and spent several hours cleaning but the smell seemed as determined to hang around as the shame. Now that the previous day's apocalyptic hangover had passed, the guilt had the freedom to run amok in his sodden mind and it was taking full advantage. That took up most of Saturday. He sat on the sofa, eating toast while his mind swapped between re-running the shameful highlights of Thursday night and generating worst-case scenarios to fill in the parts of the evening he'd blacked out.

He nodded off and awoke screaming at 2am from a dream he remembered all too well. Apparently his subconscious had thought of something it couldn't bring to his over-worked conscious mind's attention – which was why he'd been chased in his head by a massive baby with pink hair, carrying a pack of condoms screaming, "Why daddy, why?!?"

He ran through scenarios in his mind. He was in absolutely no doubt that as soon as Jessica got within five yards of the door when she returned, she'd sense his guilt, not to mention smell it. His best idea was setting the flat on fire but he'd risk burning down the whole building. The idea of Mrs Goring glaring her disapproval at him while being engulfed in flames didn't appeal.

How could this have happened? How could his penis have so

brutally betrayed his heart? His penis was a total... it was at this moment he realised why slang terms for the male genitalia were appropriately used as insults. Penises were the worst and none more so than his.

There was nothing for it – full and total confession. He had to tell Jessica everything before she got home, and the true horror slapped her right in the nostrils. The more he thought about it – telling her everything, apologising and showing her how much he wanted to fix it – that had to be the way to go, didn't it? Also, on an evolutionary level – her realising he was a desirable mate to other females, that could swing things in his favour, couldn't it? That's just basic biology. Besides, throwing himself on her mercy, telling her she meant the world to him – wasn't that just a little bit romantic?

Sunday morning he summoned up all his courage and rang Jessica. In hindsight, leaving a voicemail was a big mistake. In fairness to him, he realised that half way through and started apologising for the voicemail while he was still leaving it, meaning that the apology for the infidelity had to be covered in voicemails two through four. Voicemail five was an apology for everything while six was an ill-judged attempt to play the whole thing off as a joke. Seven through nine were really voicemails two through four reworked to no noticeable improvement.

After that he stopped leaving voicemails but kept ringing. She never picked up but at a certain point it changed to going straight to voicemail. By 11pm she'd not returned home. Maybe something terrible had happened? Even as he thought this, he was ashamed as a wave of relief washed over him – if Jessica had been hit by a car, she might not have listened to her voicemails. He could delete them and be the loving boyfriend who nursed her back to health. He'd spend every day of the rest of his life, making her the happiest woman alive, just as soon as he figured out how to do that.

Now paranoid about Jessica's well-being, he decided to ring her sister Clare. If he'd been asked before that phone call, he'd have said without hesitation that he was his own biggest critic. It turned out he'd have been entirely wrong in that assessment. From being talked

at by Clare it quickly became apparent that Jessica had not only heard the voicemails but that they'd actually gone down a lot worse than he'd feared. She wouldn't speak to him. She may've been sobbing in the background but it was impossible to hear over her sister's invective laden demolition of his character, not to mention a graphic description of things that should happen to him and his genitalia that was way too specific and elaborate to have been thought up entirely on the spot.

He spent Sunday night on the sofa, unsuccessfully attempting to get drunk on ouzo – the only booze left in the flat, an unloved refugee from last year's holiday in Crete. If only he'd not ... well, everything. Everything that'd happened in the last ...

In Paul's defence, when the thought suddenly struck him at 4am, he did realise how blindingly obvious it had been. He was the only man in the world who could really take it back. This had to be destiny, didn't it? He rolled over and slept the sound slumber of a guilty man who would soon become innocent again.

He was awoken the next morning by Jessica returning to grab some clothes. She had Gareth, her burly brother-in-law for company. Paul and Gareth had never got along and it was to Jessica's credit that she only let the big Welshman punch him once. As he kneeled on the carpet, clutching his freshly traumatised testicles and looking into the tear-stained eyes of the woman he loved, he swore he would fix this. She just swore, using a selection of words he'd frankly never realised she knew, much less being able to form into some very vivid sentences.

When he'd regained the ability to walk, Paul got dressed and hopped on his bike. He quickly realised that it was a far from ideal mode of transportation in his current state of testicular tenderness but time was of the essence.

When he reached the lab, he rushed to his desk. The white cylindrical device was still locked in his drawer, exactly where he'd left it. Sure – he could've built another one but there was no guarantee it'd work the same, perhaps this one was a happy accident in much the same way as his initial discovery had been?

This gave him pause for thought. Could he be certain this would work? Yes, it'd worked on Spartacus but Paul was considerably bigger than a rabbit. Come to that, how did he know it'd really worked on the rabbit? He gave Spartacus, still in his supposedly temporary accommodation beside Daniel's desk, an appraising look. He didn't look mentally or physically impaired but then, what did a mentally impaired rabbit look like?

Yes – on one hand, the plan was very high risk but on the other hand, he'd shat the bed – both metaphorically and literally. He checked his watch – he didn't even know exactly how far the rabbit had been sent back. It had been approximately four days but that meant he could already be too late.

He strode purposefully over to Toshiko's workstation where she was industriously beavering away with that look of absolute concentration she always wore. Paul cleared his throat dramatically. "Toshiko, I know we don't know each other very well but I have to go somewhere and, while I hope this isn't the case, I may not be back. I have some things I need to say and I need you to please pass on these words to my loved ones. OK?"

She regarded him suspiciously before giving him a curt nod.

Paul closed his eyes and spoke from the heart. He was profound, sincere, even funny in places. This was really good stuff. He was being downright eloquent, where'd this guy been when he was leaving nine disastrously inept voicemails for the woman he loved? He wondered if perhaps he should record this as...

Paul opened his eyes to find that Toshiko had wandered off. He really didn't like her.

Screw it. He looked at the device and with a deep breath, pressed the button. Nothing happened. He examined it more closely and discovered it needed to be twisted to spring the button into the fully upright position. That made sense; it obviously needed a safety mechanism. He mentally congratulated the version of him that'd actually built it on this entirely sensible piece of design. That was a good point, if he was now here on the day Spartacus had been sent back, who made the device? Figuring that out would take some

serious thought about the nature of time, causality, stuff like that. He didn't have that kind of time. He took a deep breath and pressed the button again.

The lights went out and Paul felt a sensation like every molecule in his body jumping two feet to the left. For a moment he thought he'd blown a fuse in the lab but then he noticed that it was dark outside the windows too. He'd just become the first human in history to travel backwards through time. He instantly regretted not doing it in front of Toshiko while saying something devastatingly witty like 'time flies' – no, 'time to go' or 'time waits for no man'. OK – maybe he was better just going.

He found his way to his workstation and checked the time – 4:27am, Thursday 7 November 2018. It'd been about 11:15am on Monday 11th when he pressed the button. That meant the device had sent him back about four days, six hours and forty-eight minutes. He'd have to leave the main lights off, he didn't want to get thrown out by campus security; his bed was currently occupied.

That was a thought. He was about to have his second go at November 7 but his first attempt was still out there, sleeping amidst unsullied sheets with the woman he loved. He felt a pang of jealousy. It dawned on him that he'd just effectively invented cloning as well. He was really racking up the giant leaps forward in scientific understanding this week – suck on it Einstein!

Paul had a few hours to kill so he googled when nominations for the Nobel Prize for Physics closed. Damn it – September, he'd have to wait until next year's. He then looked up time travel paradoxes on physics forums. There was a school of thought that said that if he were to ever meet himself, the universe would implode. That was worrying but then most of the people who thought that also didn't seem to be able to get over Buffy getting cancelled. Surely the same would happen when two versions of Spartacus had existed in the same time stream? Hey – that was a point, where was...

Before Paul could finish the thought, there was an electrical sizzling noise and the rabbit popped into being on the workbench beside him. It was a coincidence but the week he was having, it didn't

feel like it was worth thinking about. Two separate versions of the future were now effectively looping back into this present. He could feel a migraine coming on. He made what felt like a sensible decision in the circumstances, to just roll with it and assume everything would be fine. 'Experts' could hypothesise all they liked but seeing as he'd actually invented time travel, surely his opinion counted for more?

He stole Toshiko's biscuits from her desk and downloaded an illegal copy of *Back To The Future* for himself and Spartacus to kill some time watching. The main message of the film seemed to be, if you travel back in time – don't sleep with your mother. Paul couldn't help but think the first half of that sentence was entirely redundant.

Toshiko chained her bike up outside the Sciences building at exactly 8:15am, same as always. Two minutes later as she was busy glaring at the empty packet of biscuits on her desk, Paul was busy 'borrowing' her bike with the spare key she kept in her filing cabinet. He considered it karmic payback for her walking out on his awesome death speech – although yes, this version of Toshiko had not technically done that.

Her bike was a bit small but on the upside, it did have a nice wicker basket for Spartacus to sit in. He'd decided to take the rabbit with him, feeling a bond between them that nobody else could ever fully understand. He was aware that he was technically altering the course of history and yada yada yada, but he didn't care. He'd have to do a whole lot more messing with recent history before the night was over, causality could go take a running jump.

While it made sense to get far away from the University to minimise the opportunities for further complications, he'd nowhere particular to go. He didn't have a fully formed plan but he realised that whatever needed to happen couldn't happen before the time was right. Spartacus and he spent a rather nice day down by the pier. They played games in the arcades, walked along the beach, caught a regrettable Adam Sandler film and then ate a hearty Italian meal. It struck Paul that, now he had a second chance at life, he should do something similar with the female human he loved as soon as possible.

And so it was at 9:32pm, through the small glass window in the lab door, Paul watched the version of himself, who for the sake of his own mental health he was thinking of as 'Past Paul', make the greatest discovery in the history of science. He'd been planning this moment all day, running through snappy opening lines he could use. With Spartacus in his arms, he theatrically walked through the door – and promptly got covered in red paint.

"Ah for F..."

Paul looked up at the pot of paint dangling upside-down over the door. His past self gawped at him in disbelief. It was the weirdest of sensations – like seeing someone you've known all your life and at the same time, not quite being able to place them.

"You're..." the past stammered.

"Yeah, You – from the future. Why am I covered in fecking paint?"

Past Paul stood and started backing away. "Ehm, Daniel booby-trapped it because the bunny boilers broke in last night and stole Toshiko's biscuits."

"Well – you've ruined one of the greatest moments in history, I hope you're happy," Paul snapped.

"It shouldn't have gone off yet. Daniel said it'd be harmless until I..." The Past trailed off, staring at his future self in a way that was increasingly irritating Paul.

"This isn't possible," the past stammered.

Paul pointed at the computer. "It is, you've just seen that it is."

"If you're me – what number am I thinking of right now?"

"How the fuck should I know? I'm you from next Monday – you don't develop psychic powers over the weekend."

Paul realised his temper was further ruining the moment but he'd just noticed that poor Spartacus's white fur was now matted with red paint. The bunny had a sorrowful look in his eyes.

"So you're..."

"You from about five days in the future and this is Spartacus, a formerly white rabbit..." Paul stopped himself and took a breath.

Something was wrong, very wrong. None of this was going the way it should. It felt like there was a dark portentous cloud hanging

over them, an oppressive electrical tension in the air that indicated a storm was coming. Two versions of the same person being in the same place IN the same time hadn't caused the universe to implode but it didn't mean it was happy about it. They say nature abhors a vacuum; maybe it's none too keen on repeats either.

Paul took a deep breath, time to calm down and regain control of the situation. "OK look – I know it sounds crazy but you've discovered time travel and yes – I am you from the future."

"Shit the bed!"

"DO NOT say that."

Past Paul backed away nervously. "Why're you here?"

For lack of a better idea, Paul told the truth. He looked at the floor and as calmly as he could, he explained it all – Jessica, Orla, the voicemails, the weekend of bad decisions and bodily functions that'd led to him losing the woman he loved. Saying it all out loud made his heart ache all over again.

When he'd finished, he looked up to see the disconcerting sight of his own face, sneering at him in disgust.

"I can't believe you did that."

The thunder roared and the clouds opened. It happened fast – too fast.

It was his first fight since primary school. What it lacked in technique, it made up for in sheer brutality. They were crazed animals. His past sunk his teeth into his neck; Paul gouged an eye in response and revelled in the subsequent scream. A flailing knee connected with his genitals, still bruised and sore from earlier that day in another life. Before he knew what was happening, the past had a chokehold on him and he was gasping shallow breathes while colours flashed before his eyes. He staggered, unable to shake his limpet-like twin, as they clattered back and forth against the workbenches. As the light faded, his desperately grasping hands found something – Toshiko's oscilloscope; a two-foot by six-inch metal box for measuring voltage. He heaved it over his left shoulder and heard a sickening crunch as it made contact with bone. The other fell to

his knees, hands holding his face from which blood was now pumping.

Paul raised the spectroscope and brought it crashing down… and again… and again. All he could see was that look in Jessica's eyes as she'd walked out of his life for good. At some point he must've slipped in the blood because when the spectroscope came down for the last couple of times, he was on his knees. He was dimly aware that it was making an increasingly loud noise. As he started to lose consciousness, he realised it was because there was now precious little skull left between it and the floor.

He flopped over onto his side; the floor tile felt cool against his skin. It hurt to breathe and his throat made a weird clicking noise every time he did. The last thing he recalled was watching Spartacus hop across his field of vision, leaving a trail of bloodied footprints behind him.

---

His own voice echoed in his head – 'Wake up, wake up… wake the fuck up!' Cold water hit him in the face, jarring him awake. He opened his eyes and images began to slowly swim into focus.

Someone was standing over him… It was… him.

'Oh thank God, I thought I'd…'

The other Paul spoke in a calm voice. 'Killed me? No.'

He moved to the side and Paul saw the bloody mess on the floor. A body with most of its head gone.

'But here's one you prepared earlier.'

---

Paul stared out the rain-splattered window at the lights of the passing cars as Spartacus nuzzled against his chest. Once 'Future Paul' had got through with the explanation, there'd not been a lot else to say and they were understandably keen to avoid any possibility of a

confrontation. He was still woozy from his injuries and the unpleasant clicking noise remained each time he drew breath.

As 'The Future' explained it, the last time around Paul had been awoken at 11:46pm by the screams of Margo from the microbiologists upstairs, who'd come in to put mice in Daniel's desk, only to be confronted by a bloodbath. He'd tried to explain but she'd run and in a state of panic, Paul had run too.

He'd headed for his own flat initially, lying on the sofa and replaying in horrific detail the memories of the madness. As the adrenalin wore off, he threw up the Italian meal from earlier. About 3am he'd got out of his flat, realising just in time that the Gardaí would soon be pointed in that direction. He hid out down by the pier overnight, washing himself as best he could in the sea. The next morning, he'd watched from the park across the street as a police car had pulled up to Daniel's house and he'd gone off with them, looking pale.

When he'd returned that afternoon, unbeknownst to him, Paul was hiding in his attic – having let himself into the empty house with the spare key. Paul listened quietly as his friend explained everything to his housemate Seamus, when he'd returned from lectures. Paul was dead. They'd done DNA tests on the body. Daniel had cried as he told Seamus how, at least initially, he'd clearly been a suspect in his best friend's murder. Finally, they'd mange to verify that he'd been at a pub quiz the night before – luckily his presence had been memorable, as he had been ejected for googling. Paul had wanted to go down and explain it all to Daniel there and then but he didn't, he couldn't.

He'd tried to use the device several times since what happened in the lab but it hadn't worked. He had a theory he was clinging to, hoping against hope he was right. Otherwise, he was set for another first, being the first man put on trial for his own murder. Luckily Daniel went home to be with his family and Seamus was off to Dublin for a dirty weekend. Paul knew this as he'd unwillingly overheard Seamus's phone call with his girlfriend, where he'd

described the frankly impractical sexual acts he intended them to spend the weekend performing.

Paul spent the weekend like a ghost in someone else's digs, watching news reports on the manhunt for his own killer. The Gardaí were clearly clueless but they were making plenty of noise nevertheless. They couldn't let students get bludgeoned to death or else the psychos might move on to real people. Seamus returned home on Sunday night, by which time Paul was back in the attic – having taken most of the remaining food in the house with him. Seamus bitched and moaned about his useless housemate and then ordered a pizza. Later on, he had a frosty conversation with his soon-to-be former girlfriend. Apparently her front teeth had made contact with a bedpost during coitus convolutedus and come off much the worse.

Paul killed time until 4:22am on Tuesday 12 November 2018 – four days, six hours and forty-eight minutes after the horrific moments he'd relived over and over again in the last few days. All he had left was a theory. He pressed the button and was proven right. The device wouldn't let him go back to before the fight – maybe no more than two iterations of a person could exist in the same time, or maybe you could cheat time but not Death.

And so, at 9:34pm on Thursday 7 November 2018, while Paul was bludgeoning his past self to death in their lab, his future self was popping back in time to Daniel's attic – just in time to hear Seamus having a vigorous moment with himself while watching German porn on the internet. Paul guessed this was where Seamus had got the truly dreadful idea of something to try over the weekend that would result in his girlfriend losing a tooth, and Seamus losing a girlfriend.

Paul crept by Seamus's bedroom door and grabbed the spare keys to Daniel's Skoda from the kitchen. Then he'd gone to the shed and taken Daniel's canvas surfboard carrying bag, a can of diesel, a shovel and some paint. Which is how at 11:46pm, Brigit the Microbiologist had entered the Physics lab to be covered in red paint from a refilled booby-trap. Weirdly, the rest of the lab had red paint thrown all over

it too, which happened to cover any blood that might be knocking about from a body that was now in a surfboard bag in a Skoda's boot on its way up the Galway mountains.

---

Paul wordlessly shovelled some more dirt out of the makeshift grave. Future Paul had done most of the grunt work as he was still feeling light-headed thanks to his injuries from the fight. Still, he'd felt he should do something so he'd offered to take over for the last bit. Digging a grave is surprisingly hard work, even in the soft boggy ground they'd found so far off the beaten track you could probably build a house and nobody would see it.

'That's enough I reckon,' said Future Paul. Paul looked around at the three-foot-deep hole he was now standing in and nodded in agreement. He used the shovel to prop himself up as he struggled out. Future Paul made as if to help him and then thought better of it. They'd both avoided touching each other so far, to be on the safe side. They heaved the surfboard bag into the hole. They looked at each other and then back at the makeshift grave.

'Shouldn't we... I dunno, say something?' said Paul.

'I suppose so.'

'You do it – you've had more time to think about this than I have.'

Future Paul glared at him. He held his hands out in a placating gesture. 'I didn't mean anything by that. We both... this is nobody's fault.'

Future Paul looked at his past self, remembering the horrors of the first night dealing with this and took pity.

He closed his eyes. 'Our Father—'

The shovel hit him square in the face.

When 'the future' came to, he felt his arms and legs bound with cord from the boot. He was lying on something lumpy. Of course, it was a surfboard bag containing most of a body. He looked up to see Paul standing over him and laughed through shattered teeth, the hard bitter laugh of someone who'd just gotten the joke and, while it

wasn't that funny, it did at least make a twisted sense. Paul glared down at him. 'Be honest, you'd have done the same. It makes sense – we can only have one of us existing if it's to go back to the way it was.'

'There can be only one!'

The laughter and Highlander quotes were disconcerting. Paul was prepared for anger, pleading – but not that. 'Stop it!'

'You don't get it, do you? You've got a great future behind you.'

Paul raised the shovel, closed his eyes and finished it. Then he'd poured the diesel, started a fire and watched it burn. He filled the hole in after.

---

And so ten days later, Paul stood and admired the view. He'd got the joke now – it was pretty damn funny. The last couple of weeks had proven two things: firstly that he'd a spectacular capacity for screwing up and secondly, he was ultimately willing to do whatever was necessary to fix it, even killing.

And that was where the problem lay.

The next time he screwed up, he'd do it again. He'd go back and fix the problem like he'd done twice already. He was a killer now. How could he be protected from his own future self? Destroy the device? He could build another. Remain vigilant? You can't fool someone who remembers exactly what you did and had a whole four days, six hours and forty-eight minutes to figure out a way around it. Outrunning your own past is difficult; outrunning your own future is damn near impossible.

He'd finally figured it out, the only way he could escape.

He turned around and took a step backwards into nothing. As the wind rushed by his ears, he looked back up towards the bridge where he could just make out the twitchy little ears of a white rabbit watching him fall.

The third time was the easiest of all.

# EVERYBODY KILLS HITLER

Warning: The following short story contains more time travel, although a rather different take on it. Rest assured, what happens in this story has definitely not happened, yet.

---

A sullen silence hung in the air as four men named John pointedly didn't look at each other. That was trickier to achieve than it sounds, as they each sat behind desks at the sides of a 20-foot by 20-foot enclosure that was open to the glowering sky. A foot-thick padded yellow crash mat sat on the ground in the centre of the space. As they each stared at a different corner of the enclosure, huddled in their winter coats, their cold breath fogged in the air like bulls threatening to charge.

All four men being called John was a coincidence that they had laughed about in lighter moments. The German was actually a Hans and the Frenchman a Jean but still, they were four soldiers who shared a name if not a great deal else.

The American at twenty-three was the junior member of the

quartet, although he did not view himself in that light. The German and Englishman were of a similar age, both in their late thirties. The Frenchman was forty-one and looked it but for reasons not even truly known to himself, he'd lied and said he was thirty-six. Perhaps in a matter of international security as this was, he felt deep down that no information should be given cheaply.

The German drummed his fingers on his desk but stopped quickly when he noticed the Frenchman glaring at him. This was all indirectly Hans's fault although he had meant well. Day after day, the four men had sat in this enclosure between the hours of 8am and 8pm. It could be dull, tedious and depressing work – some days it would come in wave upon wave, other days almost nothing.

One Friday in an effort to be a good host, Hans had brought in some of his wife's strudel which had been greatly appreciated by the others, all the more so given the current rationing situation. Hans was a kind-hearted man but from a young age, he'd found it difficult to make friends. He was cursed with never being entirely sure whether someone was joking or not and this made him a terrible audience for a story, forever looking for someone else's reactions to mirror for fear of causing offence. A few years ago by accident, he'd stumbled upon the bridge-building powers of his blessed wife's cooking – a discovery that had served him well. It was in fact the reason he had pulled this favourable duty. It may be dull work, but it was sitting down work and that was a position to be cherished in any man's army.

The week after the strudel, the Frenchman had brought in some pain au chocolat; a tradition had now been established and a gauntlet thrown down. The following Friday, the Englishman had furnished his fellow Johns with clotted cream scones and a small flask of Scotch, to give their coffee a little assistance in fending off the biting Berlin winds. Hans considered the whisky to be English John slyly slipping his thumb onto the scales but he hadn't mentioned it, and it had certainly hit the spot.

Drawn by movement, the German's eyes instinctively flicked towards the Englishman. The waspishly thin Yorkshireman's

experiences in the Great War had left him with a nervous twitch of the left arm and an involuntary strangled yelp that sounded like 'Gren!' It seemed to worsen under stressful circumstances, which meant the current sullen silence could actually only be considered one out of politeness. In his idle moments, Hans had amused himself with the unkind thought that the Englishman was constantly holding himself back from pointing and loudly proclaiming where Grenoble was. He felt guilty for this; of the trio, he'd felt the strongest kinship with the John from Yorkshire. Over those scones, they'd discovered they'd both fought on the same field at the Somme twelve years ago. The young American had reacted to this revelation as if expecting it to be a source of tension, hiding his disappointment badly when it wasn't. That was the ignorance of youth, of one who had never seen the workings of the great bloody machine up close. The enemy had never been in the other trenches. No pacifist could match the disregard for the military high command that the career soldier held.

With great effort, the German did not look at his French counterpart. His plump features gave him a rather bovine quality, especially when he chewed his lunch in the irritatingly vulgar open-mouthed manner he had. The lazy eye, which Hans could only assume was a birth defect, gave Jean an unfair advantage in the current circumstance. Even though he was staring resolutely at the opposite corner, you couldn't shake the feeling he was also looking at you. It had been the Frenchman's explosion earlier that had sucked all of the air out of this room that was not a room.

The German did not dislike the American John. He'd hinted that he'd like to be referred to as 'Big John' but nobody had taken him up on the offer. In this situation, all Johns had to be equal as a matter of national pride. His shaggy blond hair hung just above piercing blue eyes that sparkled when he rolled out one of his stories, liberally sprinkled with untruth. He didn't seem to realise that those present had now heard many of his tales several times – although they were never the same twice, each new rendition having picked up another verse in the retelling. Hans supposed he was just trying to impress

the older men and his lies were at least entertainingly told. In an otherwise empty space, open to the harsh elements, the ability to fill time was not a skill to be underestimated, especially to Hans who was so lacking in that area. If nothing else, listening to him had greatly improved Hans's English.

All week, the American had been talking up the doughnuts. He had found a Berlin baker who could speak English and so American John spent what little free time he'd had instructing him in the art of making the perfect 'American style' doughnut. He certainly could sell it; each night the other men had gone home salivating at the thought of the treat awaiting them at the end of their week.

Then Friday morning had rolled around without the much-anticipated doughnuts making an appearance. The American had made profuse apologies and promises about the supply issues that he was determined to resolve. If he'd have left it there, maybe everything would've been fine. Later that morning he'd made a crack about French women and the Gallic temper had exploded. It turned out that the Frenchman, billeted in the same guest house for the duration of his stay in Berlin, had seen the American sneaking across the road the night before to pay a visit to the widowed landlady of the ale house opposite. In his hands had been a baker's cardboard box.

The floodgates had opened – the Great War, the current crisis, hundreds of years of world history and weeks of pet peeves and minor irritations had been weaponised and brought to bear in a four-way war without winners. Now nobody was talking to anybody else. It says something for the level of tension that they were each secretly relieved when the familiar feeling of electricity in the air made the hairs on the back of their necks stand on end. They each drew their sidearm as per procedure and held them pointing upwards at the ready. With his free left hand, Hans calmly took a form from the pile beside him and picked up his pen.

Then a hole opened up in the sky above them and a man from the future fell through.

He landed on the padded mat with a girlish yelp and looked around him in wide-eyed disbelief. The four men looked back with

what could be described as, at best, mild interest. He was predictably mid-forties, overweight and wearing the black linen suit so many of them had. Many of them were older, a few younger and although rarer still, some were even women. All-in-all though, this one was very much the typical. His skin had a dark complexion that implied he was used to seeing considerably more sun than any of those present and it had an unnervingly smooth look to it. At least this one had come through wearing clothes; many had not. Hans had a sneaking suspicion that this was nothing to do with the technology as they had been told but a cruel joke played by someone at the other end.

Hans cleared his throat and rolled into the agreed upon script.

"Bleiben Sie ruhig. Wir schreiben das Jahr 1928, die Sie nicht in Gefahr sind. Welchem Land kommst du her?"

The man from the future gave him a look of terrified incomprehension that the quartet of Johns were all too familiar with. Hans had long ago stop being surprised how many of their guests spoke not a word of German. Some had landed and occasionally proclaimed themselves a jelly doughnut which had lightened the mood, although today of all days, that was to be avoided. Others embarrassed themselves by attempting to speak English with what they believe to be a German accent, as if that would do. To Hans, the future seemed to be a paradise built by geniuses and populated by idiots.

The others looked at the man nobody referred to as Big John, who rolled his eyes and softly swore under his breath before trotting out the speech in English.

"Remain calm. The year is 1928, you are not in danger. Which country do you come from?"

The man from the future gawped at the man nobody called Big John, who took this as a signal to speak slightly more loudly.

"Remain calm. The year is..."

The Futurian, as many had taken to calling them, interrupted. "You're... American?"

After a while in this job, you couldn't help but develop an ear for

accents. There was a clicking sound as in near perfect synchronicity, Jean, Hans and Yorkshire John put their pens down and leaned back in their chairs, still keeping their revolvers trained on the visitor. Not-big-John grumpily started to fill out a form.

"Where in the United States are you from, sir?"

The man from the future continued to stare around him. "Where am I?"

"Just outside Berlin, now where are you from?"

"Why've you all got guns?"

"Just stay calm and you won't need to find out. Answer the question sir, where are you from?"

"California."

Not-Big-John shook his head.

"Figures."

Not-Big-John then proceeded to read out the long statement, full of clauses and legal language, where the US Government acknowledged the new arrivals claim of US citizenship and promised to process it when possible. This was a part of the process Hans considered utterly pointless. Every time the Futurian stared blankly around them not taking anything in, wearing a facial expression akin to a dog who had just been shown a card trick.

Not all of the Futurians were American of course, far from it. There had been numerous Germans, British, French – people from almost every country in the world, some of which didn't even exist. They had a lot from a place called Israel – that had proven particularly tricky in the beginning.

"Where am I?"

Not-Big-John rolled his eyes "Berlin, 1928, remember, sir? We've covered this. What's your name?"

The man from a country called Tonga who arrived a few weeks ago had been an unexpected variation from the norm. His English had been very poor and his German non-existent. Luckily, he had understood the universal language of four revolvers being pointed at him and he had seemed surprisingly cheerful given the

circumstances. Occasionally some new arrivals attempted to fight their way out. Thankfully the warning shot in the air generally calmed them down, although Jean had been forced to shoot a Japanese man in the leg two months ago. Nobody felt comfortable shooting an unarmed man but orders were very clear on this. The paperwork had been most tiresome.

"I demand to speak to President Hoover."

It was a curiosity that almost every American requested this. This man at least knew the name of the man he wanted to speak to, so many didn't. It seemed to be an ingrained belief within them, that their leader would have nothing better to do than talk to them. It was a wonder the man got anything done.

"Sure, who can I tell him is calling?"

"My name is John Geraldo..."

The man looked slightly disconcerted. He wasn't to know why all of the other men smiled briefly before remembering they were mad at each other.

"I have vital information about the future of mankind."

It was a dislikable trait of Not-Big-John's that he would occasionally seek to have fun at a new arrival's expense.

"Golly gosh, mister – you should have said!" He picked up an invisible phone and pretended to dial it, before holding the invisible receiver to his lips. "Mister President, this is Big John Gordon over here in Berlin. There's a Mister Geraldo here from the future, he wants you to know that there's mean old guy called Hitler that's gonna try and take over the world and it'd be just peachy if you could stop him."

The Future John understood he was being mocked and it just made him more irritated. "Wait, how did you know? Is this some kind of a joke?"

He made to move towards Not Big John's desk but paused at the sound of three safeties being taken off.

"Alright, that's enough." The Englishman's deeper voice carried a calmer tone of natural authority.

Not Big John flashed annoyance as his audience turned to face the Englishman.

"Relax, Mr... Geraldo, was it?"

He nodded.

"The year is 1928, you are just outside of Berlin at a League of Nations facility. The man you know as Hitler is not alive – in fact, he never has been."

This was true. Scientists had speculated as to why this was when so many people came back looking for him. No record could be found beyond the year 1827 of anyone with that family name. One theory was that someone had found a way to go further back in time, chopping down the Hitler family tree much nearer the root. Another, that such a man had never existed. Many patriotic Germans, when faced with the horrific version of future events presented by Futurians, chose to believe that they had all been fed a fiction. Hans wanted to believe that and yet he had been in the Great War. In his experience, circumstance could make a monster of any man.

"... Similarly – there is no organisation known as the Nazis or the Third Reich."

The new arrival looked around the room as the four men behind the desks nodded at him in turn. Jean did so while picking at his teeth distractedly with his pen. He really did have such appalling habits.

"In which case... my work here is done!"

Normally, a prisoner making a sudden move for an object stuck into the back of their trousers would stand a very high probability of getting shot. Luckily for him, the men with the guns had all seen this manoeuvre before. Future John snatched the grenade-sized device from his belt, held it above his head and dramatically pressed the button.

Nothing happened.

He opened one eye and glanced around briefly, to confirm to himself that indeed nothing had happened.

He closed his eyes again and pressed the button a few more times. They waited patiently. The first few times he'd watched this

pantomime, Hans had to admit it had been amusing but it had long passed that point – now becoming only a depressing monument to mankind's naivety. Of course, nobody wanted a one-way trip, however heroic they considered their mission to be. That's why they'd all been given the return button. It did make some sense – if they could invent the technology to send you back through time, why couldn't they return you forward again afterwards?

They gave him a few more moments of hopeless button pressing before Not-Big-John cleared his throat and resumed with his questions. After that point, the subjects almost always became more compliant, once the reality of where they were had begun to sink in. He was from the year 2067, and like the others he'd been approached by the friend of a friend of a friend who had just made an incredible discovery. How would he like to change the world? Not for the first time, Hans thought how much he'd like to get hold of the charlatans at the other end. They'd tried burying capsules with messages begging future generations to ban the technology, but to no effect. Apparently this told a lot of very clever people a lot of very important things about how time worked.

Once processed, Hans offered to escort the new arrival to Section 4. He enjoyed getting out of his seat when possible, especially today. They would soon be back to the same sullen silence, broken only by the Yorkshireman involuntarily 'Gren'-ing and the Frenchman picking at his teeth.

Back in his own time, the latest arrival had been something called a 'brand cohesion manager' – putting him into the 97% of Futurians who had no appreciable skills. For scientifically advanced people, they seemed almost wilfully ignorant of how any of their technologies worked. Clearly somebody must know but those people never seemed to get sent back.

The man walked in front of Hans as Jean opened the door of enclosure 23. Hans nodded a cursory greeting to the two guards stationed outside. Occasionally somebody would try and make a run for it but most quickly realised the futility of such a measure. The man had many questions and Hans answered what he could, as he

led him past the concrete buildings of the Supply depot. When they turned the corner, the conversation stopped. The elevated ground they were on offered a relatively expansive view of the camps as they stretched out before them. As far as the eye could see, men in raggedy clothing looked out from behind barbed wire at the time to which they did not belong.

The new arrival looked back at Hans in disbelief.

Hans hated this moment.

"There are thirty-four other such holes as the one you came through in Germany, another seventeen in France, and two dozen or so more scattered across Europe. Each one averages eighty-three new arrivals in each 24-hour period and you started coming through eight years ago. That's the best part of one and a half million men a year."

"But I didn't..."

"You didn't travel back as far as some, many came from two centuries after you did. Each of you, I'm afraid, believing that they too were the first. You have arrived in the midst of a global economic crisis. Ever since the great crash of 1921..."

He looked panicked now. "But the crash happens in 1929?!"

"Yes, so the first of you told us. Men falling from the sky, telling us the sky is about to fall – it caused a great panic."

"But... I'm an American citizen."

"And the German government 100% supports your claim. Sadly, the American government does not."

Hans pointed towards the various sections as they stretched out into the distance before them.

"Such claims are also not acknowledged by the governments of Britain, China, Russia, Japan... You are all men out of place and time. Twenty million and counting."

The new arrival looked numb. The Section 4 guards saluted as they came to take him away.

They would burn his clothes and delouse him to prevent the spread of disease. Then – to aid with the administrative nightmare that the ever-growing camps had become – the League of Nation guards inside would issue him with a number, tattooed on his arm.

Hans trudged back toward enclosure 23, pulling his coat tight around him as the chill wind caught it. As he passed through the door, the hair on the back of his neck stood up. He reclaimed his seat and once again drew his revolver, as a man from the future fell from the sky.

# REGRETS

WARNING: THE BELOW IS A PIECE OF FLASH FICTION, WHICH MEANS IT IS EITHER; A) A STORY TOLD IN UNDER 250 WORDS, B) A STORY ABOUT THAT SUPERHERO WHO IS VERY FAST, OR C) A STORY ABOUT A DIRTY OLD MAN EXPOSING HIS DANGLY BITS TO PEOPLE IN A PARK. SPOILER — THE ANSWER IS A — ALTHOUGH I AM NOW SORELY TEMPTED TO WRITE SOMETHING THAT COMBINES ALL THREE.

---

Jacob awoke to the unpleasant sensation of a gun in his mouth.

The balaclava-clad man at the other end looked down at him, a finger held to his lips.

"In sixty seconds, you are going to die, accept it. Before you do, I want you to tell me, now that your life is over, what you regret."

In one swift motion, the barrel of the gun is out of Jacob's mouth and pressed against his forehead.

"I have money."

"Not in... fifty-three seconds you won't."

The gun is cocked.

"I... I regret whatever I've done to you."

A fist slams into Jacob's kidneys.

"We've never met – regrets!"

"I… the kids, Emma and Graham – I mean, not seeing them grow up, not being there … and Carol…" Jacob's eyes widen in panic and swivel to the left. Relief washes over him as he remembers she is visiting her sister.

"I love her, Christ – I really do. I had an affair, just – pure pathetic ego – stupid, so stupid! The job – why did I care so much about a fucking job?! It was never supposed to be … I forgot. I wanted to be… we were going to travel but …"

"Time is up."

Jacob closes his eyes tightly and waits.

And waits…

Nothing happens and continues to do so for some time, until the following morning when everything changes.

And tomorrow night, someone else will awake to the unpleasant sensation of a gun in their mouth.

# THE GOLUM

WARNING: THE FOLLOWING STORY ISN'T EVEN TRYING TO BE FUNNY. ON THE UPSIDE, THIS MEANS THERE IS LESS CHANCE OF SOMEONE BEING WALLOPED IN THE KNACKERS.

---

In a dusty and careworn room, an emaciated man weeps.

He isn't aware of his own tears. His mind is elsewhere. His face is a mask of pained concentration – eyes shut tightly, teeth clenched. He sits in a large armchair, his frail body lost in a vastly over-sized t-shirt that envelops his frail form. You couldn't be blamed for looking at him and thinking that it might be kinder if whatever was killing him would just hurry up and finish the job.

In a brief moment of respite, his eyelids open, to reveal two gaping holes where eyeballs should be. He looks up at a ceiling that he cannot see. His spindly hand uses the corner of his t-shirt sleeve to dab at tears of blood on his face.

Another wave hits and his pain-filled vigil resumes.

---

Frank took out his rag and carefully cleaned the already spotless glass.

"If you're not careful, you're going to wear a hole in it."

His face reddened as he turned and saw his niece Gina beaming at him from behind the counter. "I'm paying you to make pizza, not laugh at me."

"I know, Uncle Frank. I consider it my bonus."

He playfully tossed the rag at her, but Gina ducked and giggled, avoiding it with ease. "I'll make up some boxes and let you get back to admiring your view."

"Yeah, you do that."

Frank stepped back and looked through the window; he did, he really did – he had a view. Not much of one, sure, but a view nonetheless. The Falls had been his home since he was a boy so he knew all too well that it was nobody's idea of a tourist attraction. In fact, until recently – if anybody from out-of-town was unlucky enough to stumble into this neighbourhood – they were in for the worst and possibly last day of their lives.

It hadn't always been like that. Sure, in his childhood it had been no Eden, but it had been a community. Most people had had work and, more importantly, pride. You might be struggling to make the rent, but the stoop outside your house was still going to gleam. Your body might've ached from hard manual labour but you still took the trash out on a Thursday and cleaned the windows.

And then, the trade from the docks had moved down the coast and taken the jobs with it. Those who were smart got out and took their pride with them. In came the drugs, the gangs, the whores and worse. At some point, what had been a working class neighborhood became a ghetto and the gleaming windows got replaced with battered chipboard. At his aunt's pleading, Frank had taken over the place after uncle Tony had been stabbed by a junkie for the twenty-three bucks in the cash register. Tony had retired upstate, his farewell gifts being the steel mesh over the windows and the loaded shotgun under the counter.

That had been twelve years ago and The Falls had only sunk deeper and deeper into the mire. Politicians and promises had come and gone. Soon the darkness of the night had encroached further and further into the day, as the sickness had spread and the whole body had become infected. It hadn't been long before not even the daylight offered protection. The police now always had somewhere else to be. The Falls had become lost, and lost all hope with it. That was until he had come.

Frank noticed old Mrs Granger across the street, out walking that yappy little dog of hers, and waved. She waved back. Imagine that, an old lady bringing her dog out for an evening stroll in The Falls. He couldn't help but shake his head in wonder. How times had changed.

"Is that him?!" Gina squealed excitedly as she rushed to the window. Frank snapped out of his reverie and looked where she was pointing. There he stood, on the roof of the Brownstone opposite. He'd been referred to by many names: The Angel, The Guardian of The Falls, and so on. People needed heroes. The name that had stuck, though, had been the Golem.

Gina had never seen him before. Frank had only allowed her to come work for him a few weeks ago when things had become safer.

"Yeah that's him," he said.

"Oh." Gina sounded disappointed. "I was expecting somebody, I dunno... bigger."

She had a point. The Golem didn't look all that. He was the size of a well-built man of average-to-stocky frame, blond-haired and wearing a battered pair of patched and ill-fitting overalls. Not exactly what the comic books would lead you to expect, he looked more the wholesome farm-boy type than anything otherworldly. It was only when you got closer that you sensed it. First you'd notice the weird vacant smile – like he was a little bit spaced out. Stoned, but not. It was like you were part of his bad trip. He never spoke, never even made a sound – just walked silently, like a ghost amongst men. What made it real were those eyes. Frank had seen them up close a couple of times – ice-blue and piercing.

"Although, he is kinda cute," said Gina. "Do you think he has a girlfriend?"

"Never you mind, young lady! Get back to work. You leave that man well enough alone, you hear me?"

He saw the wounded look in her eyes and instantly knew he'd gone too far.

"I didn't – I mean ..."

She turned and walked quickly around the counter and off into the back. Frank felt like a Grade A asshole. He'd apologise later – maybe let her go home early.

He turned back in time to see the Golem casually step off the roof and drop five floors to the alley below.

If an ordinary man survived that fall at all, he'd probably wish he hadn't, being broken seven ways from Sunday. The Golem landed unnaturally – like he had no bones at all within his body, as if he'd just stepped off the kerb. It seemed like gravity didn't dictate to him, but that he'd play along with it if he felt like it. Those piercing blue eyes turned towards Frank, and he started as an involuntary shiver shimmied down his spine. He reddened and looked away, before thinking better of it and waving nervously. He didn't want to appear ungrateful.

Then, Frank turned away and started fussing about with the napkins on the counter.

A minute later, the bell over the shop door tinkled and Frank turned to see Father Pat beaming at him from the doorway.

"Do these old eyes deceive me or does somebody have a window?"

Frank couldn't help but grin. "Installed fresh this morning, Father."

Father Pat stepped into the shop and theatrically gave the window an appraising look. "Well now, ain't she a thing of beauty?"

You couldn't help but like the old priest; seventy if he was a day and possessed of a distinctive Irish lilt despite having never left the state in his whole life. These days, he was more like the man Frank remembered from his youth – quick to laugh, a glint in his eye and

the kind of lively spirit that could get a smile out of even the surliest of teenagers. Frank loved to see him like this. Back in the dark days, he'd maybe gone from liking a drink to needing it and the glint had been dulled.

Today the old man was positively beaming. "I've just been around to meet that new couple that moved in down the block. As sweet as pie and they've a little angel with them. We're going to be having a christening a week on Saturday!"

"That's wonderful."

It was, too. Frank couldn't remember the last time somebody had actually moved to The Falls. It wasn't somewhere you moved to, it was somewhere you ended up when hope, money and the will to fight had left you.

"You should see their building as well," continued Father Pat, "looking mighty nice, almost back to its old self." A silent moment passed between the two men as they shared a memory they'd both rather forget. That had been Leon's building. He'd been a security guard, and a good man, even if his temper had blown a little hot at times. That's what had done for him in the end. He'd been crazy enough to stand up to The Skulls after one of their little joyrides had left his son in the hospital. He'd given them a piece of his mind.

They'd hung Leon's battered body off the roof so everybody could see. It'd been there for a day and a night before the fire brigade had been willing to come in with a heavy police escort to cut it down.

Father Pat snapped back to the present as Gina emerged from the kitchen. "And who, pray tell, is this vision of loveliness?"

It was Gina's turn to look a little embarrassed. "This is my niece Gina, Father. She's been kind enough to come help out her poor uncle. She's been doing a stellar job."

Gina smiled shyly – an acknowledgement that the harsh words of earlier had been forgotten. Father Pat bowed theatrically.

"Charmed to make your acquaintance, m'lady. I hope this reprobate isn't being too much of an ogre to work for?"

Gina grinned again. "Oh, he has his moments."

"Gina is my sister Carol's youngest."

Father Pat clapped his hands with delight. "Of course! Do tell her I was asking after her."

"Sure thing. Now, what can I get you?"

Father Pat stepped back and perused the menu above the counter with great ceremony. "I will have... an Americana with cheese, please, my dear."

"Great. That'll be—"

Frank cut across her. "Oh, no. The Padre's money is no good here."

Pat made a face and pulled out his wallet. "Don't be silly, Francis. Are we going have to have this fight every time I come in here?"

"Only until you give in and just accept it."

"Oh, you're a terrible man."

"That's why I need God on my side. If you like, you can shave off a few Hail Marys from my penance next week."

Father Pat slipped his wallet back into his pocket. "Ahhh, there ain't nothing in this life for free."

Gina slipped a pie into the pizza oven and then walloped the door to get it to close. Father Pat looked up with a start.

"Yeah, I've a new oven coming next month," said Frank, "and I'm thinking of getting some tables and chairs for outside too. Y'know, for the summer."

"Well I'll be. Al fresco dining in the Falls. Who'd a thunk it?" said Father Pat. "And how're you affording all this expansion?"

"Well, now I don't have to pay protection any more, this place is finally making some money..."

"Thanks be to God."

"... and the Whale," interjected Gina.

Father Pat looked confused and Frank cursed his big mouth. He should never have said anything to Gina, but she'd kept on asking. She'd wanted to know where he kept disappearing to every day.

'The Whale' as Gina had dubbed him was Frank's best customer. Hell, back in the bad old days, him moving into the neighborhood had singlehandedly kept the business afloat. Well, that and the fact

that the bank didn't want to foreclose on a property nobody in their right mind would want to buy.

He was a shut-in over on Broadhurst. A nice enough guy, once you got used to the look of him and the... well, Frank hated to admit it but the guy really stank.

He'd moved back in to his Grandma's place when she'd died and, as far as Frank could tell, he hadn't left since. He'd apparently lived there as a child, but there'd been some trouble and he'd been sent away. It was nothing terrible, as Frank understood it. He was maybe just an odd kid – he sure was an odd adult.

Every day, he ordered a dozen pies, a bucket load of sides and three quarts of soda, and he paid in cash, plus a big tip for delivery. It had been the only delivery Frank would make back in the dark days – that good a customer was worth the risk. The guy must've weighed 500 pounds easy, and Frank couldn't help but feel bad about it. He'd made the mistake of telling Carol and she'd said he was something Oprah called 'an enabler'. Was it Frank's business how someone chose to live their life? If he didn't make the delivery, somebody else would. He'd never mentioned it to Father Pat though, not even in confession. You can't confess a sin if you know you're going to be committing it again tomorrow and the next day. Gina was like her mother – she could never keep a secret either. Frank needed a change of subject, and luckily one occurred to him.

"Did you hear?" said Frank, looking out the window. "Jimmy has been onto the city council again, and he says they're definitely coming out next week to fix the streetlights."

"That's fantastic news because..." Father Pat tailed off, noticing Frank's distraction.

Frank stared, a feeling of dread building inside him. Sometimes in life, you can see exactly what's going to happen, but you're powerless to stop it – like a car crash on an icy road. When the skid starts and the vehicle goes from under you, all you can do is watch with that sinking feeling in your stomach. That was what it was like now.

A car had pulled up across the street and a kid not much older

than Gina was getting out. The driver looked older, like maybe he was the brains of the outfit – everything is relative. The kid wore a jacket that was too heavy for the weather and a look on his face that Frank had seen before. That pissed off at the world look that a nervous person gets when they've fired themselves up to do something. Add in that junkie twitch, and this kid was only going to be bad news. Frank would've reacted sooner back in the old days, but he'd stopped expecting trouble around every corner. This trouble, though, was walking right in the front door.

Father Pat was turning his head to look, as the bell above the door tinkled and the kid was already half through, pulling the gun Frank had known would be there. He held it a foot from the old priest's head and scanned the room anxiously.

"Nobody fucking move, you hear me?"

Frank looked to see Gina frozen in horror behind the counter. On her first day he'd told her – first sign of trouble, get down, stay down, no matter what. Now that the moment had arrived, she'd frozen like a rabbit in the headlights.

"OK, son," said Frank, "just take it easy."

That got the gun turned on him for his trouble. "I ain't your fucking son, motherfucker."

Frank raised his hands slowly to show he meant no harm. The kid's eyes darted to Gina.

"Gimme the register, bitch. All of it."

Somewhere inside, scared as she was, Gina was still her mother's daughter. That was a great thing in Frank's eyes almost all the time, but not now.

"I ain't a bitch."

"What did you say... bitch?"

Frank moved fast to stay in front of the gun as it swung around to point at her. "She said nothing. Gina, give the man what's in the register."

"But—"

"Now!" The sharpness in his tone and the pleading look in his

eyes made her start doing as he asked. She opened the drawer and began placing the money on the counter.

Father Pat spoke in a near whisper. "Do you know where you are, lad? This is The Falls."

"What do I care where the hell I am?"

Frank was surprised when the next person that spoke turned out to be him. "Oh God. You don't know. You're from out of town, aren't you?"

The kid's eyes widened at this, confusion and panic threatening to overwhelm him. This in turn scared Frank – a frightened man with a gun is capable of anything.

"Just take the money and—"

The kid cracked Frank above the ear with the handle of the gun and grabbed for the money on the counter.

"UNCLE FRANK!"

Frank's knees buckled, but Father Pat grabbed him under the arm. The old man was deceptively strong for one so slight.

The kid dropped some of the money as he rushed for the door, but he kept on running. Coins tinkled all around on the tiled floor.

They watched him dive into the back seat of the waiting car. The tyres raised smoke as it sped away. Gina rushed around the counter and kneeled down beside Frank.

Then there was a moment of stillness. Gina looked at Frank, but Frank and Father Pat only stared out the window at the now empty street.

"Maybe he's not watching," said Father Pat.

Frank put his hand to the side of his head to feel for blood. "He's always watching."

The car made it all of thirty yards before it coming to a juddering halt. The Golem had fallen from the sky and landed on the bonnet – crushing the front of the vehicle in a cacophony of tortured machinery. The driver didn't get much of a chance to consider the utter impossibility of a man doing that to a couple of tonnes of metal. He can't have been wearing a seatbelt because he came hurtling out through the front window. The Golem calmly extended

his right hand and caught him like he was fielding a frisbee tossed by an eight-year-old. The last thing the driver saw was the Golem looking at him with those piercing blue eyes and that vacant grin on his face.

"What the f—"

The Golem ripped him clean in half – lengthways. It was like he was just tearing through tissue paper. The front of his overalls and his face were now covered in blood and God knows what else. Still that smile remained fixed in place.

Meanwhile, the kid with the gun had made it out. He was limping badly, blood staining the front left thigh of his jeans as he dragged a gimpy leg with every ounce of energy he had.

"C'mon, kid, move!" said Frank. "Before—"

The kid stopped as something landed in front of him. Frank craned to make out what it was, and then wished he hadn't. It was the driver's head, still with half a spinal cord attached.

The kid turned to see The Golem standing behind him, that eerily calm grin on his face, as if the blood was just a light shower of rain he'd been caught in. The eyes were the worst part, thought Frank. It wasn't the anger; it was the joy.

The kid drew his gun and the Golem danced as half a dozen bullets ripped into his torso. They entered him but never left. He didn't flinch or stumble. The Golem's overalls would need some more patches, but even now Frank could see the flesh reforming around what you could hardly call a wound. It was like shooting sand.

The kid looked in bewilderment at his gun, then at the Golem, then back to the gun. Frank's stomach turned as he watched the Golem's slow advance. He wished the poor fool would just run, while at the same time he knew it would be utterly pointless. Instead, the kid dropped to his knees and started begging for his life. The Golem stood above him and calmly looked down as he pleaded his case.

He reached out his left hand and softly stroked the boy's face, an incongruous act that, if judged in isolation, would look loving, veering towards sensuous. Then with his right hand he lightly tapped him on the other cheek. Frank didn't need to see the boy's eyes to

know that suddenly there would be hope there amidst the terror and confusion.

Then the Golem's left hand slapped his cheek almost playfully...

Then the right, a little harder...

Frank looked down at the floor, unable to watch. He'd seen Carol's cat do this with a mouse once. Father Pat similarly looked away, mumbling softly to ease his conscience. "Somebody should do something."

Maybe somebody should, but Frank looked into his soul and knew it wouldn't be him. Even if he'd wanted to, what good would it do? And while he might end up tossing and turning at night, haunted by the memory, he knew deep down he didn't want to do anything. He wished things were different, but he also remembered what it had been like before.

There ain't nothing in this life for free.

Frank must've been lost in his own thoughts, desperate to block out the sight of the kid's hands uselessly trying to fend off the blows as the Golem built towards a crescendo. That could be the only explanation for why he'd not heard the bell over the door.

"STOP IT!"

Frank looked up just in time to see Gina grab at the Golem's right arm as she rushed towards him. She collided with his backswing and was tossed back through the air maybe ten feet, slamming into the side of a parked Buick.

The Golem stopped and turned his head towards Gina.

Time slowed to a crawl. Frank's feet carried him out to the street while his mind filled with memories of the past and visions of the future. Carol with her beautiful new baby in her arms – joy, pride, terror and exhaustion mixed together in a new mother's smile. Gina's first communion, the look of feisty tomboy indignation in her eyes, daring the world to tell her she looked pretty. Then the conversation with Carol to explain what'd happened. He could hear his own hollow words echoing back to him, his meaningless platitudes of sorrow for the loss of her sweet innocent daughter.

And then – finally – he was there, standing between the two of them. Those cold blue eyes stared right at him.

“Please… she didn’t mean it. She doesn’t understand.”

Gina cradled her broken arm against her as she slowly and painfully propped herself against the car and then began to push herself to her feet.

“I understand fine. He’s a monster.”

“She doesn’t—”

“I do!” Her voice was stronger now, as she looked straight into the Golem’s eyes. “You’re a monster. You don’t have the right to… You’re not God!”

Frank held his breath as the Golem looked at Gina, then down into the poor pathetic face of the kid. Frank looked down at him too. Even amongst all the blood and swollen flesh you couldn’t help but see he was, after all, just a kid. The fear and incomprehension were there, but more cruelly hope. He stared up into the Golem’s cold eyes and every inch of his being pleaded for mercy. He looked upwards as if to a saviour, forgetting what he was looking to be saved from.

The Golem turned to Gina, a look in his eyes that may have said a lot but none of it in a language Frank could understand. As their eyes met, they held the moment for what felt like the longest time. Gina was transfixed, so much so that she didn’t realise that the casual flick of the Golem’s wrist was him breaking the kid’s neck.

And with a casual step, the Golem leaped to the top of the brownstone building. As Gina’s scream reverberated around the neighborhood.

Frank thought that the look in her eyes as she’d watched the Golem leave was the worst thing he’d ever seen. Then she looked at him and he realised he’d been wrong.

---

In a dusty and careworn room, an emaciated man weeps.

He stops his slow rocking back and forth as the figure of the Golem towers over him. The Golem looks down at the frail figure,

extends his hand and they touch. The weeping man's spindly hand looks so frail as it rests in the other's large, blood-stained fingers.

The frail man grows and the Golem shrinks away, until in a matter of minutes both have disappeared. They're replaced by the morbidly obese frame of a 500-pound man, who is stretching the t-shirt he wears to its absolute limit and beyond.

His piercing blue eyes stare up at the ceiling and he sighs deeply. He is the kind of tired that never goes away.

Ain't nothing in this life for free.

# AUTHOR'S NOTE

Hey you!

So there you go, did you enjoy that? I hope so, otherwise you've only read this far looking for the phone number for the complaints department and there isn't one.

If you've not read any of my other work, well you're in luck! I've only gone and written a wheelbarrow full of novels, check the following page for details.

If you have already read them, you'd be doing me a great favour by bunging up an honest review on Amazon. It is still the best way to help other readers find my books and ergo encourage me to keep writing 'em.

Thanks for reading,

Caimh

# ALSO BY CAIMH MCDONNELL

## THE DUBLIN TRILOGY (FEATURING BUNNY MCGARRY)

**A Man With One of Those Faces** (Book 1)

**The Day That Never Comes** (Book 2)

**Angels in the Moonlight** (A prequel that we're calling Book 3 as it needs to be read before...)

**Last Orders** (Book 4)

## MCGARRY STATESIDE

**Disaster Inc (Book 1)**

**I Have Sinned (Book 2)**

And go to www.WhiteHairedIrishman.com to get the latest updates on Caimh's books

25964765R00149

Printed in Great Britain
by Amazon